## About the Author

When Canadian **Dani Collins** found romance novels in high school she wondered how one trained for such an awesome job. She wrote for over two decades without publishing, but remained inspired by the romance message that if you hang in there you'll find a happy ending. In May of 2012, Mills & Boon bought her manuscript in a two-book deal. She's since published more than thirty books with them and is definitely living happily ever after.

D1391011

# Hot Picks

## COLLECTION

# Hot Picks:
# Secrets and Lies

DANI COLLINS

**MILLS & BOON**

First Published in Great Britain 2020
By Mills & Boon, an imprint of HarperCollins*Publishers*
1 London Bridge Street, London, SE1 9GF

HOT PICKS: SECRETS AND LIES © 2020 Harlequin Books S.A.

*His Mistress with Two Secrets* © 2017 Dani Collins
*More than a Convenient Marriage?* © 2013 Dani Collins
*A Debt Paid in Passion* © 2014 Dani Collins

ISBN: 978-0-263-28084-5

0120

MIX
Paper from
responsible sources
FSC™ C007454

This book is produced from independently certified FSC™ paper to ensure responsible forest management.

For more information visit: www.harpercollins.co.uk/green

Printed and bound in Spain
by CPI, Barcelona

# HIS MISTRESS WITH
# TWO SECRETS

For my parents, who are celebrating their 50<sup>th</sup> wedding anniversary as I write this. Much love always from #1.

# PROLOGUE

As she entered the clinic from the stairwell, Cinnia Whitley almost knocked the door into a woman standing inside. Cinnia murmured a distracted apology, thinking she might have seen her before, but not here. She would remember someone so tall and stiff and alert standing in that particular place.

Wait. Was she a guard? It was an odd place to hover. Maybe that's why she seemed so familiar. After spending two years with sober-faced watchmen dogging her movements, perhaps it wasn't the face she recognized so much as the attitude.

Because, if the woman was merely a relative waiting on a patient, there was a very comfortable lounge at the front of the clinic. The back entrance was for people like Cinnia, the paranoid ones who crept in through the building's underground car park in hopes of keeping her visit to this prenatal specialist strictly confidential.

Cinnia didn't bother speculating who the celebrity patient could be. She had bigger fish to fry. She was here for a scan to confirm suspicions on why she was expanding so quickly.

*No*, she kept thinking, absolutely refusing to entertain the most likely reason. She had a lot of work to get through in the next twenty-two weeks and had struggled to find time for another morning off for this test. If the doctor's suspicions were correct, her entire future would have to be recalibrated.

Twins? Really? *No*. Multiple births weren't even hereditary when they were identical and she thought only mothers passed along the fraternal trait. A father with an identical brother and two younger, identical twin sisters couldn't pass that to his offspring.

Could he?

Henri did whatever he wanted. She knew that much.

She did not miss that arrogance, or him, or the life he led with guards like that one dogging his every step, she assured herself with another flick of a glance at the woman by the door.

So why did she spend her mornings combing through online gossip pages, reading every scrap she could find about him? Reading that Henri was back to his old ways of dating and dropping was pure self-destruction, but at least there wasn't much written about that. His twin, Ramon, was stealing all the thunder, still racing and winning while doubling down with his own passionate exploits through a rotation of women who were loved and left.

The Sauveterres were a private lot, despite their domination of the media. But in her time with Henri, Cinnia had noticed that Ramon always seemed to make a splash in the papers when something was going on with the family, like he was deliberately pulling the attention.

Her breakup with Henri was two months ago. Old news by now. It must be Angelique he was trying to cover for.

The brothers were insanely protective of their younger sisters, which was understandable given Trella's kidnapping when she was a child. Angelique was the only one seen in public these days and was becoming quite notorious, what with her affair with the Prince of Zhamair—or rather both him *and* the Prince of Elazar, if the online rags were to be believed.

Cinnia frowned, still thinking there was something about the photo of Angelique with the Prince of Elazar that wasn't right. Impossibly, she had thought it was actually Trella in that photo, but Trella was a recluse. Cinnia had only met her in person a couple of times.

The nurse was on the phone and finally noticed her. Cinnia waved a greeting and tried to smile past her jumbled thoughts. Tried not to think of Henri and twins. It was too big and scary to absorb unless she was forced to.

The nurse indicated to a clerk that Cinnia was here. The clerk nodded and turned to the cabinet to pick out her file.

Cinnia loosened her scarf and started to unbutton her coat, pleased to be warm and dry when it was such a tremendously miserable day, even by London's late-February standards.

Behind her, a door to an exam room opened, startling her into stepping out of the way and turning.

"Oh. Excuse me," the woman said.

"My fault—" Cinnia began, then blurted, "Oh, my God!" as she recognized that model-like physique and those aristocratic features. "I was just thinking about you!"

"Cinnia!" Angelique beamed and they went in for a hug like long-lost sisters, affection squeezing Cinnia's arms tight around the other woman, her excitement completely overriding what should have been *way* more caution on her part.

The reality of Cinnia's situation hit belatedly and continued to strike in successive slaps over the next few seconds.

Cinnia felt Henri's sister stiffen as she came up against Cinnia's baby bump beneath the layers of her clothes.

*Don't tell him*, Cinnia thought with panic.

They drew back. Cinnia knew she wore a look of horror, which was awful when she was actually happy about the baby, happy to see—

"Oh, my *God*," Cinnia whispered. "I thought you were your sister."

Cinnia had always been able to tell the twins apart quite easily. It had been surprise and a quick glance and an even quicker assumption that had made her mistake Trella for Angelique. Trella never left the compound in Spain without one of her siblings accompanying her.

Did that mean Henri was here? Cinnia looked around with alarm, only seeing the guard.

Of course—that's why the guard seemed familiar. She'd seen her at Sus Brazos, the Sauveterre family home in Spain. This was Trella, even though there was nothing distinct to tell the women apart, Cinnia just knew by something in their demeanor. Angelique had that hint of reserve that Henri wore, while Trella had the radiance of warmth that Ramon projected.

Then it hit that not only was it odd for Trella to be out in public, with no family in sight, but *she was also in a prenatal clinic.*

"Oh. My. *God.*"

What was the normally cloistered Sauveterre twin doing in London? Holding a bottle of prenatal vitamins and looking guilty as hell? How did a woman who lived like a nun and had female guards get herself pregnant? Henri was going to lose his mind!

Trella tucked the bottle behind her back and opened her mouth, but only a weak *um* came out.

Cinnia's eyes were widening to the point they stung. She was pretty sure they were going to fall right out of her head.

She watched Trella's gaze narrow as the full scope of

where they were and why penetrated her side. Cinnia's blood pressure had been stable so far, but her limbs began to tingle and her head went so hot she felt like her hair was on fire. She was pretty sure whatever breaths she was managing to draw lost all their oxygen before hitting her lungs.

"Are you…okay?" Cinnia asked hesitantly. She didn't know exactly what Trella had been through when she had been kidnapped, but she knew it had left her afraid of men for a long time. Afraid of a lot of things.

Trella, being an enormously resilient and self-deprecating person, let out a choke of hysterical laughter and rolled her eyes. It was a "look where I am," and her shrug conveyed that she was dealing with an unplanned pregnancy, but not one caused by something traumatic.

"How about you?" she challenged with wry cheer, then sobered. She frowned at Cinnia's middle. "Is it…?" She glanced around.

*Henri's.* That's what she was asking.

Cinnia's eyes teared up. *Please don't tell him*, she silently pleaded.

This was part sitcom, part Greek tragedy. Her own hysterical laugh pressed for escape, but her tight throat wouldn't release it.

Trella straightened her spine so she was that little bit taller than Cinnia. She gave her wavy dark hair a toss.

"We'll pretend this didn't happen." She was a stunning woman in her midtwenties, but she looked nine years old, hiding stolen candy and bravely pretending it wasn't in her red-hot hand.

This was the sister Henri had told Cinnia had existed in his childhood, the brat who had driven him crazy getting herself into trouble, always needing her big brother to step in and fix it.

Cinnia wanted to hug her again. She was so proud of

Trella, even if conquering her past had led to a complicated future.

And she desperately wanted to share this moment with Henri, instinctively knowing that after the shock, this sign of healing in Trella would be a much-needed bright spot.

Or not. Worrying about any Sauveterre would sit heavily on him. Taking care of his mother and sisters was as much responsibility as he was willing to shoulder. That's why he'd drawn such a hard line against marrying and procreating.

A wistful sigh filled her, but she held it in. Ironic that she wanted to be there for him as he dealt with his sister's news knowing full well he would lose his mind once he learned Cinnia was carrying *his* child.

*I told you from the beginning I would never marry you.*

Her heart clenched afresh, abraded and stung. *Scorned.*

"Ms. Whitley," the nurse said behind her. "I can take you now."

"It's really good to see you," Cinnia said to Trella, holding out her arms for another quick hug. "I've missed all of you."

Most of Cinnia's interactions with Henri's family had been over the tablet, but she felt the loss of connection to the Sauveterre clan quite deeply.

"I would ask you to give my regards to everyone, but…" Cinnia trailed off.

Trella's arms were firm and strong around her. She pulled away slowly, tilting her head so they were eye-to-eye. Would her baby have those Sauveterre eyes, Cinnia wondered with a pang? *Babies?*

"You and I can stay in touch now," Trella said with a conspiratorial twitch at the corners of her mouth. Her expression sobered to concern. "*Can* I call you? I'd like to know why…"

Cinnia knew that keeping the pregnancy from Henri was a losing battle. She just wanted a plan in place before he found out so he wouldn't feel trapped. Trella was far too close to her siblings to keep her own pregnancy a secret from them for long. Once she spilled those beans, Cinnia's condition would be quick to follow.

But if she could buy a little time to get her ducks in a row, maybe find out exactly how many babies she was actually having...

She nodded. "If you're still in London at the end of the week, why don't we have dinner?"

# CHAPTER ONE

*Two years ago...*

CINNIA WAS NOT a social climber, but her roommate, Vera, was. Cheerfully and without apology. Thus, when Vera wangled opening-night tickets from the owner of *the* hottest new nightclub in London, she demanded Cinnia accompany her.

"I told him about your title," Vera said. "That's how I got him to say yes to our coming."

"The title that belongs to my great-uncle a million times removed whom I've never met and who wouldn't know me from Eve?"

"I might have exaggerated how close you are. But I told him about your granny's vintage tiara and since his theme is 'flappers and gangsters,' and he wants window dressing, he said we could come as staff. No swag," Vera said with a dismayed wrinkle of her nose. "Just mingle with the guests. Be first on the dance floor, that sort of thing."

Cinnia was reluctant. Her weekends were her only time away from her job at a wealth management firm to put the pieces in place for striking out on her own. She had set September as her goal and had a mile-long list of to-dos to make it happen.

"You work too hard," Vera groaned. "Look at it as a

chance to rub elbows with potential clients. This will be wall-to-wall, top-tier, A-list celebs."

"That's not how it works."

Cinnia's mother saw a different opportunity when Cinnia spoke to her over the tablet. "Tell me I can't wear the tiara so I can tell Vera there's no point."

"Nonsense. We'll get my dress out of storage, too. It's time they both saw some use. You, too, for that matter." Her mother had purposely held a Roaring Twenties party on her tenth anniversary so she could wear her grandmother's modest, heirloom tiara. She had had a beaded dress made special for the occasion.

"You wouldn't get the tiara from the safe-deposit box when we were broke and I wanted to sell it, but you'll let me wear it to a nightclub?" Cinnia asked, askance.

"This is why I kept it, for you girls to wear on special occasions. Go. Have fun. There's bound to be some nice men there."

"Rich husbands, you mean? They don't sell them at the bar, Mum."

"Of course not. It will be an open bar for something like this, won't it?" her mother returned tartly.

There was a reason she and her sisters called their mum Mrs. Bennet. She was forever trying to find their golden ticket of a husband. There was also a reason she was so determined to do so. The Whitleys had descended from aristocracy. The blue blood cells had been significantly diluted by bright, peasant red, but Milly Whitley was determined that her daughters *would* make good matches and the Whitleys *would* return to the lofty position they'd all enjoyed before Mr. Whitley had died and his fragile financial house of cards had toppled around them.

Until then, they would dress the part and hang on to a

house that was a money pit and they would attend the sorts of occasions that told the world they hadn't gone anywhere.

"I daresay you'll find a better class of suitor than your usual struggling students and apron clingers," her mother added snobbishly.

*All they needed was one man with deep pockets.*

Or, as Cinnia had said countless times, they could all get proper jobs like normal people.

Her two middle sisters decried that as blasphemy.

Priscilla, her first younger sister, was a *model*. Genuinely pretty, but not in high demand. Two years out of school and she had barely worked at all. She just needed a better head shot or a new outfit or a change of hairstyle and her career would take off, she kept assuring them. Completing a course in hairstyling or something useful like that would only hold her back.

Nell, their stunning little party girl, didn't need a job. Boys already bought her things and *she* was the one who would land them the Big Fish when the time came. If Cinnia could somehow keep her in school long enough to complete her A levels without getting pregnant, she'd be thrilled.

Thankfully Dorry had a brain and ten times anyone's ambition to use it. Their youngest sister had been babysitting from the moment she was old enough to wipe a nose and currently had a job in a fish-and-chip truck, much to their mother's repulsion. Dorry squirreled her money before anyone saw it and kept her head down, usually bent over a book. If something happened to Cinnia, she had every confidence her baby sister would keep the rest of them fed and sheltered.

She was trying not to put that on poor Dorry. After trying to help her mother win a fight against owing back taxes and other debts associated with her father's estate,

Cinnia had taken an interest in wills and estate planning. As careers went, it paid well enough, was stable and flexible and she found it intellectually challenging.

Her mother said she might as well be an undertaker.

Vera said, "No matter what, do not tell any men we chat up what you do for a living. Not unless we're trying to get away from them."

Cinnia didn't have Vera's interest in meeting men. Her mother's lack of a career to fall back on had been their downfall. All Milly was qualified to do was take in university students as boarders because she had a big house, which was how she paid the bills, much to her everlasting embarrassment. She spun it as a lark when people asked about it. She liked to be surrounded by young people, she said, playing eccentric.

Cinnia was determined never to have her back against the wall like that. She was already self-supporting and, even though she knew running her own agency came with risk, she had hit the ceiling where she was. The next step was to become her own boss.

Thus, she was thinking about how to build her client list as she stood with Vera, chatting to an unassuming musician and a nerdy social-media magnate. The men were ridiculously wealthy and equally shy, which was why bubbly women like Vera had been called in, Cinnia supposed, letting her gaze stray to take in an evening beyond any she would experience again in this lifetime.

The nightclub was in a reclaimed industrial building, tricked out with steel and glass and modern art. Top-shelf liquor was served in cut-crystal glasses by uniformed bartenders. The main room was open to the upper floor, making the place feel airy despite the crush of people in the low-slung chairs and standing in groups around the full dance floor.

Tonight, the tables had been covered with velvet table-cloths and the place was littered with feather boas and faux furs. The typical nightclub black light had been replaced with a sultry red. It threw sexy shadows into every corner and gave faces a warm glow. The DJ was mashing old jazz and modern hits with delightful results while a bouncer guarded stairs that rose to a walk-around gallery on the upper level. When they'd arrived, they'd been given a peek into the ultraposh, private entertainment rooms reserved for the most exclusive guests.

Judging by the movie stars and the other celebrities *not* gaining access, those rooms would be used by a very rich and exalted personality indeed.

Cinnia wasn't impressed with money and fame, but she would love to take on any of these pocketbooks as clients. Sadly, people with this much money to throw around were not interested in a boutique agency still smelling of builder's dust. She had known from the outset that nothing would come of this evening beyond a few lost hours and a cute entry in the logbook of appearances made by her great-granny's tiara. *C'est la vie.*

Then she saw *him*.

Them, really. The Sauveterre twins. The male pair. The same gorgeous man in duplicate arrived at the top of the short flight of entrance stairs, where they overlooked the sunken area of the main lounge.

Her pulse stumbled.

She was startled to see them in person. And curious, of course. She'd been eleven when their sister had been kidnapped, old enough to follow the story as intently as the rest of the world. It had had a profound impact on her. To this day it made her heart feel stretched and tense just thinking about it.

The family name had turned up in a million news stories and gossip magazines and online hits since then. That's how she knew, despite the distance across the dimly lit room, that they were as handsome as they seemed from afar.

They had identical dark hair cut close under matching black fedoras tilted slyly to the left. While every other man had turned up in a baggy, striped suit with a red tie and carried a violin case, these two wore crisp black shirts with the cuffs rolled back, high-waisted, tailored black pants held up with white suspenders and smart white ties.

The sharp look accentuated their muscled shoulders and neat hips, while the narrow cut of the pants drew her eye to their matching black-and-white wing tips. They *looked* like gangsters of old, but the really dangerous ones. The ones so powerful and commanding, they didn't have to swagger. They killed with a blink.

They wore exactly the same expression of bored tolerance as they pushed their hands in their pockets and scanned the room.

It was funny to see them move in unison, which held her attention until one stopped. He turned his head from the direction of the stairs, barely moving, but it was as if he sensed her attention and met her gaze all the way from across the club.

Cinnia's heart took a funny bounce. She told herself it was the embarrassment of being caught gawking coupled with the shock of recognizing a celebrity. Catching a glimpse of the Sauveterre twins, even in a place filled with faux royals and rock stars, was a big deal. She knew they were regular people underneath the reputation, not something to get fluttery over, but she was rather giddy holding this man's gaze.

*There's my rich husband, Mum.* The thought made her smile at herself.

His head tilted just a little and he gave a slight nod. It was a very understated acknowledgement. *Hello.*

"Who do you see?" Vera asked, and followed Cinnia's gaze, whispering under her breath, "Oh, my *gawd.*"

The men moved down the stairs onto the dance floor, leaving Cinnia swallowing and trying to recover from something that had been nothing. Why did her blood feel as though it was stinging her veins?

"We have to meet them," Vera insisted.

"Shh." Cinnia protested, forcing her gaze back to the crooner. She and Vera were supposed to be circulating and making small talk. "Who needs another Gin Rickey?" she asked the men.

She absolutely refused to look around and see if *he* looked at her again. Why would he? Still, she remained attuned to him, feeling prickly and hypersensitive, like she was in grade school and her first crush had entered the room. She knew exactly where he was as they both moved around the room for the next half hour.

Vera leaned into her. "They're by the bar. Let's get into their line of sight."

"Vera."

"We'll just see if we can say hi. Besides, there will be a stampede for drinks when it's time to toast. We should freshen ours now, so we can take them outside for the fireworks."

She and Vera quickly realized they'd be swimming upstream trying to get nearer the twins *or* the bar. They moved to safer ground near the bottom of the stairs and stood with attentive expressions as the club owner quieted the room and thanked everyone for coming.

Or rather, Cinnia gave their host her polite attention while Vera visually cruised for fresh prospects.

Vera would flirt with anyone. She was fun loving, pretty

and had a knockout figure that reeled men in from across a pub or wherever she dragged Cinnia for a night out. They'd met at university and Vera was not only loyal, funny and caring, but also the absolute best at keeping Cinnia from becoming the stick-in-the-mud that Vera always called her.

Cinnia wasn't as curvy as Vera, but she drew her share of male attention. She might not try to get by on her looks the way her mother thought she could, but she knew her wavy blond hair and patrician features gave her certain advantages. They were also a perfect foil for Vera's darker looks, which *Vera* used to her advantage.

Cinnia didn't date so much as play Vera's wingwoman. She had come out tonight knowing they would very likely wind up departing the club with whomever Vera had set her sights on. But, while Vera often went home with men she barely knew, Cinnia fully expected to find her way back to their flat alone.

As the speeches finished up and the fireworks were promised to start soon, there was a minor lull in noise.

"It'd be nice if we could find some men to buy us a drink."

It was classic Vera, spoken mostly in jest because she knew it got under Cinnia's skin. She knew Cinnia believed women should be self-reliant and not look to men for anything.

Cinnia bit back her knee-jerk lecture on feminism, refusing to let her friend get a rise out of her.

Behind them, a male voice said, "Ladies? Are you going up?"

Henri recognized the blonde as they made their way toward the stairs. She had a serene profile and a graceful figure draped in a vintage-style dress that he imagined his sisters would coo over. They were the fashion aficionados, but he knew quality when he saw it.

Everything about this woman was understated elegance. In a sea of heavy makeup and over-the-top flapper gear, she wore a short black number that shimmered with fringe. Her hair was pressed into the pinched waves of old and a simple line of diamonds banded it. One side of her delicate tiara was bedecked with a leafy filigree and a single feather.

She looked smart and feminine without even trying.

She had smiled at him earlier, which was nothing new. People stared and acted like they knew him all the time. Heads in the crowd were turning to do it now. He usually ignored it, but he had looked back at her for a full thirty seconds because, why not? She was beautiful. It hadn't been a chore.

Neither was this side of her. The dress didn't need to hug her figure to show off her pert ass and slender thighs. It was rather erotic in the way it only suggested at the curves it disguised.

"Company?" he suggested.

Possessing exactly as healthy a libido as Henri, Ramon followed his gaze, saw the stacked brunette beside her and commented, "Good eye."

They easily operated as one unit without preplanning. Henri paused beside the women in time to hear them wish for a man to buy them drinks.

Ramon stepped past them to open the chain on the bottom of the stairs himself, not bothering to identify himself to the bouncer. Everyone knew them on sight.

"Ladies? Are you going up?" Ramon's gaze flicked back to Henri. He'd heard their lament and Henri very subtly signaled he didn't care.

They were targets of gold diggers all the time. They had

both learned to take care of themselves. It didn't mean a good time couldn't be had by all.

The brunette blushed and smiled, standing taller, shoulders going back. She was dazzled and very receptive. "Yes. We are." She nodded confidently despite the fact they all knew who moved freely up these upstairs and who did not. She nudged the blonde.

The blonde pursed her mouth with dismay. Embarrassed at being overheard as a mercenary? No need. Henri found that to be the easiest and most convenient of traits to manage in a woman.

The music started up again, increasing his desire to leave the noise and crowd behind.

The blonde looked warily between him and his brother, giving Henri the sense she was trying to work out which one of them had met her gaze earlier.

He and Ramon didn't fight over women. There was no point since neither of them wanted long-term relationships. Women seemed to view them as interchangeable anyway. But Henri found himself annoyed by the idea she might decide to go with Ramon.

What had been a generic restlessness responding to the gaze of a beautiful female ticked up into a desire to have this one in particular.

"Watch the fireworks from our suite," Ramon said with easy command, waving an invitation. "Save me from staring at my own face."

"Why would you stare at your brother when you'll be watching the fireworks?" the brunette asked with a cheeky bat of her lashes. "Maybe if you didn't dress alike you wouldn't feel like you were talking into a mirror?"

"We don't do it intentionally." Ramon offered his arm to escort her up the stairs. "It happens even when we're half the world away from each other. We've stopped fighting it."

"Really!"

The pair was quickly lost in the shadows of the gallery.

The blonde gazed after her friend, biting her lip, then relaxed her mouth and licked her lips as she glanced at Henri. It almost seemed a nervous response, but the action flooded color into a mouth that now looked dewy and soft as rose petals, shiny and kissable. A very enticing move.

His gaze lingered on the sight, as his mind slid naturally into the pleasant fantasy of crushing her mouth with his.

"Shall we?"

She fell into step beside him.

This was not his first time picking up women with his brother. He and Ramon had long ago concluded that if they were saddled with being *the Sauveterre twins* they were damned well going to take advantage of the one outstanding benefit. Startlingly good looks, times two, along with buckets of money and celebrity status meant that the sweetest companions were in endless supply.

"Was that true?" the blonde asked, leaning in to be heard. "That you dress alike at other times, not just tonight?"

"Yes." Henri hated talking about himself and loathed even more talking about his family, but this was one of those innocuous tidbits that strangers loved to hear. The mystery of being a twin was infinitely fascinating to those who weren't. He accepted it and had stopped fighting it, as well.

At least tonight it gave him an excuse to hold her arm as he leaned down to speak in her ear, liking the silken brush of her hair against his nose as he inhaled a scent that was cool English roses and warm woman.

"In fact, when one of us changes out of what the other is wearing, we inevitably spill something and have to go back to the first outfit."

"You're joking."

He shrugged off her skepticism. His sisters were connected on an emotional level. He and his brother were more outwardly aligned. They had very different personalities, were competitive as hell with each other, but often spoke in unison or followed a similar thought process, inevitably arriving at the same end result. As Henri had been calling his brother to suggest they host this year's planning sessions in London instead of their usual Paris or Madrid, Ramon had been accepting the invite to this club opening.

"I'm, um, Cinnia. Whitley." She offered her hand as they arrived on the upper floor.

"Henri." Her skin felt as soft as it looked and was warmer than the pale tone suggested. She had a firm grip for a woman. He didn't want to let her go, but she pulled her hand free to glance behind him at Guy, who had followed them, then frowned at Oscar ahead of them, already stepping through the door to the suite where Ramon waited with her friend.

"Do you have bodyguards?"

"It's just a precaution." They followed into them the suite.

While Oscar inspected the room, Guy brought out his phone and sent a brief text—a request for a background check on both women no doubt. Helping Guy along, Henri introduced himself to the brunette, learning her name was Vera Phipps.

Aside from relying on men's wallets rather than their own, Henri judged both women to be harmless. Vera sent a "jackpot" look to Cinnia when a butler arrived to take their order, then she followed Oscar's path through the room, trailing fingers on the low-slung sofa and chairs as she circled, glancing to the flat screen hung on the wall, and stepped onto the balcony for a quick sniff of the air off the Thames.

She came back just as quickly to fetch one of the swag bags from the coffee table. "Oh! A gold one! Everyone below got silver. And yours is bigger."

"I hear that a lot," Ramon said with a smirk, making Vera laugh throatily.

"I bet you do. May I look?" She batted her lashes suggestively.

Cinnia did not flirt so blatantly. She offered a demure thank-you as the butler poured their champagne and moved outside to glance at the colored lights swirling on the water. In the middle of the river, the technicians on the float set off a test flare.

It was a warm evening without a breeze. Her gaze lifted to the sparkle of lights across the water and up to the stars.

"I'm surprised you stayed below as long as you did when you had this to retreat to," she said as Henri padded out to join her. He was compelled. Drawn. It was strange and not something he would typically indulge. The strength of his attraction made him a little uncomfortable.

Below them, people began filing out to the outdoor lounge while the music followed them.

Ramon was the one who liked crowds. Henri preferred a quieter atmosphere, but he said smoothly, "Good thing we did or I wouldn't have met you."

Her snort was delicate, if disparaging. Most blondes with blue eyes played up the suggestion of vulnerable innocence in their coloring. Not Cinnia. Her vintage hairstyle framed her face in a waifish way, but her brows had a sharp, intelligent angle. Her lashes stayed low and her gaze watchful, not cynical, but not goggling or overly impressed by any of this.

He liked that sign of inner confidence and strength. It

was compelling, sparking his curiosity. "You feel differently?"

"I feel this is a well-oiled machine you two are operating." She flicked her glance to the plate of canapés that appeared like magic on the glass table next to them.

"I would call that distrustful," he said, waiting until the server had gone to swing his gaze back to hers. "If I didn't think you two were running a similar routine. I'll call it hypocritical instead."

Her blue gaze flashed to his, but inside the suite, Vera was laughing at something Ramon had said. The two were meshing like cogs rolling against one another to turn out a foregone conclusion. Cinnia's mouth tightened.

"Unable to deny it?" he taunted gently.

"You approached us," she reminded with enough pique to amuse him.

"I was invited."

"I didn't mean to stare." Her gaze returned to the view, chin coming up.

It had been more than a stare. She had smiled at him.

He watched with fascination as the fringe across her breasts quivered under an indignant breath. He would bet her cheeks were pink if the light was high enough to tell.

"I doubt I'm the first to be curious about the pair of you. You make a fetching couple." Her smile was pure aspartame.

Her eyes, however, were a spun sugar blue. That was unmistakable as a huge white light swirled down from a helicopter, rousing the crowd below into cheering.

Her beauty gave him a sudden kick in the chest. It wasn't a trick of makeup because she wore very little. The requisite eyeliner made her eyes stand out, but she'd only darkened her lashes a little. They weren't lengthened with false ones like so many women wore these days. A shimmery blue streaked across her lids, but otherwise her features were clean and her skin fine and creamy.

"Did you really know it was me who looked back at you, or is that an assumption? Because it usually takes people months, even years to tell us apart." It was easy once a person realized Henri was left-handed and Ramon right, or that Henri tended to speak French as his default while Ramon preferred Spanish, but few noticed those details.

"You are remarkably alike, but…" She glanced into the suite, to where Ramon was holding open the designer bag, listening politely to Vera wax in delight over the contents. They usually let their mother pick over the contents of those bags, then handed the rest to their PAs, but Henri was just as happy to let these women take them home.

He took advantage of Cinnia's distraction to glance at his phone. The bullet points backed up what he'd already assumed. Her mother was wellborn, but the family was broke. Cinnia worked for a wealth management firm and was listed on their website as an intern. Filing and fetching coffee, he assumed. The only risk Cinnia Whitley posed was financial and he was quite sure he could afford her.

He tucked his phone away, irritated to note she was still eyeing his brother, brows pulled together in consternation.

"But?" he prompted, having to stand close to be heard over the music below.

"I don't know. I don't read auras or anything like that, but… Never mind." She flashed him another look, this one self-conscious.

Sexually aware?

"That's interesting." His annoyance evaporated, replaced by intensified attraction. He leaned his elbow on the rail so he was even closer to her, edging into her space, liking the way she tried to quell a little shiver. She smelled like roses and tropics and something earthy that further turned him on.

"Wh-what is?" She was trying to look blasé, but he knew the signs of physical magnetism. There was a pulse beating fast in her throat, but it wasn't fear. She wasn't moving away. She was skimming her gaze across his shoulders and down his chest.

Chemistry was such a wonderful thing. He didn't move, allowing the primal signals to bounce between them, stimulating him and heightening his senses. Sex was the cheapest and best high in the world as far as he was concerned.

"You react to me, but not to him."

"I didn't say that!"

"Didn't you? My mistake."

"You *are* mistaken," she assured him hotly. "Whatever you're thinking about me—*us*—and why we came up here, forget it."

She wasn't used to being so attracted to the men she exploited, he surmised. Poor thing. This must be very disconcerting for her. With that reserved personality, he bet she usually did quite well at stringing a man along. Was she afraid she wouldn't be able to hold out with him until she had squeezed all she could from him?

"I'm thinking you're here to watch the fireworks. What did you think I was thinking?"

She spun back to the view, setting her chin.

He smiled. "Listen." He very lightly stroked the back of his bent finger down her bare arm, entranced when goose pimples chased the same path.

She shot him a look that was startled and uncertain, quickly rubbing the bumps away.

"I don't have to work this hard to get a woman to sleep with me. This is how I live." He waved his champagne glass at the opulence around them. "Enjoy it without feeling obligated."

"You won't expect anything after?" she scoffed.

"By *anything*, do you mean that?" He thumbed to where Vera was on tiptoe inside the suite, painting herself against Ramon, lips firmly locked over his.

Cinnia made a pained noise and looked out across the river again. As strategies went, her friend was overplaying her hand.

"I shall remain hopeful," Henri drawled.

"Yes, you will remain that way," Cinnia assured him.

He hid a silent laugh behind the glass he lifted to his lips, deciding he wanted her quite badly and was willing to pay whatever it cost. He respected people who knew what they were worth.

But he only said, "Don't make promises unless you can keep them, *chérie*."

# CHAPTER TWO

VERA, THE *TRAITOR*, left with Ramon before the fireworks started.

"That's what you two were talking about in Spanish?" Cinnia hissed as she had three seconds alone on the balcony to react.

"I told you a language degree opened doors," Vera joked, then rolled her eyes at the face Cinnia was making. "Come *on*. Look at them! Surely you're tempted? It's long past time you worked Avery out of your system, you know."

She knew. And, of course, she was tempted. She wasn't in Vera's league when it came to sexual gymnastics, but she'd had a couple of long-term relationships that had been nice until they'd gone bad. The first had been an immature thing that should have ended before they went off to separate universities, but she'd clung to what they'd had and he'd wound up cheating. Her heart had been battered at the time, but looking back she knew they'd been far too young for the level of commitment she had expected.

Avery, however, had broken her heart in two, professing love for her while they'd both been struggling through a heavy course load and then trying to make ends meet when they moved to London together. Then he had come into some money and cut her off cold, stating bluntly that her family was too much of a handful and he didn't need the dead weight. Thankfully Vera had been there for her when he'd kicked her out.

Since then, Cinnia had stayed out of the relationship arena, thinking it wiser to concentrate on getting her career off the ground.

Not that Henri would offer a relationship. She knew *that* without asking. But she couldn't deny she was intrigued by him. Every time he glanced at her with male appreciation oozing out of his pores, her hormones swayed in an erotic dance of come-hither. Like the extravagance of the night itself, she kept trying to rationalize indulging in whatever he was offering.

She didn't do one-time hookups, though. And even if she did sleep with him purely for the fun of it, he would *believe* she'd done it in exchange for being wined and dined here in this heavenly suite. She hated the idea of him thinking she could be bought. It went right to the core of the insecurities Avery had instilled in her.

"It's quite a signature for the autograph book," Vera murmured with a self-satisfied grin. "You know your mother would approve. There's a first-class trip to Australia in that bag, you know. And a smartwatch and a year's lease on a sports car. Get what you can out of it!"

Henri came back from taking a call, probably overhearing Vera's vulgar suggestion—like he needed any more ammunition to believe they were a pair of opportunists.

Seconds later, Ramon came out and said, "The car is waiting. Lovely to meet you, Cinnia."

He and Vera disappeared like a snuffed flame leaving a wisp of burned friendship hanging in the air.

Henri sat down across from Cinnia at the high-top table, mouth relaxed, but she had the sense he was laughing at her ill-disguised panic. He signaled to the butler to freshen their drinks.

"Where do you think he's taking her?" she asked as the butler left.

"The nearest hotel with a vacant room, I imagine."

She shouldn't have asked.

"Why does it bother you?"

"It doesn't."

"You're judging," he accused. "Why?"

She wanted to deny it. She considered herself open-minded and forward thinking. She didn't slut-shame. Women had needs and Vera was no one's victim.

"Vera can do whatever she wants. I don't like the idea that you're judging me by her choices, though." She hated it. Avery's awful accusations came back to her and she felt raw all over again. Worse even, as she thought of this man who *lived like this* thinking she wanted a shortcut to the same lifestyle. "I don't sleep with men for a swag bag. I have a job. I buy what I need and if I can't afford something, I live without it."

"What do you do?" He looked like he was asking out of politeness, not like he really believed her speech on self-sufficiency.

She almost blurted "funeral arrangements" just to put him off.

"I have a business degree and I'm a qualified financial advisor, but my focus is estate planning and trust management."

His stall of surprise was painful in how loudly it spoke of his having underestimated her.

"I'm a very boring person," she said, wishing she could be more smug at defying his assumptions about her, but she only felt the difference in their stations more keenly. He had obviously written her off as trifling. And yes, she was trying to climb higher than where she'd wound up, but through honest hard work. Still, she would never reach his level and that put *him* well beyond her reach.

Not that she wanted him.

Did she?

With an uncomfortable sting in her blood, she picked up her champagne then remembered she had decided to stop drinking now that Vera was gone. She took a sip of water instead.

"I wasn't expecting that," he admitted.

"You thought I was a secretary? Airline hostess? Model? Even if I was, those are all honest careers in their own right."

"They are. And you could model. You're very beautiful."

"So could you. You have a face so nice, God made it twice."

He snorted. "Point to you," he conceded with a grimace. "I absolutely hate to be reduced to 'one of the Sauveterre twins.' We are all more than we appear on the surface, aren't we?"

Oh, the bastard, now she couldn't hate him unequivocally.

"Is it bad?" she asked, feeling compelled to do so. "I mean, I see things online all the time that I know have to be pure rubbish. The same nonsense that shows up about all celebrities, saying you're having an alien's baby or whatever. Does it bother you, though? Do you resent being famous because of an accident of birth?"

He took a moment to answer.

"I don't resent being who I am. I don't talk about my family—" his gaze shot to hers in warning to stay well back "—but I wouldn't trade them for anything. The attention is a pain in the ass and not something we invite. It annoys me, but I've learned to pick my battles." He said it flatly, but the nail beds of his fingers were white where he gripped his glass.

"Well, I—" She stopped herself, holding out a hand. "Message received about your family," she assured him. "You've earned the right to privacy. But I hope she's well. Your sister, I mean."

She was tempted to say more, weirdly yearning to explain that his family's pain had rippled out to her in the strangest way. She'd been as taken as anyone with the Sauveterre twins. The girls were a little younger than her, but they had seemed like an ideal worth emulating, living much larger than Cinnia even though her family had been doing quite well in those days.

Then Trella had been kidnapped and she'd been terrified for the girl. Of course, she had been compelled to follow the rest of the family's exploits forevermore. She was as curious as anyone about why his youngest sister had dropped out of the public eye in her teens. Had she gone into rehab? A madhouse? A nunnery? Theories abounded, but Cinnia kept her lips sealed against asking for the truth.

Against asking him if he was still dealing with the fallout.

The butler brought another plate of hors d'oeuvres, this one with tiny deviled quail eggs, caviar and stuffed olives and a whipped salmon mousse with narrow fingers of toasted bread. It was exquisite and she kept her gaze on it to hide how thinking of his past had altered her perception of him. She wanted to dismiss him as a womanizer who should be avoided, but he was human. He'd been hurt. Scarred.

"Why estate planning?"

She dragged her gaze off the plate, heart taking a skip as she met his gaze.

"Many reasons. I started looking into it after my father died. There was a lot to untangle and as I learned what he could have done, I kept wondering why he hadn't set it up this way or that. My mother would have had it easier if he'd shown some foresight. Looking at it as a career, I saw it was flexible, something you could do without a lot of overhead. You can even work from home if you have to. Everyone needs a will, whether they know it or not. And it's one of those things that if you're good and fast, you can make a decent living. I didn't see a downside beyond its lack of sex appeal."

"Which you more than make up for in being yourself."

He said it with gentle mockery. She knew he meant it as over-the-top flattery, but her cheeks still warmed. She tried to hide how affected she was with a dry "I try."

The fireworks started and they turned to watch.

She was more aware of him than the performance. He was very charismatic with his air of aloof charm and hint of a French accent. He was also subtly demonstrative, lightly caressing her wrist as he drew her attention to the flotilla of boats coming in to watch.

Everything he did made her very aware of herself. Her breaths felt deliberate, her skin sensitized, her movements a dance of grace. She was being seduced and he wasn't even making an effort to do it. Her mind drifted to thoughts of kissing him. Feeling his weight against her.

Her skin warmed, her nipples tingled and she pressed her knees together to ease the ache in the fork of her thighs.

She was sorry when the fireworks ended and her excuse for being here was over.

"Oh, no," she said quickly, declining the butler's offer to bring strawberries and cream with a fresh bottle of champagne as he removed their plate of finger foods.

"Do *not* worry about your figure," Henri said, nodding to the butler.

"I'm worried about my *survival*. I'm allergic. I have a pen for emergencies and everything." She nodded at her clutch.

"It's that bad?" He held up a hand to halt the butler.

"I nearly died at a sleepover once, because my friend didn't want to fess up that she'd stolen a bottle of her dad's best wine for homemade sangria." She rolled her eyes, making light of what a frightening near miss she'd had.

He refused the strawberries and told the butler he would press the call button when they were ready for more champagne.

"Have them if you want them," Cinnia protested. "It's not so bad I can't watch someone else eat them."

He tucked his chin, leaning forward as the butler closed the door behind himself. "But I can't kiss you if I've eaten them. Can I?"

His words made her ears ring. She stole a long, subtle inhale, holding his gaze while she tried not to let him see how easily he sent her blood pressure into the stratosphere.

"Remaining hopeful?" Her gaze dropped to his mouth.

"Very much so."

She forced herself to slide off her tall chair, excusing herself to the attached powder room. *Time to go*, she told her reflection. The woman in the mirror was entirely too heavy lidded, her defenses against Henri thinning by the second.

When she returned, Henri was inside the suite. The lighting fell in subdued angles off the wall sconces and from the patio lanterns below the balcony, setting an intimate tone while the music inside the club pulsed in muted rhythm through the walls.

Henri had raided his swag bag for a box of chocolate

truffles with a Belgian label and was opening one wrapped in gold foil. A ball of discarded foil was already on the table next to the box.

"I have a sweet tooth," he admitted ruefully, offering the truffle.

"No, thanks. I'll, um, go. This was nice. Thank you." She stuck out her hand, feeling like an idiot the moment she did it.

He set aside the chocolate and brought out his phone. "I'll order the car and take you."

"I can manage."

He gave her a pithy look. "I meant it about not feeling obligated. I can drive you home without attacking you. I've made my appearance here. I don't plan to stay."

It wasn't him she was worried about. She was half-tempted to ask him to find the nearest vacant hotel room. Vera's voice was playing in her head, extolling the virtues of being a modern woman who owned her sexuality. *You eat if you're hungry, don't you?*

Cinnia was sexually hungry. She put it down to the excitement of dressing up for an extravagant evening, the soft breeze caressing her skin and champagne relaxing her. Henri was very attractive and she would bet any money he easily satisfied the most exotic of appetites.

"I think it's best if we end it here." She felt like a coward and couldn't help looking at his mouth again. She wanted him to kiss her. She really did. Her blood thickened in her arteries, throbbing with anticipation.

He quirked his lips. "If you tell me you have an allergy to chocolate, I'm going to be disappointed."

"I'll survive," she murmured, recognizing that she was consenting to a kiss. "My affairs are in order if I don't. And what a story to tell my grandchildren if I do." She said it to be cheeky, to keep this light and disguise that she was intrigued by him.

His breath rushed out in an incredulous *ha*, but he wasn't deterred. He crowded close, hands opening on her waist and drawing her forward into him.

"I'd best make it memorable then."

She wore low kitten heels and he was very tall, well over six feet and overwhelming as he bent his head to brush his mouth against hers.

She clutched his shoulders for balance, shivering lightly, head instantly swimming. Was that it? She swallowed and wet her lips then parted them, inviting a more thorough goodbye than that.

He started to smile and she knew his move had been a deliberate tease to make her want more. He moved in like a damned marauder then covered her mouth fully, angling to plunder. *Claiming.*

She curled her fingers against his shoulders, feeling them tense as he drew her closer. She moaned as she kissed him back, quickly over her head and suddenly drowning. He buffeted her senses, filling her brain with the faint scent of aftershave and masculinity, enfolding her as she melted under a flood of arousal. His tongue came into her mouth and she tasted dark chocolate and darker intention.

He wanted her. She could feel how hard he was against her stomach. Her own body grew hot and achy in seconds. Longing struck her loins and she looped her arms fully around his neck to mash her breasts against his chest.

Too much, she thought as she did it, knowing it was a signal of receptiveness, but it was pure instinct. Wanton need.

She drew back, gasped once for air, then found herself kissing him again. Just once more. Okay twice. The third time she might have found her willpower, but the solidness of a wall arrived at her back. He ran his lips down her throat and slid his hand to cradle her breast.

"Oh," she breathed, loving the gentle way he massaged, then found her nipple through the fringe, circling and teasing. Her knee came up to his thigh of its own accord, making space for him to settle against her aching mons.

He growled his approval and ran his hand up her thigh, taking the hem of her dress up to her waist, hooking his forearm behind her knee and caressing her bottom as she picked her hips up off the wall and met his suggestive thrust.

He kissed her deeply, tongue delving into her mouth as he fondled her breast and the skin of her bottom exposed by her thong. They rocked in mock lovemaking, their sighs too low to be heard over the noise of the crowd and music drifting in from the open doors of the balcony.

This was so not her. She liked sex, but she had never behaved like this. It had never *felt* like this. She might actually climax fooling around fully clothed, grinding herself against him if he kept up that perfectly delicious rhythm. The hard length of him was right where it needed to be, rubbing against her most sensitized flesh. She was *so* turned on and really tempted to let it happen. It was like they were dancing. The song's beat was picking up, growing more intense. Tension was gathering in her abdomen and lower, in the flesh he was stimulating so erotically.

Dropping her head back against the wall, she bit her bottom lip, one hand bracing on his shoulder. They had to stop. They were practically in public and she was *so* close!

He whispered something in French that sounded like encouragement and reached one hand to lock the door. "It's okay. Come."

"I'm not—"

"*Oui, chérie*, you are. Very close. I can feel you trembling. It's exciting. Come."

She wanted to tell him he didn't know how she felt, but he kissed her like he had the first time, barely grazing her mouth so she turned her head, seeking further contact and clinging to his lips with her own.

"Let me give you this," he whispered as he broke away and shifted to bring his hand between them, gently tracing her tender flesh through the damp layer of black silk.

She stopped breathing. Anticipation held her very still as he drew light patterns over the silk of her thong. Her entire being narrowed to the touch of his fingertip, which was so light, yet made her throb with need. She waited in agony for his caress to steal beneath the elastic and...

"Mmm," she moaned when he finally did it.

"You like?" He stroked her *exactly* the way she needed, unhurried, kissing and drawing away, stoking her arousal, kissing her more deeply, gently penetrating, then whispering praise, promising to make it so good for her. "Come. I want you to."

She was going out of her mind, but his control was equally crazy making. She wanted to let go but she couldn't stand that he was doing this *to* her.

"Do you have a condom?" she gasped when he let her breathe again.

He stilled, eyes a silvery glimmer in the low light, gaze burning into hers.

"You want to make love?" he asked on a rasp.

Oh, please. His hand was in her knickers. He knew what she *wanted*. She was dying. But she wanted climaxing to be something they did together.

She slid her hands down to his fly, hands shaking so much with anticipation she was clumsy as she tried to open his pants.

He removed his hand and hooked her thong to peel it down, letting her leg drop so the silk slid to her ankles. Then he shrugged out of his suspenders and finished opening his pants, bringing a condom from his pocket before he hitched his pants low on his hips and revealed himself.

It ought to have been the moment she woke up and realized this was way beyond where it was supposed to go. Across the suite, the doors were open to a crowd of famous faces, hidden just below the rail.

Her world became a narrow, shadowed one where her blood was on fire. Every breath she drew was filled with his spicy, masculine scent. She admired the shape of him in the low light as she watched him roll the condom down his length. She was so filled with anticipation her loins clenched in pangs of yearning.

He nudged his feet between hers, stepping the thong off her ankle as he settled against her again, the heat of his body a type of deliverance. She gathered her skirt and lifted her leg, hooking her calf against his buttocks, offering herself. He bent his knees and glided to caress, teasing her a moment, wetting the tip before he nudged for entry. He pressed, finding no resistance, and thrust smoothly into her slick channel, so she dug her nails into the back of his neck and made a keening noise at the intensity of his thickness filling her.

"Hurt?" he grunted with surprise, pulling back a little.

"Oh, no," she breathed. "So good." She tightened her foot into the back of his thigh, urging him deeper.

He growled a noise of agreement and pressed all the way in, giving her a moment to greet his intrusion with little rippling hugs of her inner muscles, joyous at the invasion of that hot, hard length. So rock hard. They kissed like that, joined, barely moving as they stood against the wall, tongues laving against each other, bodies quaking with holding back, hot, so hot.

She had never been so overcome by desire that she stood against a damned wall with a stranger. She had never felt so desperate for *more*. She nudged to signal him that he was making her wait too long. Her arousal was a screaming pitch of need.

He breathed a soft laugh against her mouth and began to move with heavy purpose, not rough, but thorough, drawing out each movement so the pleasure went to its furthest degree each time, dragging tingles to the tips of her extremities. It was so sweet it made her teeth ache. She kept thinking it couldn't possibly get better, then he thrust heavily, landing deep, and it was fantastic.

She ceased thinking about where she was or who he was. Their lovemaking became her entire focus. Nothing mattered except that he was moving within her in that exquisitely perfect way. It was earthy and uncivilized, yet so finely tuned it was art. She wanted him with her in this place where he'd propelled her, where nothing existed except this pleasure.

She ran her tongue up his neck and sucked his earlobe and angled to take him as deeply as she could. She kissed him back with abandon and brought his hand up under her dress to her breast, then slid her own under his shirt to caress his tense stomach. She whispered, "I can't believe we're doing this."

He said something in French, his whole body shaking, as though he was in the same state of straining to hold back because this was too good to release.

"You're killing me, *chérie*. I can't hold on. Are you ready?"

"I don't want it to end," she gasped, turning her open

mouth against his neck and gently biting as the crisis threatened.

"Neither do I, but—ah!"

"Yes. Oh, Henri."

*"Oui. Ensemble. Maintenant."* He thrust harder. Faster.

Glory rose up in a gathering wave, locking them together in ecstatic culmination.

# CHAPTER THREE

IT WAS WEEKS after the nightclub before Henri found himself in London again. He hadn't stopped thinking about Cinnia Whitley and he didn't know why. Their evening together had followed exactly the pattern he'd assumed it would and it wasn't a new one.

Well, he usually closed an encounter with more grace, but she was the one who had disappeared when he'd stepped away to take what he thought might be an emergency call from his sister.

Regardless, it wasn't as if Ramon was giving a second thought to her friend Vera, so he didn't know why he couldn't stop thinking about Cinnia. Maybe it was because she hadn't behaved as predictably as her friend.

Vera had posted the selfie she'd taken with the four of them when they'd first entered the hospitality suite. She was using her rub with a Sauveterre to gain some celebrity status of her own. Absolutely nothing new and he didn't even bother feeling disgusted by it.

Cinnia hadn't shared the selfie to her own account, though. The one online quote he'd found attributed to her about him was "I met him briefly. There's nothing else to say."

Not one to kiss and tell, obviously.

Neither was he, so he appreciated her discretion.

Of course, what could one say about their lovemaking without sounding like a blatant liar or an overly romantic poet? He liked an involved partner and always did what he could to ensure the woman got as much from their lovemaking as he did. But to say he and Cinnia had had sex, or had given each other an orgasm, was to completely understate the act.

He kept rationalizing what had made it seem so powerful. She'd been resisting their attraction in a slow burn that had made her capitulation all the sweeter. The partially public location had held a titillating appeal. Their chemistry was very compatible.

As he'd leaned against the soft cushion of her body, barely able to keep his knees from buckling, he'd been… He wanted to call it empty, but even though he'd felt drained, he'd also felt utterly satisfied.

At peace.

All the responsibilities that weighed on him were still there. He hadn't stopped caring about them, but in that moment of euphoria, he'd accepted it all. If that was what had made him into the man who could be there with that woman, forehead tilted against the wall, cheek pressed to hers, inhaling her scent and twitching with reaction long after the pulses of orgasm had faded, feeling the very light stroke of her fingertips at his spine…

So be it.

Then he had heard Trella's ringtone and his demanding life had rushed back in to consume him. He had stepped away from Cinnia and straightened himself, snatching up the phone and answering it without visuals, stepping outside in case Trella was in crisis and he needed to talk her down.

Looking back, he knew he had reacted almost like a shock victim, rushing to get on with his life after a collision that had nearly taken his life. His head had been spinning, his body firing with adrenaline.

Since then, he had been telling himself he was wrong. Their lovemaking hadn't been anywhere near so profound as he recollected. Even if it had been the best sex of his life with a woman who possessed an ounce of discretion, so what? He wasn't in the market for a relationship and given the life he led, never would be.

At best, he might have stretched their association into the rest of the weekend, if she hadn't disappeared like the fire bell had rung. When he had realized she hadn't just ducked into the ladies' room, he had told himself it was for the best and asked for his order of strawberries.

The berries had been both sweet and tart, imprinting on his memory a little deeper with each bite. He suspected he would think of her every time he glimpsed a strawberry for a very long time and would wonder if she was managing to stay away from them.

Why? Such a ridiculous question to clog up his brain.

And yet, weeks later, as he entered a party he had no desire to attend and spotted her, his first thought was *so far so good*. She was alive and well, not having succumbed to fruit poisoning.

Her blond hair was gathered in a knot and held in place with a couple of sticks, but a few delicate spirals fell around her face. Her shoulders were bared by her white summer dress, her heels an attractive spike that showed off her legs. She wore only a pair of silver hoop earrings for jewelry.

She was as casually beautiful as he remembered, her expression serene as she listened to a man who wasn't her date, but looked like he wanted to be.

As was his habit, Henri had insisted his security be given the finalized guest list before he accepted the invitation. If people wanted him to show up to their affairs, they complied. That's how he had known Cinnia would be here and he'd made himself take a full ten minutes of sober second thought before he'd accepted the invite himself—without a plus one, as she had also done.

His heart started to thud with male need as he looked at her. He knew what lurked beneath that air of containment and he'd be damned if that gangly pontificator would discover it, as well.

Cinnia had convinced herself this engagement party for her friend from uni was yet another good "networking opportunity," even though she knew why she'd been invited. Once Vera's photo of the two of them with the twins had made the rounds, Cinnia had been inundated by old acquaintances eager to reach out. She was part of the "it" crowd now and her mother couldn't be happier.

If only she was in a position to decline, but she was too practical to be proud. Her friend was marrying into a very wealthy family from New York and their circle of friends included the types of fortunes that were just complex enough to need a qualified manager.

Unfortunately, you couldn't reply to casual questions about your career with "I'm drumming up biz for the agency I'm opening." Evenings like this were about making introductions and impressions, keeping the talk light yet memorable, then somehow finding an excuse at a point down the road to contact the same people and ask, "Do you have a plan for your eventual death?"

Since she didn't have a man in her life who was eager to put on a tie and show up to a stranger's engagement party, she had come alone and was now a target for the stags in rut. Gerald, here, was a perfect example, shadowing her through her last two attempts to ditch him. She swore if he asked for her number, she would give him her business card and tell him to call when he was ready to discuss his final wishes.

"Don't look now, but guess who just walked in," the woman across from her said with a sparkle in her eye. "I think you know him, Cinnia."

Of course Cinnia looked.

And promptly felt stretched thin as a strand of glass, so brittle she would break if a wrong word was breathed in her direction. Her throat closed and her chest stung from the inside. It took everything in her to keep a look of nonchalance on her face while her heart bolted for the nearest exit.

He was looking right at her, gorgeous in tailored grey pants and a black shirt *sans* tie, hat or suspenders. His forest green linen jacket should have looked affected, but, of course, it was a simple statement that he was gorgeous *and* stylish in modern garb as well as vintage.

"Not really," she said, turning back to her group, *begging* her cheeks not to go hot with betrayal. "I only met them briefly," she lied. For the millionth time.

It was an open secret that Vera had slept with Ramon. She hadn't just notched her bedpost, but had engraved the words *A Sauveterre Slept Here* on her headboard. *Every-one* assumed Cinnia had put out as well and it had taken her weeks to convince the world at large she hadn't.

Because, when a man could walk into a room and create a stir without doing a damned thing, what red-blooded woman *wouldn't* sleep with him the first chance she got?

Guilty as charged, obviously, but Cinnia was far too mortified to admit it. Why, why, why had he affected her so strongly she'd gone against her basic principles? She could already feel him creating the same wicked stir in her—which was unconscionable now she understood he hadn't just been availing himself but *cheating*.

"Friends with the groom, I guess?" Gerald murmured. "Looks like it. Not your date then, Cinnia?"

"No," she asserted, refusing to look at Henri again. *Refusing.* Burning inside with rejection. "I'm not even sure which one that is," she said, utterly bald-faced.

But she knew that was Henri. It didn't make sense to her that her body recognized him at a basic level while regarding his brother like any other man, but there it was. She was attuned and susceptible to *this* twin.

Please, God, don't let him know how susceptible. Would it be too obvious if she excused herself to the ladies' room and caught a cab away from here?

"What did you get for the happy couple?" she asked, trying to steer the conversation off Henri. "I saw they'd registered for one of those bullets to make smoothies, but someone beat me to it. I got them the yogurt maker instead."

"He's coming," the woman said, barely moving her lips, then pasting on a big smile. "Mr. Sauveterre. It's so nice to meet you."

*"Bonjour."* He nodded and set his wide hand on Cinnia's lower back as he leaned in to shake the offered hand. She stiffened, burned by the imprint of his touch through the satin of her dress. "Cinnia. Nice to see you again. Will you introduce me to your friends?"

She could hardly breathe with his palm sending waves of sensual excitement through her.

"Of course, um—" she squinted at him, making a show of guessing "—Henri?"

His gaze flashed and his thumb and finger dug into her waist in a suggestion of a pinch, promising retribution. *"Oui."*

He was a master at the small talk game, asking people how they knew the betrothed couple, discovering occupations and commenting on places of travel without offering a single detail about himself.

She stood dumbly paralyzed by his hand resting against her spine, telling herself to walk away, but unable to. Her entire body was reacting with the tingling memory of his muscled body moving against hers. Within her. It was all she could do not to betray that she was growing aroused by standing next to him. If she walked away, she'd only draw attention to how gripped she was by her reaction.

"Oh, Cinnia, there's someone you should meet. Let me introduce you."

Henri smoothly snagged her hand and drew her away while Gerald stammered, "Nice chatting with you, Cinnia…" in their wake.

Enough. She had to get away. She tugged at her hand. "I'm leaving," she told him.

"Excellent. Me, too."

*Oh, nice one.* She had walked blindly into *that*.

"But I do have to say hello to this couple." Apparently he knew them from New York. He drew her across the room.

She followed to avoid making a scene and they chatted for a few minutes. Cinnia quietly fumed, hating him and herself for still reacting. She was just about to make her escape by excusing herself to the powder room and crawling out a window when Henri tightened his grip on the hand she was subtly working free of his.

"I'm afraid we have to run. We should say good night to our hosts," he added to Cinnia, exactly as if they were a couple who had arrived together.

"They" were not a couple. He had demonstrated that clearly enough at the nightclub. Growing hot with fresh outrage, she waited until they'd left the prospective bride and groom and their roomful of friends with a meaty chunk of gossip to chew over before saying, "Why are you doing this? You're ruining my reputation."

"Untrue. Nothing a Sauveterre touches turns to anything but gold. You can thank me later."

*"How?"* she demanded with undisguised bitterness.

"Don't be crass." He steadied her with a hand under her elbow as he walked her down the stairs and out through the lobby of the hotel. A car glided to the curb before them. His guard reached around them to open the back door. "Where can I take you?"

"I think you know where I want you to go. I prefer you go alone."

"So hostile. You can't possibly be upset about how we left things since it was your choice to leave. Let's have this conversation away from our audience."

Flashes started going off and she realized paparazzi were swarming like mosquitos scenting fresh blood.

She slid into the car and he followed, reaching forward to close the privacy screen before the door had been slammed behind him.

His guard moved into the passenger seat and the car pulled away.

"I didn't expect such a cold greeting."

She made a choked noise. "I can imagine how you thought I'd greet you, given the way I behaved, but forget it. That was me getting over an old boyfriend. *That's all.*"

That's what she kept telling herself and she believed it about as well as anyone else believed she hadn't slept with Henri Sauveterre.

*"Vraiment?"* His tone chilled by several thousand degrees.

"Oh, I'm sorry, do you find that insulting?" She flicked her head around to send him a haughty look. "At least he and I were completely over. I didn't take his call while you and I were still—"

She wouldn't say it. It was too humiliating. Her cheeks hurt with a painful blush.

Giving in to the urge to make love with him on such short acquaintance was a tolerable mistake. Yes, she'd been weak enough to succumb to a player's best moves, but from a purely physical standpoint—pun intended—it had been great. She hadn't had any regrets as he'd leaned against her, both of them damp and still breathing hard.

Then the ring of his mobile had galvanized him into withdrawing and straightening himself, as he grabbed the phone and said, "Bella." He had gone outside, seeking privacy.

He might as well have smacked her. *Of course* he had other women in his life. Maybe their lovemaking had been profound and unique for her, but it was routine for him. She was no more than the stick of gum he chewed for fifteen minutes to freshen his breath!

Cinnia had tugged on her knickers and got the hell out of there.

"Are you serious?" he muttered now. "The call was from my sister."

"Not any less offensive," she declared, turning her disconcerted frown to the window, cautioning herself not to believe him. *Fool me twice...*

"*D'accord.* You're right. It was rude," he said begrudgingly. "But there are circumstances. I don't ignore her calls."

"That's nice. Tell your driver I'm on the other side of London. He's going the wrong way."

"Cinnia," Henri growled. "Have some compassion. There are *reasons*."

The kidnapping? The isolation? She glanced at him,

desperately wanting to throw his words back in his face, but he didn't look manipulative or even like he was trying to cajole. He looked frustrated and, beneath it, troubled.

She recalled him saying he never spoke about his family and sighed. Perhaps she would have to take him at his word, but it was still insulting as hell.

"Fine," she muttered.

"Do you mean that? Or is it a passive-aggressive *fine*?"

"Does it matter? I could ask you to tell me what those circumstances are, but you're not going to, are you?"

"No." His expression darkened.

She shrugged, hiding that his reticence struck her as lack of trust, which hurt far more deeply than it had a right to.

"So what do you care if I'm fine or not? Even if we'd ended things on a warmer note that night, you were never going to call me after. We both know that, so who cares how we end things now?"

"I care, obviously."

"No, you don't!" she cried on a scoffing laugh. "You walked into that party and saw the easiest girl in the room." If she could take back her capitulation… Would she? Oh, it was lowering to admit it, but probably not. Regardless, she'd be a fool to repeat it.

"You're looking for a do-over," she accused. Her voice cracked and she forced out a tight *no, thanks.*

*"Au contraire,"* he said, his voice so sharp and hard it stabbed through the thick plate she was trying to hold over her chest. "At least three women in that room were far easier. Trust me. I've met them in the past. Not slept with them," he quickly clarified. "But I've been invited to on very short acquaintance. I came tonight because you were on the guest list."

Her emotions were taking a bumpy ride despite the

smoothness of the car's suspension. He'd come to see *her*? She didn't want to believe that. It would make her soften toward him and she was already struggling to keep him at arm's length.

"I wish you hadn't. My supervisor already suggested it would be a good career move if I sent you a letter of introduction for the firm." She turned her face to the window again. "Now he'll be even more of a pain about it. *Thanks*."

"You want me to come into his office and let him give me his spiel? Fine."

"No, Henri, I don't!" She swung her head around, barely able to keep a civil tone. "What message does that send? Next he'll *tell* me who to sleep with in order to land a client. Men! Are you really that obtuse? Your notoriety is not 'gold' for me. It's a scarlet letter. Don't do me any favors."

He sat back, a ring of white appearing around his tight mouth.

"I can't help who I am, Cinnia. I can't help that people want to use me, or use anyone who comes close to me to get to me. If I could change it, I would, but I *can't*!" His voice rang through the small space like a thunderclap, rife with incensed frustration.

His outburst was so shocking, she sat in silence a moment, absorbing what he'd revealed—reluctantly, judging by the way he shut down immediately after.

Empathy rolled into the spaces he'd blown open in her. She couldn't help feeling bad for him then, especially as a motor scooter buzzed up alongside the car and the passenger on the back aimed a camera at the darkened window. It flashed, perhaps catching her frown of dismay.

He pinched the bridge of his nose, making a visible effort to maintain his strained control.

"Trella—Trella Bella as we call her, or Bella—has a particular struggle. Partly it's due to the attention we draw.

I make myself available to her when she needs it. We all do. If she had called Ramon, your friend Vera would be the one feeling slighted. Trella's situation is a fact of my life. That's all I'm saying on the topic and you can believe it or not or post it to your damned news feed if that will make you feel better."

"Of course I wouldn't," she said crossly. "Why would I deliberately hurt someone I don't even know?"

Now she would dwell forever on the struggles of that poor girl who had surely been through enough just from being kidnapped. No public statements had ever been made about what had really happened to her during the five days she was missing. Terrible things had been theorized, though. Cinnia dearly hoped none of them were true, but judging by Henri's grim expression, his sister had a lot to deal with.

She had such an urge to reach out to him in that moment, she had to clench her fingers together in her lap.

"Has the attention been bad?" he asked. "Are you being harassed by cameras outside your home? It's so rare I meet anyone who feels like I do, I didn't imagine it would be a burden for you."

She shrugged. "Mostly just friends and family are asking about it. I didn't say much and that's not out of character because I keep a low profile as a rule."

He glanced inquiringly, so she explained further.

"My kind of work is like banking or the law. Clients expect confidentiality and no one wants to give their portfolio to a woman who's posting party photos or running with a sketchy crowd, so I live quietly and don't put much online. But as you say, people put a lot of stock in the Sauveterre name. I realize it's not really a detriment to be associated with it. It would shatter my ego completely, however, to have people say I only succeeded because of who I know. And to have my boss pressure me like that? I was really annoyed."

"Did you report him to your HR?"

"There's no point."

"There is. Speaking as the president of a huge company, I can't fix what I don't know is broken. I need reports of that sort of thing so I can take action or it will keep happening."

She hadn't thought of it that way, only that she was leaving soon. "Fine. I will."

"Good."

Great. Annoying-boss issue resolved. "Can you take me home now, please?"

"I would like to have dinner with you."

"You don't want dinner, Henri." That damned crack was back in her voice, betraying that she was still feeling slighted because even if he hadn't been cheating when he'd made love to her, it had been nothing more than a casual hookup. "You want to go to bed with me."

"I do," he said baldly, face tightening at her tone. "Tell me you're not interested and I'll take you home. *Be honest.*"

She wanted to look away, but his intense gaze held hers, peeling back her layers of defensiveness as the streetlights flashed by. She knew she was flushing with guilty anticipation. She had managed to hate him for weeks because he had taken his girlfriend's call after their lovemaking, but that's not what he'd done. Her best reason for resisting him was nullified.

She jerked her head around, staring blindly at the passage of headlights and darkened shop windows.

"*Ça va?*"

"You could have called," she muttered. "You're not going to call tomorrow if I sleep with you tonight."

"Since you'll be with me at breakfast, there will be no need."

She snorted at his arrogance.

"You were not planning to sleep with me that night." Something in his quiet tone made her listen. It was as if he was reflecting fondly and it gave her a small shiver of pleasure because she was part of a memory he was recollecting warmly. "At first I thought it was your game to resist, but you really were intending to leave. You didn't. You were carried away by a kiss and didn't even take one of those silly gift bags on your way out. Yes, I took note of that detail," he said as she swung a scowl at him.

As if she would have sex for a BPA-free water bottle and the latest reality star's brand of lip gloss!

"You went away feeling ill used and I regret that," he continued. "But I am used by women *all the time*. Put yourself in my shoes and imagine how singular and exciting it is for me to have met a woman who not only responds so strongly to me she lost her willpower against *herself*, but doesn't want to write a damned online diary about it. Yes, I want to experience that again. You're damned right I do."

"I don't *like* that I was carried away like that. It makes me feel cheap."

"Cheap! *Why?*"

"Because you expected it. You expected me to behave that badly and I did."

"I *wanted* you to make love with me. I didn't *expect* it. And there was nothing bad about it. You have a real hang-up about when it's permissible to have sex, don't you?"

"Yes, all right? I do! I've had two lovers and I thought I loved both of them. I don't have sex with random strangers for whom I feel mostly annoyance."

He blinked once, taking a moment to pick apart her

words. She expected him to take issue with her calling him annoying, but he only repeated, "*Thought* you loved."

She looked away, aware of tension in the hands that had become fists on her thighs, and said nothing.

"Tell me about this boyfriend you were exorcising."

"No." She craned her neck to look past him. They were pulling up in front of a posh hotel. "What are we doing here?"

"We have dinner reservations."

She had eaten exactly one stuffed mushroom cap at the engagement party. She was starving. Nevertheless, she glared at him.

To hide the fact she was scared.

And shamefully thrilled they weren't parting ways yet. This man utterly fascinated her and it was so dangerous. Like swimming in petrol under a rainstorm of flaming comets.

"Why?" she asked, stalling.

"It's a *date*, Cinnia. Surely that doesn't go too harshly against your precious rules for how to behave with a man?"

She looked at her nails. "No, but I have one about providing the lion's share of sarcasm in a relationship. I suggest you take it down a notch or things could become quite scathing."

He tsk-tsked and started to open his door. His guard finished the job, but Henri held out his hand himself to help her out.

Then he kept his fingers firmly entwined with hers as he walked her through the glittering gold-and-glass entrance of the hotel, across the marble tiles and around the lobby fountain, up the red-carpeted staircase and into a restaurant where a harpist played. The maître d' exclaimed delight that she could join them when Henri introduced her.

The moment they were alone, she said drily, "And I

won't feel obligated after this to go upstairs to the room you've booked."

"No," he assured her. "You won't feel *obligated*." He gathered her hands across the white tablecloth and gave her a slow and anticipatory smile. "But I hope very much you'll feel inclined."

# CHAPTER FOUR

CINNIA WOKE TO a room that was nearly pitch-black, Henri's arm heavy across her waist. They were naked, front to front, legs entwined. She wanted to press her lips into the smoothness of his shoulder and kiss his skin.

What the hell was she *doing*?

Succumbing to hormones. And charm. Henri was very engaging when he wanted to be. He smoothly deflected from anything too personal, but he was keenly intelligent and had exchanged lively opinions with her on everything from world politics to pop music. He had asked her advice about a point of estate law, which she had thought was pure pandering, but she soon realized he was serious and had to tell him he was better off consulting someone who specialized in international trusts.

Then the evening's trio had arrived and he had taken her to the dance floor and *seduced* her, right there in front of the world. Not that he was obvious about it. Henri was far too subtle for that. No, it had been a light brush of his chest against her breasts, a whisper that she smelled delicious, a brief contact with his hips so she knew he was aroused.

"I can't help it, *chérie*. You have that effect on me," he had said without embarrassment.

Dessert had arrived, a caramel flan they'd shared, but

they hadn't even finished when he said, "Will you come upstairs? I'm dying to kiss you."

They both knew how she reacted to his kiss.

They might have made love in the elevator if his guard hadn't been with them, standing discreetly at the front of the car with his back to them so Henri could steal a first kiss, then a second, longer, more passionate one.

Inside the suite, they'd barely made it to the bed.

How had she been so aroused? Until that moment, he'd barely touched her.

But even as she lay here next to him, thinking about the way he'd hurriedly skimmed away her knickers and covered himself with a shaking hand, she was growing wet and achy. She had been pure butter beneath him, locking her legs around his waist and lifting into his heavy thrusts.

She should go home. She didn't want to do the walk of shame in the morning, not when she already knew the paparazzi were on to them.

But she found herself slithering closer, sliding her legs against his and giving in to the temptation to taste his skin. He smelled sharp and masculine against his neck. His stubble abraded her nose and lips, but in a sexy way that turned her on because it accented how different they were. Female and male, meant to come together like pieces of a puzzle.

*"Encore?"* he murmured, moving against her, hardening at her first touch.

"What's wrong with me?"

"Not a damned thing, *chérie*. Ah, this," he growled with satisfaction as he trailed his hand between her legs and found her juicy and plump. "I'm addicted. I have to taste you again." He slid down, pressing her legs open.

She moaned at the sheer indulgence of being pleasured by him like this. He made her feel like she was giving him something when she allowed this, which maybe she was because he pretty much took ownership of her. This act lowered her defenses completely so she was without inhibition, ready to beg when he drew back before she'd climaxed.

"I need to be inside you, *chérie*. I can't wait." He rolled her over and brought her onto her hands and knees.

He covered her like a male animal dominating his mate, filling her with a possessive thrust, so deliciously hard where she was soft and needy. One wide hand slid over her breasts, teased her nipples, rubbed her stomach, then fondled where they were joined as he moved in lusty thrusts.

She received him with cries of encouragement and abandon, so caught up in the raw excitement of it, she didn't care who might hear or what he thought of her behavior. When she climaxed, the paroxysm locked a scream in her throat while he shuddered over and around her, his noises guttural and final. She was *his*. Neither of them could deny it.

That was in the dark.

When she woke in the light of day, and recalled all they'd done, she wanted to *die*.

Why, oh, *why* couldn't she resist him?

Henri had been tempted to join Cinnia in the shower when he woke and heard her starting the water, but he forced himself to put a small distance between them while he contemplated a decision that had been rooting a little deeper into his mind with each hour of lovemaking that had ticked by.

He had never had a mistress, had never wanted anything long-term at all. Not since…

The wrenching memory struck like a kick in the stomach, ambushing him as that dark day sometimes did.

*Do you love me?*

She had been a pretty thing with caramel eyes and a mouth he'd been trying to kiss for weeks. They were cornered in a stairwell and he was flushed with more attraction than he'd ever felt. Suddenly there was Trella, telling him it was time to *go*.

*Go, then*, he told her. *Little sisters are such a pain*, he had told the object of his affection, as Trella ran off to be stolen by Gili's—their affectionate name for Angelique—math tutor. *I do*, he had assured the caramel eyes as they were given privacy again. At least, he supposed it was love. He grew excited seeing this girl in the distance. He wanted to hold her hand, touch her all the time. He could hardly take his eyes off her when she was anywhere near him.

And then their friend Sadiq had shouted his name, telling him, "Trella's been taken."

He had seen that girl again, after Trella was home and he and Ramon returned to school. She'd tried to talk to him, but he'd avoided her.

After that, if girls and women came on to him, if they wanted to give up their bodies for mutual physical pleasure, fine. But he was never going to make the mistake of letting a female mean something to him. It put him off his game, exposed a flank.

It could cost the life of someone near and dear.

Romantic love, he had determined, was a weakness he couldn't afford.

Taking a mistress, however, was a slightly less dangerous risk.

He presumed, wondering if he was rationalizing.

Dressing in his pants and shrugging on his open shirt, he moved into the lounge, where he called in an order for breakfast, put in a request for the boutiques to send a selection for them and picked up the paper left outside his door.

*"Bon matin,"* he said to Pierre, who had relieved Guy overnight. "Anything I should know about?"

"All the coverage seems run-of-the-mill, but fresh posts are still coming out. We're keeping an eye out."

Henri nodded, thoughtful, as he closed the door.

He'd never taken a mistress for the same reason he refused to marry and have children: the threat of kidnapping. Women who were only briefly linked to his name were not likely to be targeted or used against him. Precautions would have to be extended to Cinnia if he went through with this.

He scanned the headlines, then picked up his phone to see a text from Ramon. A question mark. Obviously he'd seen the headlines and wondered why Henri was seeing that woman from the nightclub again.

Henri ignored it and returned a text from Angelique with a video call.

*"Problème?"* he asked, continuing in French. "That was a cryptic message. Why are you worried about something you said to Trella about Sadiq? Are they having a romance I don't know about?"

"What? No! Of course not. No, I think he's falling for someone back in Zhamair. Do you know if that's true?"

"He didn't say anything when I spoke to him last." Sadiq might be the best friend he and his brother had, but they did not discuss their love lives. They talked about important things like stock prices and politics.

"Why does that affect Trella?" he prompted.

"I don't know." She frowned in her introspective way and he knew to give her a moment to gather her thoughts. Angelique was a quieter personality, more like him, preferring solitude, while Trella and Ramon were the extroverts. Everything Trella did was full bore, including a nervous breakdown. She had been making him mad with worry since her birth, when she had turned blue in his arms the first time he held her.

He often thought that if it *had* been Angelique outside the day of the kidnapping, and her tutor had called her over, planning to stuff her in his van, she would have waited for Ramon and insisted he hold her hand and come with her. Shyness had been a hurdle for her, but it was a type of self-protection that served her well.

Trella had possessed none of that. She had run headlong over to the tutor, eager to be helpful and say she wasn't Angelique.

They had stolen her despite her kicks and screams, because how effective was a nine-year-old girl against two strong men?

The trauma affected his sister to this day, which made him blind with fury if he didn't carefully drip-feed himself those memories. It made him want to hurry Angelique to tell him how she imagined Sadiq, their friend who had actually helped save Trella, could be a threat to their sister now.

"I was just talking to her about him," Angelique continued as though still gathering her thoughts. "And saying it was bound to happen that he would marry someday, even if he's not in love now. She got really quiet. Now I feel…" She shrugged. "You know. Like she's upset."

"Deeply upset?"

"No." She said the word on a rush of relief. "Normal upset. But I think she's worried that if he did get married, she wouldn't be able to go to his wedding."

"We can cross that bridge when we come to it," he said. "But thank you for telling me."

Trella had been stable for half a year. They were all holding their collective breath that this time she was actually conquering her panic attacks.

He heard Cinnia and glanced up to see her with dry, windswept hair, wearing one of the hotel robes. "I, um, just want my phone." She scurried to where he had set her handbag on a table after finding it on the floor, where she'd dropped it last night.

"Who's that?" Angelique asked.

"A friend." A very beautiful goddess who had done wicked, devilish things with him in the night. He had not misremembered the power of their chemistry. He kept reminding himself he wasn't a man to be led by his organ, but as many times as they'd made love last night, it wasn't enough. That's what he kept coming back to. He wasn't prepared to go another few weeks, let alone a lifetime, without making love to her again.

"Don't run away," he ordered Cinnia before she could lock herself in the bedroom. "I'm finishing up here." To his sister, he said, "I'll touch base with her later. Let me know if anything changes."

He ended the call and stood, still conflicted now his sister had reminded him of the threats they faced daily and their far-reaching effects.

At the same time, his hands rolled of their own accord, silently inviting Cinnia to come to him.

She didn't move, only hugged herself and flicked her glance to his phone. "Who was that?"

"Gili. Angelique. My other sister."

"You're very close to your siblings."

"They're the only people I trust completely."

She looked at her bare toes. "I speak French. I wasn't trying to eavesdrop, but I heard a little."

"And?"

"And nothing." She shrugged. "I feel bad for your sister. I don't imagine something like that is anything you get over. I mean, I still cry about losing my dad and it's been over a decade, but it sounds like she's quite haunted and I'm sorry she's still affected." She glanced up, expression so soft with compassion it cracked things inside him. "I know you lost your father, as well. I'm sorry for that, too."

"You're sorry for a lot of things." Deepening their relationship would come with many types of risk, he realized. Long-term relationships demanded more of this sort of thing. He was not eager to open up to her, but he hated the distance she was keeping between them right now. The physical distance, at least.

"Are you sorry about last night?" he asked, trying to understand why she wasn't rushing into his arms.

"A little," she mumbled.

"Why?" he demanded, not pleased to hear it.

She kept her head down, but he could see her growing red. With embarrassment?

He swore and went to her, tugging her close with gentle roughness so they knocked together and she threw back her head to scowl at him.

The vulnerability in her eyes made his heart swerve. He was not the only one disturbed by the level of intimacy between them. He found himself rubbing his thumbs against her upper arms where he gripped her, trying to offer reassurance.

"We gave each other a great deal of pleasure. That's not something to be ashamed of."

She swallowed and hid her thoughts with a lowered gaze. Her mouth pouted, maybe even showed a hint of bruising from their thousand rapacious kisses.

Oddly, that hint of injury was the turning point, allowing him to make his decision. They needed time so they could pace themselves. Otherwise, they were liable to kill each other.

"I *like* that you held nothing back," he told her. "Quit being shy about it or I'll do all those same things to you right here on the floor in the lounge. In *daylight*."

Cinnia was tempted to scoff and say, "You can try," but she had a feeling he *would*.

And she'd let him.

He started to kiss her, but the knock on the door interrupted. "Breakfast," he said with a small grimace, releasing her to let in room service.

She touched fingertips to her tingling lips, scolding herself for being disappointed. She was achy and exhausted, very tender in delicate places, and all she could think about was how much she wanted to feel his touch on all those sensitized places again.

Other staff came in with the wheeled table of covered dishes. A woman brought an assortment of outfits and held up each in turn for approval.

"Not that one. It's hideous," Henri said as the woman showed them a green dress. "Why does it even exist? That one, the blue. To match your eyes," he told Cinnia.

He accepted a striped button shirt and the boutique owner left clean underthings for both of them. Cinnia waited until everyone was gone to check the price tags.

"You're not paying for those," Henri said, barely glancing up from the plates he uncovered.

"Neither are you. I guess I'm going home in last night's dress."

"You're my guest. I will provide everything you need while you're with me."

Something in her midsection did a little curl and twist, anchoring and panging inside her. *Get what you can.*

"Are you going to join me? Surely you're as hungry as I am."

"Are you going to keep teasing me about it?" she demanded.

"Last night? Did that sound like teasing? I mean it as praise and gratitude." He looked at her and his shoulders relaxed as he gave her a perplexed look. "*Vraiment*, why does it bother you that we spent a night making love?"

He had stripped her bare, not just physically, but down to her soul. She was never going to be the same. He would always be the man who had done those things and made her feel that way and he would always *know* it. *She* would always know it and compare future lovers and feel wistful. Cheated, even.

"I told you," she muttered, moving to sit across from him, absolutely starving from her expenditure of calories, but feeling defenseless and needy. Tired, she assured herself. She was just tired. And filled with impossible yearning. "I don't do this."

"If you think last night was common for me, you're overestimating my libido."

"Oh, I have a healthy respect for that animal, believe me." *Coffee*. She poured a cup for each of them with shaking hands and quickly doctored hers, sighing with her first sip even though it burned her tongue.

When she glanced at him, he was watching her with an enigmatic look.

"You're also underestimating your effect on me. We have a unique connection." He seemed to choose his words very carefully. "We could leave things here and go on with our lives. I would probably call you the next time I was in London. I will optimistically believe you would be available and want to see me."

*That* was what was killing her right now. She had been able to put him mostly out of her mind after the first time because she'd been angry and genuinely hadn't thought she would see him again. For him to show up and pursue her so blatantly, however, set her up for believing he would do it again in the future.

She would counsel any girlfriend or sister to *never* wait on a man or give him so much power over her personal happiness, but here she sat, looking into her coffee because she didn't want Henri to see that he already held her on the end of a leash and all he had to do was tug for her to come to heel.

That's where her shame was coming from. Her eyes stung and she made herself blink to stem the tears of humility at being his sexual pet.

"What do I assume by your lack of response, Cinnia? That you would be agreeable to that arrangement?"

"I'm not going to hold a reservation for you," she lied, setting her cup into its saucer with a hard clink and a little slosh of coffee over the rim.

"Exactly what I thought you'd say." He braced his elbows on the table, hands loosely linked above his plate. "Much of your appeal for me is that you expect so little of me. You're very independent. But I do not care to take my chances with your accessibility. I would like to propose a different arrangement."

When she glanced up, his gaze was waiting to snare hers. The hazel-green tone was very, very green. Avid in a possessive, masculine way. *Mine.*

Her stomach swooped and she scented danger, yet it was the lofty danger of swinging out on a rope over a cliff on a bottomless lake. Life threatening, but exhilarating.

"A retainer?" she mocked.

"Of a sort. I've never had a mistress, but I begin to see the benefits."

She was knocked speechless. For a few painful heartbeats, she could only stare, then pointed out, "So. Not a proposal. A *proposition*."

Her pulse raced in panic and she looked across the room at the pretty clothes he was already trying to purchase for her.

*Get what you can.*

"I believe there are websites where women advertise for sponsors. Perhaps start *there*," she suggested thinly.

"I don't want *a* mistress. I want *you*. Look." He waved at the plates they hadn't yet touched. "I can eat plain scrambled eggs and there's nothing wrong with that, especially when I'm hungry, but if I have the option to eat one poached to perfection, delicately spiced and accompanied by a tempting banquet of other flavors, one that not only sates the appetite but is a joy with every bite, why the hell wouldn't I want the quality ones?"

"And since you're used to buying the best, I'm sure you think you can afford the eggs you see in front of you today. In this case, you can't."

"I'm very rich."

"I'd rather go hungry than sell myself."

He made a noise that was decidedly French. "Forget the metaphors and eat the damned eggs before they go cold."

After they'd both taken a couple of bites, he said, "I'm never going to marry. Long-term dating, in the traditional sense, is a false promise I won't make. Women come to me, come *on to* me, at a steady enough rate that I've never lacked for company."

"I kind of prefer the not calling over this turn of conversation." She flashed a humorless smile. "Just saying."

"But if I expect a woman to make herself exclusive to me, I ought to provide something in return."

"Your charm isn't enough?" She blinked in fake shock.

"Have you heard of erotic spanking, Cinnia? Some

women find it pleasurable and deliberately test a man's patience with backchat, looking for a hot bottom." He showed his teeth. "Just saying."

Wicked, evil man. For one second, she thought about that. Started to blush, and told herself to smarten up.

"You want it straight, Henri?" she challenged, stomach twisting. "Not shaken nor stirred? Fine."

She seemed to have no pride where he was concerned anyway. She dropped back in her chair and gave him a hate-filled glare for forcing her to bring up the pathetic mistakes of her past.

"I told you my father left his estate in a mess. We were in dire straits, actually. Really dire. Mum and my sisters have a hard time seeing it, especially Mum. She has this throwback notion that if one of us marries well, all our problems will be solved. You asked me last night what happened with my ex-boyfriend. That's what happened."

"He was rich and didn't want to marry you?"

"Exactly. Except that we'd been poor together, struggling through school and scrambling for rent every month for a year when we moved here to the city. I was actually the one making more money for the first while. I thought we were in love and that we would get married. Then his folks sold a piece of property and said they were going to split the money between their children. It was a few hundred thousand each, enough to make a nice down payment on a good home. I honestly thought he was being cagey for the weeks following the sale because he was shopping for an engagement ring and planning how to propose."

*"Non?"* He was holding on to a very neutral tone, betraying nothing of what he might be thinking.

"Hell, no! He was telling his parents to hold off doling out his portion so I couldn't put a claim on it, then he siphoned off half of what was in our shared accounts and kicked me out of our flat the day we were supposed to renew the lease."

She looked at her eggs and knew Avery had been dry, white toast at best while Henri was a mouthwatering croissant.

"I know my family is a handful. I know Mum came on strong when she learned his news. She was on the phone calling local churches that *day.* She flat out told him he should sink his money into her house and said we should move in with her. I never would have let that happen, though. I'll never live with her again if I can help it. She makes me bananas."

She crossed her legs and adjusted the fall of the robe, noting her hand was trembling. She was trying hard to keep a grip, but she still felt so *stupid.* She had thought Avery loved her and it had shaken her confidence in herself, in her belief that she could judge a character and even in her belief that she was lovable. Her voice quavered with old emotion and she couldn't seem to steady it.

"Even though he had known me all that time, he wrote me off as only wanting his bank balance. He said I had always known his parents were sitting on that potential, that I had known money would come to him, and that everything I had done was a calculated investment in getting a piece of it. I did know about it. I had counseled his parents on whether it was better to sell the land before their death or leave it as part of their estate. *Because he asked me to.* And I didn't charge them, by the way. Friends-and-family discount." She picked up her fork and stabbed her egg and watched the yolk bleed out.

Henri reached for his phone and said very casually, "What is his name?"

"Jerkface McPants on Fire. Don't bother ordering a hit. He's not worth the bullet."

He set down his phone again. "This is why you're so sensitive about letting me buy you a meal or a dress?"

"Or a hotel room or a favor with my boss or a rental agreement as a mistress. I earn my keep, Henri. I refuse—I absolutely refuse—to become a kept woman. I'm aiming to start my own agency. I will not work my butt off to succeed only to have people say it's because I was sleeping with a sexy French tycoon."

"My sisters are constantly accused of succeeding with their design house because Sauveterre International underwrote it. Do you know how they respond to that accusation?"

"How?"

"By ignoring it. You do not owe explanations to anyone. You certainly don't have to justify yourself to McFacey man. Stop worrying about what he thinks of you. As for opening an agency, I encourage you to send us a business plan regardless of the terms you and I negotiate for our personal partnership. Ramon and I are investors. We invested in Maison des Jumeaux because Trella wrote a solid plan that has exceeded all of our expectations. If yours shows promise, we may extend you a start-up loan. It won't be nepotism. We do not offer friends-and-family discounts. When it comes to money, neither of us is influenced by sentiment or sexual infatuation. That's why we're rich."

He was not joking.

She was crushed by his reduction of her to a sexual infatuation, but suffered an immediate urge to knock his socks off with her business acumen, wanting to secure a loan from him simply for the achievement of it.

She murmured, "I'll think about it," and returned to eating.

He made short work of his plate and freshened their coffee.

"I like the idea of you working for yourself," he said.

"Why?"

"Because I have a very busy life. It would be hard to find time to be together if you had a strict workweek."

"I love the way you talk like I'm going to agree to be your—oh!" She leaned forward with mock delight. "Let's use the French term, shall we? *Courtisane.*"

He gave her a flat look that grew into a considering one.

"An educated woman who values herself and her time? One who is not ashamed of her sex drive? *Is* that you, Cinnia?"

She sat back. "You're trying to make it sound like that's all it is. It's not."

"No, it's potentially quite complicated. But seeing as you are so smart, walk through this with me. I am based in Paris, but I travel to New York at least once a month. I have an office here in London. I could work some of my time out of it, perhaps one week a month. Ramon and I would like to expand into Asia, but we're already stretched thin. And I occasionally drop everything to fly home to Spain if my sister needs me. Tell me how much time we'll have together unless you come with me for some of that travel."

"Presuming I want to spend time with you," she said tartly.

"Look at me," he commanded in such a stern voice her heart stalled and her gaze flashed up to his. "Were you there last night? The bed is a pile of ashes, we set it so completely on fire. If you don't want to do that again, fine. Get dressed and leave. I'll never bother you again."

His words spiked through her heart and she found herself pushing to her feet in a rush of pique, catching the wild flare of something in his eyes before she turned away and—

She halted, unable to make herself take another step.

Something hooked sharp and fierce behind her breast-bone. Tears slammed into her eyes. She brought her fists up and pushed the heels of her hands into her clenched lids, catching a shattered breath. She couldn't move. Couldn't walk away from him.

*"Idiot,"* he said behind her, chair scraping before he pulled her back against his chest, strong arms encasing her, but in a way that felt secure and reassuring.

"I don't want to feel this way," she said in a whisper, voice breaking. All of her breaking. She was self-reliant. She didn't need anything from a man.

But she needed *him. This* man. Who offered *things,* not his heart.

"How do you feel? Hmm?" One hand stole into the front of her robe and he cupped her bare breast, flicked her nipple.

She made a noise of pleasure-pain, instantly catapulted into memory and desire, but her nipples were so tender she covered his hand and stilled his caress.

"Sore?" he asked against her ear, nibbling in a way that sent shivers down her nape, all the way to the small of her back.

She arched, pushing her bottom into the hardness at his loins.

"You're going to kill me, Henri. I ache all over and I don't care. I want you anyway."

*"Ah, chérie.* You're hurting like this because you don't want our time to end. I feel the same." His mouth opened on the side of her neck, delicately sucking a mark into her skin. "But I will be very, very careful with you, I promise."

His free hand went in below the belt and found her naked and slippery, already responding to being close to him. "You like that?"

"You know I do," she breathed, tilting her head to the

side so his kisses could reach all down the side of her neck. "But I don't think I can."

"Come here." He backed up, bringing her with him.

She heard him unzip his pants and turned to see him putting on a condom. He sat in the chair and drew her to straddle him.

"Gently," he murmured, taking it slow as he drew her down.

Even though she was tender, she breathed a sigh of relief when she was seated on him, full of his turgid heat and completely possessed by this terribly wicked sorcerer of a man.

He opened her belt and spread the robe, looking down at her breasts. His hands moved on her thighs and buttocks, caressing without urging her to move. Then he kissed her, gently and sweetly. Slowly and languorously.

"See?" he breathed against her lips. "We don't have to be greedy if we know we have time."

She was greedy anyway, running her hands across his chest to spread his shirt, then placing kisses there, pinching his nipples and feeling his response inside her. She smiled with secretive joy.

And she began to move instinctively, riding him in an abbreviated rock. She was so tender and sensitive she was gasping in moments, squeezing him with her powerful orgasm.

"*Magnifique.*" He stroked her hair back from her face, set light kisses on her cheekbone and brow and the tip of her nose. His eyes were bright green with arousal. "Do you want to stop? I don't want to hurt you."

"You didn't finish," she said in an urge for him to do so, nerve endings coming alive under the fresh stimulation. She was nearly in tears because it was such an intense sensation.

"I will later, when you're feeling better." He cupped her face, thumbs coming together in the center of her lips, then parting to rest in the corners.

"You're shameless, aren't you?" she said on a trembling breath, frightened by his assumption she would be there for him later today and every day from now on. Maybe she would. Right in this second, she wanted to be whatever he needed her to be. "Don't manipulate me through my body's response to yours."

"Now you won't even accept an orgasm given freely? You are a difficult woman to please."

She ducked her head out of his hands and tucked her forehead against his throat, nose to his collarbone so his scent filled her head.

"You won't ever marry me." She didn't know if it was a refusal, an accusation, or merely a statement of terms.

He tensed, but said firmly, "*Oui.* I will never marry you."

She waited for some kind of repugnance to arrive and prompt her to reject him. All she could think was that at least she would have this, him, for a little while. She closed her eyes, still swimming in the high of orgasm while tendrils of fresh arousal wound around her. He was offering a sensual, sexual contract of association, that was all, but it would be such a pleasurable one.

"I want to marry and have children. Someday. I'm not going to give you all of my best years and wonder what happened when you throw me over for a younger model."

His fingers were under the fall of her hair, working upward in a comb to the back of her skull.

"I'll let you go when you're ready for that. You're not searching for those things today, are you? Be with me until you are."

A half sob pressed out of her. Was she really going to agree to this?

"If either of us was willing to give this up, *chérie*, you would have left in the middle of the night."

"I know," she said on a sob of surrender. "Please don't be smug."

"It's not comfortable for me to be this taken by you." He massaged her scalp, holding her in compassionate, irrevocable intimacy. "I am yielding, too."

It didn't feel like it. He was still hard inside her. She moved restlessly, drawing back to nip his chin, then looked into his eyes. "I bet I'll get there before you do."

"I bet I'll make sure of it." He threw himself forward, swooping her to the floor beneath him, sending them both soaring with the masterful thrust of his hips.

# CHAPTER FIVE

*Present day...*

"KILLIAN." HENRI STOOD and rounded his desk to greet the owner of Tec-Sec Industries as he was shown into Henri's Paris office. They shook hands and Henri asked, "How are Melodie and the baby?"

"Well. Thank you."

Henri wasn't surprised by Killian's succinct reply. Cinnia had summed it up nicely when she had first met the man who was an international security specialist and held the contract for the Sauveterre family's safety. *Did you meet at reticence school? He doesn't care for small talk, does he?*

They had met eight years ago, when Killian had come to Sauveterre International seeking investment capital to expand his global security outfit. Underwriting Killian's ambitions had been one of the first really big risks Henri and Ramon had taken with their father's money after their initial power struggles with the board. A year into watching Killian skyrocket with his business model and suite of military-grade services, they had hired him themselves.

That had been another type of gamble, a move Henri had not made without a great deal of reflection. Ramon operated on gut instinct while Henri was more fact driven. Killian had a good track record, but not a long one.

Ramon had left the final decision to Henri, after making a very good case for the change. "But we both have to believe in this. If you don't like it, we won't do it," his brother had said.

Which had left the massive responsibility for any muck-ups squarely on Henri's shoulders—where the weight still sat. Heavily.

Fortunately, Killian was a brilliant mind hidden behind an impassive face. Nothing escaped him. Aside from the occasional blip of overly exercised caution, they hadn't had one security incident since signing contracts with him.

Not that Henri planned to become complacent as a result, but he felt he and his family were in very good hands. Even marriage and the arrival of his first child hadn't thrown Killian off his focus on business.

"Coffee? Something stronger?" Henri offered.

"I won't be here long," Killian said with a wave of his hand and hitched his pants to sit.

Henri was relieved Killian was so reserved, not trying to bend Henri's ear about the wonders of fatherhood. Henri didn't need to hear what he was missing. Not when he was still stinging over Cinnia's departure for that very reason.

The recollection jabbed like a rapier into his gut, swift and unexpected. She had left him to find the man who would give her the family she craved. Thinking of it sent a reverberation of frustrated agony through him every time he thought of it, so he refused to think of it and quickly pushed aside the temptation to brood today.

He took the chair opposite, distracting himself by getting to business. "You said it wasn't an emergency. I assume it's a price increase?"

"No, although there will be one at the end of the year

to go with a system upgrade. The briefing for that will come through regular channels. No, this is something I thought was best dealt with promptly and face-to-face. One of my guards—I should say, one of the Sauveterre guards—brought me an ethical dilemma." Killian braced his elbows on the chair's arms and steepled his fingers. "In performing regular duties, this guard became aware of a situation that will be of interest to you, but the guard couldn't come to you without compromising the privacy of your sibling."

Henri frowned. "Which one?"

Killian canted his head. "I work for all of you, Henri. I won't betray the trust of one to another. You'd fire me yourself if I did. This guard was reluctant to say anything, but brought it to me because Tec-Sec is charged with protecting the *entire* Sauveterre family. We take that responsibility very seriously."

"Ramon has an illegitimate child somewhere," Henri deduced, and was struck by something he rarely felt, but it was most acute if it happened to involve his brother. Ramon had something he wanted.

He didn't want children, though. He didn't want the responsibility. He had decided that long ago.

Nevertheless, the idea of his brother becoming a father seared his bloodstream with envy so sharp it felt like pure acid.

Then he heard Killian say, "I would take that up with Ramon, wouldn't I?"

Henri's mind blanked as it tried to recalibrate.

There was no humor in Killian's face, no judgment, no emotion whatsoever. He was a master at hiding his feelings, which was one of the reasons Henri liked working with him. Their dealings were always straightforward and unsentimental.

"One of the girls?" he said, hazarding a guess. It was impossible in Trella's case. There had been that one night three months ago, when she'd slipped out in public as Angelique. She'd been photographed kissing a man—a prince, no less—but she had sworn to Henri that's all that had happened.

Gili was tangled up with a prince of her own, had even taken off into the desert overnight with Kasim while they'd all been in Zhamair for Sadiq's wedding. He'd had a message this morning to say that things were back on, but hadn't had a chance to catch up with her about it.

Even if she was back with Kasim, Gili was so cautious he couldn't imagine her failing to take steps to prevent a pregnancy. She would definitely make arrangements to protect her child if she did happen to fall pregnant. Killian wouldn't have to bring it up with Henri. Same went for Trella, for that matter.

Which had to mean...

"You can't mean me," Henri said dismissively. "Cinnia is the only woman I've been with—"

He ran straight into it like he was in one of Ramon's high-performance race cars and hadn't seen the big, red, tightly stacked, rough-edged bricks cemented into a giant wall that had arrived right in front of his nose.

*I didn't ask if you wanted to marry me. I asked if you loved me.*

*And the reason you're asking is because you want to change things between us. I told you I'd never marry you.*

He'd been taken aback that morning three months ago, not having seen that conversation coming, either. They were comfortable as they were. He'd grown quietly furious as she had put him on the spot with her "do you love me?"

He *couldn't*. Too much was at stake.

From there, the separation had unfolded like surgery

without anesthetic. He'd endured it with stoicism so he wouldn't betray how much he begrudged her not being content with what they had. That's all he could offer her. She knew that. *He* had to accept it. Why couldn't she?

*I would say that things have already changed, but they really haven't. I've always wanted children. You said when I was ready to start a family, you would let me go. Are you going to keep your word?*

*Of course.* He didn't make promises he wouldn't keep.

They had parted with as much civility as possible. Hell, he'd left the flat and come back a week after she was packed and gone. He hadn't looked her up on social media. There was no point. She rarely posted and the last thing he needed was to see whom she was dating in her quest to marry and procreate.

Now he knew she wasn't dating anyone.

*Because she was having his child.*

It couldn't be true. *Couldn't.* She would have told him. Unless…

The next thought that followed was a screamingly jagged "was it even his?"

Of course it was. It had to be. Killian wouldn't have brought this news to him otherwise and Henri couldn't imagine… Didn't want to imagine… No. Cinnia was highly independent, stubborn to a fault and honest. She would not sneak around having affairs behind his back. When would she have found the time? One way or another, they had shared a bed most nights and while she had been extremely passionate between the sheets, she had never been promiscuous.

No, if she was pregnant, the baby was his.

But how? She knew he didn't want children. On that point he had been blunt, so what the hell had happened?

Had she stopped taking her pill? Was this pregnancy deliberate?

Did she not realize how dangerous that was?

From the moment the responsibility of protecting his family had become his, he had felt as though a Russian roulette gun was pressed to his head. The mere suggestion he had a child on the way slid an extra bullet into one of its chambers. She wouldn't put that on him. Would she?

An excruciating twist of betrayal wrung out the muscle behind his breastbone as he took in that she had disregarded his wishes.

"I see I've given you a lot to think about," Killian said, rising.

"You have." Henri stood, brain exploding. He was coated in a cold sweat beneath his tailored suit. It was all he could do to form civil words as his mind raced to Cinnia and a demand for answers. Somehow he managed to grasp the relevant threads of this conversation and tie them off. "Ensure the guard in question receives a suitable bonus."

"Of course."

"And submit a quote for extending your services to include my growing family." There were times when he recklessly played tennis in the heat and wound up this light-headed, walking through gelatin. He could barely breathe.

"The proposal is being prepared along with a selection of suitable résumés. Are you headed to London? I have staff on standby if you need them. Let me know."

"I'll go straight to her flat, but didn't you put someone on her the minute you learned she was pregnant?" He snapped the words, straining to hold on to his temper, not wanting the pregnancy to be real, but slamming walls of protection into place with reflexive force anyway.

This would be the longest flight of his life. His palms

were clammy, he was so fixated on ensuring the safety of his child. If she was pregnant, he wouldn't breathe easy until he had Cinnia locked behind the Sauveterre vault-like doors.

"I came here the minute I learned," Killian said. "Less than two hours ago. Although I gather the guard has been aware for a few weeks. Preliminary surveillance reveals she's paying one of my competitors to keep the paparazzi at a distance. They're good enough they would notice if someone started watching her, so we're maintaining a distance. She's staying at her mother's, by the way."

Henri nodded and shook Killian's hand.

*"Merci,"* he said distantly. "And one of my siblings knows about this?" He struggled to take in that incredulous piece of the news along with the rest.

"Yes." Killian refused to say which one.

From there, Henri operated like a robot in a sci-fi thriller. *Get to her.* Order the car, text his pilot they were flying to London, climb on the plane, blow through any obstacle without regard.

*Wring Ramon's neck.* It had to be Ramon. Was he still in touch with that friend of Cinnia's? Cinnia had told him Vera had married last year.

Henri couldn't imagine either of his sisters learning something of this magnitude and keeping it from him. They were far too softhearted to leave him in the dark, knowing how heavily the family's security weighed on him.

But Ramon would have taken the necessary steps to guard her. He wouldn't be satisfied with leaving Cinnia to make her own arrangements.

It was all a jumble and nothing would make sense until Henri saw her. Topmost in his mind would be… *What the hell had she been thinking?*

\* \* \*

Cinnia was tired. Not just tired because she was building two more human bodies with her own, but because today was one thing after another. Nell had been quick to tell her it was because Mercury was in retrograde, when she'd used the phone from the pub where she worked to say that the Wi-Fi was on the blink at the flat.

Perhaps it was true, since Cinnia's new partner running her London office was having phone and network issues. She was forwarding all the office calls and emails to Cinnia today. Cinnia had asked her tech guy to check both, but he was stuck in traffic. Again, thanks to a certain planet traveling backward, *apparently*.

Dorry, bless her, had something going on at school. She was doing most of her learning online these days, accelerating to finish early. She usually sat at the desk in the parlor across the hall, answering the handful of calls Cinnia typically received, allowing Cinnia to concentrate on the piles of work in front of her.

Not today. Nope. Today Dorry was out and their mother was "pitching in." Which meant rather than screen calls and take a message, or look up a price and answer a simple question, she said things like, "Sorry to interrupt, love, but they want to set up a video chat. How do I do that again?"

When her mother knocked for the billionth time, and pushed in without waiting for an invitation, and the phone hadn't even rung this time, Cinnia snapped, "*Mum.* I'm *working.*"

"Well, he wasn't going away, was he?"

Cinnia glanced up and the sight of Henri struck her like an asteroid. Like an atomic bomb that had been packed with nuclear energy bottled up by the weeks of being apart from him. Instantly she shattered into a million pieces—

and had to sit there trying not to show it. Her entire body stung with the force.

He was painfully gorgeous. Cutting-edge dark blue suit, a narrow line of ruthless red in his striped tie, clean shaven, tall and trim and larger than life, as always. His intense personality honed in on her with that piercing quality that made her insides twist with joyful reunion.

It was quickly choked off with a quake of abject fear.

She wasn't ready for this.

Because the flutters in her belly were not just the butterflies of excitement he always inspired. They were the movement of his offspring.

She said a word that was *very* unladylike.

"Lovely to see you, too." His mouth curled in something that was the furthest thing from a smile.

"You called him?" she accused her mother, because that's what one did in times of deep stress: attack the people who loved you unconditionally.

She couldn't believe it, though. She'd been so careful to hide her pregnancy, practically living like a shut-in since she had begun to show. In the most uncompromising of terms, she had bribed and cajoled and threatened her family into silence. How had he found out?

"I did not." Her mother chucked up her chin in offense, silver coif trembling. "But it's long past time you did, isn't it? Shall I hold your calls?"

"Oh, thanks, Mum. That would be great." Cinnia rolled her eyes as her mother closed the door, locking Henri into the library with her.

"Trella told you?" She lowered the angle of her laptop screen to see him better over it, but quavered behind it.

"Trella?" His sister's name came out with the weight of grim consideration. "I was wondering which one of them it was. How the hell does my sister—" He held up a hand. "We will come back to that."

"You haven't talked to her?" Oh, damn. *Sorry, Trell.*

Cinnia glanced at her phone, wanting to warn her friend that big brother was on the warpath, but she had to survive his wrath first.

She took in the way he looked like a caged lion, tail flicking and muscles bunched, ready to pounce. They had argued in the past, but he'd never been this angry. He'd never looked at her like this—as though whatever he'd felt for her was completely *gone*.

Their breakup had been agony for her, but it was nothing compared to the raw squirming torment that accosted her under that accusatory glare of his.

"How, um…" Wait. If Trella hadn't told him, did he even know she was pregnant?

She scooched her chair a little tighter to the desk and tugged her lapels over her noticeably more ample breasts, adjusting the angle of her laptop one more inch, hoping to hide what was pressing up against the edge of her desk.

"Why are you here?" she asked shakily.

"You know damned well why I'm here." He planted his hands on the two-hundred-fifty-year-old Chippendale masterpiece that her mother refused to sell. "Stand up."

"You came to school me on my manners?" She pretended she wasn't torn to shreds inside and lifted haughty brows. "Sorry I didn't rush around to greet you like a long-lost relative!"

He made a choked noise.

"Yes, *chérie.* I think there is a certain courtesy concerning relatives that you have grossly overlooked." His hazel-green eyes were stainless steel. Chop-chop, his gaze warned. Prepare to be sliced and diced.

She had known he would be angry, but this was so unfair. Her hand wanted to go protectively to the bump that had sent him away and was now bringing him back, but not with so much as a hint of pleasure at seeing her again.

She had been trying to work up the courage to call him. Her ego had held her back. Pride and ego. Pride because she was still devastated that he had let her go, obviously feeling nothing toward her despite the fact they'd essentially been living together, and ego because she looked ridiculous.

She gathered her courage and stood, bracing to take it on the chin.

He slid his gaze down and jerked, pushing off the desk, clearly taken aback by the small planet that shot straight out of her middle and arrived a full minute before she did in any room she entered.

*"Thanks,"* she said acerbically, but couldn't blame him. While she was a little plumper in the face and chest, she really hadn't gained much weight except in her middle, where she looked like she'd stuffed a sofa cushion under her shirt. The whole sofa, actually, and she was only midway through this pregnancy!

Henri took a long inhale, cheeks hollowing as he stared at her belly with such laser focus she was compelled to block his fierce stare with her hand.

His own hand went into his hair. His nostrils flared as that cutting glance swung up to pierce hers. "Why would you do this?"

He was gray beneath his swarthy skin. Obviously he was shocked.

She had expected this accusation. It was precisely the reason why she had left him and had worked so hard to put in place a means to do this alone. It still went into her like a knife. Nearly two years, *two years* of never asking him for one damned thing except "do you love me?"

"*I* did this to *you*?" she said, barely managing to keep a level tone. Oh, she felt so discarded and misused in that moment, worse even than when he'd shrugged off their breakup. "I suggest you take a hard look at which one of us is carrying three stone of our combined DNA." It was closer to five, but shut up, bathroom scale.

"You were supposed to be taking your pill."

"And I had the flu for a week last fall."

"I used condoms after," he reminded her, stabbing the top of the desk with his finger.

"I thought we were fine, too. What am I? A reproductive scientist? I don't know how it happened! Sometimes when people have sex, they make babies. Super weird that it could happen to us, right? 'Cause we hardly ever had sex."

Every night. All the time. She wanted to have sex with him right now, the bastard, coming in here smelling all yummy with that aftershave that drove her crazy and not having gained an ounce. If anything, he was sculpted into an even harder, sharper version of the man she had lusted after without reserve.

She looked away, hating her cheeks for flushing with awareness and her body for *remembering*.

If her eyes began to tear, she would throw herself through the curtain-cloaked window behind her.

"I never wanted this responsibility!" Henri blurted, like he'd been saving that statement for miles and miles. All his life. "You *knew* that."

"Then you should have kept your pants on," she hissed back at him.

He glared at her like he was furious with her for forever tempting that beast from behind his zipper. Like he resented her and her pregnancy and everything they'd shared.

Well, she was as volatile as any pregnant woman. Probably twice as emotional as the average. Salty tears rushed up to sting her eyes. Her throat closed with emotion and her inner mercury shot up so high it bounced off the inside of her skull.

"Don't feel you have to accept any responsibility today." She rounded the desk and headed for the door. "This is all my fault. You're completely innocent and have no obligation. I am more than capable of parenting without you." She pulled the door inward and waved an arm to invite him to exit. "Fly. Be free."

He folded his arms, such a filthy glare on his face she should have been turned to stone.

"I'm serious," she said, not caring if her mother was in earshot. She'd heard it all and the rest of the house was empty. "I'm one hundred percent ready to do this on my own. As you can see, I've started working here, where Mum and Dorry have agreed to help with child care. The London office is paying for itself and turning a small profit. So is my flat. Nell and her friends are renting it, but I give what I make on that to Mum since I've kicked out all her boarders. This place has been outfitted with a security system—"

"I'm supposed to imagine that my child is safe in a house where strangers—I'm sorry, *potential clients*—are coming and going?"

"You're supposed to imagine that I did not do this on purpose and I am *not* trapping myself a wealthy husband, as you obviously thought when you came storming in here on your high horse. I knew you would think that of me. I *knew*. Why else did I send back all your stupid jewelry? I could have kept it and sold it, you know! That money would be really handy right now, and God knows I earned it, didn't I? But I never asked you for it, Henri. I never asked you for *anything*."

"Calm down," he growled.

"You calm down! I never wanted to be pregnant by accident! I wanted it to be something I did *on purpose*. With the man I *loved*!"

His head went back like she'd clawed at his cheek. Her own emotions were clawing open her chest, leaving her heart exposed, raw and vulnerable. She railed on, protecting herself the only way she could, with mean, nasty words.

"I never asked for anything until that last morning and I would have settled for you telling me you *cared*. I would have settled for you asking me not to *leave*. But you didn't give one solid damn that I wanted to end it. Bye-bye, Cin. Nice having sex with you. Take your pretty payoffs. And all you can think about right now is how hard this is for you? Try hiding this from paparazzi!" She pointed at her massive bump. "Congratulations on being as big an ass as I thought you would be."

"Are you finished?"

"Really?" she cried. "You're going to take that patronizing tone with me? No, I'm not finished! I'm allowed to freak out! While you've spent the last twelve weeks screwing other women and carrying on with your completely unaffected life, I've been overhauling mine. I've been working damned hard so you never have to be inconvenienced by something that *we* did *together*. Say 'Thank you, Cinnia' and get the hell out of my house."

"Well aren't you the great martyr," he scoffed. "Excuse me for not being grateful when I wasn't given a choice in the matter, was I?"

"Oh, you had choices. And you made them. I'm making the same one, which means getting on with *my* life without *you*. Ta-ta," she sang in a jagged, off-key tone. "I have to get back to work now." After bawling her eyes out over this stupid man and his complete lack of regard for her.

"That's very cute. You know I have no choice. Neither do you," he warned, chin low, brows flat and ominous.

That did it. Her heart broke along old lines and her eyes filled up with hot, fat tears.

"Right," she said in a voice that cracked. "Your only choice is to be saddled with a woman you don't want. A gold digger, obviously, who had her eye on your money all along." She couldn't do this. She started to leave the room.

"Don't put words in my mouth." He caught at her arm.

She shook him off and blinked rapidly, but her lashes were matted together and her composure was thinning to the breaking point.

"Don't put babies in my belly."

"I'll confine it to one, trust me."

"Too late!" It came out shrill and loud. She spun to leave again, but quickly found herself halted and turned back to face him.

Through her tears, he was a blur of ashen skin.

"What?"

"Oh, look at me, Henri!" she intoned. "Have you ever been satisfied with only giving me *one* orgasm? Of course, you had to give me *two* babies!" Her fists clenched and she wanted to pound them against him, against the wall of his chest, as if she could break past the invisible wall he presented to hold off everyone.

Including her.

Especially her.

Instead she found herself stumbling across the hall as he dragged her with him. He plonked himself onto the love seat in the parlor and tugged her to sit beside him.

She was shaking so badly she let it happen and sat beside him in stiff silence, trying to hold her threadbare self together.

He sat with his elbows on his thighs and his face pressed into his wide hands.

She reminded herself she'd had weeks to process her pregnancy and the fact it was twins. He'd had, well, she would guess a few hours on the first baby and about ninety seconds on the second.

Oh, she didn't want to feel sorry for him! Maybe the idea of being a father was hard for him, but it didn't change the fact he'd thought awful things about her and hadn't tried *at all* to hang on to what they'd had.

What had they had? she asked herself for the millionth time. Sex. So much sex and yes, a few good laughs and many excellent meals. But while they'd been profoundly intimate physically, on an emotional level he'd held her off in a dozen subtle ways. Two years she had spent banging her head against that reserve of his and yes, she knew things about him like his taste in music and had a handful more facts on his family than the average person did, but he had never let her into his heart.

How many times had she counseled a girlfriend not to let a man own her soul without giving back a piece of his? Dear God, it was easier to give that advice than take it.

She reached for a tissue off the side table and blew her nose, fighting to pull herself together. She hadn't realized how much poison she'd been harboring over all of this. At one point her mother had accused her of punishing Henri by keeping the pregnancy from him and Cinnia had denied it, vehemently.

Just as she had vehemently done her best to annihilate him in every possible way today, holding off on stabbing him with the fact it was twins so she could do maximum damage when his shields were down.

Because she was crushed and she wanted him to join her in her anguish. She wanted to know she *could* hurt him.

Taking a shaky breath, she started to rise.

His hand shot out and he kept her on the sofa.

"I have to use the toilet. It's nonnegotiable."

He released her and she went, then lingered after washing her hands, studying the profile of her body while avoiding her gaze in the mirror.

She had come from a loving, nuclear family. It was what she had always aspired to have for herself and had never been comfortable as Henri's mistress. He had called her his friend and his companion, sometimes even his lover, but the lack of emotional commitment had always stung.

Part of her had wanted to believe Henri did love her deep down, but she had believed Avery had loved her because he *had said the words* and he hadn't. Even her first boyfriend, who had possessed her whole heart, had let her down. So she had tried to hold off giving up too much of herself to Henri. Had tried to stay autonomous and strong.

Still, she had hoped they were moving toward *something*. When she had turned up pregnant, however, she had had to face how superficial their relationship really was. She hadn't been able to stay with him at that point, not if she had any self-respect left.

At the same time, she knew how he would react to a pregnancy. Ties. Short, cold chains and tall, barbed wire fences.

It wouldn't be easy to hold herself apart from him while he tried to do what she knew he would want to do: pull her inside his castle and shut the drawbridge. *That* was why she had held off telling him. She couldn't be dragged back into his life knowing she meant nothing to him.

That was why she had to find the strength to continue resisting him now.

# CHAPTER SIX

THE RATTLE OF china made Henri lift his head.

Millicent Whitley—Milly—came in with a tea tray. She set it up on the coffee table before him. The only noise was the sound of the dishes, but she made a statement with the force with which she served him.

He knew that Cinnia had had words with her mother at different times about their relationship and his refusal to offer a ring. Milly had never said a word to him about it, though. She was too wellborn, too possessed of impeccable manners.

Today, however, she brilliantly conveyed that she would love to see him choke to death on his petit four.

"Thanks, Mum," Cinnia said in a subdued tone as she came back.

"Eat one of the sandwiches," Milly said to her, pointing at the stack of crustless triangles as she straightened with the now empty tray, adding as she passed her daughter at the door, "You're behaving like a harridan."

"Gosh, I hope I haven't ruined my chances for a proposal."

Her mother shut the door on that comment and Cinnia made a face.

"How is your health?" Henri asked her, grasping for a lifeline of fact and logic to keep from being blown into the abyss of unknowns circling in his periphery.

Cinnia blew out a breath that lifted her fringe and came to perch next to him. She reached for a sandwich. "No issues. The weight packs on fast, which is expected. I'm not watching calories, but I try to avoid the empty ones. I've started drinking my tea black and I skip things like mayonnaise and sweets."

He nodded, watching her bite into what looked like plain tuna with a slice of tomato between two dry pieces of bread. Her lips looked fuller. Plump and kissable.

"There haven't been other women." His voice came out a shade too low.

She choked, hand going to her mouth before she reached for her tea and took a cautious sip, clearing her throat and flashing him a persecuted look.

"I'm ready to be civilized, but let's agree to be honest, shall we?"

"I had to date, you know I did." If she was offended that he'd accused her of deliberately getting pregnant, he was insulted that she believed he'd slept with all those women—*any* woman—since her. "Our breakup was well documented. I couldn't appear to be carrying a torch, could I? That wouldn't be safe for you." He'd been plagued by concerns regardless, teetering on wishing she would find a man to look out for her while passionately hating the idea.

"Well, you did an excellent job of convincing *me* you weren't carrying one."

He waited for her gaze to come to his, but she kept her attention on the plate she held.

Her features were softer and, if anything, prettier for it. More feminine. She wasn't wearing makeup, her hair was clipped at her nape, but he found her casual elegance as fascinating as ever.

He wanted her, every bit as much as ever.

He pushed to his feet, restlessly moving away from temptation. He was still processing that she was pregnant. His brain was not ready to take in twins and he was still very much reeling from the anger she'd thrown at him.

"There were no other women," he repeated. "I'm not going to say it again."

It was too much of a blow to his ego. He *couldn't* screw other women. She wanted them to throw toxins at one another? Fine. He would love to tell her how much he resented her grip on him. He felt like a cheat merely allowing another woman's hand to rest on his arm. Had he realized that would be a by-product of a long-term, monogamous relationship, he never would have entered into one.

Damn. He wished that was true, but Cinnia had entranced him from the first time he'd seen her. She still did, sitting there cutting a suspicious glare at him from beneath pulled brows. This connection between them was as base as an alpha wolf imprinted by a mate.

He wasn't comfortable being ruled by anything so visceral, but even now, as he was reeling from this life-altering news, part of him was soaring with the knowledge that he now had the perfect excuse to yank her back into his bed.

"As for expecting things of me, you expected me to behave badly and set me up to do so." He pushed his hands into his pockets. "How long did you think you could hide this? I can see if you had a single baby, you might have convinced the press it was someone else's, maybe pretended your infidelity was the reason we broke up. But twins? Of course they'll assume they're mine and go stark raving mad! How did that even happen?" He tried to wrap his brain around it. "Are they identical? Do you know?"

"One placenta," she said with a bemused shrug. "I realize it's like your family has been struck by lightning three times. I'm buying lotto tickets, but I'm told that's not how it works…"

Her joke fell flat.

She had finished her sandwich and was nursing her tea, brow furrowed in contemplation. He always had an urge to kiss that little wrinkle in her brow when she looked like that. She always tsk-tsked at him when he did, complaining it broke her train of thought.

Because he invariably wound up kissing her mouth next, and that led to making love.

That's probably why he liked to kiss her brow.

*Could* they make love? What the hell was wrong with him that that was all he could think about as he faced such a daunting prospect? Escape, he supposed. Making love with Cinnia had always provided him with a sense of peace to balance the rapid juggling of priorities that was the rest of his life.

She rubbed between her brows with two fingers, like tension sat there.

"I knew I'd have to tell you," she mumbled in a disheartened tone. "I was putting it off because I know what you're going to say, and…" She dropped her hand and said firmly, "I don't want to marry you."

In his lifetime, there were a handful of words that had gone through him like bullets. *Trella's been taken. Your father is gone.* Now, *I don't want to marry you.*

He'd been trying to ignore what she'd said earlier about wanting children with the man she loved. He had been fairly convinced she was in love with him, even though she'd never said the words. Then she had left him.

Today, all that rage she'd aimed at him? His brain told him that came from a scorned heart. He *had* scorned her.

*Bye-bye, Cinnia.* Yes, he had let her go without a fight. What was he supposed to have done? Denied her the family she had told him from the beginning that she wanted? If she had been telling the truth on her way out the door, and really *had* wanted to run off and find Mr. Right, to make a family with that unknown man, Henri had been honor bound to let her.

She hadn't been telling the truth, though. She'd been *testing* him.

He'd failed, obviously.

Had his rejection killed whatever she *had* felt?

He pinched the bridge of his nose. It didn't matter.

"You still have to do it," he informed her.

"No. I—"

"Cinnia," he interrupted, unequivocal. "I will accommodate your career if you want to keep working. Dorry can be our nanny. I will give you just about anything you ask of me, but you know that you are coming with me today. Our children must be protected. *You know I won't negotiate on this.*"

"No."

Cinnia had never been a pushover, something he had always admired in her, but Henri had written the book on how to get your way. He didn't bother saying anything, only gave her a look that warned she was wasting both their time.

"Divorced people raise children apart. If you want to amp up my security, that's your prerogative, but I'm handling things just fine."

"Are you?" He scratched his cheek and glanced toward the draped window. "Shall I open those curtains and we'll see how well you're keeping the world at bay?"

"Oh, you didn't drag a swarm of those buzzards here, did you?"

He could have taken steps to lose the cameras they'd picked up at the airport, but he'd been too intent on getting here. "You know what my life is like."

"I do!" she asserted with a crack in her voice as the words burst out of her. "And I put up with your guards and all the awful trolls who post those nasty things and I never made a peep because it was my choice to be with you. I could have walked away anytime if I didn't like it. And I did! So don't ask me to sign up for a lifetime of it. Don't try to *make* me."

His fuse, the one that had slowly been burning down since Killian had set a match to it, reached powder.

"Do you honestly think either of us has a choice?" He managed to keep his voice under a roar, but it was fierce with the bitter vehemence he normally kept pent up. "Don't tell me how hard it is to live under such attention. I know, damn you."

She sat back, intimidated by his muted explosion, but he couldn't contain it. Not if she was going to throw it in his face as the reason she didn't want to marry him. Damn it, she *would* understand, if nothing else, that it wasn't just a nuisance, but a life-threatening menace.

"Trella wasn't kidnapped because we're *rich*. We were valuable because we'd been portrayed as a national treasure. *I* didn't sign up for that. None of us did! And did they have the decency to give us privacy after she was rescued? Hell, no! It was worse!"

He thought of all the ugly conjecture that had followed them for years.

"They pushed her into a breakdown and I swear they caused my father's death. He might have withstood nearly losing his child, but trying to keep us out of that microscope? There was no pity for the pressure he was under! If he showed signs of cracking, they turned it higher. *I know.*" He smacked his hand into his chest. "I stepped into his shoes. The corporation is enough for any man and then to be worried sick for the rest of your life that another attempt would be made? All because those vipers insist on making us into demigods?"

He threw an accusatory point at the closed curtain, vainly wishing, yearning, for the ability to incinerate every camera on earth.

"I hate them. I bloody well hate them. They're vile and they set us up to be victimized in every way—by trolls, by opportunists, by criminals who want to steal a child for profit."

He ran his hand down his face, trying not to think of such a thing happening to *his* child. He pointed a railing finger at her.

"You have no idea what they're really capable of. And you definitely don't have the resources to hold them at a decent distance. So, no. Do not think for a minute that I will leave it to you to 'handle' security. I can't even say I will take the babies and let you live your life away from us because you are part of this now, like it or not. So you *will* come to Paris with me and *I* will handle security."

At some point she had pulled a cushion across her chest and had drawn her knees up, buffering herself against his outburst.

He pushed his fingers through his hair, scratching at his tight scalp, feeling like a bully now that the worst of his temper was spent, but—

"This was why I didn't want children. This is how I knew it would be." He was defeated by circumstance. "But we're here now, so we'll do what we must. You'll marry me."

"No," she said in a husk of a voice, lips white.

He drew in a tested breath, frustration returning in a

flood of heat. "Did you hear what I just said? *You can't stay here.*"

"Yes, I heard you. Fine. I'll live behind your iron curtain, but—" She swallowed. "But I won't marry you." Her chin came up in what he knew was her stand-ground face.

His ears buzzed as he sifted through her words. "What do you mean?"

"I mean I'll live with you, but I won't *live* with you." She flushed and pulled her shoulders up defensively around her ears.

"You don't want to sleep with me?" His heart bottomed out. She couldn't mean that.

She flinched and looked away, blinking hard. "No. I don't."

"Liar." It came out of him as a breath of absolute truth. A dying wish.

She made a face that held shame and guilt and self-contempt, but when she brought her gaze back to his, she didn't try to convince him she was being honest. She couldn't.

The naked vulnerability in her expression caught at something inside him, though. It was out of character and gut-wrenching, making him tamp it down with resistance. Cinnia was tough. He had always liked that about her. He needed her to be resilient and as impermeable as he was. It was too much on him if she was fragile.

Despite the revelation of weakness, however, she was resolved.

"We can carry on pretty much as we did before." Her voice was a tangle of conflicted emotions. "I'll work remotely around your schedule and go into my office when I can. I'll have to see what my doctor says about travel, but I'm not up for a lot. I was planning to take a few months off work when the babies come, but I don't care where we are when that happens. We can figure that out as we go along, but I'm not going to take up with you again."

"It's not 'taking up.' It's *marriage*." Did she realize how deeply she was insulting him? "Are you trying to make some kind of point? Damn it, Cinnia, are you still trying to prove something to a man in your past who has nothing to do with me?" He wanted to physically hunt down the jerk and shake him.

Her stare flattened to a tundra wasteland of blue that chilled him to the marrow.

"Do you *want* to marry me, Henri? If I wasn't pregnant, would you even be here right now? If I had ended things purely because I wanted to marry and have children, would you have crossed a street to even say, 'Nice to see you'? No. So, no, I'm not being perverse. Yes, this has everything to do with you. If you want to marry me, you can damn well get down on one knee, ask nicely and *mean it*."

Cinnia went upstairs to pack.

Henri forced himself to sit and drink his cold tea while he ate a sandwich, determined to regain his composure after his flare-up.

He hadn't meant to ignite like that, but Ramon was the only one who really understood how dark that time had been after their father's death. Grief had crippled all of them, but a fresh round of attention had fallen on them with the funeral—the girls especially. At fifteen, they'd been long-legged fillies, striking in their youthful blossom of womanhood, hauntingly beautiful in their sorrow.

He and Ramon were used to being sexually objectified by then, but nothing had prepared any of them for the reprehensible, predatory way strange men had begun stalking the girls once the photos were published. For Trella, it had been particularly insidious, sparking panic attacks that had been debilitating.

While other young men his age were drinking themselves stupid, hooking up and partying, he and Ramon had been forced to a level of maturity that exceeded any geezer on the board.

In some ways, combating those dinosaurs for control of Sauveterre International had been a much-appreciated outlet. Ramon was the verbal one, passionately arguing their case and hotly quitting a tense meeting to let off steam by racing cars.

Henri had retreated to spreadsheets and numbers, facts and figures that fueled his ruthless pushback against attempts to sideline him.

He couldn't count the nights he'd sat in a room lit only by the screen of his laptop, angry with his father for abandoning him to this, but sorry for him. Empathizing with him while silently begging for advice on how best to protect his mother and sisters.

Things had grown easier as the girls had matured and taken more responsibility for their own safety. Hell, Trella's self-imposed seclusion had been a relief when it came to how vigilant they all had to be, not that Henri would have ever asked her to go to those lengths.

But he'd never forgotten those first years of wearing his father's mantle, wondering how he would withstand the next day or the one after that. The pressure was too much to expect of anyone. It had hardened his resolve against ever having children and being charged with their safety.

Yet here he was. With Cinnia.

Leaning on his elbows, he rested his tight lips against his linked fingers, examining the assumption he had made before he'd even confirmed her pregnancy. Of course they would marry. For all his reluctance to become a family man, he was the product of one. He and Cinnia were compatible in many ways. It was a natural conclusion.

But she didn't want to rekindle their physical relationship. If the reason was medical, she would have said, "I can't," but her words had been "I won't."

Because she wanted more than sex?

*Do you love me?*

He jerked to his feet as though he could escape his own ruminations by physically running from them. Now, more than ever, he couldn't afford such distractions. Look at him, dwelling on things that couldn't be changed when he should be putting wheels into motion for all that *had* changed.

He shook off his introspection, decided to tell his mother when Cinnia was with him, and video-called Ramon.

When he and his brother had been children, his mother had always spoken Spanish while their father had used his native French. They had wanted their boys to be fluent in both. Before he and Ramon went to school and learned otherwise, they had thought that if someone spoke to them in Spanish, they had to reply in French. It had amused Ramon to no end when the girls had come along and done the same thing. They were all still guilty of reverting to the habit in private conversations with each other.

"Cinnia is pregnant," Henri announced in French.

Ramon visibly flinched. "*Es lamentable.* Who is the father?"

"Me. I am the father," Henri said through his teeth, offended his brother would think otherwise. "The babies are mine." He was still assimilating that outlandish fact. Saying it aloud made it real and all the more heart-stopping.

"'Babies?' *Twins?*" Ramon choked out with disbelief. He swore. Let out a laugh, then swore and laughed again. "*Es verdad?*"

"So real." Henri wiped his hand down his face, trying to keep it from melting off. "You and I need to talk. She has four months to go, but they'll probably come early. I'll have to curtail most of my travel this year. We'll station in Paris, but you and I must discuss how we'll restructure. The press will be a nightmare." His knee-jerk response when thinking about their name in the press was to worry about how it affected Trella, which reminded him... "Trella knew. Did she say anything to you?"

"Knew that Cinnia was pregnant? *No dijo nada.*"

"She's still in Paris?"

"*España.* But go easy." Ramon held up his hand in caution. "She's doing so well. Don't give her a setback."

Henri took that with a grain of salt. His sisters often accused him of smothering, but he still tried to head off potential problems before they triggered one of Trella's attacks. Given how agonizing the episodes were for her, he would never forgive himself if he *caused* one.

He didn't bother defending himself to his brother, though. The warning was pure hypocrisy, coming from Ramon. Ramon and Trella had the most volatile relationship among the four of them. Where Angelique was so sensitive she had always cried if her sister said one cross word in her direction, and Henri was so pragmatic and coolheaded he refused to engage when Trella was in a snit, Ramon had always been more than eager to give her a fight if she wanted one.

But Ramon and only Ramon was allowed to get into a yelling match with their baby sister. Somehow it never caused an attack and sometimes, they all suspected, it had been the only way for Trella to release her pent-up frustrations in a way that didn't leave her fetal and shattered.

Nevertheless, Ramon would not stand between Henri and Trella on this.

"There is no good explanation for leaving me in ignorance." If something had happened before he'd been able to set precautions in place... He refused to even consider it. "It was cavalier and reckless."

"I'll speak to her about it," Ramon said.

Henri made a mental note to be in another country when that happened, saying only, "Meet me in Paris. I'm taking Cinnia there as soon as she packs."

He ended the call and tried Trella. After a few rings, she came on the screen shoulder-to-shoulder with Angelique, both of them wearing a look of apprehension.

"I forgot you were home, too, Gili," he said as he recognized the lounge at Sus Brazos. "Is Mama there?"

"Siesta," they said in unison.

He nodded. Seeing them side-by-side like that, he was struck by Trella's very slight weight gain. It allowed him to get a firmer grasp on the temper he was already holding on a tight leash. After the kidnapping, she'd gone through a heavy period. Comfort eating, her therapist had called it. Insulating. The press had labeled her The Fat One and that had been only the tip of the iceberg with the ugly things printed and said about her.

By the time their father had died, her eating habits had gone the other way and she'd been starving herself. They'd worried about how underweight she was and then the panic attacks had arrived, carrying on for years. After a lengthy bout of trying different medications, which had amounted to drug dependency more than once, she had removed herself from the public eye. Eventually her moods had stabilized, then her weight and overall health had, too.

Things had been going so well that, when Sadiq had announced he was marrying last year, Trella had insisted on coming out of isolation to attend his wedding a few weeks ago. The event had forced her back into the public eye and he and his siblings had been walking on eggshells since, holding their breaths in fear she'd backslide.

Henri wanted her to live as normal a life as their family was capable of, but that fullness in her cheeks and the trepidation in her eyes made him worry that she was not coping as well as they all hoped. He was angry, but forced himself to tread gently.

"I'm at Cinnia's mother's," he began.

"I know. Cin texted me."

That was a surprise. He hadn't seen Cinnia fetch her phone. "Am I to understand you knew about this, too, Gili?"

"Not about Cinnia, no. Trella just explained that bit after she got the text that you were there. Congratulations." Her smile grew to such bright warmth and sincere joy he wanted to groan. Leave it to Gili to undermine his bad mood with her soft heart and warm enthusiasm. *"Twins?"* She patted her hands together in a little clap of excitement. "We each get one! *Merci*, Henri!"

He and Ramon had thought the same thing when their mother had produced a pair of girls when they were six, one for each of them. He might have rolled his eyes, but something in what she'd said niggled.

"What do you mean, you didn't know about *Cinnia?* What *did* you know that I don't?"

Angelique looked at their sister.

"Um." Trella's mouth twisted as she bit the corner of her lip. She held Gili's gaze with a pleading one of her own.

Gili put her arm around her, bolstering her. "*Ça va,* Bella. Just tell him."

"Cinnia didn't tell you where we bumped into each other?" Trella asked, catching his gaze in the screen, then flicking hers away.

"Here in London, I presume. You've been coming to see a client the last few weeks, haven't you?"

"Sort of. Cinnia is a client, right? She couldn't buy maternity wear from anyone else without risking a tip-off to the press."

"Bella," he said in his most carefully modulated tone. "I'm trying very hard not to be angry with you, but I have every right to be. Don't make it worse. Whatever you need to tell me, spit it out."

Her eyelashes lifted and she finally looked at him, speaking swiftly and sharply. "We saw each other at the clinic. The prenatal one. I'm pregnant."

He sat back, absorbing that along with the three dependents he'd just picked up—six, actually, because Cinnia's family would be under his protection, as well. Now, his vulnerable, fragile baby sister was…

He closed his eyes, unable to take it in.

"How…?"

"I was blessed by God, *obviously*. Same as Cinnia," Trella said with a bite in her tone. Then she picked at a nail and mumbled, "It wasn't anything bad. I had a chance to be with someone—"

"The prince. The one you were photographed with a few months ago?" His sisters were even more difficult to tell apart than he and Ramon, especially in photos, but he'd known at the first glance that Trella had been the one caught kissing the Prince of Elazar. Since he'd helped her impersonate Gili himself as part of her process of moving in public again, he hadn't been too hard on her for going rogue.

Now, however…

"You didn't even know him."

"I won't confirm or deny until I've figured out what I'm going to do," Trella mumbled.

"Speaking as a man who just missed several weeks of impending fatherhood, *don't do that, Trella*. It's bad form."

"I'm the one who told her to hire guards and I offered to pay if she couldn't. And speaking as a woman facing an unplanned pregnancy, *this isn't about you*. I *will* handle this, Henri. But I have enough on my plate worrying about myself and my baby without bringing the father into the mix. So does Cinnia, by the way, except she has *two* babies to worry about. Plus, you were the idiot who didn't ask her to stay when you had the chance. *That's* why you missed those weeks, so don't throw that on me. Ugh. I have to go to the bathroom." She pushed to her feet.

As Trella stormed off, Gili gave him a sympathetic look. "Pregnant women are moody." She skipped her gaze in the direction Trella had gone. "Don't tell her I said that. But, you know, keep it in mind with Cinnia."

"How is she, really?" he asked.

Gili's brow pulled with worry, but there was a wistful, pained quality to it. "She's trying so hard not to lean on *anyone*, especially me. Obviously it's a lot to deal with, but I think that's why she's refusing to, you know, tell the father. She doesn't want to feel like a burden again. Give her some time, okay?"

"Oh, I have quite enough to keep me busy here. But you'll tell me if she needs me."

"I will," she promised.

"And how are you?" Had it really only been yesterday that she'd sent him that beaming photo of her with Kasim? She had captioned it "this time we're serious."

He expected a joyful response to his question, but she pulled a sad face.

"Kasim had to go back to Zhamair. I won't see him again until the end of the month. But we want to have a little engagement party." Now came the smile and she was incandescent. "That will take a few weeks to organize, given all our schedules, but I'd like to do it here. Now I'm wondering about Cinnia traveling?"

"We'll have to check with her doctor."

"Please do. If we have to go to London, we will, but I'd rather stay here."

"Agreed." They all relaxed at their childhood home in a way they never could anywhere else.

Besides, he anticipated making his home there with Cinnia, at least at first. His mother still lived there, but she would be thrilled to have them while they worked out exactly where they wanted to live and built their own heavily guarded accommodation. She had despaired for years at having no grandchildren and had been fond of Cinnia. She would express only delight when she heard they were reunited and expecting.

He ended his call with Gili and took the tray to the kitchen, checking in with Milly.

"Thanks, love," Cinnia's mother murmured. She was leafing through an old-fashioned telephone book, flipping through the *C* section, he noted as he set the tray on the island across from where she stood.

"If you're looking up churches, don't bother. She said she'll live with me, but refuses to marry me." He skipped the part where she'd refused to "take up" with him—it still stung.

"Mmm. Claims to be the sensible one." *Flip.* "Perverse is what she is. My husband was the same. It's his fault she's like that, too. The mess he left when he died. Same reason, too. Figured he knew better and the government could go hang with their taxes and formalities and such." *Flip.*

"She seems to be doing well for herself, helping people

navigate those regulations and avoid that kind of debt."
He had to defend Cinnia. She worked hard. Surely her
mother saw that.

"Oh, she does. I only mean she has that same streak of
independence my husband had. And his stubborn… She
calls it a failure to plan, but no, it was a kind of anarchy,
his refusal to fall in with what was clearly the accepted
approach. He was being a bit of an ass, trying to prove he
knew better. She's the same, completely determined to
show her dead father the choices he should have made.
And show me that a woman should never rely on a man,"
she added pithily. "The exact same obstinacy channeled in
a different direction. But you're quite right. I'd have been
in the poor house long ago if not for Cinnia knuckling
down with her career and sorting things out for all of us."

*Flip.*

Henri thought again about how hard life had been after
his father had passed. Their situations were very different, but Cinnia's devotion to her family, her desire to look
out for them, was every bit as strong as his. She must have
been overwhelmed.

"How old was Cinnia when you lost your husband?"

"Fourteen."

"Fourteen," he repeated, wondering why he didn't know
that already. For all the times she'd admonished him as
being reticent, she wasn't terribly forthcoming about herself. "That must have been a lot on you at the time."

"On Cinnia," she amended with dismay. "Little Dorry
was barely walking. I was a wreck. Well, you know. It's
devastating for the whole family when the cornerstone is
gone, but I was completely unprepared. I didn't know how
to even pay a bill. Genuinely didn't know how to write a
check or how to call a plumber if the sink backed up. All
I knew was that I needed to keep my girls in this house.

It's the only home they knew. That's all you think, isn't it?" She set her hand on the open book and looked at him, old grief heavy in her expression. "Hang on to what's left so you can stay on your feet after such a terrible blow."

Henri nodded. She was stating it exactly right. His mother had been shattered, his sisters distraught, he and Ramon overwhelmed.

"Cinnia doubled up with Dorry so we could let her old room along with the rest. It wasn't worth asking the other two to share. You've met them. You know what I mean," she said with an exasperated shake of her head. "The blood wouldn't have come out of the carpets, but at least they express themselves. Not Cinnia. No, she and Dorry bottle everything up and use it like fuel to get where they're going. Heaven help you if you try to give either a leg up. Dorry is allowed to answer the phone because Cinnia pays her to do it. Quid pro quo, but if I so much as pick it up so it stops ringing? Well!"

Henri folded his arms, thinking of the way Cinnia had refused to let him glance over her business plan until after she'd secured financing elsewhere. Then there had been her reluctance to tell him what she was looking for in a flat, let alone the location she preferred or the price range she could afford. As it turned out, living above her office space had been her plan all along, and a sensible one, but he'd been in the dark on the entire thing until she'd closed the deal. It wasn't just that she hadn't wanted his help, he was seeing, but she needed every last shred of credit to be hers. She *was* independent to a fault.

"That self-sufficiency isn't just because of your husband's situation, though, is it? Tell me about that boyfriend she lived with in London."

"Avery? That is a perfect example of how obdurate she can be. She let that, well, it's not fair to call him a ne'er-do-well, but you could tell at first glance he wouldn't amount to much. I made the mistake of saying I thought she could do better and that was it." Her hand went up in surrender. "She let that boy attach to her like a lamprey. I say 'boy' deliberately. Her first suitor wasn't ready to act like a man, but you could see straight away he had some stones. You remind me of him, if you want the truth."

Henri wasn't sure how to take that, especially when Milly was taking his measure with such a shrewd eye. He didn't like talking about Cinnia's past, either. Not when it included men her mother knew so well.

Aside from Cinnia, his mother had rarely met any woman he'd slept with. Cinnia was the only woman he'd ever trusted enough. First he'd taken her to watch Ramon race a few times, then he'd included her in a dinner with Gili in Paris after she began staying with him there. They'd been seeing each other a full year before he'd taken her to Spain for his birthday, where she'd finally met Trella and his mother.

Those had been big steps for him and she hadn't pressed him to meet and mingle with her family, either, disappearing for a dozen lunches and overnights to see them before she'd started inviting him to accompany her.

He'd been relieved, but now it irritated him that other men had come and gone from this kitchen. He'd had many lovers before Cinnia. Why did he care that she'd had *two*?

"James would have been a good match for her, but they met too young. He let her down," Milly continued with a disheartened sigh. "She went to the opposite end of the spectrum with Avery. Saw him as safe, I suppose. Not so capable of breaking her heart."

*That* was why he hated the thought of her previous lovers. No other women had impacted him the way Cinnia had, but those other men had been fixtures in her life. They'd shaped her. They affected how she reacted to *him*.

"Avery could barely spoon his own oatmeal. It was my fault she got in so deep with him, of course. 'Mum thinks we should marry for money.' I never said that." She held up an admonishing finger, then waved it away. "But that doesn't matter. She had to prove she's a feminist who can support a man, like someone would pin her with a Victoria Cross for *that*. Oh, she wanted so desperately to make me eat my words about him. And how did that turn out? He was a complete waste of her time and stole a thick slice of her savings, didn't he? Exactly as I called it."

She lowered her nose to the book and gave another page a loud flip.

Everything she'd said had given him a fresh view of Cinnia. Not so much a new angle, as a deeper understanding of her edges and shadows. Was this why she was holding him off? He came on strong at the best of times and his children's safety was a red line for him. She *had* to live with him.

He shouldn't have lost his temper, though. That must have scared her.

At the same time, she must also know he wouldn't let her down the way those other men had. He kept his promises.

*You said when I was ready to start a family, you would let me go. Are you going to keep your word?*

*Of course.*

The pit of his belly roiled.

"I have my opinions about you, too, Henri," Milly told him without looking up. "Not *all* of you falls short so if my daughter decided to marry you, I would support her decision." Her head came up and her mouth was tight, her brows arched. "Exactly as I will if she refuses."

He was absorbing that statement as she dropped her attention to the book, adjusted her glasses and set a fingernail onto the page.

"There we are. Classifieds. If she's leaving, I can let out the rooms again, can't I?"

# CHAPTER SEVEN

CINNIA DIDN'T HAVE much to pack. Her sisters had been through her wardrobe like locusts once she had grown too big to wear most of it. Trella had been incredibly generous, bringing her maternity clothes and refusing to let her pay. Cinnia had given things back as she grew out of them.

She and Trella had been meeting in secret every other week and without her, Cinnia would have fallen apart by now.

Burying herself in work had also helped her cope. She'd busied herself with bringing on her partner who was taking over the payments on her start-up loan. Then there'd been all the arrangements to set up an office here at the house. For hours, sometimes days at a time, she could forget she was sitting on a ticking time bomb.

But she had always known that Henri would have to be told.

And that he would insist on her coming back for safety reasons. She didn't blame him for that, she didn't, especially after he had pulled back the curtain on how he really felt about the press.

She was still shaken by the bitterness he had revealed. And defeated. Her firm intentions to make her own way had buckled not from his show of temper, but from his helpless anguish. She couldn't, absolutely couldn't, make things harder for him. Not in good conscience.

But her life would change irrevocably now. It would have anyway, she supposed. Twins did that to a woman. But things with Henri would be profoundly different this time. She would no longer be his equal.

Not that she'd been his equal in the past, but she had been able to pretend they were traveling in parallel lanes, living their own lives and intersecting when it suited them for the same reason: sex.

Even before she had turned up pregnant, however, she had known she was following more than pacing. She was becoming more emotionally invested than he was, wrapping her life around his. She had hid it from herself as much as him, but the pregnancy had forced her to confront it. She'd had to ask herself, and him, how deeply he was involved.

"Do you love me?" she had asked him that morning in January, making sure to wait until they'd returned to London so she had an escape strategy that didn't involve getting herself to the ferry.

In typical Henri fashion, he had dodged the question with a faintly bored "If you're looking for a proposal—"

"I didn't ask if you wanted to marry me," she had interrupted sharply, hiding that his attitude stung like a scald. "I asked if you loved me."

"And the reason you're asking is because you want to change things between us." He hadn't even looked up from whatever he was reading on his tablet, like this was a tiresome conversation. "I told you I'd never marry you."

She had sat there with her sip of orange juice eating a hole in her stomach.

Her pregnancy had already been weighing on her conscience for two weeks, earning her a few queries from him about why she was so withdrawn and distracted. He'd even set a hand on her forehead at one point, looking concerned when he asked if she was coming down sick again.

She had been heartsick, aware that he would not be happy about the pregnancy, while deep in her soul, she was *so* happy. There was no man whose baby she would want more.

But not like this. Not so he would feel manipulated and forced into marrying her. Not when she might be a little in love while he clearly didn't have any deep feelings on his side.

So, yes, she had set him up to disappoint her. Maybe if she had said "I love you" first, he might have found some tender words of his own. Perhaps they could have progressed amicably toward an arrangement from there.

She hadn't. She had locked her own heart down tight, preparing herself for rejection and yes, even engineering it so she could walk away wounded yet righteous.

"I've always wanted children," she had reminded him, nearly trembling she was holding herself so tightly together as she gave the greatest shake of dice in her life. "You said when I was ready to start a family, you would let me go. Are you going to keep your word?"

"Of course."

Two words. Bam, bam.

Why couldn't he have at least said he was fond of her in that moment? Why hadn't he said he would miss her? Or acted in some small way like he didn't want her to go? He had spent all the time they'd been together making her think he felt something, even if it was just affection. He was terribly protective of her and often expressed admiration at how hard she worked and what she accomplished. Maybe he didn't laugh outright at all her jokes, sometimes he even gave her a look that scolded her for crossing a line, but he invariably smirked. He appreciated her snark, whether it was witty or facetious.

Why else would she feel so much for him if he didn't at least appear to care for her, too? She wasn't a self-destructive idiot.

Was she?

Did he really feel nothing? From the moment he had walked in here, he hadn't betrayed one iota of pleasure in seeing her again. Just anger and resentment.

*You want to change things*, he had accused her that day.

She hadn't, she really hadn't. Things had changed all by themselves. Cells had split.

Then she and Henri had.

Her eyes welled as she recognized that nothing had changed between then and now. Absence hadn't made his heart grow fonder. He still felt nothing.

Despair accosted her afresh.

*Don't be stupid*, she told herself as the pressure built behind her eyes and in her throat. She only cried late in the night, when she lay awake in the dark, missing him, curled around their babies, freezing to death because his side of the bed was empty.

During the day, she was pragmatic and confident.

Which had been easy when she'd been convinced she would hold her position and stay right here in this room.

How would she protect her heart if she was living with him again, seeing him every day?

The pressure behind her eyes built as she contemplated how hard this was going to be. Her breaths were already coming in shaky jags of panic.

She told herself to quit being so silly, but her hand pulled a tissue from the box, then kept grabbing a string of them as she felt her world crumbling around her. The agony of not having his love rose, too much for one or two measly tissues. It was a freight train bearing down on her, filling her throat with a wail of agony that she held her breath against releasing.

She didn't want to love him. It was too big, too hard. It hurt too much.

She buried her face in the cloud of tissues, but this swell of emotion wouldn't be stemmed. Her whole body became wracked by anguish. She had tried to keep everything together and was falling apart. Everything was splitting and rending. She gasped for a breath and it was a ragged sob.

"Cinnia."

His voice, so gentle, so tender, was the last straw. How did he do that? How did he sound like he cared when he didn't?

Her heart broke open and she started to buckle forward, knees giving way under a keening moan.

Strong arms caught her, gathering her, muscles flexing as he picked her up, breath rushing out with the effort. She gave his shoulder a knock with her closed fist, hating him for being virile and powerful when she was fat and weak and falling apart.

He laid her on the bed, coming down alongside her, gathering her into his chest and pressing his lips against her brow, murmuring in French.

She tried to stop crying and listen and wound up wailing, "I don't understand you!" She didn't mean because he was speaking French, but because he was being so *nice*.

"I'm telling you not to be afraid, *chérie*. I shouldn't have scared you, saying those things about being a target. You're safe. I promise I will keep you and the babies safe."

He had it all wrong, but she was so shaken to be held by him, so relieved, she surrendered to emotion and let the pain of these weeks without him release.

He continued to stroke her hair and murmur reassurances. She knew he had probably done this with Trella. Henri had spent fifteen years trying to help his sister recover from something that never should have happened. It was no wonder he drew such a thick line around himself and his family, holding everyone else at a distance.

But even though he begrudged Cinnia for daring to get pregnant, here he was, making promises, letting her burrow into his warmth. It was sweet and right and she cried all the harder.

Bastard. How dare he keep this good, generous heart of his out of her reach?

"Shh. Calm yourself, *chérie.*"

"I don't think I can do this," she said, feeling pitiful as she admitted it.

He misunderstood her again. "It's not all on you, Cinnia. You can trust me." He rubbed her back and smoothed his lips against her brow. "I'm here now."

"But you don't want to be." That was the crux of the matter.

He held his mouth against her forehead for a long moment, then sighed a warm breath against her hairline.

"You're fair to berate me for that."

She waited, but he didn't say anything else. Despair rose afresh and she started to roll away.

He tightened his arms, keeping her against his warmth.

"It was painful enough that the kidnapping happened," he said in a low voice that sounded like it barely scraped through a dry throat. "It was frightening enough to live with the knowledge that we're not impervious. But then I became the one responsible for standing watch. Of course I will always look after my mother and sisters, but I never wanted to take on a wife and child. A *child*, Cinnia. If you knew what my parents looked like when Trella was missing."

She swallowed, shocked out of her desolation. He never talked about the kidnapping.

"*I* was in agony. My mother… It was inhuman what they did to her by taking her daughter. And what they did to Trella? I have *never* wanted to bring the potential for more suffering into my life by having children. That sounds cowardly, I know, but I couldn't volunteer for it."

"I'm sorry," she said, wilting in helplessness, voice nothing but a rasp as she realized he would never forgive her.

*"Non,"* he insisted. "You are not sorry. Neither am I. I'm not." He cupped her face, tilting it up so she could see he was sincere. "I am concerned. I will worry about our children for the rest of my life. But I'm not sorry to be their father."

She could hardly see him through her swollen eyes as they filled with tears of tentative hope.

He caressed her cheek with his thumb. "Our children are not something either of us will regret." He tucked his chin to send his gaze down to her belly and very carefully set his hand on the firm, round bump. "These babies are wanted. By both of their parents. *Oui?*"

Being held by him had already warmed her through, but that touch, the reverence in his gentle, splayed hand, sent joyous light through her, so sharp and sweet she had to close her eyes to withstand it. She ducked her head against his collarbone, feeling all the sharp edges of her broken heart shifting, trying to find a way to fit back together.

"Yes." Her lips trembled as she felt his hand move, lightly exploring. It was pure magic.

"How are there two in there, Cinnia? That's unbelievable."

As if they knew it was him and wanted to say hello,

a tiny rolling sensation went through her abdomen. She choked on a little laugh.

"Did you feel that? Maybe it's not strong enough—"

"Shh." He seemed to hold his breath as they both held very still.

Pressure nudged where his hot hand rested. He let out a breath of wonder.

"Is that really them?" he whispered.

"You don't have to whisper. They're not sleeping." She tilted her face to look at him again, unable to hold back her smile. He was too devoted to his siblings to withhold his love from his children. She'd always known that, deep down, but she was still relieved to see him react with the beginning of parental love. She was overjoyed. "It's incredible, isn't it?"

"It is nothing like I imagined it could be." He shifted so her head was pillowed on his shoulder.

She relaxed, comforted by his seeming desire to get to know his babies through the wall of her belly. But she had to ask—with more than a little trepidation. "You really don't hate me for this? I swear I didn't do it on purpose."

A pause, then his voice was very grave, rumbling beneath her ear. "I know. And I could never hate you."

Not "I love you." Not even "I care." Just "I don't hate you."

Fresh despondency closed her eyes, but she had to wonder if he was withholding his heart because he was afraid of being too attached. What if something happened? As he said, he had every reason to believe bad things could happen if he wasn't vigilant.

Oddly, she found herself thinking of his young self, fifteen and worrying about his missing sister. Her arm went across his chest and she tucked her face into his neck, hugging him tight. Saying nothing, but offering belated comfort.

"Are you changing your mind, *chérie*?" he asked, snuggling her closer with hands that cruised in a familiar way. "Would you like to make love?"

She suspected if this silly belly wasn't in the way, she would feel he was aroused. She was growing warm and boneless, feeling him against her like this.

"No," she lied, shifting so her head was on the pillow, putting space between them. "No, I—" She sighed, confronted by how difficult it would be, living with him again, resisting not just him, but herself. "No." Just *no*.

She wondered how long she'd be able to keep saying that.

They didn't make it to Paris until late the next day.

Cinnia was subdued, making Henri think of those days leading up to their breakup. He'd churned through those moments of pale silence a few times since, always concluding she had been deciding whether she wanted to leave him.

He saw it differently now. She had known she was pregnant. Along with that weighty knowledge, her body had already been under a lot of demands. The Cinnia he thought of as quite tough and impervious had fallen apart in his arms last night, then crashed for almost three hours.

Her mother had cautioned him to let her sleep, implying Cinnia didn't always take as much care of herself as she should in her condition, which didn't surprise him. She was as driven by ambition as he was. But her tears and exhaustion had thrust an unpleasant sensation upon him. Humbleness.

She had been carrying more than his children. Guilt. Fear that he would hate her. He had been honest when he'd told her he could never hate her, but he couldn't give her the love she sought, either.

To counter some of that disappointment for her, he had stood in the doorway of her sister's bedroom, cutting a deal with Dorry.

"My preference is to make Spain our base," he had said. "My mother will be there, but she will be Abuela. We'll need an au pair. Since you were already planning to nanny for Cinnia, I'd like you to come with us, at least for the short term."

"Really?" Dorry's quizzical eyebrow had gone up behind the round rims of her glasses. "Wouldn't you rather, like, have someone professional? Who knows karate?"

"The babies will have their own bodyguards, *absolument*, but the guards' duties will be protection, not feeding and changing. And Cinnia may be homesick without family nearby. It would be nice to have you there." Cinnia often talked about her mother and sisters in a tone of exasperation, but she loved them to pieces. "We both trust you, and you and I get along well."

"Also, his brother won't try to hook up with you," Cinnia had called sleepily through the cracked door of the darkened room behind him.

Henri had shaken his head, secretly delighted to hear her rallying, but sometimes her remarks were in such poor taste.

Dorry hadn't flinched or laughed. She'd given him her sister's exact deadpan look and said, "Forget it then."

"I take it back," he'd told the girl. "Two sharp Whitley tongues under one roof is too many."

He hadn't meant it. They'd all convened in the dining room for a late dinner, Dorry contemplating a year in Spain. He had also negotiated with her mother to bring in staff to serve as security and run the family mansion as a B and B if she wanted to continue letting rooms, but he promised to find her a flat near them in Spain so she could come and go as it suited her, and see her grandchildren.

Those were the simple details. There were a million more complex ones still to work through, but he found himself unable to catch at any of them as they entered his penthouse, tired from a long day.

They had slept last night in the London flat, arriving very late and using separate rooms, then visited her doctor first thing this morning, ensuring she was safe to travel and transferring her file to a specialist here in Paris—whom they'd briefly met on arrival in the city.

He liked the London flat fine. He and Cinnia had made it a sort of base in the past and had been comfortable there, but family came and went from that residence.

This penthouse was his. With six bedrooms, his family each had a room here, but only stayed occasionally. His mother and sisters typically put themselves up in the secure flat atop the girls' design house, Maison des Jumeaux, while his brother made do with hotels—so he could have a guest if he desired.

Henri preferred these spacious rooms with their modern decor and plethora of conveniences. It was his retreat, a space he had purchased for himself for the private terrace overlooking the Eiffel Tower and the Seine.

Cinnia let out a sigh as they entered, exactly expressing how he felt.

She had always been a pleasant companion, providing a side commentary that made cocktail parties or gala dinners that much easier to endure, but always as relieved as he was to close the door on the world.

She took off her coat and hung it herself like she'd arrived into her own home.

He watched with a twist in his gut, realizing how much

he'd taken her place in his life for granted. He'd been impatient when she had sounded like she wasn't satisfied with their arrangement. He had been. Eminently. You didn't mess with perfection.

He'd been furious with her that morning. He'd not only resisted allowing her to stir things in a different direction, but he'd also let her go to prove to himself he would quickly get past any disappointment at her departure.

He hadn't. Her absence had been eating a hole in him, not least of which because he had no interest in other women. It was the longest stretch in his life he'd been abstinent since discovering what the opposite sex had to offer.

She had her back to him, not even looking pregnant from this angle. She was his ever-alluring Cinnia with her wavy blond hair falling down her narrow back and her lovely round bottom creating an exquisitely feminine hourglass below her wide shoulders. Her supple backside flexed as she kicked off her shoes into the closet.

He wanted her. *Craved* her. Had for months.

Hell. When had he not hungered for her? From the first moment he'd seen her, he'd been captivated.

Now, finally alone with her, the talons of lust were taking a firm hold in him—destructive lust, since the press already knew something was up, forcing a lot of trying detours today. He needed to keep his head, his mind, focused.

He ought to keep his distance, but he moved to stand beside her and toed off his own shoes.

He could smell that familiar, elusive scent of hers. Subtle. She never wore anything overpowering. He always had to get in close to catch the faint hints of rain and roses in her hair, lavender and geranium on her skin.

Her profile was stark, shadows playing deep into the contours of her face, making her look pale and shell-shocked. She stared into the closet like she was searching for a passageway to another world.

"What's wrong?" His arm went out in a reflexive need to catch and hold. He hooked it across the top of her chest, pivoting to draw her back into him.

"Nothing." His action turned her and she lifted her gaze to where they were reflected in the mirror by the door. Her hands came up to hold on to his forearm, but she didn't press him to remove his touch.

He looked at their reflection.

Her brow pleated with accusation before hurt clouded into her sky blue eyes. She lowered her lashes to hide it, but her mouth remained pouted with disappointment.

In him.

He tightened his arm on her.

"I didn't think I had to ask why you wanted to leave, *chérie*. You told me why. You're not allowed to hate me for letting you go when you said it's what you wanted. I'm not a barbarian. I wasn't going to keep you against your will."

Laughter burst out of her. "Really? Where am I now? With how much choice?"

He folded his other arm across her, splaying a hand over the babies he would protect with his life. "You could have been honest. *You* decided to make this hard by not telling me."

Her lips trembled and she tightened her mouth to steady them. "Two years is a long time to be a courtesan, Henri. I wanted to know I meant more to you than sex for hire."

"You do."

"Do I?" Her gaze flashed back to his in the mirror, filled with dejection as she nudged her bottom into his groin. Where he was hard. "That's all you ever gave me. That and jewelry, and now a pair of babies. Never *you*."

"This *is* me," he said through gritted teeth, barely containing himself as a rush of excitement went through him at the press of her soft cheek. He chucked his chin at his reflection. "This man who is obsessed enough to risk bringing you into my home, where you can see the inner workings of my life. Do you honestly think our affair was something I took on lightly? No, damn you, it wasn't. It's a weakness. A dangerous indulgence. But I wanted you. I want you all the time. Do you really expect me to apologize for giving in to that? When you want me every bit as much?"

She tried to glare him down in the mirror, challenging his claim, but he dismissed her bravado with a scoffing breath of a laugh.

"You're nipples are hard, *chérie*. Think I haven't noticed?" He slid his hand to cup her breast, full enough now to make him splay his fingers to contain the abundant flesh.

She gasped and hunched away from his touch, bumping into him to escape the pressure.

He released her with a jolt of shock. "I hurt you?"

"They're really tender." Her eyes were shiny with tears.

He turned her to face him and asked, "*Can* you make love?" The doctor had said it was safe, but if it would be painful for her—

She threw back her head and he braced for another rejection.

But as he held her gaze, unable to disguise how ferociously he ached to make love with her, the glow of outrage dimmed in her eyes.

His pulse hammered in his throat, in his chest, in his groin. He might have tightened his hands on her arms, unconsciously urging her to match his need. He couldn't be the only one affected this deeply. It was too much to bear.

Her blue irises began to swim with longing and her weight pressed into his hold. Her shoulders dropped in capitulation.

He swore, control snapping. He cupped her face and kissed her. He tried to be gentle, tried to hang on to a semblance of control, but damn it, it had been *so long*. He opened his mouth wider to take full possession of hers, finally tasting her again and feasting on what he'd been missing. He curled his fist into the silken tresses that had grazed every inch of his naked skin at one time or another, wrapped his other arm around her so his hand braced between her flexing shoulder blades, and he kissed her without restraint. He took.

Raided.

Owned.

And she gave.

She slid her fingers into his hair and pressed him to kiss her harder, opened her mouth beneath his and met his tongue with hers. She scraped her teeth against his lips and clung across his shoulders with a slender arm and let her knee crook up to his thigh.

She moaned in the way that begged him to take her to bed and find fulfillment with her. Within her.

His skin stung, feeling too tight for the heat of desire exploding in him. It was a monster that wanted to consume both of them. He scraped his teeth down her throat to where her neck joined her shoulder. That fantastic, exciting place that always made her gasp and shiver and soften her knees so she wilted in his embrace.

*Mine.*

"Henri," she moaned and pushed at him.

Pregnant, he reminded himself dimly, saying, "Bed," as he took a half step back.

"Damn you," she whispered in pained despair. "I need more than sex!"

# CHAPTER EIGHT

CINNIA WAS SHOWERED, dressed and putting the final touches on her makeup when Henri knocked and came into her bedroom. He had knocked once, an hour ago, telling her without inflection that he'd let her sleep as long as he could, but that they had a busy day and she should get up.

"Ramon is en route. PR will be tricky. I'll want you in several of my meetings. There will be photos."

He'd been on the phone with someone when she'd slipped into the kitchen for a glass of orange juice and scrambled eggs. She'd stolen a yearning look at his back, admiring the way his white shirt clung across his shoulders and his belted pants outlined his firm butt.

Now she was forced to look him in the eye for the first time since he'd walked away from her last night, stepping onto the terrace and staying there, despite the pecking rain.

She hadn't slept well, having sat on the edge of her bed half the night, fighting the temptation to go to him and damn herself and her stubborn principles all to hell.

Was she just being pigheaded, as her mother sometimes accused? She didn't think so. Henri was an easy man to yield to. To drown in. If she started having sex with him, she would let him take over her entire life—become dependent. She couldn't allow herself to become that weak.

But she suspected he would always be stronger than

her, always, which was unnerving, especially when he strode with that easy, panther-like confidence toward her.

"Yours." He placed an open envelope on the vanity before her.

She recognized it and her heart fell into her toes. It was the courier envelope with her own handwriting. She had stuffed it full of all the jewelry he'd given her and sent it back to him right after their breakup.

His expression was implacable. Confrontational.

There'd been no reaction out of him when she'd done it, which had fed her misery. Now she saw there were very strong feelings on his side, so strong she had to look away, getting the sense he was barely holding back a blast at her that had nothing to do with being rebuffed from her bed.

She twisted her mascara back into its base and set it aside. "Is Ramon here?"

"Any minute."

*Damn. Hurry up, Ramon.*

She took a half step back from the mirror, gave her hair a flick so it was behind her shoulders and wondered if Henri liked what he saw, then heard her own thoughts and wanted to groan. She wore a blue wrap dress with a satin belt and a tulip cut to the hem. As with any Maison des Jumeaux creation, it was incredibly flattering. Of course, she looked her best.

She still longed for his approval. His hot stare was making her skin sizzle.

"You're not going to see if it's all there?" Henri challenged. "Perhaps accuse me of bringing that in here to persuade you into bed?"

She kept her gaze on her reflection, feeling the sting as her cheeks flooded with color, but refused to let her attention drop to the envelope or even back to what she sensed would be his hardened expression. His voice sounded like granite.

"You said last night that all I ever gave you was sex and jewelry. Jewelry *for* sex, in fact. Whereas I thought we'd settled that argument with this one." He spoke in a tone that held an undercurrent of danger. He plucked out a bracelet, the first thing he'd ever given her, and dropped it onto the vanity with an air of dismissal. Disgust even.

She gave a cry of protest and reached to catch it before it slithered off the edge and onto the floor. Then she stared at the puddled jewels in her palm, inordinately pleased to cradle them again.

She had worn this bracelet almost every day. It was a line of individually set rubies and diamonds. A tennis bracelet, some called it. "Fireworks," he had said of the color in the stones when he'd presented it. "I saw it and thought of our first night."

She had gone through the roof, accusing him of paying her for sex. They'd had a rousing big fight about it. He had been more offended than she was.

"If I wanted to pay for sex, I would have grabbed the first gaudy piece of trash that came along. *Same goes for a woman.* No, I saw something that made me think of the night we met and I wanted you to have it, because I will always remember—"

He had cut himself off and walked away.

*Her? Their first time? That night?*

Chastened, she had put on the bracelet and had only taken it off to bathe or if she happened to wear something else for an evening.

"Do you know how angry I was when this showed up?" he said now, the steadiness of his tone belying the latent fury within. He tipped the envelope so everything tumbled out.

She flinched and threw out her free hand, keeping everything on the vanity top.

"This—" he snatched up a bejeweled pendant in the shape of a key "—was never, ever about sex and you know it. It was something I wanted you to have."

He had given it to her a few days after she'd closed on her office and flat. They hadn't even made love there until she'd taken possession and she had had the carpets replaced so, no, it absolutely had nothing to do with sex.

"I'm proud of you," he had said as he had pushed the little velvet box across the restaurant table where they were celebrating. "You worked hard to achieve something and did it. Hell, you're walking around sparkling with such pride in yourself, I thought you should have something sparkly to commemorate it."

She'd been bemused yet touched, and had often worn the pendant when she happened to be having a rough time with a work file or even just a gray day. It never failed to pick her up and make her feel good about who she was and how far she'd come.

"This?" He held up an anklet from their first trip to New York. "What sex was I paying for with this?"

She pinched her mouth shut, knowing full well it had been a silly joke between them. She had bemoaned the fact that the Americans seemed to have a fixation with shoes, but she had no interest in which designer was which. He'd given her that cord of gold, the reticulated links heavy on her skin and always a more pleasant conversation piece when the shoe topic came up. She had threatened to get herself a charm of the Statue of Liberty to hang off it, which had earned her such a stare of revulsion, she still snickered thinking of it.

"I enjoyed having you with me in New York. That's all

I was saying when I gave this to you," he said, shaking the little snake of gold.

"Don't," she muttered, worried he would kink a link. She stole it from him and closed it in her fist against her heart.

"What do you care what happens to it? This is a pile of junk, isn't it?" He gave a solid platinum arm cuff a disdainful bat with his fingertips. "It's not like each one represents a special memory between us. It's not like I spent any time choosing these things specifically for *you*. You're right. They're meaningless and I should have thrown the works in the garbage when they came back. I'll do that now."

"Don't you dare!" she cried, knocking his hands away from sweeping everything back into the envelope. "You made me feel lousy, acting like you didn't give a damn that I was leaving, so I tried to do the same to you. All right?"

She pushed herself between him and the trove of emeralds and diamonds, gold and platinum.

"Message received. Our two years together weren't even worth remembering. When that came back, I wanted to—" In her periphery, she saw his fists clench, but his jaw pulsed. His brow flinched. "We had more than sex." His voice was raw, the words bit out between clenched teeth.

Funny thing about trying to hurt someone you cared about. It wasn't nearly as satisfying as you thought it would be.

She dared a glance up into his face, fearing she'd see anger or resentment. There was only regret. Apology, even.

"Is that why you're refusing to marry me? We're good together, Cinnia. Not just there." He pointed at the bed where she had tossed and turned. *"Everywhere."*

She waited, but he didn't profess undying love.

She looked away, blinking at the sting in her eyes. It wasn't so much disappointment as a feeling of inevitability. What would it even prove if he did say the words? She wouldn't believe him.

A painful jolt went through her, realization striking like a hard pulse of electricity, making her catch her breath. She hadn't just been testing him when she'd left. She'd been driving him away, *afraid* to want his love. Proving to herself she didn't need it.

She was still holding him off to protect herself.

"I care about you. *Ça va?*" He ground out the words like he begrudged even giving her that much.

"No," she said, voice strained, facing something she had barely peered into that day in January. She threw back her head, ignoring the dampness on her lashes as she stared into his wary expression. "It's not okay. Because even if you'd said the words that day…"

Her voice thinned and her throat strained to swallow.

"I've heard them before and it didn't matter. I still wound up hurt and on my own. So yes, I knew deep down that you meant these as signs of affection…" She waved at the jewelry. "But I expected to be left to fend for myself eventually. And was."

"That won't happen again," he vowed fiercely. "It's different."

"Is it? I won't take any chances, will I?"

He started to argue further, but they both heard the door chime.

He swore. "That's Ramon."

"I'll be out in a moment," she promised and turned away to fix her makeup.

Henri ruminated as he watched his brother greet Cinnia. Ramon genuinely liked her, probably because she expected even less from him than she had ever demanded of Henri.

Henri disguised a wince, thinking of what she'd said

moments ago. He supposed he should be relieved that she'd essentially told him she didn't want his declaration of love, since she wouldn't believe him anyway, but it was as much a slap in the face as her return of his jewelry.

He couldn't believe she had so little faith in him.

She was pale and Henri imagined that if his brother noticed, he put it down to her delicate condition.

Ramon, however, being an inveterate flirt, still went out of his way to charm her.

In a moment of shaken confidence, Henri watched closely for her reaction. Cinnia tended to respond with smiles of amused tolerance when his brother turned on the charisma, occasionally flattered, but never swayed, never tempted.

He'd seen it the first day they met, of course, but her preference for him hadn't been fully cemented in his mind until the first time he'd taken her to watch his brother race in Nürburg. It had been a good trip, the first one where he introduced her to perhaps not the family's *inner* circle, but people in their regular social circle. She had fit in well. They had all enjoyed the race day and danced the night away afterward.

The next morning, Henri had taken her down to breakfast only to receive a call as they were entering the restaurant. She had gone ahead to the table with Sadiq and some others from their group. While Henri had watched from afar, Ramon had arrived.

Of course Ramon was wearing the same shirt Henri already wore and of course Ramon had tried to trick Cinnia into believing he was Henri.

Henri's hand had tightened on his phone and he'd missed what his executive was telling him as he watched Ramon come up behind Cinnia and set a familiar hand on her shoulder *exactly* as Henri might have done. Without a doubt, Ramon had said something like "*Je m'excuse, chérie.* I'm here now."

Then his bastard brother had leaned down to kiss her in greeting, exactly as Henri would have done.

Cinnia had paused in midconversation, lifted her mouth in absent acceptance of his arrival and kiss—and had nearly leaped out of her chair before Ramon's lips touched hers. Henri had heard her scream of surprise through the window. If Ramon hadn't caught her and kept her on her feet, she would have stumbled to the floor.

Henri might have found it as funny as everyone else if he hadn't been worried she had hurt herself. He'd cut short his call and hurried into the restaurant, where Cinnia, being a good sport, was laughing at herself even as she scolded Ramon to never *ever* do that to her again.

Henri had then heard every account from every other person who had witnessed it, all ringing with great humor and awe that she could tell the brothers apart so easily. Most of them had also presumed Ramon had been Henri. Pretty much the entire party had been taken in by his joke *except* Cinnia.

Cinnia didn't react to Ramon the way she reacted to him.

He might have been reassured by that, but her heart, he was realizing, was as out of reach as his own. It made him jealous of the rapport Ramon still had with her.

"If you laugh…" Cinnia warned with a sideways look.

"I said you look stunning. As always." Ramon held Cinnia's hands out at her sides. His mouth twitched as he took in her belly.

"I look like a boa constrictor after it swallowed a goat."

"Two. Let's be honest," Ramon said, then he laughed as he dodged her attempt to slug his belly. "Small ones. Kids!" He gathered her into a gentle bear hug and kissed her hair, exactly as he would do if he'd teased one of their sisters into reacting.

"You're a brat!" She playfully shoved out of his arms.

Henri was forced to turn away as the doorman rang to announce their second guest. "*Oui*, send her up."

"Who else is coming?" Cinnia asked as Ramon dropped his hand from her arm and frowned a similar inquiry.

"Isidora Garcia." He didn't bother moving away from the door since she would be knocking momentarily. "You would have met her father, Bernardo, at my mother's birthday."

"Oh, yes! He's lovely."

"He doesn't retire until next month." Ramon's scowl held more than confusion. "We have a team of people under him. I thought we agreed to promote Etienne."

"We have a lot of sensitive information to manage. Angelique and Kasim will go public with their engagement in a few months and you spoke with Bella?"

"I did." His brother's mouth flattened and he shot a look at Cinnia. "Do *you* know who the father is? Is it that Prince of Elazar?"

"She wanted me to have plausible deniability," Cinnia told him with a rueful moue. "She refused to say."

Ramon made a noise of dismay. "Regardless, I don't see why you think we need—"

The knock on the door interrupted him.

Henri opened it and greeted Isidora.

She was a Spanish beauty with a fiery hint of auburn in her long dark hair. Her warm brown eyes were framed in thick, sooty lashes. She took after her notorious socialite mother far more than the short, barrel-chested man she called Papa. Henri privately had his doubts that Bernardo *was* her father, biologically, but had never asked. Bernardo had always guarded the Sauveterre family secrets so diligently, he allowed the man his own.

"*Bonjour*, Isidora. Thank you for coming."

"Of course. It's always lovely to see you." They exchanged cheek kisses. Hers were well-defined and aristocratic, perfumed and soft. She turned to greet Cinnia.

Her smile fell away as she saw Ramon.

"Ramon," she greeted flatly.

Isidora was a little younger than their sisters. Given her father's close relationship with their own, and Trella's homeschooling after the kidnapping, at times Isidora had been one of the few playmates the girls had had. The adoring crush she had developed on Ramon through her adolescence had been awkward, but they had never teased her over it. She was too nice. And Ramon had never encouraged her. She'd been too young, for starters, and he was too conscious of her father's protectiveness of her virtue.

As she had grown into womanhood, however, and developed curves that didn't quit, Henri had thought his brother might be tempted. Now, seeing the frost Isidora directed toward Ramon, Henri had to wonder if his twin had finally raced those curves and left a trail of dust.

He introduced her to Cinnia, adding, "I was just explaining to Cinnia that your father has always been a trusted leader of our team. He's more than entitled to enjoy his golden years, but we are very disappointed to lose him, especially since our lives have become very complicated. We need a delicate touch."

"So Papa said," Isidora murmured. "I don't mean he gave me details," she clarified quickly. "Only said he would feel better if it was me, which I took to mean sensitive information." Her gaze flicked to Cinnia's belly.

"He put the thumbscrews to you?" Henri asked, making a mental note to double Bernardo's retirement bonus for coaxing Isidora to take them on. "I've always said we would hire you when you completed your degree," he reminded her.

"I'm only finishing now. That's why I was in London. And I have never wanted to ride Papa's coattails. You know that." She flashed a glance at Ramon. Didn't want to ride with *him*, she seemed to imply.

"I've been badgering Isidora to join our team since she decided to follow her father into PR," Henri told Cinnia. "She would rather work her way up the ranks of an independent career. Does she remind you of anyone?"

"Look at that. I have a twin myself." She smiled at Isidora. "Would you like something? I was about to make tea."

"I'll help you." Isidora allowed Henri to take her coat before she disappeared into the kitchen with Cinnia. He had the impression she was distancing herself from Ramon.

He threw his brother an admonishing look. "You slept with her?"

"I was turned down," Ramon said blithely, but it didn't sound like the whole story—which surprised Henri. The two of them kept little from each other.

"That happens?" Henri asked drily, allowing his brother his privacy.

"I was shocked, too." Ramon threw off his suit jacket as if he was too warm, leaving it draped across the back of the sofa. Business shirts were all the same, especially white ones, but Ramon's wore the exact crest that embroidered the pocket of Henri's. His pants were an identical shade of gray and even his belt was the same.

Henri didn't even bother remarking on it, only asked, "Is it going to affect her work? Tell me now. We need someone in our midst for months. Not Etienne. He's good on the professional side, but with this much personal information…"

"*Sí*, I know." Ramon shook his head in exasperation. "How am I the only one not causing a stir in the press right now?"

"Meaning you won't be working directly with her. Is that your only reason for hesitating? Because she has always shown excellent potential. We saw it when she was a teenager." She'd begun coming to the office on Take Your Daughter to Work days, drafting soft press releases that had shown better composition than finished work turned out by some of their long-standing professionals. "She's as discreet as they come. Learned that at her papa's knee, I imagine."

"There are other reasons she keeps her own counsel," Ramon said cryptically. "But, *sí*, you are right. She's a good fit. She can't stand me, but she's fond of Gili and Bella. They will be far more comfortable with her than anyone else. Cinnia already likes her." He nodded at where the women's laughter drifted from the kitchen.

Henri nodded, satisfied, but caught the look of inquisition his brother sent him.

"*Qu'est-ce que c'est?*" Henri prompted, even though he knew where Ramon's thoughts had gone.

"I thought we signed a blood oath not to have children." Ramon was a master at affecting a light attitude, but he was far from as shallow as he pretended. His voice was dry, but his expression grave.

"This isn't entrapment." Henri grimaced. "It's an oldfashioned slipup. She left because she was trying to spare me."

Ramon dismissed that with a wave of his hand. "*Pah.* It doesn't matter if you didn't ask for the responsibility. We would never leave one of our own at risk. She must have known you would step up."

*"Oui."* But given how much he now had at stake, he wouldn't have gone after her without the pregnancy as incentive.

The knowledge caused a white light to shoot through him, jagged as lightning, rending something in him. What if she hadn't been pregnant? What if he really had spent the rest of his life without her?

Ramon slapped his shoulder, yanking him back from staring into a bleak void.

"I have your back, *hermano*. Together we'll keep *tus niños* safe. Your wife is my wife."

"A comforting sentiment," Henri said with a humorless snort. "If she was willing to marry me. She's not."

"That happens?" Ramon stepped back, astonished.

"Apparently."

*Do you love me?*

Did it matter?

Given all he faced, he couldn't allow himself to be preoccupied with courtship. It was better that she was holding him off.

Still, as the women came back and Cinnia's smile of good humor fell away, he found himself snaring her gaze and holding it, searching for something he couldn't name.

"I was just telling Isidora that I don't even want to *think* about a wedding dress until I've got my figure back," she said, expression neutral.

The singed edges of his ego continued to smolder, filling his throat with an acrid aftertaste.

The media circus was in full swing by the end of the month.

They had released a photograph with their statement that they were delighted to announce the upcoming birth of twins, but that wasn't enough. The paparazzi went berserk. Cinnia only went out a handful of times, once for a checkup with her new doctor and twice to visit Henri's sisters at the design house. She was mobbed every time. Her guards earned their exorbitant paychecks, practically needing a whip and a chair to keep the lions at bay.

What made her groan loudest, however, was how many of the photographers didn't even bother capturing her face. Shots of her belly cluttered every gossip rag as if the twins she carried were visible if you looked hard enough. It could have been any woman's swollen abdomen. She told Henri she was going to start wearing T-shirts with obscene logos and vulgar catchphrases.

He gave her his don't-you-dare look, but then suggested something decidedly unprintable, making her snort.

Henri, who rarely spoke to the press unless it was through a prepared statement that invariably pertained to the business of Sauveterre International, became old news. Why photograph any of the adult Sauveterre twins when they could harangue the mother of the newest set? Even Ramon's best efforts to draw fire with his racing antics and half-naked supermodels failed.

Henri would have taken the attention off her if he could. They were living in an armed truce, managing to be civil and, in some ways, falling into their old routine very easily. Most days he worked at his Paris office while she worked out of his home office at the flat, exactly as she used to when staying with him here in Paris. Their evenings were filled with arrangements for their future: how they would modify the family home in Spain to accommodate the twins, signing up for a private birthing class, reviewing résumés for the babies' security staff.

He took pains to include her in all of it, but she felt the undercurrents of being one more thing he had to manage. Maybe some of that was sexual tension, since they were still sleeping separately, but she saw how frustrated he was with the press and precautions and the sheer volume of to-dos.

It fueled her sense that things were tenuous between them, making her all the more determined to maintain her own income and have a fallback position. Which made *him* say she was working too hard, forcing *her* to point out they had enough topics to debate without throwing her career into the mix.

He began swearing yet again as their car was swarmed when they arrived at a hotel in Milan.

Already prickly and nervous, she flinched at his tone.

"You told me the day we met that you've learned to pick your battles," she reminded him, forcing herself to bite back a reflexive apology. It wasn't her fault she was pregnant. She told herself that every day.

"You should be able to move in public without being harassed," he growled as he helped her from the car and held her arm up the red carpet.

She wore sunglasses, but was still terrified the flashes were going to blind her into stumbling. She clung to Henri's arm as she walked. At twenty-four weeks, she was already ungainly, and tonight she'd put on proper heels, wanting one thing to feel normal after so many changes.

They were attending a charity gala put on by a banking family he worked with regularly. Ramon had taken on all the long-distance travel, but Henri was still covering Europe.

She had vainly hoped this weekend would be a break from the paparazzi. She was due for a night out at the very least, even if it was only a business appearance.

It was decidedly more peaceful inside, thank goodness. The hotel was one of the most exclusive in Europe, the guest list for this ten-thousand-euro-per-plate dinner tightly vetted.

Henri guided her through a grand lobby inspired by a fourteenth century Venetian palace. Marble columns rose like massive sentries above them. The wide staircase spilled a line of royal red carpet down its center. Above, crystal chandeliers sparkled and threw glints of burnished light off the gold leaf accents.

Strangers, all dressed in tuxedos and evening gowns, turned to smile at them.

Cinnia had learned to keep a serene smile on her face and keep moving.

They arrived at the coat check and she let Henri take her sunglasses along with her light full-length jacket. It was faintly medieval in its generous cut and flared sleeves. The gray fabric was shot with threads of silver detailing by Trella's clever hand. Her gown was Angelique's finest work, a Grecian style with a halter bodice and an empire waist. The miles of gathered white silk could drape her growing form with elegance through the rest of her pregnancy.

She wanted to believe she looked attractive, but it was hard when her body was so different and the man at her side had grown even more contained as their relationship solidified behind lines of abstinence.

Maybe she should have sex with him, if only to feel close to him again. Of course, her sexual confidence was eroding as quickly as her waistline was expanding. It didn't help that he was acting like he was escorting his sister. He was solicitous, ensured she had a drink, held her chair when they sat for the dinner, but it wasn't the way it used to be. His touch on her was light and incidental, not carrying the possessive, proprietary weight of the past. No stolen caresses or tender brushes of his lips against a bare shoulder.

After dinner, they made the rounds, spoke with their

hosts, Paolo and Lauren Donatelli, along with Paolo's cousin Vito and his new wife, Gwyn. Cinnia had met them a handful of times in the past and they warmly congratulated her.

The music started and Henri asked her to dance.

In the past, she would have slid naturally into the space against his ruffled tuxedo shirt and tucked her hair beneath his chin, enjoying the light foreplay of moving against him.

Tonight they had to angle their bodies to accommodate her bump. She gave a wistful sigh.

"These events are tiresome, I know, but I'd forgotten how much more bearable they are when you're with me." His thumb caressed where his hand was splayed against her rib cage.

He found an extravagant evening like this "tiresome"? Her mouth twitched as she recalled him telling her the first night they met, *This is how I live.* At the same time, she couldn't help softening toward him, flushing with sweetness at his saying he liked having her at his side.

"I should have taken you on a proper date before this, but things have been..."

"I know." She looked up at him, rueful, startled to find his gaze on her mouth. Her foot slipped.

He caught her close with strong arms. Her hip brushed his fly.

*Hard?*

Her eyes widened and a flood of sensual heat went through her.

He guided them back into the waltz, but there was a flash of something dangerous in his gaze. "Don't look surprised. You know your effect on me," he said in a quiet rasp.

"It's hard to feel desirable when you're pregnant," she mumbled, blushing with self-conscious pleasure.

"Is *that* why you're still holding me off? Because you have nothing to worry about. You're sexier than ever. It's all I can do to behave like a gentleman."

She would have stumbled again if she hadn't been clinging to his shoulders. His hands firmed on her and stayed that way, deliciously possessive. The rest of the dance became as subtly erotic as any they'd ever shared.

She floated in a sea of possibility after that, deeply tempted. As she freshened her lipstick in the powder room, she gave herself a stern lecture about keeping her head and not succumbing to his charms.

But, oh, it would feel so good.

Then she made the mistake of checking her email and her heart stuttered. She had become enough of a liability to turn him off completely.

Who is Avery Benson? Isidora asked. He just sold a story claiming you went after his money in the past. We should refute his accusation that your pregnancy is a deliberate ploy to snare a piece of the Sauveterre wealth.

Suddenly the sideways looks she'd been receiving all evening were explained—and intolerable. Cinnia felt sick. Of course people would speculate, but to have it stated like that, by *Avery*...

She turned her ankle returning to the ballroom, having to catch herself on the back of a nearby chair, which only added to the humiliation as people turned their heads to stare even harder.

*Yes, I'm drunk along with being a gold digger*, she wanted to lash out.

Henri was watching for her and rushed to meet her. "Are you all right?"

"I have a headache." Her throat was so tight, words barely fought their way through it. "Can we go?"

"Of course." He waited until they were in the back of

the car, then said sharply, "You're white as a ghost. Should we go to the hospital?"

"No. Read your email." Isidora had sent it to both of them. There was no use trying to hide from this degradation. She stared out the side window, the darkened Milan streets a blur through her tear-filled eyes.

Henri said nothing, but she heard a couple of taps and a phone call being placed.

"Avery Benson," he requested.

She swung her head around. "How do you have his number?"

Henri covered her hand on the seat between them and squeezed a signal for quiet. "I don't care if he's having tea with the queen. Tell him it's Henri Sauveterre."

"Don't make it worse." Cinnia reached for his phone.

Henri fended her off, giving her a dark glower. "No, this is not a joke," he told his caller. "Retract your story."

"He won't," Cinnia warned.

"No, *you* listen," Henri said in a voice that made her sit back and hold very still.

She hadn't thought he could sound more deadly than he had the day he had railed about paparazzi. He could. He definitely could. Ice formed somewhere between her heart and her stomach, deep against her spine.

"You were on my watch list and have now been elevated to my red list. I take the security of my family *very* seriously—why were you on my watch list? Because you're a known opportunist who can't be trusted. I had a dossier prepared with your contact details for just this possibility. If you had remained in the background, I wouldn't have given you another thought, but now you've shown yourself willing to profit off my family. That makes you a threat so I must neutralize. No, I don't intend to kill you!"

Henri cast her an impatient look.

"I wouldn't call you to warn you, would I? You would be at the bottom of the ocean with an explanation for your disappearance concocted. No, I prefer you alive to see how I dismantle everything you've acquired after Cinnia gave you a leg up... Oh, she did. You had her convince your parents to sell and stole half her savings on your way out the door. Now if you value your house and your job, you will retract your story and never speak of us again."

Henri paused briefly, then sighed.

"Say you were drunk, on drugs, owed gambling debts. I don't care *how* you explain it, just retract it. Prove to me you are not intending harm to my family or I will push you to my blacklist and I can assure you, your prospects for a promotion, or refinancing your mortgage, or for buying that boat you're looking at, will evaporate. I will sue you into obscurity. Cinnia is not a tool you can use. Ever. Not even just this once."

Henri listened again.

"You will not do that. I've just explained what it means to be on my blacklist and that's where I'll put you if you do anything but retract your story. No, she didn't put me up to this. You poked the bear. This is the consequence. Be smart or lose everything."

Henri ended the call.

"I can fight my own battles," Cinnia muttered, mortified.

Henri kept his gaze on his phone as he tapped out a text. "I'll have Isidora help him. He really does need to be spoon-fed, doesn't he? What did you ever see in him?"

Cheeks stinging, Cinnia looked out the side window again, listening to his phone ping a few times with an exchange of messages, presumably with Isidora.

"Hmm?" Henri prompted a moment later. "I'm curious.

What drew you to such a weak man? You're far too smart to be taken advantage of. Why did you let him use you?"

She shifted, uncomfortable. "You didn't have to be such a sledgehammer. We could have talked first and I could have called him."

"You want to *protect* him?" Henri asked, astounded.

"No. But you didn't even… *I can fight my own battles,*" she repeated.

"This isn't your battle. It's ours."

"It was about me. He wasn't really intending—"

"Do not ever be naive about people's intentions, Cinnia," he interrupted, sharp and severe. "Promise me that. Trusting someone who seems harmless is a mistake."

*Like a math tutor.*

She swallowed and nodded. "Fine. But you could have let me do it. You didn't have to make it seem like I was…"

"What?" he prompted.

"I don't know. Not capable or something."

Henri swore under his breath. "This is about your precious independence? You know, when Trella was four, she went through an annoying phase where she wouldn't let me tie her shoes or zip her jacket. You don't have to do every single thing yourself."

"Name calling isn't any more mature than toddler level, you know."

"Did you *want* to talk to him? Because I don't understand what we're fighting about."

"Do you rely on me for anything?" she demanded as she swung around, thinking maybe, just maybe, if she thought she fulfilled some corner of his life that was more than arm candy at a banquet, they had a chance. "Beyond sex and, you know, building two babies you didn't ask for?"

"Pleasant companionship?" he suggested.

"I loved my first boyfriend, you know." She threw it

at him and should have been more pleased at the way he stiffened as it struck, but she just felt raw. "Maybe it was puppy love, but James felt the same. I knew better than to let a man hold too much sway over my life, though. Learned that from losing Dad, right? So I didn't change my plans and follow James to the school he preferred. I followed my own path, thought we could weather it, but he cheated on me and it felt *awful*."

"Your mother said she thought you picked Avery because he was safe. Is that what she meant?"

"Yes." She shrugged off how self-delusional it had been. "He was nice, but socially awkward and, yes, he was the beta in the relationship. Okay? It felt good to be the one in control. To feel adored without risking too much. *You know how great that feels.*"

They held a locked stare. His jaw was granite, shadows flicking in his face as the angle of lighting changed. The car was pulling into the underground parking of the hotel where they were staying.

"Maybe I unconsciously thought if I took care of him, he wouldn't cheat or leave," Cinnia muttered, gathering her purse and straightening in preparation for the dash to the elevator. "Even if he did, it wouldn't hurt like it had with James, but Avery still found a way to make me feel horrible for believing he cared and, yes, that left me convinced I need to do things myself. I hate needing a man for *anything*. Thank you, Guy," she said as the door beside her opened and the guard offered his hand.

She even needed a man's help crawling from a car these days. It was pathetic.

Oscar already had the elevator open. Cameras flashed from between the shrubs outside the open grill windows as they scurried the short distance into the lift.

They didn't speak again until they were inside their

suite at the top of the building. The space was full of plush furniture in burnt reds and toasted golds, welcoming with fresh flowers and bowls of fruit. None of it softened her mood.

Henri took her coat to hang it and she went to the sofa, sitting to remove the stupid shoes that were killing her feet. That's when she remembered she'd had to ask him to buckle them for her earlier.

She let out a muted scream of frustration and dropped onto her side, burying her face in a tasseled pillow. It was that or break down altogether.

Warm hands gathered her ankles and he lifted her feet out of the way to sit, then set her shoes in his lap and worked on a buckle.

"I hate being weak," she said, shifting the pillow so it covered her ear and she spoke from beneath it, arm curled to hold it in place. "I hate that I can't get through a day without a nap. I hate that I can't sit long enough to get through all the work that needs to be done so I can put away the money that you keep telling me I don't need. I hate that you're taking over my bills and won't let me pay for groceries. I hate that no matter how hard I try, I'm becoming dependent on you."

He dropped her shoes away and kept her bare feet in his lap, rubbing them. It felt wonderful and tender and it was one more way she was letting him do something for her. Her breath caught, nearly becoming a sob.

"I hate that those men hurt you and you don't trust me as a result," he said gravely. "You're right that I crave control even more than you do. At your expense, even. I wasn't trying to make you feel weak when I called him, though. I was reacting." He squeezed her feet, warming them. "I would have preferred to kill him, if you want the truth. Apparently there are laws."

He was trying to make light, but she had heard his tone in the car and heard that same ruthlessness now.

"I used to find it so refreshing that you were self-sufficient. Lately, I find it insulting. You *can* entrust yourself to me, Cinnia. I know that's not easy for you, I understand why you're so reluctant, but I have already put many things in place that will ensure you never want. You'll always be comfortable and, to the extent I can manage it, safe from harm. We are a team where these babies are concerned. It's basic parenting dynamics that I do the providing and protecting so you can do the birthing and nurturing."

"If that's you trying to get out of nappy duty already..."

"And she rallies," he said with a warm stroke of his hand up her calf. "You are never weak, *chérie*. It is the last word I would use to describe you. All of those things you are trying to do before the babies come? You are doing them while building those babies. Why can you not see how much you are accomplishing? I can't help you with the pregnancy, so why can't you let me help you with the rest? Hmm?"

Because it would make her love him even more.

And then what? He wouldn't leave. She knew that much. He wouldn't let her leave, either. Not again. Not ever.

It was oddly humbling to realize that.

She flipped the pillow away and looked at him. He had loosened his bow tie and opened a couple of shirt buttons, which only made his tuxedo look sexier.

"Do you feel stuck with me?" she asked, confronting the root question.

"No." He looked affronted she would ask. "I feel privileged that I'm starting a family with someone I respect and admire. You are the one who is stuck, *chérie*. You will always be the mother of Sauveterre twins. My mother can tell you that comes with serious drawbacks." He reached higher to set his hand on the side of her belly. "*I have placed a burden on* you. At least let me carry what I can of it."

She considered that as she looked into his hazel-green eyes. She loved him *so much*. What was the point in keeping hostility between them when they would be together for the rest of their lives? Holding him at arm's length certainly wasn't the way to win his heart. Letting him see how much she cared might.

"Can I sleep in your bed tonight?"

Something flashed in his gaze and his body tensed. "I won't let you leave it," he warned.

Oddly, as monumental and terrifying as his implacable possessiveness was, it also reassured her that they were a unit, moving into the future *together*.

"I know," she whispered.

He rose in a fluid motion, drawing her up with him, then letting her lead him to the room he was using.

He closed the door and turned on the light.

"Don't!" She shot out an anxious hand.

He released a ragged laugh and pulled at his clothes so roughly she could hear how little care he was taking.

Despite the near blackness, she moved to the blinds and gave them an extra twist then tugged the drapes fully closed.

"You really think the dark offers you any sort of protection, *chérie*?"

He was suddenly behind her, naked. She started at the touch of his hands, not because she hadn't heard him coming, but at the zing of electricity he sent through her.

He gathered her hair out of the way and found the zipper on her dress.

As it loosened, she turned in his arms and put hers around his neck, offering her mouth to his hot, hungry kiss. She moaned, closing her eyes in the darkness, but feeling dampness against her lashes as emotion welled. She kissed him back, hard.

"You missed this, too." He slid the fabric away and pressed his lips to her neck. "But don't be frantic. We have a lifetime now. I'll take care of you, but *gently.*"

She wanted to protest and tell him to go fast, but he kissed her again, languorously, smoothly skimming her dress away, then taking his time tracing the lace across her hips, slowly, slowly working it down her thighs.

She panted as she waited for it to fall away, to be bare to his touch.

He turned her and leaned to set light kisses across her upper chest, skin brushing skin in a whisper. His hand drifted to pet her mound.

"Yes. Please." She covered his hand.

"Shh. I'll make it good, I promise." He explored deeper, carefully.

She caught her breath and arched into his touch, reaching to hold on to him as she let him take control of her pleasure.

"*Oui, chérie*, you love this, don't you? I do, too."

The closest he'd ever come to telling her he loved her and she could only gasp, digging fingernails behind his neck as she responded to his touch with a rock of her hips.

"That feels so good." She rubbed her face into the spicy aftershave in his throat, purring like a cat enjoying strokes.

How had she resisted this for all these weeks? *Why?*

His free hand moved over her, shaping her hip, cupping her bottom, encouraging her to move against the hand still nestled between her thighs.

They shifted hot skin against one another, trying to get closer, angling this way and that, finding each other's lips and kissing. Kissing and kissing for eternity.

"You're so hot." She slid her hand down his front, finding where he was pulled taut with arousal and clasping him, remembering all the ways to make him groan and push into her touch.

"Say it," he commanded her. "Tell me exactly what you want, *chérie*. I won't have accusations in the morning."

"I want you inside me, Henri. This." She caressed his smooth, hard shape and ran her thumb into the point beneath the tip, feeling him pulse in her palm. *"Please."*

He pressed a groan of abject hunger into her neck, opened his mouth to suck a love bite there. The sting caused a delicious counterpoint to the sweet pleasure of his touch parting her wet folds. She clenched on his fingers and cried out, holding tight to him as climax flooded through her in a rush, so powerful her knees folded.

He held her up, one hard arm around her back, releasing a jagged laugh of triumph against her skin, soothing, caressing, keeping her pulses going and maintaining her arousal.

"Nothing excites me more than knowing I do that to you," he told her, backing her toward the bed. "Nothing makes me want you more. I want to eat you alive. Have you in a thousand ways. Tie us both to this bed and never leave it."

He pressed her onto her back at the edge, leaning on one hand, looming over her as he guided himself against her, rubbing and nudging where she was plump and slippery and welcoming. Still tingling.

"Don't tease," she protested.

"Want?"

"So much."

"How much?" He gave her just the tip.

"More." She used her heel in his buttock to urge him deeper, releasing an unfettered groan as he sank into her.

For a moment there was nothing except the pleasure of returning to this place of joy. Ecstasy.

He said, "Cinnia," like he was exactly as overcome. Then, after a long time, he said, "I don't want to hurt you. Tell me if it's too deep." He caught under her legs and offered a few shallow strokes. His whole body was trembling with strain.

"Show me you want me, Henri."

"How can you doubt it?" he growled. "I'm so hard I hurt." He moved with deliberation, carefully withdrew then pressed as deeply as he could. Tingling sensations pushed into her, so sharp they were almost too much to bear.

"There," she cried as she lifted her hips to meet his and he folded over her. They melded together, mouths, bodies, kissing deeply with abandon. Then she slapped her hands far out to her sides and nudged her hips up against his, urging him to move with more purpose. "Take me."

He ground out a few muttered imprecations, trying to hold a civilized pace, but they were on a plateau of acute, mutual pleasure. Each stroke was a delicate torture that kept her on exactly the knife's edge of wanting orgasm, but withholding it.

She caught at his shoulders and dragged her nails down his arms. "You're not going to break me," she said fiercely. "*Do* it. Harder. Faster."

"You are going to break *me*." He thrust with more power. "Stop me if—"

"Yes!" she cried. "Like that!" She moved with him, meeting his thrusts, keening under the onslaught of pleasure. And there it was. Culmination. Hovering before her, detonating around them.

"Now, Henri. Please… With me," she gasped, shuddering with climax.

He abandoned his grip on his restraint, and let out a

shout of gratification, holding himself deep inside her as they both shattered with rapture.

It was beautiful and perfect and she smiled as he shifted them into the bed and settled her to fall asleep in his arms.

But just as she began to drift, her smile faded. She opened her eyes to the dark. He hadn't answered her question. In fact, as her pregnancy continued to take a toll and she leaned on him more and more, the answer became obvious.

Henri didn't *need* her for one single thing.

# CHAPTER NINE

CINNIA WAS ENTERING her thirty-first week, feeling big as a house, but healthy enough that her doctor agreed she could travel to Spain for a few days. Angelique and Kasim were hosting a very small, private engagement party of immediate relatives in the Sauveterre compound. The formal announcement wouldn't be made for a few more months, due to Kasim's situation in Zhamair, but they were eager for their siblings to get to know one another.

The gathering was relaxing and lovely, giving Cinnia something she had longed for the first time with Henri: a sense of being a real part of his family. She and Trella had grown closer since their pregnancies, and Angelique had always been warm and welcoming. Now the twins felt like real sisters, calling her into their rooms to try on this draped top or one-size skirt, sharing little confidences along with a sample of hand cream or asking an opinion on a color of lipstick. His mother trimmed her hair when Cinnia bemoaned that going to the stylist was too much trouble when it was such a horrid crush of cameras.

Then there was Hasna, Sadiq's new wife and Kasim's sister.

Angelique had met Kasim when she and Trella had been designing Hasna's wedding gown. Cinnia already knew Sadiq. He was the most trusted friend Henri and Ramon had. She had actually been invited to the wedding in Zhamair, but she and Henri had broken up right before it.

Hasna made her feel like an integral part of the inner circle when she told her in private that Sadiq was very happy to see her again. "He was *so* upset when he heard that you and Henri had split. It bothered him for weeks."

"Sadiq and Hasna seem really happy," Cinnia said to Henri later, as they were preparing for bed. "I've missed him."

"Me, too," Henri said drily. "This is the first time I've seen him since the wedding. But yes, they do seem happy. I'm pleased for him."

"I don't think I've ever asked how he became such a fixture in your lives. I mean he's not—" She took off her earrings, recalling how often Henri had switched plans to accommodate his friend coming into town or making a point of catching up with him if they had an opportunity. "I'm trying to figure out how to say this nicely. He's not like most of the people I've met through you. He always came out to Ramon's races, but he didn't care about cars. I guess you do business together, but he seems more passionate about computers and software. I'm trying to figure out what you and Ramon have in common with him."

Sadiq was soft-spoken and quick to laugh, but didn't make jokes or put forth strong opinions. He was the male version of a wallflower when he was around the Sauveterre men.

"I see so many people trying to *gain* your attention," she pointed out. "He isn't like that at all. Which answers my question about why you like him, but I'm still wondering how you ever got to know him well enough in the first place, to know that he would make such a good friend."

Henri was silent as he removed his shirt and unbuckled his pants.

"We met at school." He stripped to his snug navy blue underwear. "The day Trella was taken." He folded his pants on a hanger and placed them on the rung. "He was on the steps next to Ramon. Saw it happen and ran in to find me."

"Oh." She was already in her nightgown and paused in pulling back the sheets. "I had no idea."

"I don't talk about it," he said flatly. "But he was instrumental in our locating her. He *is* passionate about his computers and was able to help the police by hacking into the math tutor's computer. Afterward, he was one of the few men Trella could tolerate being around other than family. Maybe because he saved her, maybe because his personality is, as you say, low-key. Either way, we didn't care. He was a hero in our eyes and has always been a true friend."

He turned off the closet light and moved into the bathroom to brush his teeth.

Cinnia crawled into bed, stunned by Henri being so open, but thinking, *be careful what you wish for.* It was so disturbing. She hurt terribly for him.

But she was oddly encouraged that he'd chosen to share this with her. Their relationship wasn't perfect, but she was back to believing he cared for her to some degree. Perhaps he was coming to entrust her with his heart if he was willing to entrust her with his most painful memory.

When he came to bed a few minutes later, she snuggled close, wanting to offer comfort even though he was stiff and unreceptive.

"I didn't mean to bring up bad memories," she said, fitting herself under his arm and kissing his shoulder. "Every time I think of it, I wish that I could take away how scared you must have been."

"I wasn't scared, I was *guilty*," Henri acknowledged in a soft hiss.

Cinnia drew back a fraction, trying to see him in the filtered light. "How?" She knew the whole family had had therapy at different times in their efforts to heal from the incident. He must know he wasn't at fault. "You were fifteen. Victims are never to blame for the hurt done to them."

"I was talking to a girl."

His tone reminded her of the day he'd let his hatred of the press burst out of him, like he had kept it pent up too long. There was also a quality of confessing the worst crime in history, as if he'd never told anyone what he was saying to her now.

"Trella came by and said she was going outside. I told her to *go*. I wanted privacy, but Trella was *my* responsibility. That's how it always was with the four of us. Ramon kept an eye on Gili, I watched out for Bella. I might as well have handed her to them."

Her heart stalled. This poor man.

"Henri, if you had been outside to stop Trella, they would have gone for Angelique," she argued, lifting on an elbow. "That's not a better outcome."

"If they'd called out to Angelique, she would have made Ramon go with her. She was shy. We might have had a fighting chance at stopping it before it happened. I should have told Trella to wait for me, but I didn't." He pinched the bridge of his nose.

"Because you were talking to a girl."

She was trying to make him see how insignificant that was, but a chill moved into her heart. A realization was dawning, but it was a dark one. More like a shadow dimming the landscape inside her.

"Who was she?" Her ears rang, making it nearly impossible to hear his response.

"Just a girl."

Cinnia pulled all the way back onto her own pillow, no longer touching him. She wanted to ease his conscience, she really did, but said, "No, she wasn't." She didn't know how she knew it, she just did. "There were lots of girls after that. She wasn't *just* a girl."

"I don't want to talk about this. Go to sleep."

"You cared about her," she said in realization. It hurt. Oh, it hurt like acid and corrosive and nuclear waste, all being poured over her heart.

"*Mon Dieu.* It was puppy love, Cinnia. You had that yourself and know it means nothing."

"No, it doesn't. Not when it means... This is why you won't let yourself care for me. You're worried it will impact your ability to take care of the rest of your family."

"I *care* for you, damn it."

"But you don't *love* me. You're never going to love me, are you? You will never let yourself feel anything like it because you think it takes too much of your attention. Do you know how hard this is, Henri?" She gave the mattress a smack with her fist. "I've fought and fought falling in love with you. I've let myself rely on you. I sleep with you and I'm having children with you. And you can't even love me back? You won't even *try*."

"You love me?" He rolled toward her.

"Yes, and I'm *sorry*. I know it's one more burden you don't want!"

"That's not true." He reached for her.

"I keep telling myself to give you time, that you'll come around, but you are never going to relent, are you? It's not because I'm not lovable. You're just that stubborn!"

"Cinnia." He tried to gather her into his front.

"No." She rolled so her back was toward him. "I want to go to sleep."

"Cin," he cajoled, pressing his lips to her shoulder as he fit himself behind her.

"Don't touch me." She pushed at his leg with her foot and brushed his hand off her hip. "It's one thing to put something in a cage because you love it and want to protect it, but when you don't actually care, it just makes me a prisoner. So forget it. No conjugal visit."

"Stop it. You're blowing this out of proportion." His hand settled on her waist.

"I'm *tired*." Her voice broke. She was *so* tired of wishing and yearning and winding up empty. She pushed his hand off her, wriggling so she was on the very edge of the bed. "Leave me alone."

He swore and threw off the covers, leaving the bed and their room.

Cinnia woke late, alone, eyes like sandpaper. She held a cold compress on them, somehow pulled herself together with a comb and a toothbrush, put on a sundress that wasn't too much like a circus tent and went downstairs, raw as an exposed nerve.

Everyone was outside, seeming in good spirits, which made her depression all the harder to disguise. She pretended she was merely tired when she joined Hasna at the table under the umbrella. Trella was on a nearby lounger, showing something to her mother on her tablet. Kasim and Sadiq stood with Angelique at the rail, laying bets on the tennis match below.

Henri and Ramon were on the court, trying to kill one another. She'd seen them play before and they were hideously competitive, equally strong and skilled, and they knew each other's weaknesses. Their games could go on for ages.

"They're so well matched," Hasna said, craning her

neck. "I suppose loyalty demands you put your money on Henri."

In the mood he was in, yes, he would likely prevail. In the mood she was in? She'd love to see him lose abysmally, especially to Ramon. That always annoyed the hell out of him.

"Is this the yogurt we heard so much about yesterday?" Cinnia looked over the tubs set in ice. "They got away okay this morning?" she asked of the guests who'd brought it.

"They did and, yes, it is," Hasna said with an absent smile. "Ooh, that's tied it up again. Goodness, this is a nail-biter. The muesli is very good, too," she added over her shoulder, then looked back to the rapid *plonk, plonk* of the ball.

Cinnia avoided the pink-tinged yogurt and went for the plain, sprinkling muesli without really looking and re-seated herself to take a bite. She started to ask Trella what she was reading and felt the first tingle streak from the roof of her mouth down the back of her throat.

She swore. "The muesli." She grabbed Hasna's wrist. "Does it have dried strawberries? Call an ambulance." Her tongue felt like it was swelling as she spoke. "Call Henri. Tell him I need my pen."

"What?" Hasna asked with incomprehension.

"I'm allergic." Her throat was growing raspy. She watched Hasna's fear turning to pain as Cinnia increased her grip, driven by terror to impress how bad this was. She was barely able to force out the rest of her words. "To strawberries."

"Henri!" Hasna screamed at the top of her lungs, standing to wave at him. "Cinnia ate a strawberry!"

Distantly she heard Trella say something, maybe that she would call an ambulance. Cinnia wasn't tracking, just closed her eyes and gripped the edge of the table, concentrating on breathing, managing long, slow, strained wheezes. Rapid footsteps ran toward her and hard hands grasped her, moving her to a lounger. She kept her eyes closed, feeling like she was sipping tiny drinks of air through a narrow straw. A tiny, hollow piece of dry grass. Her throat strained, trying to pull her breaths through the constriction.

Henri's voice was hard as he shouted for her purse. She opened her eyes. He looked gray. Angry.

*Scared.*

There was a spare pen behind the mirror in their bathroom. Did he remember that? She wanted to reach out to him, grab him, but her limbs felt heavy and her hands were on fire. Her ears itched inside her head and her brain had gone swimming.

A sting went into her thigh, like a bite or the snap of a rubber band.

"That's one," Henri said, cupping the side of her face very forcefully. "Stay with me, *chérie*. Breathe."

She tried. *The babies*, she tried to say, but her lips were fat and numb. Tears filled her eyes. She was scared. Her entire body felt as though it was glowing with fire, her skin cooking, too tight to contain all this heat. What if her carelessness hurt the twins?

Henri took his hand away from her cheek as he accepted something. Another stab went into her thigh and he rubbed it hard.

She closed her eyes, begging the medicine to work, trying to listen for the ambulance, but her heart was pounding so loud she couldn't hear anything. It took everything in her to draw a breath, then to focus on pulling in one more.

Her hand hurt. Henri was holding it and his voice was *furious*. "Cinnia. *Breathe*."

She was *trying*.

* * *

Cinnia had been right last night, but he'd refused to admit it. He was being stubborn. He had shut her down. Shut her out.

But even as he had left her, fully aware she was beginning to cry, he had told himself this was for her own good. He was keeping her *safe* by keeping a clear head and withholding his heart.

Her safety meant everything.

Then he'd heard Hasna scream, *"Cinnia ate a strawberry!"*

He added it to the list of worst phrases he'd ever heard.

"We're here." Ramon appeared at his side and clamped a hard arm across his shoulders.

Henri staggered, only then realizing he was swaying on his feet.

On his other side, Trella took his arm. "Where is she? What did they say?"

Henri realized he was standing in the middle of the hospital hallway, staring at the doors where Cinnia had been whisked away from him. Of course Ramon was here on the heels of the ambulance. Of course their pregnant sister had climbed into the passenger seat for that hair-raising ride.

"Her blood pressure dropped," Henri said, repeating all the terrible, terrible words. They detonated fresh explosions of despair as they left his lips and hit on fresh ears. "They said the babies might not be getting enough oxygen. They're taking them."

"Taking—" Trella gasped. Ramon swore.

"I should call her mother," Henri said, dreading it. He had failed. *I'm so sorry.*

He didn't think he could manage it.

"Mama is calling her. Kasim said he would arrange a flight to bring her." Trella pulled out her phone while

Ramon physically helped Henri to sit. "I'll relay that she's gone into surgery. Was she conscious in the ambulance? They gave her something, right? Medicine? She was breathing? She'll be okay?"

"She was trying," Henri said, throat raw from shouting at her, as if that would help. "They put a tube in her throat. Then she had a seizure. She wasn't conscious after that."

Ramon was crushing him with that hard arm across his shoulders, but Henri crumpled forward, elbows on his knees, stomach churning. Putting his hands over his eyes didn't help. He still saw her blue lips, still felt the strength go out of her grip.

"Oh, Henri." He could hear the plea for reassurance in his sister's voice, but he had none to offer. He was terrified.

"I saw the yogurt this morning. I saw it had strawberries and I made a mental note she shouldn't have any." He had been restless, hadn't slept properly. He'd been feeling guilty and angry and small. Defensive.

When Ramon had asked if he wanted to play tennis, he'd let the activity consume him, working out his frustrations in a hail of powerful volleys.

"I shouldn't have been playing tennis. I should have been there, at the table, waiting for her, ready to warn her."

"We all knew she was allergic. You told us last year when she came for your birthday. We just weren't thinking," Trella soothed. "Cinnia is always careful, too. She always asks. I don't know why she didn't today."

"We'd had a fight. She wasn't thinking."

"This is not your fault, Henri." Trella's small hand dug into his arm, trying to press the words into him.

It *was* his fault.

If he had said the words that Cinnia had asked for last night, the ones that had burst out of him in the ambulance, everything would be different right now.

*I know it's one more burden you don't want...*

She loved him. He'd been touched, elated, filled with such tenderness he had reached to gather her in, wanting to hold her against his heart.

Then she had said something about feeling like a prisoner and kicked him out of bed.

He had walked out on a sense of righteousness, telling himself he would not let her make him feel obligated, but when had Cinnia ever done that to him? She had begun to lean on him lately, literally holding his arm out of physical exhaustion, but she had been carrying her love for him like a dogged little soldier, refusing to *burden* him with it.

He had always expected to feel hampered by love, but *Cinnia's* love? Her sunny smiles and cheeky asides, her passion and even that streak of pigheadedness had kept him going for two years, not that he'd realized it at the time. It was only as he looked back on their separation, recalled how short-tempered he'd been after Cinnia had left, picking fights with Gili, of all people, that he recognized how badly he'd been missing Cinnia.

Since she'd been back with him, it had been one adjustment after another, but he'd attacked all of the changes with determined energy, eager to carve out her permanent place in his life. He hadn't just accommodated her. He'd made her part of his foundation. He wanted to *marry* her.

Because he couldn't live without her. There was no point.

Why hadn't he told her all of that last night?

"I tried to tell her I loved her. In the ambulance. I don't think she heard me."

"She knows," Trella said, brushing the tickling wetness from his cheek. "She knows, Henri. I promise you."

"No. She doesn't." Because he had refused to say it. Refused to admit it even to himself until it was too late. "I do all these things, go to such great lengths, to try to keep us all safe. I told her she could trust me and what happens? *A goddamned strawberry.* What am I going to do if I lose her? What if I lose all of them?"

# CHAPTER TEN

CINNIA OPENED HER eyes to such bright light, she immediately shut them again. Where was she? She peeked again at the tiled ceiling, the stainless-steel contraption beside her with an IV bag hanging off it.

Hospital?

Oh, right. She winced and tried to touch her belly, apprehensive because it didn't feel nearly so heavy as it should.

Someone had hold of her hand.

*"Chérie."* Henri's whisper had grit in it. He carried the back of her hand to his closed mouth as he stood to loom over her.

She peered from one eye. He looked gorgeous even when he looked horrible. His eyes were sunk into dark sockets, his jaw coated in stubble, his clothes wrinkled.

Her eyes welled with fear.

She tried to say *the babies?* but her throat was a desert that caught fire as she tried to speak.

*"Les filles sont très bien.* Our daughters are beautiful," Henri said with quiet urgency, setting his hand on the side of her face. "They're very small, but they're little fighters." He stroked her cheek. "Just like their mama. And so alike, Cinnia." He gave his head a bemused shake. "They are the most magical thing I have ever seen."

She started to smile, but her mouth trembled with emotion. "Can I—" She cut herself off with a wince and a moan, touching her throat. Talking really hurt, but she glanced toward the door. She wanted to see them. *Bring them to me.*

"You had a tube in your throat. That's why it hurts." He leaned to press the call button. "The nurse was just in here, said your vitals are good, but the doctor will want to come now you're awake. I'll get the girls."

First he lowered to set his mouth on her forehead, holding the kiss for a long moment, slowly drawing back with such a look in his eyes it made her throat ache in a different way.

"Do not ever do that to me again. Not ever," he said gravely.

"Deliver twins?" she joked in a dry whisper.

"Not funny." His eyes winced shut, lashes appearing matted with wetness when he opened them. They were practically nose to nose. The emotion in his eyes made her catch her breath. He stroked the backs of his fingers against her cheek and started to say something.

The nurse bustled in, forcing him to straighten in a jerk and cast a scowl at the poor woman.

Minutes later, Cinnia met her daughters, tearing up all over again as Henri and a nurse set their tiny swaddled forms into her shaking arms.

"You're sure they're okay?" She wanted to squish them tight, but held them like fragile eggshells. She couldn't take her eyes off their identical little faces with their rosebud mouths and button noses, one sleeping soundly, the other blinking blue eyes at her.

"Colette needed a little oxygen at first and they're both still working on regulating their body temperatures, but they're taking a bottle and squawking when they want more." Henri's hand looked ridiculously huge, overwhelming the tiny form as he splayed his fingers ever so gently on the infant in her right arm.

"Colette?" That was not a name she had had on her mental list, but it suited the inquisitive gaze that met hers.

"And Rosalina," he said with a rueful smile, moving to use one fingertip to adjust the edge of the blanket away from Rosalina's cheek. "We are under no obligation to keep those names, but my sisters refused to call them Twin One and Twin Two. Given the custody battle going on in the nursery between them and the grandmothers, we'll be lucky to have our *own* names on the birth certificates."

"They're perfect. *Hola*, Rosalina. *Bonjour*, Colette," she whispered, pressing a kiss to each girl's warm, soft forehead. "Wait. Grandmothers? Mum is here?"

"*Oui.* And she's as anxious to see you as you were to see *your* daughters. Let's let the doctor do his thing so we can reassure her you're recovering."

Cinnia allowed the babies to be whisked back to the nursery and thirty minutes of playing snakes and ladders with her dignity followed. She suffered exams and questions and prodding. On the plus side, she was allowed a drink of water, a facecloth, a hairbrush and, best of all, a *toothbrush*.

She learned they were well into the afternoon of the day *after* she had taken her near-fatal taste of strawberry-tainted muesli.

"I'm going to devote my life to eradicating that particular fruit from the planet," Henri muttered as the doctor finished up his own riot act about the dangers of anaphylactic shock while pregnant.

"I'm *sorry*," Cinnia said, wincing at the trouble she'd caused.

The doctor pronounced her well enough to be wheeled down the hall to try nursing the twins and the nurse left to fetch a chair.

As they were left alone, Henri hitched his hip on the bed beside her. At least she was sitting up now, beginning to feel human again.

"I am sorry," she said with genuine remorse, unnerved by the way he looked at her with such deep emotion in his eyes. It made her feel compressed. Breathless. "I saw the pink yogurt and thought the plain would be fine. I didn't even look properly at the muesli."

"*I* am sorry, *chérie*," Henri took her hand and handled it very gently, turning it over as though examining it. "I keep expecting to see bruises. Your bones could have broken, I was holding on to you so tightly. I was so afraid it wouldn't be tight enough."

"Mum is going to ground me for sure," she said, trying to make light because his shaken tone made her insides tremble. "Has anyone told my sisters? They won't let me hear the end of it."

"Ramon is at the airport, collecting them."

"Oh, no, seriously? I'm *so* sorry."

"I'm not trying to make you feel guilty. I'm telling you we were worried. We all love you very much. We didn't want to lose you."

Her heart caught and she tried to pull her hand from his.

He made a noise of refusal and held on. "You didn't hear me in the ambulance. I *love* you, Cinnia."

"You don't have to say that just because—"

"I *do* need to say it. I should have said it when you asked back in January. Before that even." He scowled in self-re-crimination. "Hospitals are excellent places for confronting your failings. Cowardice. Wrongful thinking. Time wasted that could have been spent with someone who brings joy into your life. I can spell out all my mistakes, but I don't have to because you know all of them. You know *me*. You say I'm a closed book, but you know me, Cinnia. In ways no one else does."

He pressed her hand to his thigh, looked into her eyes with so much openness it was like standing over the Grand Canyon, her mind incapable of taking in the vastness before her.

"I took you for granted. I expected you to just *be* there," he continued. "But that *is* all I need from you, *mon amour*. I know you want to help me pay the bills or make my dental appointments. You want to play a role so you feel you are pulling your weight, but what I need most from you is *you*. I need you to *be* with me. *Alive*."

The corners of her mouth pulled, lips trembling, chastised, but deeply touched. "It's hard to feel like I'm enough," she confessed, stroking his thigh. "When you're…you."

"Who else can I trust with my heart? Hmm?" He cupped the side of her face. "I didn't ask you to carry it, but you picked it up and took such care with it all this time."

She had, and all the while she had felt like it was turned away from her. Now, suddenly, love was shining back at her, gleaming from his eyes and his heart and his soul, bathing her in a light so blinding her eyes watered.

"I want yours, *chérie*," he said tenderly. "Will you give it to me?"

Her throat closed and her chest felt tight. "It's always been yours."

He shifted, rising to stand, then set his knee on the mattress beside her hip. "You told me to get down on one knee, but I'll be damned if I'll do that on a hospital floor."

She caught back a laugh even as she caught her breath.

"I mean this, *chérie*."

She knew what was coming, but was still unprepared.

"I love you, Cinnia. Will you marry me?"

The words expanded the air around them so everything disappeared except this beautiful man holding her hand, holding her gaze. Her heart grew so big, pounded so hard, she thought it would burst with happiness. Her eyes flooded and such love filled her, she could only lift her arms and say, "Yes. Of course. I love you. Yes."

He gathered her close and they kissed, first briefly, tenderly, then with deeper feeling. Passion, but something else that was healing and unifying, solemn and binding.

"Enough of that," the nurse said as she interrupted. "The babies you've already made are still fresh. And hungry, Mama. Let's take you to them."

Henri wheeled her, impulsively kissing the top of her hair as they went into the warm nursery. Her mother was cradling a sleeping Rosalina while Elisa Sauveterre was fending off her daughters from Colette, who was fussing and rooting with hunger.

"Oh, love," Milly said, letting Henri take Rosalina so she could hug Cinnia. "This is the last time you do this, do you hear me?"

"Get engaged?" Cinnia teased, sending a cheeky wink to Henri. "Agreed."

The women erupted in excitement, kissing and congratulating Henri.

"Have you set a date?" Angelique demanded, clasping her hands with excitement. "Have a double ceremony with me and Kasim!"

"I don't want to wait that long." Henri was still holding Rosalina, but he grazed the backs of his fingers against Cinnia's cheek in a tender caress. "We can wait until you're discharged if we have to, but right after. *Oui?*"

"Why wait until I'm discharged?" Cinnia held his gaze

in a small dare. "What do you think, Mum? Could you arrange something for tomorrow? Since everyone is here?"

"What?"

"Are you serious?" A smile grew on Henri's lips.

"Are you?"

"Never more." There wasn't a shred of hesitation in his expression. "I love you with everything in me. I can't wait to call you my wife."

"Then yes, let's do it." She lifted her lips for a quick, sweet kiss, then gave her attention to the women. "Ladies, your assignment, if you choose to accept it, is to plan a wedding for tomorrow."

"Way to clear a room," Henri said drily a moment later, as she latched the hungry Colette.

"Do you want something more formal?" she asked with sudden concern. "A longer engagement?"

"Hell, no. Once you see what's going on outside these walls, you won't want anything to do with being a Sauveterre. No, I am perfectly happy to keep the wedding small and fast and do it while we have a semblance of privacy."

For a ceremony thrown together at the last minute in the hospital chapel, it was touching and beautiful. Cinnia wore an ivory sundress altered by the twin designers into an elegant afternoon wedding creation. Her sister Priscilla brought all her modeling skills to bear as she did Cinnia's makeup and hair. Nell handled the music, the grandmothers took care of the bouquet and flowers, Ramon stood up for Henri and Dorry witnessed for Cinnia.

The rings were tied to ribbons around their swaddled daughters, who were held tenderly by the aunties who had named them. Fortunately the aisle was short since Cinnia could only manage a few steps.

Her husband put a possessive, bolstering arm around her

as she arrived next to him. He was rested, clean shaven, wore a tailored gray suit and had a fresh haircut. The pride and contentment in his expression as he gazed down on her made her tuck her face into his shoulder, too moved to withstand how much she loved him.

But as they spoke their vows and exchanged their rings, she knew he loved her just as much. In this, the most important way, they were equal.

# EPILOGUE

*Four years later...*

CINNIA MADE THE mistake of thinking that if the girls weren't with her, she could walk the few blocks from the clinic to her mother's flat without being noticed.

It was a nice day. She was wearing a sun hat and sunglasses. She was in a good mood and wanted to feel the early summer sun beaming down on her. The city wasn't yet overrun with tourists. Surely she could get away with it?

*Not.*

A Swedish couple noticed her and the selfies started. Her guards helped her navigate the handful of pedestrians who then accosted her. Everyone was very polite, but very quickly there were too many of them. She skipped with a sigh of relief into the quiet of the lobby, where she waved at the doorman and headed to the lift.

Henri was waiting for her when she entered. "I thought you'd be here ahead of me."

"I walked. Big mistake. Now the paparazzi will be waiting when we leave. Sorry."

"Such a scandal, to be caught meeting my wife for an afternoon tryst in her mother's empty apartment," he said, scooping her into his arms and kissing her with enough enthusiasm to make her heart race as quickly as it had the first time he'd kissed her. He drew back. "How was the appointment?"

"We can go." She smiled with anticipation. They occasionally managed a weekend away, leaving the girls with family, but most of their alone time was stolen here in an afternoon. Which was lovely, but with another baby coming, they'd decided to book a week on an island so long as she was cleared to travel.

"And?" he prompted.

"One." She set aside her sunglasses and handbag, then linked her arms around his neck. Her tennis bracelet slid down from her left wrist and her stylish and subtle, beautifully engraved, gold allergy bracelet skimmed down her right. It didn't do a thing to protect her really, except to remind her daily to be very careful what she ate, but Henri liked her to wear it, so she did.

"Are you disappointed?"

"Never." He closed one eye, considering. "But I think you will get an earful from other quarters."

"I know, right?" She wrinkled her nose in amusement.

Their daughters had recently reached an age of enough understanding to ask where Mama's twin was. Papa had a twin. *They* had a twin. Where was Mama's twin?

Cinnia had explained about singles and twins. They had cousins who were singles, remember? Not everyone had a twin.

Colette, being her father's daughter, had taken the explanation with equanimity. She had snuggled into Cinnia's lap with a despondent little sigh and said, "That's sad." A hug and a kiss later, she'd been off to other more important things, like learning to write her name.

Rosy had been beside herself. That was *not* right, she insisted crossly. Mama *must* have a twin. Where was she? *Go get her.* She had cried on and off for days.

*"Merci, chérie."*

"For?" she asked, smiling up at him.

"Our children. The joy you give me, every day."

"We're not even in bed yet." She nudged her hips into his, feeling him harden against her as she gave him a smoky look. "Take me there. I'll show you joy."

"I *love* your libido when you're pregnant. Do you know that? I love *you*." He backed her toward the wall.

"Ooh. Look who's feeling sentimental. Shall we open the windows? Have you arranged fireworks?"

"You deliver joy, I deliver fireworks," he vowed, catching at her mouth with a brief kiss. "I think about our first time often. Don't you? It's one of my favorite memories."

"It *was* a good night," she acknowledged.

"It was very good. Let me remind you *how* good."

Lucky her, he had an excellent talent for recall.

\* \* \* \* \*

# MORE THAN A
# CONVENIENT
# MARRIAGE?

For my sisters, 'cause they live far away and
I miss 'em.

# CHAPTER ONE

GIDEON VOZARAS USED all his discipline to keep his foot light on the accelerator as he followed the rented car, forcing himself to maintain an unhurried pace along the narrow island road while he gripped the wheel in white-knuckled fists. When the other car parked outside the palatial gate of an estate, he pulled his own rental onto the shoulder a discreet distance back then stayed in his vehicle to see if the other driver noticed. As he cut the engine, the AC stopped. Heat enveloped him.

*Welcome to hell.*

He hated Greece at the best of times and today was predicted to be one of the hottest on record. The air shimmered under the relentless sun and it wasn't even ten o'clock yet. But the weather was barely worth noticing.

The gates of the estate were open. The other car could have driven straight through and up to the house, but stayed parked outside. He watched the female driver emerge and take a moment to consider the unguarded entrance. Her shoulders gave a lift and drop as though she screwed up her courage before she took action and walked in.

As she disappeared between imposing brick posts, Gideon left his own car and followed at a measured pace, gut knotting with every step. Outrage stung his veins.

He wanted to believe that wasn't his wife, but there was no mistaking Adara Vozaras. Not for him. Maybe her tourist clothes of flip-flops, jeans chopped above the knees, a sleeveless top and a pair of pigtails didn't fit her usual professional élan, but he knew that backside. The tug it caused in his blood was indisputable. No other woman made an immediate sexual fire crackle awake in him like this. His relentless hunger for Adara had always been his cross to bear and today it was particularly unwelcome.

*Spending the week with her mother.* This ain't Chatham, sweetheart.

He paused as he came alongside her car, glancing inside to see a map of the island on the passenger seat. A logo in its corner matched the hotel he'd been told she was booked into. And now she was advising her lover where to meet her? Walking bold as you please up his million-dollar driveway to his billion-dollar house? The only clue to the estate's ownership, the shields welded to the gate, were turned back against the brick wall that fenced the estate from the road.

Gideon's entire body twitched with an urge to slip his reins of control. He was not a poor man. He'd got past envying other men their wealth once he'd acquired a certain level of his own. Nevertheless, a niggle of his dock-rat inferiority complex wormed to life as he took in what he could see of the shoreline property that rolled into a vineyard and orange grove. The towering stone house, three stories with turrets on each corner, belonged on an English estate, not a Greek island. It was twenty bedrooms minimum. If this was the owner's weekend retreat, he was an obscenely rich man.

Not that Adara needed a rich man. She had grown up wanting for nothing. She had a fortune in her own right plus half of Gideon's, so what was the attraction here?

*Sex.*

The insidious whisper formed a knot of betrayal behind his breastbone. Was this why she hadn't shared that stacked body of hers with him for weeks? His hands curled into fists as he tried to swallow back his gall.

Dreading what he might see as he looked to the front door, he shifted for a full view. Adara had paused halfway to the house to speak with a gardener. A truck overflowing with landscaping tools was parked midway up the driveway and workers were crawling like bees over the blooming gardens.

The sun seared the back of Gideon's neck, strong enough to burn through his shirt to his shoulders, making sweat pool between his shoulder blades and trickle annoyingly down his spine.

They had arrived early this morning, Adara off the ferry, Gideon following in a powerboat he was "test-piloting." She'd been driving a car she'd rented in Athens. His rental had been negotiated at the marina, but the island was small. It hadn't surprised him when she'd driven right past the nose of his car as he had turned onto the main road.

No, the surprise had been the call thirty-six hours previously when their travel agent had dialed his mobile by mistake. Ever the survivor, Gideon had thought quickly. He'd mentioned that he'd like to surprise his wife by joining her and within seconds, Gideon had had all the details of Adara's clandestine trip.

Well, not all. He didn't know whom she was here to see or how she'd met her mystery man. *Why was she doing this when he gave her everything she asked for?*

He watched Adara's slender neck bow in disappointment. Ha. The bastard wasn't home. Grimly satisfied, Gideon folded his arms and waited for his wife.

Adara averted her gaze from the end of the driveway where the sun was glancing off her rented car and piercing straight into her eyes.

The grounds of this estate were an infinitely more beautiful place to look anyway. Groomed lawn gently rolled into vineyards, and a white sand beach gleamed below.

The dew was off the grass, the air moving hotly up from the water with a tang of salt on it. Everything was brilliant and elevating.

Perhaps that was just her frame of mind, but it was a refreshing change from depression and anxiety and rejection. She paused to savor the first optimistic moment she'd had in weeks. Looking out on the horizon where Mediterranean blue met cloudless sky, she sighed in contentment. She hadn't felt so relaxed since… Since ever. Early childhood maybe. Very early childhood.

And it wouldn't last. A sick ache opened in her belly as she remembered Gideon. And his PA.

Not yet, she reminded herself. This week was hers. She was stealing it for herself and her brother. If he returned. The gardener had said a few days, but Adara's research had put Nico on this island all week, so he obviously changed his schedule rapidly. Hopefully he'd return as suddenly as he'd left.

*Just call him,* she cajoled herself, but after this many years she wasn't sure he'd know who she was or want to hear from her. He'd never picked up the telephone himself. If he refused to speak to her, well, a throb of hurt pulsed in her throat as she contemplated that. She swallowed it back. She just wanted to see him, look into his eyes and learn why he'd never come home or spoken to her or her younger brothers again.

Another cleansing breath, but this one a little more troubled as she turned toward her car again. She was crestfallen Nico wasn't here, not that she'd meant to come like this to his house, first thing on arrival, but her room at the hotel hadn't been ready. On impulse she'd decided to at least find the estate, and then the gates had been open and she'd been drawn in. Now she had to wait—

"Lover boy not home?"

The familiar male voice stopped her heart and jerked

her gaze up from the chevron pattern in the cobblestones to the magnificence that was her husband. Swift, fierce attraction sliced through her, sharp and disarming as always.

Not a day passed that she didn't wonder how she'd landed such a smoking-hot man. He was shamelessly handsome, his features even and just hard enough to be undeniably masculine. He rarely smiled, but he didn't have to charm when his sophistication and intelligence commanded such respect. The sheer physical presence of him quieted a room. She always thought of him as a purebred stallion, outwardly still and disciplined, but with an invisible energy and power that warned he could explode any second.

*Don't overlook resourceful,* she thought acridly. How else had he turned up half a world from where she'd thought he would be, when she'd taken pains to keep her whereabouts strictly confidential?

Fortunately, Adara had a lot of experience hiding visceral reactions like instant animal attraction and guilty alarm. She kept her sunglasses on and willed her pulse to slow, keeping her limbs loose and her body language unreadable.

"What are you doing here?" she asked with a composed lift of her chin. "Lexi said you would be in Chile." Lexi's tone still grated, so proprietary over Gideon's schedule, so pitying as she had looked upon the ignorant wife who not only failed as a woman biologically, but no longer interested her husband sexually. Adara had wanted to erase the woman's superior smile with a swipe of her manicured nails.

"Let's turn that question around, shall we?" Gideon strolled with deadly negligence around the front of her car.

Adara had never been afraid of him, not physically, not the way she had been of her father, but somewhere along the line Gideon had developed the power to hurt her with a look or a word, without even trying, and that scared her.

She steeled herself against him, but her nerves fried with the urge to flee.

She made herself stand her ground and find the reliable armor of civility she'd grown as self-defense long ago. It had always served her well in her dealings with this man, even allowing her to engage with him intimately without losing herself. Still, she wanted higher, thicker invisible walls. Her reasons for coming to Greece were too private to share, carrying as they did such a heavy risk of rejection. That's why she hadn't told him or anyone else where she was going. Having him turn up like this put her on edge, internally windmilling her arms as she tried to hang on to unaffected nonchalance.

"I'm here on personal business," she said in a dismissive tone that didn't invite discussion.

He, in turn, should have given her his polite nod of acknowledgment that always drove home how supremely indifferent he was to what happened in her world. It might hurt a little, but far better to have her trials and triumphs disregarded than dissected and diminished.

While she, as was her habit, wouldn't bother repeating a question he had ignored, even though she really did want to know how and why he'd followed her.

No use changing tactics now, she thought. With a little adherence to form they could end this relationship as dispassionately as they'd started it.

That gave her quite a pang and oddly, even though his body language was as neutral as always, and his expression remained impassive as he squinted against the brightness of the day, she again had the sense of that coiled force drawing more tightly inside him. When he spoke, his words were even, yet she sensed an underlying ferocity.

"I can see how personal it is. Who is he?"

Her heart gave a kick. Gideon rarely got angry and even

more rarely showed it. He certainly never directed dark energy at her, but his accusation made her unaccountably defensive.

She told herself not to let his jab pierce her shell, but his charge was a shock and she couldn't believe his gall. The man was banging his secretary in the most clichéd of affairs, yet he had the nerve to dog her all the way to Greece to accuse *her* of cheating?

Fortunately, she knew from experience you didn't provoke a man in a temper. Hiding her indignation behind cool disdain, she calmly corrected his assumption. "*He* has a wife and new baby—"

Gideon's drawled sarcasm cut her off. "Cheating on one spouse wasn't enough, you have to go for two and ruin the life of a child into the mix?"

*Since when do you care about children?*

She bit back the question, but a fierce burn flared behind her eyes, completely unwanted right now when she needed to keep her head. The back of her throat stung, making her voice thick. She hoped he'd put it down to ire, not heartbreak.

"As I said, Lexi assured me you had appointments in Chile. '*We* will be flying into Valparaiso,' she told me. '*We* will be staying in the family suite at the Makricosta Grand.'" Adara impassively pronounced what Lexi hadn't said, but what had been in the woman's eyes and supercilious smile. "'*We* will be wrecking your bed and calling your staff for breakfast in the morning.' Who is cheating on whom?"

She was proud of her aloof delivery, but her underlying resentment was still more emotion than she'd ever dared reveal around him. She couldn't help it. His adultery was a blow she hadn't seen coming and she was always on guard for unearned strikes. Always. Somehow she'd convinced herself she could trust him and if she was angry with anyone, it was with herself for being so blindly oblivious. She was so furious she was having a hard time hiding that she was trembling, but she ground her teeth and willed her muscles to let go of the tension and her blood to stop boiling.

He didn't react. If she fought a daily battle to keep her emotions in reserve, his inner thoughts and feelings were downright nonexistent. His voice was crisp and glacial when he said, "Lexi did not say that because it's not true. And why would you care if she did? *We* aren't wrecking any beds, are we?"

*Ask me why,* she wanted to charge, but the words and the reason stayed bottled so deep and hard inside her she couldn't speak.

Grief threatened to overtake her then. Hopelessness crept in and defeat struck like a gong. It sent an arctic chill into her, blessed ice that let her freeze out the pain and ignore the humiliation. She wanted it all to go away.

"I want a divorce," she stated, heart throbbing in her throat.

For a second, the world stood still. She wasn't sure if she'd actually said it aloud and he didn't move, as though he either hadn't heard, or couldn't comprehend.

Then he drew in a long, sharp inhale. His shoulders pulled back and he stood taller.

Oh, God. Everything in her screamed, *Retreat.* She ducked her head and circled him, aiming for her car door.

He put out a hand and her blood gave a betraying leap. She quickly tamped down the hunger and yearning, embracing hatred instead.

"Don't think for a minute I'll let you touch me," she warned in a voice that grated.

"Right. Touching is off limits. I keep forgetting."

A stab of compunction, of incredible sadness and longing to be understood, went through her. Gideon was becoming so good at pressing on the bruises closest to her soul and all he had to do was speak the truth.

"Goodbye, Gideon." Without looking at him again, she threw herself into her car and pulled away.

# CHAPTER TWO

THE FERRY WAS gone so Adara couldn't leave the island. She drove through a blur of goat-tracked hills and tree-lined boulevards. Expansive olive branches cast rippling shadows across bobbing heads of yellow and purple wildflowers between scrupulously groomed estates and bleached-white mansions. When she happened upon a lookout, she quickly parked and tried to walk off her trembles.

She'd done it. She'd asked for a divorce.

The word cleaved her in two. She didn't want her marriage to be over. It wasn't just the failure it represented. Gideon was her husband. She wasn't a possessive person. She tried not to get too attached to anything or anyone, but until his affair had come to light, she had believed her claim on him was incontestable. That had meant something to her. She had never been allowed to have anything. Not the job she wanted, not the money in her trust fund, not the family she had briefly had as a child or the one she longed for as an adult.

Gideon was a prize coveted by every woman around her. Being his wife had given her a deep sense of pride, but he'd gone behind her back and even managed to make her writhe with self-blame that it was her fault.

She hadn't made love with him in weeks. It was true. She'd taken care of his needs, though. When he was home.

Did he realize he hadn't been home for more than one night at a stretch in months?

Pacing between guilt and virtue, she couldn't escape the position she'd put herself in. Her marriage was over. The marriage she had arranged so her father would stop trying to sell her off to bullies like himself.

Her heart compressed under the weight of remembering how she'd taken such care to ask Gideon for only what seemed reasonable to expect from a marriage: respect and fidelity. That's all. She hadn't asked for love. She barely believed in it, not when her mother still loved the man who had abused her and her children, raising his hand often enough Adara flinched just thinking about it.

No, Adara had been as practical and realistic as she could be—strengths she'd honed razor sharp out of necessity. She had found a man whose wealth was on a level with her father's fortune. She had picked one who exhibited incredible control over his emotions, trying to avoid spending her adult life ducking outbursts and negotiating emotional land mines. She had accommodated Gideon in every way, from the very fair prenup to learning how to please him in bed. She had never asked for romance or signs of affection, not even flowers when she was in hospital recovering from a miscarriage.

Her hand went instinctively to her empty womb. After the first one, she'd tried not to bother him much at all, informing him without involving him, not even telling him about the last one. Her entire being pulsated like an open wound as she recalled the silent weeks of waiting and hoping, then the first stain of blood and the painful, isolated hours that had followed.

While Gideon had been in Barcelona, faithful bitch Lexi at his side.

She had learned nothing from her mother, Adara realized with a spasm in her chest. Being complacent didn't earn you anything but a cheating husband. Her marriage was over and it left a jagged burn in her like a bolt of lightning was stuck inside her, buzzing and shorting and trying to escape.

A new life awaited though, unfurling like a rolled carpet before her. She made herself look at it, standing tall under the challenge, extending her spine to its fullest. She concentrated on hardening her resolve, staring with determination across the vista of scalloped waves to distant islands formed from granite. That's what she was now, alone, but strong and rooted.

She'd look for a new home while she was here, she decided. Greece had always been a place where she'd felt hopeful and happy. Her new life started today. Now.

After discovering his room wasn't ready, Gideon went to the patio restaurant attached to the hotel and ordered a beer. He took care of one piece of pressing business on his mobile before he sat back and brooded on what had happened with Adara.

He had never cheated on her.

But for the last year he had spent more time with his PA than his wife.

Adara had known this would be a brutal year though. They both had. Several large projects were coming online at once. He ought to be in Valparaiso right now, opening his new terminal there. It was the ticking off of another item on their five-year plan, something they had mapped out in the first months of their marriage. That plan was pulling them in different directions, her father's death last year and her mother's sinking health not helping. They were rarely in the same room, let alone the same bed, so to be fair it wasn't strictly her fault they weren't tearing up the sheets.

And there had been Lexi, guarding his time so carefully and keeping him on schedule, mentioning that her latest relationship had fallen apart because she was traveling so much, offering with artless innocence to stay in his suite with him so she could be available at any hour.

She had been offering all right, and perhaps he hadn't outright encouraged or accepted, but he was guilty of keeping his options open. Abstinence, or more specifically, Adara's avoidance of wholehearted lovemaking, had made him restless and dissatisfied. He'd begun thinking Adara wouldn't care if he had an affair. She was getting everything she wanted from this marriage: her position as CEO of her father's hotel chain, a husband who kept all the dates she put in his calendar. The penthouse in Manhattan and by the end of the year, a newly built mansion in the Hamptons.

While he'd ceased getting the primary thing *he* wanted out of their marriage: her.

So he had looked at his alternatives. The fact was, though, as easy as Lexi would be, as physically attractive as she was, he wasn't interested in her. She was too much of an opportunist. She'd obviously read into his "I'll think about it" response enough to imagine she had a claim on him.

That couldn't be what had precipitated Adara running here to Greece and another man, though. The Valparaiso arrangements had only been finalized recently. Adara wasn't that impulsive. She would have been thinking about this for a long time before taking action.

His inner core burned. A scrapper in his youth, Gideon had found other ways to channel his aggression when he'd reinvented himself as a coolheaded executive, but the basic street-life survival skill of fighting to keep what was his had never left him. Every territorial instinct he possessed was aroused by her deceit and the threat it represented to all he'd gained.

The sound of a checked footstep and a barely audible gasp lifted his gaze. He took a hit of sexual energy like he'd swallowed two-hundred-proof whiskey, while Adara lost a few shades of color behind her sunglasses. Because she could read the barely contained fury in him? Or because she was still feeling guilty at being caught out?

She gathered herself to flee, but before she could pivot away, he rose with a menacing scrape of his chair leg on the paving stones. Drawing out the chair off the corner of his table, he kept a steady gaze on her to indicate he would come after her if she chose to run. He wanted to know everything about the man who thought he could steal from him.

So he could quietly destroy him.

"The rooms aren't ready," he told her.

"So they've just informed me again." Adara's mouth firmed to a resistant angle, but she moved forward. If there was one thing he could say about her, it was that she wasn't a coward. She met confrontation with a quiet dignity that disconcerted him every time, somehow making him feel like an executioner of an innocent even though he'd never so much as raised his voice at her.

She'd never given him reason to.

Until today.

With the collected poise he found both admirable and frustrating, she set her purse to the side and lowered herself gracefully into the chair he held. He had learned early that passionate women were scene-makers and he didn't care to draw attention to himself. Adara had been a wallflower with a ton of potential, blooming with subtle brilliance as they had made their mark on the social scene in New York, London and Athens, always keeping things understated.

Which meant she didn't wear short-shorts or low-cut tops, but the way her denim cutoffs clung all the way down her toned thighs and the way the crisp cotton of her loose shirt angled over the thrust of her firm breasts was erotic in its own way.

Unwanted male hunger paced with purpose inside him. How could he still want her? He was furious with her.

Without removing her sunglasses or even looking at him as he took his seat, she opened the menu he'd been given. She didn't put it down until the server arrived, then ordered a souvlaki with salad and a glass of the house white.

"The same," Gideon said dismissively.

"You won't speak Greek even to a native in his own country?" Adara murmured in an askance tone as the man walked away.

"Did I use English? I didn't notice," Gideon lied and sensed her gaze staying on him even though she didn't challenge his assertion. Another thing he could count on with his wife: she never pushed for answers he wouldn't give.

Nevertheless, he found himself waiting for her to speak, willing her almost, which wasn't like him. He liked their quiet meals that didn't beleaguer him with small talk.

He wasn't waiting for, "How's the weather," however. He wanted answers.

Her attention lifted to the greenery forming the canopy above them, providing shade against the persistent sun. Blue pots of pink flowers and feathery palms offered a privacy barrier between their table and the empty one next to them. A colorful mosaic on the exterior wall of the restaurant held her attention for a very long time.

He realized she didn't intend to speak at all.

"Adara," he said with quiet warning.

"Yes?" Her voice was steady and thick with calm reason, but he could see her pulse racing in her throat.

She wasn't comfortable and that was a much-needed satisfaction for him since he was having a hard time keeping his balance. Maybe the comfortable routine of their marriage had grown a bit stale for both of them, but that didn't mean you threw it away and ran off to meet another man.

None of this gelled with the woman he'd always seen as ethical, coolheaded and highly averse to risk.

"Tell me why." He ground out the words, resenting the instability of this storm she'd thrown him into and the fact he wasn't weathering it up to his usual standard.

Her mouth pursed in distaste. "From the outset I made it clear that I would rather be divorced than put up with infidelity."

"And yet you sneaked away to have an affair," he charged, angry because he'd been blindsided.

"That's not—" A convulsive flinch contracted her features, half hidden by her bug-eyed glasses, but the flash of great pain was unmistakable before she smoothed her expression and tone, appearing unaffected in a familiar way that he suddenly realized was completely fake.

His fury shorted out into confusion. What else did she hide behind that serene expression of hers?

"I'm not having an affair," she said without inflection.

"No?" Gideon pressed, sitting forward, more disturbed by his stunning insight and her revelation of deep emotion than by her claim. Her anguish lifted a host of unexpected feelings in him. It roused an immediate masculine need in him to shield and protect. Something like concern or threat roiled in him, but not combat-ready threat. Something he wasn't sure how to interpret. Adara was like him, unaffected by life. If something was piercing her shell, it had to be bad and that filled him with apprehensive tension.

"Who did you come to see then?" he prodded, unconsciously bracing.

A slight hesitation, then, with her chin still tucked into her neck, she admitted, "My brother."

His tension bled away in a drain of caustic disappointment. As he fell back in his chair, he laced his Greek endearment with sarcasm. "Nice try, *matia mou*. Your brothers don't earn enough to build a castle like the one we saw today."

Her head came up and her shoulders went back. With the no-nonsense civility he so valued in her, she removed her sunglasses, folded the arms and set them beside her purse before looking him in the eye.

The golden-brown irises were practically a stranger's, he realized with a kick of unease. When was the last time she'd looked right at him? he wondered distantly, while at the same time feeling the tightening inside him that drew on the eye contact as a sexual signal. Like the rest of her, her eyes were understated yet surprisingly attractive when a man took the time to notice. Almond-shaped. Clear. Flecked with sparks of heat.

"I'm referring to my older brother."

Her words left a discordant ring in his ears, dragging him from the dangerous precipice of falling into her eyes.

The server brought their wine. Gideon kept his attention fully focused on Adara's composed expression and contentiously set chin.

"You're the eldest," he stated.

She only lifted her wine to sip while a hollow shadow drifted behind her gaze, giving him a thump of uncertainty, even though he *knew* she only had two brothers, both younger than her twenty-eight years. One was an antisocial accountant who traveled the circuit of their father's hotel chain auditing ledgers, the other a hellion with a taste for big engines and fast women, chasing skirt the way their father had.

Given her father's peccadilloes, he shouldn't be surprised a half sibling had turned up, but older? It didn't make sense and he wasn't ready to let go of his suspicions about an affair.

"How did you find out about him? Was there something in the estate papers after your father passed?"

"I've always known about him." She set aside her wine with a frown of distaste. "I think that's off."

"Always?" Gideon repeated. "You've never mentioned him."

"We don't talk, do we?" Golden orbs came back, charged with electric energy that made him jolt as though she'd touched a cattle prod to his internal organs.

No. They didn't talk. He preferred it that way.

Their server arrived with their meals. Gideon asked for Adara's wine to be changed out. With much bowing and apologies, a fresh glass was produced. Adara tried it and stated it was fine.

As the server walked away, Adara set down her glass with another grimace.

"Still no good?" Gideon tried it. It was fine, perhaps not as dry as she usually liked, but he asked, "Try again?"

"No. I feel foolish that you sent back the first one."

That was so like her to not want to make a fuss, but he considered calling back the waiter all the same. Stating that they didn't talk was an acknowledgment of an elephant. It was the first knock on a door he didn't want opened.

At the same time, he wanted to know more about this supposed brother of hers. Sharing was a two-way street though and hypocrite that he was, he'd prefer backstory to flow only one way. He glanced at the offending wine, ready to seize it as an excuse to keep things inconsequential between them.

And yet, as Adara picked up her fork and hovered it over her rice, she gave him the impression of being utterly without hope. Forlorn. The hairs rose all over his body as he picked up signals of sadness that he'd never caught an inkling of before.

"Do you want to talk about him?" he asked carefully.

She lifted her shoulder. "I've never been allowed to before so I don't suppose one more day of silence matters."

It was her conciliatory tone, the one that put everything right and allowed them to move past the slightest hiccup in their marriage.

What marriage? She wanted a divorce, he reminded himself.

Instinct warned him this was dangerous ground, but he also sensed he'd never have another chance to understand if he didn't seize this one. "Who wouldn't let you talk about him?" he asked gruffly.

A swift glance gave him the answer. Her father, of course. He'd been a hard man of strong opinions and ancient views. His daughter could run a household, but her husband would control the hotels. Her share of the family fortune wasn't hers to squander as her brothers might, but left in a trust doled out by tightly worded language, the bulk of the money to be held for her children. The male ones.

Gideon frowned, refusing to let himself be sidetracked by the painful subject of heirs.

"I assume this brother was the product of an affair? Something your father didn't want to be reminded of?"

"He was my mother's indiscretion." Adara frowned at her plate, her voice very soft, her expression disturbingly young and bewildered. "He lived with us until he left for school." She lifted anxious eyes, words pouring out of her in a rush as if she'd held on to them for decades. "My aunt explained years later that my father didn't know at first that Nico wasn't his. When he found out, he had him sent to boarding school. It was awful. That's all they'd tell me, that he'd gone to school. I knew I was starting the next year and I was terrified I'd be forgotten the same way."

A stitch pulled in his chest. His childhood predisposed him to hate the thought of any child frightened by anything. He *felt* her confusion and fear at losing her brother mixed with the terror of not knowing what would happen to herself. It made him nauseous.

Her expression eased into something poignant. "But then we saw him at my aunt's in Katarini over the summer. He was fine. He told me about his school and I couldn't wait to go myself, to be away from the angry man my father had turned into, make new friends…" Her gaze faded to somewhere in the distance. "But I was sent to day school in New York and we saw Nico only a few more times after that. One day I asked if we would see him, and my father—"

Gideon wouldn't have known what she failed to say aloud if he hadn't been watching her so intently, reading her lips because he could barely hear her. Her tongue touched the corner of her mouth where a hairline scar was sometimes visible between her morning shower and her daily application of makeup. She'd told him it had come from a childhood mishap.

A wrecking ball hit him in the middle of his chest. "He hit you?"

Her silence and embarrassed bite of her lip spoke volumes.

His torso felt as if it split open and his teeth clenched so hard he thought they'd crack. His scalp prickled and his blood turned to battery acid.

"I didn't ask again," she said in her quick, sweep-it-under-the-rug way. "I didn't let the boys say his name. I let it go. I learned to let a lot of things go."

Like equal rights. Like bad decisions with the hotel chain that were only now being repaired after her father was dead. Like the fact that her brothers were still boys because they'd been raised by a child: her.

Gideon had seen the dysfunction, the alcoholic mother and the overbearing father, the youngest son who earned his father's criticism, and the older children who hadn't, but received plenty of it anyway. Adara had always managed the volatile dynamics with equanimity, so Gideon hadn't tried to stir up change. If he had suspected physical abuse was the underbelly of it all…

His fist clenched. "You should have told me," he said.

Another slicing glance repeated the obvious. *We don't talk.*

His guts turned to water. No, they didn't and because of that he'd let her down. If there was one thing his wife had never asked of Gideon, but that he'd regarded as his sacred duty, it was his responsibility to protect her. Adara was average height and kept herself toned and in good shape, but she was undeniably female. Her bones were smaller, her muscles not as thick as a man's. She was preordained by nature to be vulnerable to a male's greater strength. Given what had happened to his own mother, he'd lay down his life for any woman, especially one who depended on him.

"At any time since I've known you," he forced himself to ask, "did he—"

"No," she answered bluntly, but her tone was tired. "I learned, Gideon."

It wasn't any sort of comfort.

How had he not seen this? He'd always assumed she was reserved because she had been raised by strict parents. She was ambitious and focused on material gain because most immigrant families to America were. *He* was.

And compliant? Well, it was just her nature.

But no, it was because she had been abused.

He couldn't help staring at her, reeling in disbelief. Not disbelieving she had been mistreated, but that he hadn't known. What else did he not know about her? he wondered uneasily.

Adara forced herself to eat as though nothing was wrong, even though Gideon's X-ray stare made her so nervous she felt as if her bones were developing radiation blisters. Why had she told him? And why did it upset her that he knew what she'd taken such pains to hide from the entire world? She had nothing to be ashamed of. Her father's abuse wasn't her fault.

Sharing her past made her squirm all the same. It was such a dark secret. So close to the heart. Shameful because she had never taken action against her father, trying instead to do everything in her power to keep what remained of her family intact. And she'd been so young.

Her eyebrows were trying to pull into a worried frown. She habitually noted the tension and concentrated on relaxing her facial muscles, hiding her turmoil. Taking a subtle breath, she begged the constriction in her throat to ease.

"He went by his father's name," she told Gideon, taking up the subject of her brother as the less volatile one and using it to distract his intense focus from her. "I found his blogs at one point, but since he had never tried to contact us I didn't know if he'd want to hear from me. I couldn't reach out anyway," she dismissed with a shrug. "Not while my father was alive." She had feared, quite genuinely, that he would kill her. "But as soon as Papa died, I started thinking about coming here."

"But never told me."

She flinched, always sensitive to censure.

Her reaction earned a short sigh.

She wasn't going to state the obvious again though, and it wasn't as if she was laying blame. The fact they didn't talk was as much her fault as his, she knew that. Talking about personal things was difficult for her. She'd grown up in silence, never acknowledging the unpleasant, always avoiding points of conflict so they didn't escalate into physical altercations. Out of self-defense she had turned into a thinker who never revealed what she wanted until she had pondered the best approach and was sure she could get it without raising waves.

"I didn't tell anyone I was coming here, not even my brothers. I didn't want anyone talking me out of it." It was a thin line in the sand. She wouldn't be persuaded to leave until she'd seen her brother. She needed Gideon to recognize that.

He didn't argue and they finished their meals with a thick cloud of tension between them. The bouzouki music from the speakers sounded overly loud as sultry heat layered the hot air into claustrophobic blankets around them.

The minute the server removed their plates, Adara stood and gathered her things, grasping at a chance to draw a full breath. "Thank you for lunch. Goodbye, Gideon."

His hand snaked out to fasten around her wrist.

Her heart gave a thump, his touch always making her pulse leap. She glared at the strong, sun-browned fingers. It wasn't a hard grip. It was warm and familiar and she hated herself for liking it. That gave her the strength to say what she had to.

"Will you contact Halbert or shall I?" She ignored the spear of anguish that pierced her as she mentioned their lawyer's name.

"I fired Lexi."

"Really." She gave her best attempt at blithe lack of interest, but her arteries constricted so each beat of her heart was like a hammer blow inside her.

He shifted his grip ever so slightly, lining up his fingertips on her wrist, no doubt able to feel the way her pulse became ferocious and strong. Not that he gave anything away. His fiercely handsome features were as watchful as a predator's, his eyes hidden behind his mirrored aviators.

"She had no right to speak to you as she did." His assertive tone came across as almost protective. "Implying things that weren't true. I haven't cheated on you, Adara. There's no reason for us to divorce."

As a spasm of agitated panic ran through her, Adara realized she'd grasped Lexi as a timely excuse. Thoughts of divorce had been floating through her mind for weeks, maybe even from the day she had realized she was pregnant again. *If I lose this one, I'll leave him and never have to go through this again.*

"Actually, Gideon," she said with a jagged edge to her hushed voice, "there's no reason for us to stay married. Let me go, please."

# CHAPTER THREE

*No reason to stay married?*

Gideon's head nearly exploded as Adara walked away. How about the luxury cruise ship they were launching next year? The ultimate merger of his shipbuilding corporation and her hotel chain, it wasn't just a crown jewel for both entities, it was a tying together of the two enterprises in a way that wouldn't be easy to untangle. They couldn't divorce at this stage of that project.

Gideon hung back to scratch his name on the bill while tension flooded back into him, returning him to a state of deep aggravation. Neither of them had cheated, but she still wanted a divorce. Why? Did she not believe him?

It was too hot to race after her, and his stride was long enough that he closed in easily as she climbed the road behind the marina shops. Resentment that he was following her at all filled him with gall. He was not a man who chased after women begging for another chance. He didn't have to.

But the fact that Adara saw no reason to continue their marriage gave him a deep sense of ignorance. They had ample financial reasons. What else did she want from the union? More communication? Fine, they could start talking.

Even as he considered it, however, resistance rose in him. And at that exact moment, as he'd almost caught up to Adara, the stench of rotting garbage came up off a restaurant Dumpster, carried on a breeze flavored with the dank smells of the marina: tidal flats, diesel exhaust and fried foods. It put him squarely back in his childhood, searching for a safe place to sleep while his mother worked the docks in Athens.

Adara didn't even know who she was married to. Divorce would mean court papers, identification, paparazzi... Marrying under an assumed name had been tricky enough and he lived a much higher profile now. He couldn't risk divorce. But if he wasn't legally married to her, did he have a right to keep her tied to him?

His clothes began to feel tight. "Adara, you'll get sunstroke. Come back to the hotel," he ordered.

She seemed to flinch at the sound of his voice. Pausing, she turned to face him, her defensive tension obvious in her stiff posture.

"Gideon—" She seemed to search for words around her feet, or perhaps she was looking for stones to scare him away. "Look, I've taken this time as vacation." She flicked her thick plait back over her shoulder. "The gardener said my brother will be back in a few days. I'm staying until I meet him. In the meantime, I might as well see the sights. There's a historical viewpoint up here. You can go back to New York or on to Valparaiso as scheduled. Legal can work out the details. I'm not going to contest anything. Neither of us will be bothered by any of this."

Not bothered? He *wished*. He was shaken to the bone by what she'd revealed, not the least bit comfortable with the fact he'd been so oblivious. It gave him new eyes on her and them and yes, he could see that they'd foundered a bit, but this wasn't so bad you abandoned ship and let it sink.

Apparently Adara was prepared to, offering up one of her patented sweep, fold, tuck maneuvers that tidied away all conflicts. *Mama's asking about Christmas. We can take two cars if you like, so you can stay in the city?*

Her accommodating nature was suddenly irritating in

the extreme, partly because he knew he *should* get back to work rather than standing here in the middle of the road in the middle of the Mediterranean watching her walk away. She might have lightened her workload in anticipation of coming here, but he hadn't. Myriad to-dos ballooned in his mind while ahead of him Adara's pert backside sashayed up the incline of the deserted street.

He wasn't stupid enough to court heat exhaustion to keep a woman, but the reality was only a very dense man would let that beautiful asset walk away from him without at least trying to coax her to stay. Admiring her round butt, he recollected it was the first thing he'd noticed about her before she'd turned around with an expression of cool composure that had assured him she was all calm water and consistent breeze.

The rest of the pieces had fallen into place like predetermined magic. Their dealings with each other had been simple and straightforward. Adara was untainted by the volatile emotions other women were prone to. Perhaps the smooth sailing of their marriage was something he'd taken for granted, but she must know that he valued it and her.

Or did she? He was about as good at expressing his feelings as he was at arranging flowers.

Disquiet nudged at him as he contemplated how to convince her to continue their marriage. He knew how to physically seduce a woman, but emotional persuasion was beyond his knowledge base.

Why in hell couldn't they just go back to the way things had been?

Not fully understanding why he did it, he caught up to her at the viewpoint. It was little more than a crosspiece of weathered wood in dry, trampled grass. A sign in English identified it as a spot from which ships had been sighted during an ancient war. It also warned about legal action should tourists attempt to climb down to the beach below. A sign in Greek cautioned the locals to swim at their own risk.

Adara shaded her eyes, but he had the sense she was shielding herself from him as much as the sun. Her breasts rose and fell with exertion and her face glowed with light perspiration, but also with mild impatience. She didn't really give a damn about old ships and history, did she? This was just an excuse to get away from him.

He experienced a pinch of compunction that he'd never bothered to find out *what* she gave a damn about. She was quiet. He liked that about her, but it bothered him that he couldn't tell what she was thinking right now. If he didn't know what she was thinking, how would he talk her round to *his* way of thinking?

Her beauty always distracted him. That was the truth of it. She was oddly youthful today with her face clean of makeup and her hair in pigtails like a schoolgirl, but dressed down or to the nines, she always stirred a twist of possessive desire in his groin.

*That* was why he didn't want a divorce.

His clamoring libido was a weakness that governed him where she was concerned. The sex had always been good, but not exactly a place where they met as equals. In the beginning he'd been favored with more experience. The leader. He wasn't hampered by shyness or other emotions that women attached to intimacy. He'd tutored her and loved it.

Adara had maintained a certain reserve in the bedroom that she had never completely allowed to let slide away, however. While the sex had always been intense and satisfying, the power had subtly shifted over time into her favor. She decided when and how much and *if*.

Resentment churned in him, bringing on a scowl. He didn't like that she was threatening him on so many levels. Yanking the rug on sex was bad enough. Now all that he'd built was on a shaky foundation.

*Why?* Did it have to do with her fear of her father? Did she fear him? Blame him? Apprehension kept him from asking.

And Adara gave no clue to her thoughts, acting preoccupied with reading the signage, ignoring him, aggravating him further.

She peered over the edge of the steep slope to where a rope was tied to the base of the wooden crosspiece and, without a word, looped the thin strap of her purse over her head and shoulder then maneuvered to the edge of the cliff. Taking up the rope, she clung to it as she began a very steep, backward descent.

Gideon was taken aback. "What the hell are you doing?"

She paused. Uncertainty made her bottom lip flinch before she firmed it. "Going swimming."

"Like hell you are." Who *was* this woman?

The anxiety that spasmed across her features transitioned through uncertainty before being overcome by quiet defiance. "I always did as I was told because I was scared my father would punish me. Unless you intend to take up controlling my behavior with violence, I'm doing what I want from now on."

The pit of his belly was still a hard knot over her revelations about her childhood. He would never hurt her or threaten to and was now even more inclined to treat her with kid gloves. At the same time, everything in him clamored to exert control over her, get what he wanted and put an end to this nonsense. The conflicting feelings, too deep for comfort, left him standing there voicelessly glaring his frustration.

Despite her bold dare, there was something incredibly vulnerable in her stance of toughness though. An air of quiet desperation surrounded her as tangibly as the hardened determination she was trying to project.

She wanted to prove something. He didn't know what it was, but bullying her into going back to the hotel wasn't the way to find out. It wouldn't earn him any points toward keeping their marriage intact either.

"It's fine, Gideon. You can go," she said in her self-possessed way. *Papa doesn't think the Paris upgrade is necessary. I'll find my own way home after our meeting.*

"And leave you to break your neck? No," he said gruffly.

The way she angled a look up at him seemed to indicate suspicion. Maybe it was deserved. He was chivalrous, always picked up her heavy bags, but neither of them were demonstrative. Maybe he'd never acted so protective before, but she'd never tried to do anything so perilous.

"I won't break my neck," she dismissed and craned it to watch as she tentatively sought a step backward.

A completely foreign clench of terror squeezed his lungs. Did she not see how dangerous this was? He skimmed his hand over his sweat-dampened hair.

"Adara, I won't hurt you, but I will get physical if you don't stop right there and at least let me get behind you so I can catch you if you slip."

She stared, mouth pursing in mutiny. "I don't have to ask your permission to live my life, Gideon." *Not anymore*, was the silent punctuation to that.

"Well, I won't ask your permission to save it. Stay put until I get behind you."

He sensed her wariness as he took his time inspecting the rope, approving its marine grade, noting it was fairly new and in good repair, as was the upright it was tied to. Assured they weren't going to plunge to their deaths, he let his loose grip slide along the rope until his hand met Adara's.

She stiffened as he brushed past her, making him clench his teeth. When had his touch become toxic?

*Ask*, he chided himself, but things were discordant enough. His assumptions about her were turned on their heads, her predictability completely blown out of the water. He didn't know what to say or what to expect next, so he picked his way down the slope in grim silence, arriving safely on to the pocket of sand between monolithic gray boulders.

The tide was receding, but the cove was steep enough it was still a short beach into a deep pool. It was the type of place young lovers would tryst, and his mind immediately turned that way. Adara wasn't even looking at him, though.

Adara shrugged against the sting of sweat and the disturbing persistence Gideon was showing. She thought they had an unspoken agreement to back off when things got personal, but even though she'd spilled way more of her family history than she'd ever meant to, he was sticking like humidity.

She didn't know how to react to that. And should she thank him for his uncharacteristic show of consideration in accompanying her down here? Or tell him again to shove off? He was so hard to be around sometimes, so unsettling. He was shorting out a brain that was already melting in the heat. She desperately wanted to cool off so she could think straight again, but she hadn't brought a bathing suit and—

Oh, to heck with it. She kicked off her flip-flops and began unbuttoning her shirt.

"Really?" he said, not hiding the startled uptick in his tone.

She didn't let herself waver. Maybe this was out of character, but this was her new life. She was tossing off fear of reprisal, embracing the freedom to follow impulse.

"I miss Greece. My aunt let us run wild here. In Katarini, not this island, but we'd do exactly this: tramp along the beach until we got hot then we'd strip to our underthings and jump in."

"Your aunt was a nudist?" he surmised.

"A free spirit. She never married, never had children—" Here Adara faltered briefly. "I intend to emulate her from now on."

She shed her shorts and ran into the water in her bra and panties, feeling terribly exposed as she left her decision to never have children evaporating on the sizzling sand.

The clear, cool water rose to her waist within a few splashing steps. She fell forward and ducked under, arrowing deep into the silken blur filled with the muted cacophony of creaks and taps and swishing currents.

When her lungs were ready to burst, she shot up for air, blinking the water from her eyes and licking the salt from her lips, baptized into a new version of herself. The campy phrase *the first day of the rest of your life* came to her with a pang of wistful anticipation.

Gideon's head appeared beside her, his broad shoulders flexing as he splayed out his arms to keep himself afloat. His dark lashes were matted and glinting, his thick hair sleeked back off his face, exposing his angular bone structure and taking her breath with his action-star handsomeness. The relief of being in the cool water relaxed his expression, while his innate confidence around the water—in any situation, really—made him incredibly compelling.

She would miss that sense of reliability, she acknowledged with a hitch of loss.

"I've never tried to curb your independence," he asserted. "Marrying me gained you your freedom."

They'd never spoken so bluntly about her motives. She'd only stated in the beginning that she'd like to keep working until they had a family, but he knew her better after her confession today. He was looking at her as though he could see right into her.

It made her uncomfortable.

"Marrying at all was a gamble," she acknowledged with

a tentative honesty that caused her veins to sting with apprehension. "But you're right. I was fairly sure I'd have more control over my life living with you than I had with my father."

She squinted against the glare off the water as she silently acknowledged that she'd learned to use Gideon to some extent, pitting him against her father when she wanted something for herself. Not often and not aggressively, just with a quiet comment that *Gideon* would prefer this or that.

"You had women working for you in high-level positions," she noted, remembering all the minute details that had added up to a risk worth taking. "You were shocked that I didn't know how to drive. You fired that man who was harassing your receptionist. I was reasonably certain my life with you would be better than it was with my father so I took a chance." She glanced at him, wondering if he judged her harshly for advancing her interests through him.

"So what's changed?" he challenged. "I taught you to drive. I put you in charge of the hotels. Do you want more responsibility? Less? Tell me. I'm not trying to hem you in."

No, Gideon wasn't a tyrant. He was ever so reasonable. She'd always liked that about him, but today that quality put her on edge. "Lexi—"

"—is a nonissue," he stated curtly. "Nothing happened and do you know why? Because I thought *you* were having an affair and got myself on a plane and chased you down. I didn't even think twice about it. Why didn't *you* do that? Why didn't you confront me? Why didn't you ask me why I'd even consider letting another woman throw herself under me?"

"You don't have to be so crude about it!" She instinctively propelled herself backward, pushing space between herself and the unbearable thought of him sleeping with another woman. She hadn't been able to face it herself, let along confront him, not with everything else that had happened.

"You said we don't talk," he said with pointed aggression. "Let's. You left me twisting with sexual frustration. Having an affair started to look like a viable option. If you didn't want me going elsewhere, why weren't you meeting my needs at home?"

"I did! I—"

"Going down isn't good enough, Adara."

His vulgarity was bad enough, but it almost sounded like a critique and she resented that. She tried hard to please him and could tell that he liked what she did, so why did he have to be so disparaging about it?

Unbearably hurt, she kicked toward shore, barely turning her head to defend, "I was pregnant. What else could I do?"

How he reacted to that news she didn't care. She just wanted to be away from him, but as her toes found cold, thick sand, she halted. Leaving the water suddenly seemed a horribly exposing thing to do. How stupid to think she could become a new person by shedding a few stitches of clothing. She was the same old worthless Adara who couldn't even keep a baby in her womb.

The sun seared across her shoulders. Her wet hair hung in her eyes and she kept her arms folded tightly across her chest, trying to hold in the agony.

She felt ridiculous, climbing down to this silly beach that was impossible to leave, revealing things that were intensely personal to her and wouldn't matter at all to him.

"What did you say?" He was too close. She flinched, feeling the sharpness of his voice like the tip of a flicking whip.

"You heard me," she managed to say even though her throat was clogging. She clenched her eyes shut, silently begging him to do what he always did. Say nothing and give her space. She didn't want to do this. She never, ever wanted to do this again.

"You *were* pregnant?" His voice moved in front of her.

She turned her head to the side, hating him for cutting off her escape to the beach, hating herself for lacking the courage to take it when she'd had the chance.

Keeping her eyes tightly closed, she dug her fingers into her arms, her whole body aching with tension. "It doesn't matter," she insisted through her teeth. "It's over and I just want a divorce."

Gideon was distantly aware of the sea trying to pull him out with the tide. His entire being was numb enough that he had to concentrate on keeping his feet rooted as he stared at Adara. She was a knot of torment. For the first time he could see her suffering and it made his heart clench. When had she started to care about the miscarriages? The last one had been called into him from across the globe, his offer to come home dismissed as unnecessary.

"Tell me—"

"What is there to tell, Gideon?" Her eyes opening into pits of hopeless fury. Her face creased with sharp lines of grief. "It was the same as every other one. I did the test and held my breath, terrified to so much as bump my hip on the edge of my desk. And just when I let myself believe this time might be different, the backache started and the spotting appeared and then it was twenty-four hours of medieval torture until I was spat out in hell with nothing to show for it. At least I didn't have the humiliation of being assaulted by the people in white coats this time."

She took a step to the side, thinking to circle him and leave the water, but he shifted into her path, his hand reaching to stop her. His expression was appalled. "What do you mean about being assaulted?"

She cringed from his touch, her recoil like a knee into his belly. Gideon clenched his abdominal muscles and curled his fingers into his palm, forcing his hand to his side under the water even though he wanted to grip her with all his strength and squeeze the answers out of her. She couldn't possibly be saying what he thought she was saying.

"What people in white coats?" he demanded, but the words sounded far away. "Are you telling me you didn't go to the hospital?" Intense, fearful dread hollowed out his chest as he watched her mask fear and compunction with a defiant thrust of her chin.

"Do you know what they do to you after you've had a miscarriage? No, you don't. But I do and I'm sick of it. So, no, I didn't go," she declared with bitter rebelliousness.

Horror washed through him in freezing waves.

"We need to get you to a doctor." He flew his gaze to the cliff, terror tightening in him. What the hell had he been thinking, letting her descend to this impossible place?

"It was three weeks ago, Gideon. If it was going to kill me, it would have by now."

"It could have," he retorted, helplessness making him brutal. "You could have bled to death."

She shrugged that off with false bravado, eyes glossy and red. "At the time that looked like a—what's the expression you used? A viable option?"

It was a vicious slap that he deserved. While he'd been contemplating an affair, she'd been losing the battle to keep their baby. Again. And she'd been filled with such dejection she'd refused medical care and courted death.

The fact she'd let herself brush elbows with the Grim Reaper made him so agitated, he clipped out a string of foul Greek curses. "Don't talk like that. Damn it, you should have told me."

"Why?" she lashed out in uncharacteristic confrontation. "Do you think I enjoy telling you what a failure I am? It's not like you care. You just go back to work while

I sit there screaming inside." She struck a fist onto the surface of the water. "I hate it. I can't go on like this. I won't. *I want a divorce.*"

She splashed clumsily from the surf, her wet underpants see-through, her staggered steps so uncoordinated and indicative of her distress it made him want to reach out for her, but he was rooted in the water, aghast.

He cared. Maybe he'd never told her, but each lost baby had scored his heart. This one, knowing he could have walked into the penthouse and found both of them dead, lanced him with such deep horror he could barely acknowledge it.

*She* was the one who had appeared not to care. The fact she'd been so distraught she hadn't sought medical attention told him how far past the end of her rope she had been, but she'd never let him see any of that.

He followed her on heavy feet, pausing where they'd left their clothes.

She gave him a stark look, her gaze filling with apprehension as she took in that he was completely naked. Her fingers hurried to button her blouse.

Hell. He wasn't trying to come on to her.

"Adara." A throb of tender empathy caught in him like a barbed hook. He reached out to cup her neck, her hair a weight on his wrist.

She stiffened, but he didn't let her pull away. He carefully took her shoulder in his opposite hand and made her face him, for once driven by a need deeper than sexual to touch her.

"I'm sorry," he said with deep sincerity. "Sorry we lost another baby, sorry you felt you couldn't tell me. I do care. You've always been stoic about it and I've followed your lead. How could I know it was devastating you like this if you didn't say?"

She shivered despite the heat. Her blink released a single tear from the corner of her eye. Her plump mouth trembled with vulnerability, and a need to comfort overwhelmed him.

Gideon gathered her in. She seemed so delicate and breakable. He touched his mouth to hers, wanting to reassure, to console.

It wasn't meant to be a pass, but she felt so good. The kiss was a soft press of a juicy fruit to the mouth of a starved man. He couldn't help opening his lips on hers, sliding his tongue along the seam then pressing in for a deep lick of her personal flavor. Involuntarily, his arms tightened while greed swelled in him. Everything in him expanded in one hard kick. His erection pulled to attention in a rush of heat, fed by the erotically familiar scent of his wife.

The feathery touch of her hands whispered from his ribs to his shoulder blades. A needy sob emanated from her throat, encouraging him.

*Here. Now.* His brain shorted into the most basic thoughts as his carnal instincts took over. He skimmed his hand to the wet underpants covering her backside, starting to slide them down even as he deepened the kiss and began to ease them both to the sand.

Adara's knees softened for one heartbeat, almost succumbing, then she broke away from their kiss with a ragged moan, stumbling backward a few steps as she shoved from him with near violence. Her flush of arousal dissolved into a bewildered glare of accusation and betrayal.

That wounded look bludgeoned him like a club.

Without speaking, face white, she gathered her things and moved to the bottom of the rope where she tried to force her wet legs into her denim shorts.

Gideon pinched the bridge of his nose, ears rushing with the blood still pumping hotly through his system, deeply aware that the distance had been closed until he'd forgotten that he was trying to comfort, not seduce. But the sexual attraction between them was something he couldn't help. He wished he could. The fact that he couldn't entirely control his hunger for her bothered him no end.

His thoughts were dark as they returned to the hotel, a fresh sweat on his salted skin as they came through the front doors, with not a word exchanged since the beach. The life he'd created with Adara, so easy on the surface, had grown choppy, teaming with undercurrents. She'd stirred up more emotion in him with this bolt to Greece than he'd suffered in years and he didn't like it.

Part of him wanted to cut and run, but it was impossible now he understood what was driving her request for a divorce: grief. He understood that frame of mind better than she would suspect. He'd even bolted across the ocean in the very same way, more than once, but he was able to think more clearly this time. Losing the baby was heartrending, but he wasn't left alone. He still had her. They needed to stick together. With careful navigation, they'd be back on course and sailing smoothly. When she came out the other side, she'd appreciate that he hadn't let her do anything rash.

He hoped.

Adara blinked as they entered the artificial light of the hotel foyer. The temperature change hit her between the eyes like a blow. The boutique accommodation was the best the island offered, but nothing like the luxury service she took for granted in her thousand-room high-rise hotels. Still, she liked the coziness of this small, out-of-the-way place. She'd give serious thought to developing some hideaways like this herself, she decided.

Another time. Right now she felt like one giant blister, hot and raw, skin so thin she could be nicked open by the tiniest harsh word.

Desire had almost overwhelmed her on the beach. Gideon's kiss had been an oasis in a desert of too many empty days and untouched nights. His heartfelt words, the way he'd enfolded her as if he could make the whole world right again, had filled her with hope and relief. For a few seconds she had felt cherished, even when his kiss had turned from tenderness to hunger. It had all been balm to her injured soul, right up until he'd begun to tilt them to the sand.

Then fear of pregnancy had undercut her arousal. Her next instinct had been to at least give him pleasure. She *liked* making him lose control, but then she'd remembered *it wasn't good enough*.

It had all crashed into her as a busload of confusing emotions: shattered confidence, anger at her own weakness and a sense of being tricked and teased with a promise that would be broken. If she had had other men, perhaps she wouldn't be so susceptible to him, but she was a neophyte where men were concerned, even after five years of marriage. She needed distance from him, to get her head straightened out and her heart put back together.

Gideon was given a room card at the same time she was.

As they departed the front desk for the elevators, she said in a ferocious undertone, "You did not get yourself added to my room." They might share a suite, but never a room. She would *die*.

"I booked my own," he said stiffly, the reserve in his voice making her feel as if she'd done something wrong. She hadn't! Had she? Should she have been more open about the miscarriages?

She shook off guilt she didn't want to feel. "Gideon—" she began to protest.

"What? You're allowed a vacation, but I'm not?"

She tilted her head in disgruntlement. That was not what she was driving at. She wanted distance from him.

"Would you like to eat here tonight or try somewhere

else?" he said in a continuation of assumptions that were making her crazy.

"It's been a lot of travel getting here and already a long day. I'm going to shower and rest, possibly sleep through dinner," she asserted, silently thinking, *Go away*. Her feelings toward him were infinitely easier to bear when half a globe separated them.

"I'll email you when I get hungry then. If you're up, you can join me. If not, I won't disturb you."

She eyed him, suspicious of yet another display of ultra-consideration, especially when he walked her to her room. At the last second, he turned to insert his card in the door across from hers.

Her heart gave a nervous jump. So close. Immediately, a jangle went through her system, eagerness and fretfulness tying her into knots. She locked herself into her room, worried that he'd badger her into spending time with him that would roll into rolling around with him. She couldn't do it. She didn't have it in her to risk pregnancy and go through another miscarriage.

Even though she ached rather desperately to feel his strong, naked body moving over and into hers.

Craving and humiliation tormented her through her shower and stayed with her when she crawled into bed. She wanted him so much. It made her bury her head under her pillow. She couldn't live with a man she had no defenses against.

Steadfast to his word, Gideon didn't disturb her. Adara woke to fading light beyond her closed curtains, startled she'd fallen asleep at all, head fuzzy from a hard four-hour nap.

Like an adolescent desperate for a hint of being popular, she checked her email before rising from bed, scrolling past the work ones that were piling up and honing in on Gideon's.

Brief and veiled as all his communications tended to be, the message was nevertheless maddeningly effective at driving her into fresh clothes and across the hall.

Your brother called. Dinner?

# CHAPTER FOUR

ADARA WAS SO anxious, she blurted out her questions before Gideon fully opened his door. "What did he say? Is he coming here?"

The swipe of her tongue over her dry lips, however, was more to do with Gideon's bare chest beneath the open buttons of his white shirt than nerves at the thought of seeing her brother. Why had he brought those wretched jeans that were more white than blue, so old they clung to his hips and thighs like a second skin? No shoes either, she noted. The man was so unconsciously sexy she couldn't handle it. She'd never known how to handle it.

It didn't help that he looked at her like he could see into the depths of her soul. All that she'd told him today, the way he'd reacted, rushed back to strip her defenses down to the bare minimum.

"He won't be back to the island for a couple of days," he said, holding his door wider. "I had a table set on my balcony. They have our order, I only need to call down to let them know we're ready for it."

Adara folded her arms across the bodice of her crinkled white sundress, grossly uncomfortable as she watched him move to the hotel phone, his buttocks positively seductive in that devoted denim.

"I'd rather go down to the restaurant," she said, stomach fluttering as she struggled to assert herself.

"It's booked. And we can talk more privately here." He projected equanimity, but he sent her an assessing glance that warned her he wasn't one hundred percent pleased by this new argumentative Adara.

She swallowed, not at ease in this skin either, but she couldn't go on the old way. At the same time, she couldn't help wondering what had transpired in his conversation with her brother that they needed privacy. Nico lived here on the island, she reminded herself. It wouldn't be fair to bandy about his private business in public.

Out of consideration to him, she stepped cautiously into Gideon's room. The layout was a mirror of her executive room with a king-size bed, lounge area and workstation. Gideon had a better view, but she had taken what they had offered, not asking for upgrades. He, on the other hand, demanded the best.

Moving into the velvety night air of his balcony, she listened to him finalize their dinner then come up behind her to pour two glasses of wine. The sunset turned the golden liquid pink as he offered her a glass.

"To improved communication," he said, touching the rim of his glass to hers.

Adara couldn't resist a facetious "Really? And how long do you intend to make me wait to hear all that you and my brother said to each other?"

"I'll tell you now and you can leave before the meals arrive, if you're going to be so suspicious." He sounded insulted.

Adara pressed the curve of her glass to her flat mouth, a tiny bit ashamed of herself. She lowered the glass without wetting her lips. "You can't deny you used his call like some kind of bait-and-switch technique."

"Only because I genuinely want to salvage this marriage. We can't do that if we don't see each other." The sincerity in his gaze made her heart trip with an unsteady thump.

Why would he want to stay married? She was giving up on children. They both had enough money of their own without needing any of each other's. She tilted her glass, sipping the chilled wine that rolled across her tongue in a tart, cool wave that... *Bleh.* An acrid stain coated her mouth.

*Stress,* she thought. Rather than being someone who drank her troubles away, she avoided alcohol when she was keyed up. The way her mother had drowned in booze, and the cruelty it had brought out in her father, had always kept Adara cautious of the stuff. Her body was telling her this was one of those times she should leave it alone.

Setting her glass on the table, she leaned her elbows on the balcony railing and said, "Would you please tell me what happened with Nico?"

"He called asking for us. The front desk tried my room first and I told him you were resting."

"How did he even know we were here?" she asked with surprise.

"Ah. Now, *that's* amusing." He didn't sound amused. He turned his back on the sunset and his cheeks hollowed as he contemplated some scowl-inducing inner thought. "I assumed he had a crack security team, but he has something far more sophisticated—an island grapevine. You didn't tell the gardener you were related to him, so a strange woman asking about him set off speculation, enough that he got a call from a well-meaning neighbor and logged in to his gate camera. He recognized you and I guess he's kept tabs on you over the years, too, because he knew your married name. The island only has four hotels, so it was quick work to track us to this one. He invited us to stay at his villa until he gets home."

"Really?" Adara rotated to Gideon like a flower to the sun, buoyed by what Nico's interest and invitation represented. *He wanted to see her.*

A thought occurred, making her clench her hand on the railing. Gideon was a very private person who kept himself removed from all but the most formal of social contact. He wouldn't want to stay in a stranger's house full of unfamiliar staff.

An excruciating pang of loss ambushed her. She would have to continue her journey alone, her request for independence and divorce granted even as her husband's desire for reconciliation hung in the air. As cavalier as she wanted to be about leaving him, it wasn't painless or easy. Her heart started to shrivel as she looked to the emptiness that was her future.

"I told him I would leave it up to you to decide," Gideon continued. "But that I expected we'd move over there tomorrow because you're eager to renew ties." He took another healthy draw from his wine.

Adara blinked, shocked that Gideon would make such a concession. It made everything he said about salvaging their marriage earnest and powerful.

"You said that?" She reached out instinctively, setting her free hand on his sleeve so he would look at her, then feeling awkward when he only stared at her narrow hand on his tense forearm. She pulled her hand away. "I didn't expect you to understand."

"I'm not an idiot. I've got the message that there's more going on than you've let me see." Now his gaze came up and his dark-chocolate irises were intensely black in the fading light. "I want you to quit keeping so much to yourself, Adara."

Longing speared into her, but so did fear. The words *I can't* lodged in her throat. She never shared, never asked for help. She didn't know how.

A knock at the door heralded room service. Gideon moved to let the server in and stood back as the meals were set out. Gideon's knowledge of her tastes and his desire to please were well at the forefront. He'd ordered prawn soup, fried calamari, and baked fish fillets on rice with eggplant. Delicious scents of scorched ouzo and tangy mint made her mouth water. Their climb to the beach, coupled with the time change, had her stomach trying to eat itself. Much as she knew it would be better not to encourage either of them that their marriage had a chance, she couldn't help sinking into the chair he held.

Winking lights bobbed on the water, live music drifted from the restaurant below and the warm evening air stroked her skin with a sensual breeze. The server closed the door on his way out and the big bed stood with inviting significance just inside the room.

And then there was the man, still barefoot, still with his shirt hanging open off his shoulders, the pattern of hair across his chest and abdomen accentuating his firm pecs and six-pack stomach. How he managed casual elegance with such a disreputable outfit, she didn't know, but the woman in her not only responded, but melted into a puddle of sexual craving.

She was in very real danger of being seduced by nothing more than his presence.

Frightened of herself, she stole a furtive glance into his face and found him watching her closely, not smug, but his gaze was sharp with awareness that she was reacting to him. Her cheeks heated with embarrassment at not being able to help this interminable attraction to him.

Gideon couldn't remember ever being so tuned to a woman, not out of bed anyway, and even at that he and Adara had fallen into certain patterns. Now that he was beginning to see how much she disguised behind a placid expression or level tone, he was determined to pick up every cue. The fact he'd just caught her lusting after him in her reserved way pleased him intensely, but her reluctance to let nature take its course confused him.

"I've been faithful to you, Adara. I hope you believe that."

She stopped chewing for a thoughtful moment. Her brows came together in a frown he couldn't interpret. Worry? Misery? Defeat?

"I do," she finally said, but her tone seemed to qualify the statement.

"But?" he prompted.

"It doesn't change the fact that one of the major reasons we married…" Her brows pulled again and this time it was pure pain, like something deeply embedded was being wrenched out of her.

He tensed, knowing what was coming and not liking the way it penetrated his walls either.

"Obviously I'm not able to give you children," she said with strained composure. "I won't even try. Not anymore."

The bitter acceptance he read beneath her mask of self-possession, her trounced distress, was so tangible, he reached across to cover her shaking hand where she gripped her knife. Her knuckles felt sharp as barnacles where they poked against his palm.

He would give anything to spare her this anguish.

"Having children was a condition that came from your side of the table. It's not a deal-breaker for me," he reassured her.

If anything, she grew more distraught. "You never wanted children?"

*Tread lightly,* he cautioned himself, touching a thoughtful tongue to his bottom lip. "It's not that I never wanted them. If that were true, I'd be a real monster for putting you through all you've suffered in trying to have one. I'm very—" *Disappointed* wasn't a strong enough word.

"I'm sad," he admitted, drawing his hand back as he took the uncharacteristic step of admitting to feelings. He'd been powerless at sea in a storm once and hadn't felt as helpless and vulnerable as he had each time she'd miscarried. This one he'd learned about today was the worst yet, filling him with visions of coming upon her dead. It was too horrifying a thing to happen to a person even once in a lifetime and he'd been through it twice already. He couldn't stomach thinking of finding her lifeless and white.

Then there was the bereft sense of loss that he'd known nothing about the baby before it was gone. He hated having no control over the situation, hated being unable to give her something she wanted that seemed as if it should be so simple. He hated how the whole thing stirred up old grief. He ought to be over forming deep attachments. He'd certainly fought against developing any. But he wished he'd known those babies and felt cheated that he hadn't been given the chance.

He swiped his clammy palm down his thigh.

"I'm sad, too," she whispered thickly, gaze fixed on her sweating glass of ice water. "I wanted a family. A real one, not a broken one like I had."

"So, it wasn't just pressure from your father to give him the heir your brothers weren't providing?"

She made a motion of negation, mouth pouted into sorrow.

*Damn,* he swore silently, thinking his version of her as merely ticking *children* off the list with everything else would have been so much easier to navigate.

"I thought you were like my father, not really wanting a family, but determined to have an heir. A boy." *Of course,* her tiny shrug added silently.

He could see wary shadows in her eyes as she confessed what had been in her mind. She wasn't any more comfortable with being honest than he was. He sure as hell didn't enjoy hearing her unflattering assessment of his attitude toward progeny.

"I wasn't taking it that lightly," he said, voice so tight she tensed. "But I didn't know how much it meant to you."

Any other time in his life he would have swiftly put an end to such a deeply personal conversation, but right now, unpleasant as it was, he had to allow Adara to see she wasn't the only one hurt by this. She wasn't the only one with misconceptions.

"I never knew my father, so that gave me certain reservations about what kind of parent I'd make. You're not anything like my mother, which is a very good thing in most ways, but she did have a strong maternal instinct. I never saw you take an interest in other people's children. Your family isn't the warmest. Frankly, I expected you to schedule a C-section, hire a nanny and mark that task 'done.'"

He'd seen this look on Adara's face before, after a particularly offside, cutting remark from her father. Her lashes swept down, her brow tensed and her nostrils pinched ever so slightly with a slow, indrawn breath. He'd always assumed she was gathering her patience, but today he saw it differently. She was absorbing a blow.

One that he had delivered. His heart clutched in his chest. *Don't put me in the same category as that man.*

"I'm just telling you how it looked, Adara." His voice was gruff enough to make her flinch.

"Like you're some kind of open book, letting me see your thoughts and feelings?" She pushed her plate away with hands that trembled. "I've told you more about myself today than I've ever shared with anyone and all I've heard back is that you're sad I miscarried. Well, I should damn well hope so! They were your babies too."

She rose and tried to escape, but he was faster, his haste sending his chair tumbling with a clatter, his hands too rough on her when he pulled her to stand in front of him, but her challenge made him slip the leash on his control.

"What do you want me to say? That I hadn't believed

in God for years, but when I took you to the hospital that first time, I gave praying a shot and felt completely betrayed when He took that baby anyway? That I got drunk so I wouldn't cry? *Every time.* Damn it, I haven't been able to close my eyes since the beach without imagining walking into your bathroom and finding you dead in a pool of blood." He gave her a little shake. "Is that the kind of sharing you need to hear?"

Her shattered gaze was more than he could bear, the searching light in them pouring over his very soul, picking out every flaw and secret he hid from the rest of the world. It was painful in the extreme and even though he would never want to inflict more suffering on her, he was relieved when she crumpled with anguish and buried her face in her hands.

He pulled her into his chest, the feel of her fragile curves a pleasure-pain sting. She stiffened as he pinned her to him, but he only dug his fingers into her loose hair, massaging her scalp and pressing his lips to her crown, forcing the embrace because he needed it as much as she did.

"It's okay, I'm not going to mess it up this time." His body was reacting to her scent and softness, always did, but he ignored it and hoped she would too. "I'm sorry we keep losing babies, Adara. I'm sorry I didn't let you see it affects me."

"I can't try anymore, Gideon." Her voice was small and thick with finality, buried in his chest.

"I know." He rubbed his chin on the silk of her hair, distantly aware how odd this was to hold her like this, not as a prelude to sex, not because they were dancing, but to reassure her. "I don't expect you to try. That's what I'm saying. We don't have to divorce over this. We can stay married."

She lifted her face, her expression devastated beyond tears, and murmured a baffled "I don't even know why you want to."

Under her searching gaze, his inner defenses instinctively locked into place. Practicalities and hard facts leaped to his lips, covering up deeper, less understood motivations. "We're five years into merging our fortunes," he pointed out.

Adara dropped her chin and gathered herself, pressing for freedom.

His answer hadn't been good enough.

His muscles flexed, reluctant to let her go, but he had to. *Feelings,* he thought, and scowled with displeasure. What was she looking for? A declaration of love? That had never been part of their bargain and it wasn't a step he was willing to take. Losing babies he hadn't known was bad enough. Caring deeply for Adara would make him too vulnerable.

He reached to right his chair, nodding at her seat when she only watched him. "Sit down, let's keep talking about this."

"What's the point?" she asked despairingly.

The coward in him wanted to agree and let this madness blow away like dead ashes from a fire. If he were a gentleman, he supposed he'd spare her this torturous raking of nearly extinguished coals. Something deeply internal and indefinable pushed him to forge ahead despite how unpleasant it was. Somehow, giving up looked bleaker than this.

"You don't salvage an agreement by walking away. You stay in the same room and hammer it out," he managed to say.

"What is there to salvage?" Adara charged with a pained throb in her voice. Her heart was lodged behind her collarbone like a sharp rock. Didn't he understand? Everything she'd brought to the table was gone.

Gideon only nodded at her chair, his expression shuttered yet insistent.

Adara dropped into her chair out of emotional exhaustion. For a few seconds she just sat there with her hands steepled before her face, eyes closed, drowning in despair.

"What do you *want,* Adara?"

She opened her eyes to find him statue hard across from her, expression unreceptive despite his demand she confide.

He was afraid it was something he couldn't give, she realized. Like love?

A barbed clamp snapped hard around her heart. She wasn't brave enough to give up that particular organ and had never fooled herself into dreaming a man could love her back, so no, she wouldn't ask him for love. She settled on part of the truth.

"I want to quit feeling so useless," she confessed, suffering the sensation of being stripped naked by the admission. "I'm predisposed to insecurity because of my upbringing, I know that. I'm not worthless, but I feel that way in this marriage. Now I can't even bring children into it. I can't live with this feeling of inadequacy, Gideon."

He stared hard at her for a long moment before letting out a snort of soul-crushing amusement.

Adara couldn't help her sharp exhale as she absorbed that strike. She tried to rise.

Gideon clamped his hand on her arm. "No. Listen. God, Adara…" He shook his head in bemusement, brow furrowed with frustration. "When you asked me to marry you—"

"Oh, don't!" she gasped, feeling her face flood with abashed color.

He tightened his grip on her wrist, keeping her at the table. "Why does that embarrass you? It's the truth. You came to me with the offer."

"I *know.* Which only reminds me how pathetically desperate I must have seemed. You didn't want me and wouldn't have chosen me if I hadn't more or less bribed you."

"Desperate?" he repeated with disbelief. "I was the desperate one, coming hat in hand to your father with a proposition I knew he'd laugh out of the room. All I had going for me was nerve."

"Someone else would have taken up the chance to invest with you, Gideon. It was a sound opportunity, which Papa saw after he got over being stubborn and shortsighted."

"After you worked on him."

She shook that off in a dismissive shrug, instantly self-conscious of the way she'd stood up for a man she'd barely known simply because she'd been intrigued by him. It had been quite a balancing act, truth be told.

"Don't pretend you didn't have anything to do with it." He sat forward. "Because this is what I'm trying to tell you. You came to me with things I didn't have. Your father's partnership. Entrée into the tightest and most influential Greek cartels in New York and Athens. I needed that, I wanted it, and I had no real belief I could actually get it."

"Well, I didn't have much else to offer, did I?" she pointed out in a remembered sense of inadequacy.

"Your virginity springs to mind, but we'll revisit that another time," he rasped, making her lock her gaze with his in shocked incredulity.

Suddenly, very involuntarily, she flashed back to her wedding night and the feel of his fingers touching her intimately, his mouth roaming from her lips to her neck to her breast and back as he teased her into wanting an even thicker penetration. She hadn't understood how his incredibly hard thrust could hurt and feel so good at the same time. Instead of being intimidated by his strength and weight, she'd basked in the sense of belonging as his solid presence moved above her, on her, and within her so smoothly, bringing such a fine tension into every cell of her being. His hard arms had surrounded and braced her, yet shielded her from all harm, making her feel safer than she'd ever felt in her life, so that when she'd shattered, she'd known he'd catch her.

Her body clenched in remembered ecstasy even as she was distantly aware of his hold on her gentling. He caressed her bare forearm and his voice lowered to the smoky tone he'd used when he'd told her how lovely she'd felt to him then. *So hot and sweet. So good.*

"Try to understand what it meant for me to form a connection to you."

Her scattered faculties couldn't tell if he was talking about her deflowering or the marriage in general. She shivered with latent arousal, pulling herself away from his touch to ground herself in the now.

"People knew I came from nothing," he said. "You want to know why I only speak Greek when I absolutely have to? Because my accent gives me away as the bottom class sailor that I am."

"It does not," she protested distractedly.

He reached to tuck a tendril of hair behind her ear, his touch lingering to trace lightly beneath her jaw. "If you want me to talk, you're going to have to listen. People respect you, Adara. Not because your father owned the company, not because of your wealth, but because of the way you conduct yourself. Everyone knew your father's faults and could see that you were above his habits of lashing out and making hasty decisions. They knew you were intelligent and fair and had influence with him."

"Now I know you're lying." She drew back, out of his reach.

"He didn't sway easily, that's true." He dropped his hands to his thighs. "But if anyone could change his mind, it was you. Everyone knew that, from the chambermaids to the suits in the boardroom. And people also knew that you were being very choosy about finding a husband. *Very* choosy."

He sat back, his demeanor solidifying into the man who headed so many boardroom tables, sharp and firm. Not someone you argued with.

"I didn't appreciate what that choosiness meant until I was by your side and suddenly I was being looked at like I had superpowers because you'd picked me. Maybe it sounds weak to say my ego needed that, but it did. I went from being an upstart no one trusted to a legitimate business-man. I had had some success before I met you, but once I married you, *I* had self-worth because *you* gave it to me."

"But—" Her heart moved into her throat. She wanted to believe him, her inner being urgently needed to believe him, but it was so far from the way she perceived herself. "You're exaggerating."

"No, I'm telling you why I'm fighting to keep you."

"But people respect you. That won't go away if we di-vorce."

"*Now* they respect me. And perhaps that wouldn't go away overnight, although I can guarantee I'd be painted the villain if we split. People would pin the blame on me because you're nice and I'm not, but I'm not saying I want to stay married so I can continue using this knighthood you've unconsciously bestowed on me. It comes down to loyalty and gratitude and my own self-respect. I *like* being your husband. I want to keep the position."

"It's not a job." She'd tried to treat Husband and Wife like spots on an organizational chart and it wasn't that sim-ple. Having a gorgeous body in a tux to escort her to fund-raisers wasn't enough. She needed someone she could call when her world was crashing in on her and she thought she was dying.

That unexpected thought disturbed her. She had learned very young to guard her feelings, never show her loneliness, be self-sufficient and never, ever imagine her needs were important enough to be met. Wanting to rely on Gideon was a foreign concept, but it was there.

Gideon was watching her like a cat, ready to react, but what would he have done if he'd come home to find her sobbing her heart out? He'd have tried to ship her into the sterile care of stiff beds and objectifying instruments.

And yet, if she had found the courage to ask, would he have stayed with her and held her hand at the hospital? Would it have made a difference if he had?

It would have made a huge difference.

Deeply conflicted, she pushed back her chair, fingers knotting into the napkin on her lap. She didn't like feeling so tempted to try when there were so many other things wrong between them. "You make it sound so easy and it's not, Gideon."

"We have a few days before your brother shows up," he cut in with quick assertion. A muscle pulsed in his jaw. "I've cleared my schedule to the end of the week. We'll spend time together and set a new course. Turn this ship around."

She wanted to quirk a smile at the shipbuilder's oh-so-typical nautical reference, but her system was flooded with adrenaline, filling her with caution.

"What if—" She stopped herself, not wanting to admit she was terrified that spending time with him would increase her feelings for him. He was trying to make her feel special and it was working, softening her toward him. That scared her. If she knew anything about her husband, and she didn't know nearly enough, she knew he wasn't the least bit sentimental. She could develop feelings for him, but they'd never be returned.

What was his real reason for wanting to stay married?

"Look how much we've weathered and worked through since this morning," he reasoned with quiet persistence, showcasing exactly how he'd pushed a struggling shipyard into a dominant global enterprise in less than a decade. "We can make this marriage work for us, Adara. Give me a few days to prove it."

Days that were going to be excruciating even without a replay of today.

Nerves accosted her each time she thought of seeing Nico again and in the end, her consideration of Gideon's demand sprang from that. She would prefer to have him with her when she met Nico again. She couldn't explain it, but so many things, from social events to family dinners, were easier to face when Gideon was with her. She'd always felt that little bit more safe and confident when he was beside her, as if he had her back.

"You'd really move over to my brother's house with me?" she asked tentatively.

"Of course."

There was no "of course" about it. He showed up for the events in his calendar because it was their deal, not because he wanted to be there for her.

At least, that was her perception, but she hadn't really asked for anything more than that, had she? He'd offered to come to the hospital each time she'd told him about another miscarriage. She was the one who'd rebuffed the suggestion, hiding her feelings, not only holding him at a distance but pushing him away, too fearful of being vulnerable to even try to rely on him.

Which hadn't made her less vulnerable, just more bereft.

She couldn't stomach feeling that isolated again, not when she had so much of herself on the line. Still, she wasn't sure how to open herself up to help either.

"If you really want to, then okay. That's fine. But no guarantees," she cautioned. "I'm not making any promises."

He flinched slightly, but nodded in cool acceptance of her terms.

# CHAPTER FIVE

GIDEON WAS A bastard, in the old-fashioned sense of the word and quite openly in the contemporary sense. When he wanted something, he found a way to get it. He wasn't always fair about it. His "bastard" moniker was even, at times, prefaced with words like *ruthless, self-serving,* and *heartless.*

When it came to other men trying to exercise power over him, he absolutely was all of those things. He fought dirty when he had to and without compunction.

He had a functioning conscience, however, especially when it came to women and kids. When it came to his wife, he was completely sincere in wanting to protect her in every way.

Except if it meant shielding her from himself. When Adara's brother, "Nic," he had called himself, had invited them to take a room at his house, that was exactly what Gideon had heard. *A room. One* bed.

Normally he would never take up such an offer. Given the unsavory elements in his background, he kept to himself whenever possible. He liked his privacy and was also a man who liked his own personal space. Even at home in New York, he and Adara slept in separate beds in separate bedrooms. He visited hers; she never came to his. When she rose to shower after their lovemaking, he took his cue and left.

That had always grated, the way she disappeared before the sweat had dried on his skin, but it was the price of autonomy so he paid it.

*Had* paid it. He was becoming damn restless for entry into the space Adara occupied—willing to do whatever it took to invade it, even put himself into the inferior position of accepting a favor from a stranger.

Irritated by these unwanted adjustments to his rigidly organized life, he listened with half an ear to the vineyard manager's wife babble about housekeepers on vacation and stocked refrigerators, trying not to betray his impatience for her to get the hell out and leave them alone.

The nervous woman insisted on orienting them in the house, which looked from the outside like an Old English rabbit warren. Once inside, however, the floor plan opened up. Half the interior walls had been knocked out, some had been left as archways and pony walls, and the exterior ones along the back had been replaced by floor-to-ceiling windows. The remodeling, skilled as it was, was obvious to Gideon's sharp eye, but he approved. The revised floor plan let the stunning view of grounds, beach and sea become the wallpaper for the airy main-floor living space.

"The code for the guest wireless is on the desk in here," the woman prattled on as she led them up the stairs and pressed open a pair of double doors.

Gideon glanced into a modern office of sleek equipment, comfortable workspaces and a stylish, old-fashioned wet bar. A frosted crest was subtly carved into the mirrored wall behind it. In the back of his mind, he heard again the male voice identifying himself when he had called the hotel, the modulated voice vaguely familiar.

*It's Nic...Makricosta. I'm looking for my sister, Adara.* Gideon had put the tiny hesitation down to anything from nerves to distraction.

Now, as he recognized the crest, he put two and two together and came up with C-4 explosive. A curse escaped him.

Both women turned startled gazes to where he lingered in the office doorway.

"You told me your brother had changed his name. I didn't realize to what," Gideon said, trying for dry and wry, but his throat had become a wasteland in the face of serious danger to his invented identity.

"Oh," Adara said with ingenuous humor. "I didn't realize I never…" A tiny smile of sheepish pride crept across her lips. "He's kind of a big deal, isn't he? It's one of the reasons I hesitated to get in touch. I thought he might dismiss me as a crackpot, or as someone trying to get money out of him."

*Kind of a big deal?* Nicodemus Marcussen was the owner and president of the world's largest media empire, not to mention a celebrated journalist in his own right. His work these days tended toward in-depth analysis of third-world coup d'état stuff, but he was no stranger to political exposés and other investigative reporting in print or on camera. Running a background check would be something he did between pouring his morning coffee and taking his first sip.

Gideon reassured himself Nic had no reason to do it, but tension still crawled though him as they continued their tour.

"My number is on the speed dial," the woman said to Adara. "Please call if you need anything. The Kyrios was most emphatic that you be looked after. He's hurrying his business in Athens as best he can, but it will be a couple of days before he's able to join you." She made the statement as she led them into a regal guest room brimming with fresh flowers, wine, a fruit basket, a private balcony with cushioned wicker furniture and a massive sleigh bed with a puffy white cover. "I trust you'll be comfortable?"

Gideon watched Adara count the number of beds in the room and become almost as pale as the pristine quilt. She looked to him, clearly expecting him to ask for a second room. Any day previous to this one he would have, without hesitation. Today he remained stubbornly silent.

Color crept under her skin as the silence stretched and she realized if anyone made an alteration to these arrangements, it would have to be her. He watched subtle, uncomfortable tension invade her posture and almost willed her to do it. He wanted to share her bed, but he suddenly saw exactly how hard it was for her to stand up for herself.

She gave a jerky little smile at the woman and said, "It's fine, thank you," and Gideon felt a pang of disappointment directed at himself. He should have made this easy for her. *But he didn't want to.*

The woman left. As the distant sound of the front door closing echoed through the quiet house, Adara looked to him as if he'd let her down.

"Do we just take another room?" A white line outlined her pursed mouth.

"Why would we need to?" he challenged lightly.

"We're not sharing a bed, Gideon." Hard and implacable, not like her at all.

"Why not?" he asked with a matching belligerence, exactly like himself because this issue was riling him right down to the cells at the very center of his being.

Her gaze became wild-eyed and full of angry anxiety. "Have you listened to me at all in the last twenty-four hours? *I don't want to get pregnant!*"

"People have felt that way for centuries. That's why they invented condoms," he retorted with equal ire. "I bought some before we left the hotel. Do you have an allergy to latex that I don't know about?"

She took a step back, her anger falling away so completely it took him aback. "I didn't think of that." Her brows came together in consternation. "You really wouldn't mind wearing one?"

He stood there flummoxed, utterly amazed. "You really didn't think of asking me to use them?"

"Well, you never have the whole time we've been married. I wasn't with anyone else before you. They're not exactly on my radar." She gave a defensive shrug of her shoulders, averting her gaze while a flush of embarrassment stained her cheekbones.

*Innocent,* he thought, and was reminded of another time when they'd stood in a bedroom, her nervous tension palpable while he was drowning in sexual hunger.

Anticipation was like a bed of nails in his back, pushing him toward her. On that first occasion, she had worn a blush-pink negligee and a cloak of reserve he'd enjoyed peeling away very, very slowly.

*Don't screw this up,* he'd told himself then, and reiterated it to himself today. The first night of their marriage, he'd had one chance to get their intimate relationship off on the right foot. He had one chance to press the reset button now.

The primal mate in him wanted to move across the room, kiss her into receptiveness and fall on the bed in a familiar act of simple, much-needed release.

But it wouldn't be enough. He saw it in the way her lashes flicked to his expression and she read the direction of his thoughts. Rather than coloring in the pretty way he so enjoyed watching when he suggested a visit to her room, she paled a little and her lips trembled before she bit them together.

"You don't…" Licking her lips, she looked to him with huge eyes that nearly brimmed with defensiveness. "You don't expect me to fall into bed with you just because you've got a condom, do you?"

Expect it? The animal in him howled, *Yes.*

"It's always been good, hasn't it?" He bit out the words, perhaps a little too confrontational, but his confidence was unexpectedly deserting him.

She crossed her arms, shoulders so tight he thought she'd snap herself in half. "It's always been fine."

"Fine?" he charged, gutted by the faint praise.

She sent him a helpless look that made him feel like a bully.

"I can hardly deny that I've enjoyed it, can I?" she said, but the undertone of something like embarrassment or shame stole all the excitement he might have felt if she'd said it another way. "I just…"

"Don't trust me." He ground out the words with realization. It was an unexpectedly harsh blow. "Come on," he said, holding out his hand before he lost what was left of his fraying self-control.

She stilled with guardedness. "What? Where?"

"Anywhere but this room or I'll be all over you and you're obviously not ready for that."

A funny little frisson went through Adara as she took in the rugged, intimidating presence that was her husband. He held out a commanding hand, as imperious and inscrutable as ever, but his words had an undercurrent of…was it compassion?

Whatever it was, it did things to her, softening her, but it scared her at the same time. She was already too susceptible to him.

And his desire for her was a seduction in itself. Her insecurity as a woman had been ramped to maximum with everything that had happened, but things had shifted in the last twenty-four hours. She was looking at him, hearing him. His sexual hunger wasn't an act. She knew the signs of interest and excitement in him. His chiseled features were tense with focus. A light flush stained his cheekbones—almost a flag of temper if not for the line of his mouth softened into a hungry, feral near smile.

Her body responded the way it always did, skin prickling with a yearning to be stroked, breasts tightening, loins clenching in longing for him.

Oh, God. If she stayed in this room, she'd *beg* him to be all over her, and where would that lead beyond a great orgasm? She didn't know what sort of relationship she wanted with Gideon, but knew unequivocally she couldn't go back to great sex and nothing else.

She moved to the door, not expecting him to fall in beside her and take her hand. A *zing* of excitement went through her as he enveloped her narrow fingers in his strong grasp. Stark defenselessness flared and she wanted to pull herself away. Why?

"It's not that I distrust you," she said, trying to convince herself as much as him while they walked down the stairs, her hand like a disembodied limb she was so aware of it in his. "I know you'd never hurt me. You can be stubborn and bossy, but you're not cruel." It still felt strange to speak her mind so openly, increasing her sense of vulnerability and risk. Her heart tremored.

"But you don't trust me with who you *are*," he goaded lightly.

Her hand betrayed her, wriggling self-consciously in his firm grip. He eyed her knowingly as he reached with his free hand to slide open the glass door on the back of the house.

An outdoor kitchen was tucked to the side of a lounge area. A free-form pool glittered a few steps away, half in the sun, the rest in the shadow of the house. The paving stones dwindled past it to a meandering path down the lawn to the beach. The grounds were bordered on one side by the vineyard and by an orange grove on the other.

"Swim?" he suggested as they stood at the edge of the pool staring into the hypnotic stillness of the turquoise water.

Working up her courage, she asked softly, "Do you trust *me,* Gideon?"

His hold on her loosened slightly and his mouth twitched with dismay. "I don't wholly trust anyone," he admitted gruffly. "It's not because I don't think you're trustworthy. It's me. The way I'm made."

"The "it's not you, it's me" brush-off. There's a firm foundation." Disgruntled, she would have walked away, but he tightened his hold on her hand and followed her into the sunshine toward the orange grove.

"Would it help to know that I've been more open with you than I've been with anyone else in my life? Ever? Perhaps you learned to keep your feelings to yourself because you were afraid of how your father would react, but after my mother died, no one responded to what I wanted or needed. Even when she was alive, she was hardly there. Not her fault, but I've had to be completely self-sufficient most of my life. It shocks me every time you appear to genuinely care what I'm thinking or feeling."

The sheer lonesomeness of what he was saying gouged a furrow into her heart. She might have a stilted relationship with her younger brothers, but they would be there if she absolutely needed them. She unconsciously tightened her hand on his and saw a subtle shift in his stony expression, as if her instinctive need to comfort him had the opposite effect, making him uncomfortable.

"You never talk about your mom. She was a single mother? Constantly working to make ends meet?"

His face became marble hard. "A child. I have a memory of asking her how old she was and she said twenty-one.

That doesn't penetrate when you're young. It sounds ancient, but if I can remember it, I was probably five or six, which puts her pregnant at fifteen or sixteen. I suspect she was a runaway, but I've never tried to investigate. I don't think I'd like any of the answers."

She understood. At best, his mother might have been shunned by her family for a teen pregnancy, forcing her to leave her home; at worst, he could be the product of rape.

A little chill went through her before she asked, "What happened after you lost her? Where did you go?"

His mouth pressed tight.

Her heart fell. This was one of those times he wouldn't answer.

He surprised her by saying gruffly, "There was a sailor who was decent to me."

"A kindly old salt?" she asked, starting to smile.

"The furthest thing from it. My palms would be wet with broken blisters and all he'd say was, 'There's no room for crybabies on a ship,' and send me back to work."

She gasped in horror, checking her footstep to pause and look at him.

He shook his head at her concern. "It's true. It wasn't a cruise liner. If you're not crew, you're cargo and cargo has to pay. If he hadn't pushed me, I wouldn't be where I am today. He taught me the ropes—that's not a pun. Everything from casting off to switching out the bilge pump. He taught me how to hang on to my money, not drink or gamble it away. Even how to fight. Solid life skills."

"Does he know where you are today? What you've made of yourself?"

"No." His stoic expression flinched and his tone went flat. "He died. He was mugged on a dock for twenty American dollars. Stabbed and left to bleed to death. I came back too late to help him."

"Oh, Gideon." She wanted to bring his hand to her aching heart. Of course he was reticent and hard-edged with that sort of pain in his background. Questions bubbled in her mind. How old had he been? What had he done next?

She bit back pressing him. Baby steps, she reminded herself, but baby steps toward what? Their marriage was broken because *they* were broken.

She frowned. The future they'd mapped out with such simplistic determination five years ago had mostly gone according to plan. When it came to goal achievement in a materialistic sense, they were an unstoppable force. A really great team.

But what use was a mansion if no patter of tiny feet filled it? Without her father goading for expansion, she was content to slow the pace and concentrate on fine-tuning what they had.

She wasn't sure what she wanted from her marriage, only knew she couldn't be what Gideon seemed to expect her to be.

Where could they go from here?

The sweet scent of orange blossoms coated the air as they wandered in silence between the rows of trees. Gideon lazily reached up to steal a flower from a branch and brought it to his nose. A bemused smile tugged at his lips.

"Your hair smelled like this on our wedding night."

Adara's abdomen contracted in a purely sensual kick of anticipation, stunning her with the wash of acute hunger his single statement provoked. She swallowed, trying to hide how such a little thing as him recalling that could affect her so deeply.

"I wore a crown of them," she said, trying to sound light and unaffected.

"I remember." He looked at her in a way that swelled the words with meaning, even though she wasn't sure what the meaning was.

A flood of pleasure and self-consciousness brimmed up in her.

"That almost sounds sentimental, but the night can only be memorable for how awkward I was," she dismissed, accosted anew by embarrassment at how gauche and inexperienced she'd been.

"Nervous," he corrected. "As nervous as you are now." He halted her and stood in front of her to drift the petal of the flower down her cheek, leaving a tickling, perfumed path. "So was I."

"I'm sure," she scoffed, lips coming alive under the feathery stroke of the blossom. She licked the sensation away. "What are you doing?"

"Seducing you. It'd be nice if you noticed."

She might have smiled, but he distracted her by brushing the flower under her chin. She lifted to escape the disturbing tickle and he stole a kiss.

It was a tender press of his mouth over hers, not demanding and possessive as she'd come to expect from him. This was more like those first kisses they'd shared a lifetime ago, during their short engagement. Brief and exploratory. Patient.

Sweet but frustrating. She was too schooled in how delicious it was to give in to passion to go back to chaste premarital nuzzling.

He drew back and looked into her eyes through a hooded gaze. "I remember every single thing about that night. How soft your skin was." The blossom dropped away as he stroked the back of his bent fingers down her cheek and into the crook of her neck. His gaze went lower and his hand followed. "I remember how I had to learn to be careful with your nipples because they're so sensitive."

They were. Sensitive and responsive. Tightening now so they poked against the dual layers of bra and shirt, standing out visibly and seeming to throb as he lightly traced a finger around the point of one. A whimper of hungry distress escaped her.

"I remember that most especially." The timbre of his voice became very low and intense. "The little noises of pleasure you made that got me so hot because it meant you liked what I was doing to you. I almost lost it the first time you came. Then you fell apart again when I was inside you and you were so tight—"

"Gideon, stop!" She grasped the hand that had drifted to the button at the waistband of her shorts. Her lungs felt as if all the air in them had evaporated and a distinctive throb pulsed between her thighs.

"I don't want to stop," he growled with masculine ferocity. "The only thing hotter than our first time together has been every time since."

She wanted to believe that, but yesterday…

Gideon watched Adara withdraw and knew he was losing her. He'd come on too strong, but hunger for her was like a wolf in him, snapping and predatory from starvation.

"What's wrong?" he demanded, then swore silently at himself when he saw that his roughened tone made her flinch. He wasn't enjoying these heart-to-hearts any more than she was, but they were necessary. He accepted that, but it was hard. He was the type to attack, not expose his throat.

Adara flicked him a wary glance and stepped back, arms crossing her chest in the way he was beginning to hate because it shut him out so effectively. She chewed her bottom lip for a few seconds before cutting him another careful glance.

"Yesterday you said… Maybe I'm being oversensitive, but what you said when we were swimming really hurt, Gideon. About me not being good enough. I *try* to give you as much pleasure as you give me—"

He cut her off with a string of Greek epithets that should have curled the leaves off the surrounding trees. "Yesterday was a completely different era in this relationship. What I said—" The chill of frustration gripped his vital organs. How could he explain that his appetite for her went beyond what even seemed human? He understood now why she'd confined their relations to oral sex, but it didn't change the fact that he ached constantly for release inside her. "I felt managed, Adara. I don't say that with blame. I'm only telling you how it seemed from what I knew then. I want you. Not other women. Not tarts like Lexi. *You.* Having you hold yourself back from me made me nuts. I need you to be as caught up as I am. To want me. It's the only way I can cope with how intense my need for you is."

She blinked at him in shock.

He rubbed a hand down his face, wishing he could wipe away his blurted confession. "If that scares the hell out of you, then I'm sorry. I probably shouldn't have told you."

"No," she breathed, head shaking in befuddlement. "But I find it hard to believe you feel like that. I'm not a siren. You're the one with all the experience, the one who thinks about using condoms because you've used them before."

"Yes, I have," he said with forcible bluntness, not liking how defensive he felt for having a sexual history when she'd come to him pristine and pure. "But you know when the last time I used one was? The night before we met. I don't remember much about the woman I was dating then, only that the next evening she left me because I asked her if she knew anything about you. Pretty crass, I know. I couldn't stop thinking about you."

Her searching gaze made him extremely uncomfortable. He jerked his chin.

"Let's keep walking."

"And talking? Because it's such fun?" Adara bent to retrieve the blossom he'd dropped and twirled it beneath her nose as they continued deeper into the orange grove. His revelations were disturbing on so many levels, most especially because they were creating emotional intimacy, something that was completely foreign to their marriage. Nevertheless, as painful as it was to dredge up her hurts, she was learning that it was cathartic to acknowledge them. Letting him explain his side lessened the hurt.

She glanced at him as they walked, no longer touching.

"I hate thinking of you with other women." The confession felt like a barbed hook dragged all the way from the center of her heart across the back of her throat. "Infidelity destroyed our family. We were quite normal at first, then Nico was sent away and it was awful. Both my parents drank. My father fooled around and made sure my mother knew about it. She was devastated. So much yelling and crying and fighting. I never wanted anything like that to happen to me."

"It won't," he assured her, reaching across with light fingers to smooth her hair off her shoulder so he could tuck his hand under the fall of loose tresses and cup the back of her neck. "But tell me you were jealous of Lexi anyway. My ego needs it."

"I felt insecure and useless," she said flatly.

He checked his step and a spasm of pain flashed across his face before he seared her with a look. "Exactly how I felt when I saw you walk up the driveway here. Like I'd been rejected because I wasn't good enough."

She bit her lips together in compunction while her heart quivered in her chest, shimmering with the kind of pain a seed must feel before the first shoot breaks through its shell. She wanted to cry and throw herself into him and run away and protect herself.

"We're never going to be able to make this work, Gideon. I don't want the power to hurt you any more than I want you to be able to hurt me. This is a mess. We're messing each other up and it's going to be—"

"Messy?" he prompted dryly. "Just take it one day at a time, Adara. That's all we can do."

She drew in and released a shaken breath, nodding tightly as they kept walking. Their steps made soft crunches in the dry grass while cicadas chirped in accompaniment. No breeze stirred beneath the trees and the heat clutched the air in a tight grip.

"Should we go back and swim?" she suggested.

"If you like."

It didn't matter what they did, she realized. They were filling time until her brother returned, distracting themselves while sexual attraction struggled for supremacy over hurt and misgivings. They should give in. Sex would take the edge off their tension and God knew she wanted him. Lovemaking with Gideon was a transcendent experience as far as she was concerned.

But she'd never felt this vulnerable with him before. It made physical intimacy seem that much more *intimate*. Her normal defenses were a trampled mess. The idea of letting him touch her and watch her lose control was terrifying. He'd see how much he meant to her and that was too much to bear.

Twenty minutes later they were in the pool. His laps were a purposeful crawl with flip turns and patterned breathing, hers a less disciplined breaststroke that made one lap to his four. Tiring, she moved to sit on one of the long tile stairs in the shallow end, half out of the water as she watched him. The pool was fully shaded now, leaving her quite comfortable watching his athletic build cut through the water.

When he stopped and joined her on the step, he was breathing heavily, probably having swum a mile though she'd lost count ages ago, distracted by the steady thrust of his arms into the water and the tight curve of his buttocks as he kicked. She really couldn't fathom what a sexy, virile man like him was doing with mousy, boring her.

And even though he'd pushed himself with thirty minutes of hard swimming, his gaze moved restlessly, as if he was looking for the next challenge.

"You're not comfortable with downtime, are you?" she said.

He glanced questioningly at her while diamond droplets glittered on his face and chest hair.

"You're driven," she expounded. "I keep thinking of all those plans we made, but what does it matter if we have a floating hotel? I know it's top-notch, but who cares? We don't need the money and the world doesn't need another behemoth cruise ship."

"It matters to the people we've employed and the ones who invested with us. But you're right, I suppose. Wealth isn't something either of us really needs. Not anymore. It's a habit I've fallen into, I guess."

"You worked hard to get here and now you don't know how to stop," she paraphrased.

He made a noise of agreement.

"If we don't have children, what would we fill our lives with? More hotels and boats?" Involuntarily, her ears strained to hear the words *each other*.

They didn't come. After a long moment he said, "Our last five-year plan took months to mold. This one can, too. There's no rush."

"There is," she insisted. "I feel like if we don't have everything sorted out before we sleep together again, our marriage will go back to the way it was and I'll be stuck in it." There. She'd said it. Her worst fear had blurted out of her.

He stared at her for a long minute, absorbing her outburst, then he chuckled softly and shook his head. "And I can't think of anything but making love to you again. New plans?" He shook his head as if she was speaking another language. "We're at quite an impasse."

He wasn't being dismissive, just blatantly honest. Her heart constricted as she absorbed that this was what he'd meant about trusting him. Somehow she had to dredge up the faith to believe he'd continue working on their marriage along with the courage to surrender herself to him. The potential for pain was enormous.

While the yearning to feel close to him was unbearable.

She looked up to where the afternoon sun had bleached the clear sky to nearly white. Not even close to evening or bedtime. She hadn't brought either her green-light or red-light nightgown. How else could she possibly signal to him that she was receptive to his advances?

*Oh, Adara, quit being such a priss.* They were learning to *communicate,* weren't they?

Her internal lecture didn't stop her heart from beating frantically in her throat as she set tentative fingertips on his wrist where it rested on his thigh. Leaning toward him, she shielded her eyes with a swoop of her lashes and watched his lips part slightly in surprise before she pressed hers to them.

Heat flooded into her. The very best kind of heat that had nothing to do with Greek sunshine and everything to do with this man's chemistry interacting with hers. He didn't move, letting her control the pressure and deepening of their kiss, but he responded with a muted groan of approval and drew on her tongue with gentle suction.

Runnels of sexual hunger poured through her system, spreading out in delicate fingers that excited her senses and made her want to tip into his lap.

Shakily she pulled back and licked the taste of him off her lips before she gripped the railing in slippery fingers and forced her weak knees to take her weight as she stood.

"Will you, um, give me a minute to shower before you

come up?" The question was so uncouched and blatant she felt as though she'd stripped herself naked here in public.

"I'll use the shower in the cabana and be up in ten," he replied gruffly, eyes like lasers that peeled her bathing suit from her body.

Adara wrapped a towel around herself and went to their room.

# CHAPTER SIX

THE PARALLEL TO their first time kept ringing in Gideon's skull. He was just as keyed up as he'd been then, his masculine need to possess twitching in him like an electric wire, while his ego inched out onto that wire, precarious as a tightrope walker.

*No room for false moves.* The message pulsed as a current, back and forth within him.

He climbed the stairs as though pulled by an invisible force. No matter how many times he told himself it was ridiculous to place so much importance on this—he'd done this before. *They* had. It didn't matter. This meant something. The last time he'd felt this sense of magnitude, Adara's initiation to sexual maturity had been on the line. He'd felt a massive responsibility to make it good for her, especially as he'd been selfishly determined he would be her only lover for the rest of their lives. The pressure to ensure they were both satisfied with that exclusivity had been enormous.

Without being too egotistical, he believed they had been. He certainly had. Her subtle beauty had flourished into his own private land of enchantment.

This ought to be a visit to the familiar, he told himself as he turned the handle on the door and pressed into their room. It wasn't. This was uncharted territory and the initiation this time was happening to both of them, moving them into some kind of emotional maturity he would have rather avoided. The tightrope he was walking didn't even feel as if it was there anymore. He was walking across thin air, reminding himself not to look down or he'd be tumbling into a bottomless crevasse.

As he leaned on the door until it clicked, she opened the bathroom door and emerged wearing one of his T-shirts. The soft white cotton clung to her damp curves and naked breasts before falling to the tops of her thighs. He couldn't tell if she wore underpants and couldn't wait to find out.

"I didn't bring anything sexy," she murmured apologetically, her eyes bigger than the black plums in the basket. Her apprehension was unmistakable.

"You look edible," he said, voice originating somewhere deep in his chest. He moved across to her. "I didn't shave." He took her hand and rubbed the heel across his jaw where a hint of stubble was coming in.

"It's okay," she murmured and pulled her hand back then wrung it with her other one. "I'm sorry. I don't know why I'm so terrified. This is silly."

A swell of tenderness rose in him. He took her hands and kissed each palm. "It's okay. I'll take it slow. As slow as the first time. I want to savor every second."

Her smile trembled. "I know it will be good, but my body seems to think we're strangers. I keep reminding myself I know everything about you. The important things, anyway."

His blood stopped in his arteries as he thought about what she didn't know about him. Important things, but so was this. He needed to cement their connection before he could even contemplate stressing it with a full exposure of who he was. And wasn't.

Adara cupped the sides of his head, trembling with nerves and anticipation, wanting the kiss that would erase all her angst and drown her in the sea of erotic sensations he always delivered.

Gideon wasn't moving, seeming to have slipped behind a veil of some kind.

"What's wrong?" she asked as doubts began to intrude.

"Nothing," he said gruffly and set his mouth on hers.

The first contact was just that, contact. Like finding the edge of the pool when your eyes were closed and head submerged and your lungs ready to give up. Relief poured through her as the familiar shape and give of his full lips compressed her own.

And then he opened his mouth in a familiar signal that she do the same and she nearly melted into a puddle of homecoming joy. His arms slid around her and pulled her into a hard embrace against his shirtless chest, muscles bulging with such strength it was almost uncomfortably hard against her tender breasts, but so welcome.

Adara curled her arms around the back of his neck and clung, kissing him unreservedly as her senses absorbed every delicious thing about him. His shoulders and back were gloriously smooth and naked, scented with body wash and rippling hotly as he moved his hands on her, awakening every nerve in her body.

The wide plant of his strong legs let her feel the brush of his hairy legs against the smoothness of her thighs. She wriggled closer, wanting to feel the hard muscle that told her he liked the feel of her against him. Her body craved contact with that gorgeous erection and she arched herself into firm pressure against the ridge she could feel behind the fly of his shorts.

"This isn't slow," he growled, straightening and grasping a handful of T-shirt between her shoulder blades.

The soft fabric stretched across the round thrust of her breasts. Her nipples stood out prominently. Eagerly. He leaned to take one in his mouth, suckling her through the fabric until she let out a keening moan of distress at the pleasure-pain. He pulled back to examine the wet stain that turned the cotton invisible, clearly revealing the sharp pink tip and shaded areola of her breast.

Adara gasped at how flagrantly erotic this was, but couldn't help arching a little in pride when she could see how excited he was by the sight. He smiled tightly before bending to do the same to her other nipple, bringing her up on her toes the sensation was so ferociously strong. A ripple of near ecstasy quavered in her abdomen, making her weak and mindless. She clung to him as if he was a life raft.

"I've always liked that, too," he said with satisfaction.

"What?" she asked breathily.

"The way you dig your kitten claws into me when you're about to come."

The heat that suffused her nearly burned her alive. "I'm not," she said in a near strangle.

"No?" A light of determination flared behind the liquid heat that had turned his dark eyes black.

Her heart skipped in alarm, but his superior strength easily backed her to the bed and levered her into the poofy cloud of the duvet. He took a moment to admire the purple undies she was wearing, the prettiest pair she'd brought, before he drew them down her legs in a deliberately slow tease of satin against skin.

The unfettered daylight and proprietary touch of his strong hands on her legs made her thighs quiver.

"Gideon," she protested.

"You're so close, *matia mou*," he cajoled, thumb stroking into her wet folds to search out the knot of sensation that was undeniably eager for his touch. She instinctively lifted her hips off the bed at the first contact. He bent and chuckled softly against her inner thigh, kissing his way to where her entire world was centered.

Latent modesty curled her fingers into his hair and she moaned indecisively, wanting badly to give in to what he offered, but she felt like such a wanton. She tossed her head back and forth, tugged on his hair, then felt the hot lick of his tongue and nearly screamed with delight. Need ravaged through her and she encouraged him, nearly begged him with the rock of her hips and clench of her fist in his hair and then—

Release seared through her like a white-hot blade, blinding in its intensity. Sensations racked her on waves of unadulterated pleasure that gripped her for an eternity, exquisite and joyous.

She came back on a sobbing pant of gratification. Aftershocks trembled through her as she became aware of Gideon kissing his way up her torso, pushing aside the T-shirt. He lifted onto an elbow to admire the quivering breasts he'd bared, then slowly lifted his gaze to her face.

Adara felt utterly defenseless and he made it worse when he said, "Now imagine how you would feel if I left you right now."

The way she had been leaving him in exactly this state for weeks.

He began to roll away and her world crashed in. "Don't!" she cried.

He showed her the condom he'd reached for. "I can't," he said with a near-bitter fatalism. He opened his shorts and pushed them down, kicking his shorts free.

The thrust of his erection was as powerfully intimidating as ever, but she positively melted with anticipation. "Can I—" She tried to help him with the condom.

"Next time, Adara. For God's sake, just let me get inside you."

He lifted to cover her, his weight a sweet dominance as he pushed into her, filling her with the heat of his length and rocking his hips so he was seated as deeply as possible. Then he weaved his fingers into her hair and nuzzled light kisses on her brow and cheekbones, giving her time to adjust to his penetration.

"You don't know what it's been like," he grumbled.

She had an idea. Her body was barely hers, responding to the feel of him so strongly that just the thick stretch of him inside her and the faint friction of their tiniest movement was setting off another detonation. It would have been humiliating if it wasn't so amazingly, sweetly incredible.

"Oh, God, Gideon. I'm sorry," she moaned and scratched at his rib cage as she tilted her hips for more pressure and shuddered into ecstasy beneath his weight.

"Oh, babe," he said consolingly against her lips, rocking lightly to increase the sensations, forcing and prolonging her climax. "You missed this, too."

She shattered, unable to stop herself gasping in joy

"Don't be arrogant," she warned a minute later, turning her face to the side in discomfiture as she tried to catch her breath.

"I'm not, I swear I'm not." His breath was hot on her ear before his tongue painted wet patterns on her nape.

"You don't seem quite as swept away as I am," she said pointedly, pressing against the wall of his chest.

"I'm barely hanging on. Can't you feel me shaking? If I was naked, I'd have been lost on the first thrust. Being inside you is so good, babe. I never want to leave. It's always like this, like I'm in heaven."

Her heart seemed to flower open to him and her hands moved on him of their own volition, absorbing that he was, indeed, trembling with strain.

"I thought I was the one shivering," she confessed softly.

"I live for this, Adara. The feel of you under me, the way you smell, the heat and the insane pleasure of feeling you around me." He pressed deep as he spoke, sparking a flare of need in her for another and another of those fiercely possessive thrusts.

"Don't stop," she begged. "It feels too good."

With an avid groan, he took her mouth in a deep soul kiss and thrust in a purposeful, primal rhythm. The sensations were nearly too much for her, but she couldn't let him go, couldn't give it up. Her legs locked around him and her heels urged him to heavier, harder slams of his hips into hers. This wasn't a man initiating a virgin; it was too halves trying to meld into a whole. The sensations were acute and glorious and feral.

And when the culmination arrived, it was a simultaneous crescendo that burst from the energy between them, surrounding and sealing them in a halo of shimmering joy as they clung tightly to the only thing left in the universe. Each other.

Gideon left Adara at a complete and utter loss. She always left the bed first, hitting the shower so she could recover her defenses after letting them fall away during sex. Lovemaking always made her feel vulnerable, and after acting so greedily and helpless to her desire for him, she needed alone time more than ever. She'd never felt so peeled down to the core in her life

But Gideon disappeared into the bathroom, stealing her favorite line of escape. She sat up, thinking to dress, but then go where?

The toilet flushed and she flicked the corner of the duvet over her nudity, not sure where to look when he came out of the bathroom. He struck a pose in the doorway with elbows braced and a near belligerence in his naked stance.

"What's wrong?" she asked, unnerved by his intense stare.

"Nothing. You?" He seemed almost confrontational and it got her back up.

"No. Of course not." Except that she'd pretty much exploded in his arms and didn't know how to handle facing down this tough guy who didn't seem to have a shred of tenderness in him anymore. She slid a foot to the edge of the bed. "I'll, um, just have a quick shower—"

"Why?" he challenged. "You just had one."

True, but where else did one ever have complete privacy except the bathroom? She'd figured that one out in grade school. It was one of her coping strategies to this day. She set her chin, trying to think up a suitable way to insist.

"I hate it when you run away after sex," he said, coming toward the bed in a stealthy, pantherlike stride. "Unless you're inviting me to join you in the shower, stay exactly where you are."

Her heart skipped, reacting to both his looming presence and the shock of his words.

"You're the one who started it, running out like you had a train to catch the first night of our honeymoon. I thought that's how we did this," she defended, going hot with indignation. "When we're done, we're done."

"Our first night was your first *time*. If I hadn't left you, I'd have made love to you all night and I didn't want to hurt you any more than I already had." He leaned over her as he spoke, forcing her onto her back.

She pressed a hand to his chest, warding him off. "Well, I didn't know that, did I? You walked out on me and I didn't like it, so I made it a habit to be the first to leave every other time."

He hung over her on straight arms, his eyes narrowed hawkishly. "So you're not running away to wash the feel of me off your skin?"

"No." That was absurd. She loved the feel and smell of him lingering on her. "Sometimes I run the shower but don't get in," she admitted sheepishly.

He muttered a curse of soft, frustrated amusement. "Then why…?"

"You make me feel like I can't resist you! Like all you have to do is look at me or say a word and I'll melt onto my back. That's not a comfortable feeling."

"That's exactly how I want you to be. I want you here, under me. I want to make love to you until we're so weak we can't lift our heads. I've never been comfortable with how insatiable I am for you. At least if we're in the same boat, I can stand it."

She almost told him then that sometimes she woke in the middle of the night and ached for him to come to her. Shyness stopped her, but she overcame it enough to reach up to the back of his head and urge him down to kiss her. She stayed on her back, under him, and moaned in welcome as he settled his hot weight on her.

He groaned in gratification.

Moonlight allowed Adara to find his T-shirt on the floor. The doors were still open and the air had cooled off to a velvety warmth that caressed her nudity. She took a moment to savor the feel of her sensitive skin stroked by the night air. It was an uncharacteristic moment of sensuality for her.

She glanced at her naked form in the mirror. The woman staring back at her through the shadows was a bit of a stranger. The dark marks of Gideon's fingerprints spotted her buttocks and thighs. They'd got a little wild at times through the afternoon and evening, definitely more voracious than either had ever revealed to the other before.

Her abdomen fluttered in speculative delight. His focus on her had shored up places inside her that had been unsteady and ready to collapse. Her footing felt stronger now, even if the rest of her still swayed and trembled.

Yes, there were still places inside her that were sensitive and vulnerable, places very close to her heart. In some ways, she was even more terrified than she'd been before they'd come up here and thrown themselves at each other, but she was glad they'd made love. Very glad.

A whisper of movement drew her glance to the bed. Gideon's arm swept her space on the bed. The covers had long been thrown off and the bottom sheet was loose from the corners. They had indisputably wrecked this bed.

The body facedown upon it, however, was exquisitely crafted to withstand the demands he'd made upon it. Adara took a mental photo of his form in the bluish light: his muscled shoulders, the slope of his spine, the taut globes of his buttocks, his lean legs, one crooking toward her vacant spot as he came up on an elbow.

His expression relaxed as he spotted her in the middle of the room. She tightened her grasp on the T-shirt she clutched to her front.

"Get back here."

The smoky timbre of his voice was a rough caress all its own, while his imperious demand made her want to grin. Despite being a naturally dominant male, he usually phrased his commands as requests when he spoke to her. That was all part of the distance between them, she realized. Part of both of them not letting the other see the real person. She ought to be affronted by his true, domineering and dictatorial colors, but she liked that he wasn't quelling that piece of his personality around her anymore.

She liked even more that she wasn't afraid of this side of him. He wasn't an easy man to resist on any level, but she wasn't afraid to stand up to him.

Even if he still made her feel inordinately shy.

"I'm thirsty. And I want to see what's in these baskets." She turned away, prickles of awareness telling her he studied her back and bottom exactly as proprietarily as she'd looked at him before he'd woken. She shrugged his T-shirt over herself.

"That's the first thing I noticed about you and I hardly ever get to see it naked."

"My bum?" Her buttocks tightened beneath the light graze of his T-shirt and she felt herself heat. She turned to bring the basket along with the wineglasses to the bed, not bothering with the wine itself. She was after the sparkling water in the green bottle.

As she placed the basket on the bed and knelt across from him, she caught a look of disgruntlement on his face.

"All of you," he clarified. "You're gorgeous and I like looking at you."

She didn't know what to say. She was flattered, but only half believed him.

Tucking her loose hair behind her ear, she confided, "I've never felt confident about the way I look. Showing any hint of trying to be sexy while my father was alive would have been a one-way ticket to hell. And I never really trusted any man enough to flirt." She gave him the bottle of water to open for her then poured two glasses, drinking greedily only to make herself hiccup.

She giggled and covered her wet lips, but sobered as she saw Gideon glowering into his glass.

"Men who hit women make me insane. I know it's not right to answer violence with violence, but if your father were still alive, the police would be involved right now, one way or another." He took a deep slug of his water, eyes remaining hooded, not meeting her shocked gaze.

His vehemence was disturbing, prompting an odd need to comfort him. She reached across to stroke his tense arm. "Gideon, it's in the past. It's okay."

"No, it's not," he said sharply, but when he looked at her, his expression softened a little. "But right now isn't the time to think about it. Get rid of that," he ordered with a jerk of his chin at the T-shirt.

"What am I? Your sex slave now?" She did feel a little enslaved, but she wasn't as resentful as she ought to be about it.

"No. You're my wife. You ought to be comfortable letting me see you naked." He set aside his glass to reach for an orange.

She finished her own water and set it aside before easing the shirt off her body and setting it aside while she continued to kneel demurely, feet alongside her buttock, arm twitching to cover her breasts. To distract herself, she watched Gideon efficiently section the orange and bring a piece to his mouth.

He clutched it in his teeth and looked at her. "Bite," he said around it.

Her heart did a somersault. "Why?" The defensive question came automatically, but then she thought, *Just do it,* and leaned down to close her mouth on the fruit.

They bit it in half at the same time. Tangy juice exploded in her mouth. At the same time, his firm lips moved on hers in an erotic, openmouthed kiss. When she would have pulled away in surprise, he set a hand behind her head and kept her close enough to enjoy the messy, sweet, thorough act of sinful wickedness.

When he finally let her pull away to finish chewing and swallow, he grinned. "You flirt just fine, Mrs. Vozaras."

"Do it again," she blurted, making herself be assertive so she'd quit letting habits of inhibition hold her back from what she wanted.

A flicker of surprise flashed in his eyes before his eyelids grew heavy and his gaze sexily watchful. In her periphery, she was aware of him growing hard and her mouth watered for that too, but she took another bite of orange and splayed her hand on his chest, leaning into him to enjoy the sticky, tart kiss.

The last shreds of her inhibitions fell away and they didn't get back to the orange for a long, long time.

* * *

"You're going to burn," Gideon said as he returned from the waves to see the sun had moved and the backs of Adara's legs were exposed to the intense rays.

She stayed on her stomach on the blanket, unmoved and unmoving, only blinking her eyes open sleepily, as if she didn't have an ounce of energy in her. Forty-eight hours of unfettered lovemaking, impulsive napping and abject laziness were taking a toll on both of them. His own ambition had frittered into an *I'll look at it later* attitude. He'd left his phone and tablet up at the house, bringing only his sunglasses and wife to the beach.

"I like being on vacation," she told him, still not moving.

He adjusted the umbrella so she was fully in the shade then flopped down beside her. "So do I. We should definitely do this more often."

A shadow passed behind her eyes before she lowered her lashes to hide it. She shifted to rest her chin on her stacked fists, the circumspect silence making him aware of all the things they'd avoided while enriching their knowledge of each other's capacity for physical pleasure. Suddenly they were back in the pool, he couldn't think beyond his sexual hunger, and she was telling him that she needed to know where their relationship was going.

Restless frustration moved through him. He didn't know what to tell her. This was perfect. Wasn't it? He couldn't think of one thing they needed besides warm sand, the reassuring swish of a calm sea, each other's heated breath while they—

A faint noise lifted his head and a preternatural tingle went through him as he noticed a speck appear in the distant sky. They hadn't been tracking time, neither of them particularly interested in a return to reality, but apparently it was descending whether they were ready for it or not.

"Babe? I think your brother's here."

# CHAPTER SEVEN

GIVEN HOW THEIR trip to Greece had started, Gideon supposed he shouldn't be surprised by Adara's reaction, but the way she paled and panicked startled him. She took herself back to the house as if her skin was on fire. In their room, she pulled on a sundress and revealed a level of agitation he'd never seen as the thwack of chopper blades became loud enough to make the house hum.

He dragged on shorts and a collared shirt, concerned by the way her hand shook as she tried to apply makeup.

"Adara, you look great," he reassured her, even though her lips were bloodless and her eyes pools of anxiety.

Coming back from a place of dark thoughts, she gripped his forearm with a clammy hand. "Thank you for being here with me. I don't know if I could have done this alone."

Shaken by the reliance and trust her statement represented, he wanted to pull her into his arms and assure her he'd always be here, but she was already pulling away from him. She had been waiting for this a long time and he could see she was both eager and filled with trepidation. Not knowing her brother or how this would go for her filled him with his own anxiety, wanting to shield her yet knowing he had to let whatever happened happen. He could only accompany her outside where the sound of the chopper blades faded to desultory pulses.

Walking out a side door, they stood on the steps, Adara's fingernails digging into his biceps as she gripped his arm.

They watched Nic Marcussen help a woman with crutches from the helicopter. Rowan Davidson was vaguely familiar to him as a moderately famous child actress who'd had a flirtation with notoriety among the euro-trash social elite. She seemed surprisingly down to earth now as she spun with lithe grace on one foot, accepting her second crutch while trying to take a bag from her husband at the same time.

Nic shouldered the bag's strap and reached back into the chopper for one more thing: an infant carrier.

As the couple made their way across the lawn toward them, Gideon felt the slicing gaze of the media magnate take his measure.

It wasn't often that Gideon met a man he considered his equal. Standing on the man's stoop didn't exactly put him on an even playing field and he might have been more uncomfortable with that if a severe expression of anguish hadn't twisted Nic's expression when he transferred his gaze to Adara.

Her tense profile barely contained the emotions Gideon sensed rising off her as viscerally as if they were his own. Everything in him wanted to pull her close and screen her from what was obviously a very painful moment. But he had to stand helplessly waiting out the silence as Nic paused at the bottom of the steps and the siblings were held in a type of stasis, staring at each other.

Like a burst of rainbows into a rainy afternoon, Rowan smiled and stepped forward. "We're so glad you came," she said in a warm Irish accent. Hitching up the steps on her crutches, she embraced Adara with one arm, kissing her cheek. "I'm Rowan. It's my fault we're late. And you're Gideon?"

She hopped over to hug him as if they were long-lost

relatives, and for once Gideon didn't take offense at an unexpected familiarity, accepting her kiss on his cheek, still
focused on his wife who seemed to be in a kind of trance.

Slowly Nic set down the baby carrier and let the bag
slide off his shoulder on his other side. He took a step forward and Adara tipped forward off the stoop, landing in
the open arms of her brother. It was beautiful and heartrending, the reunion so intense it could only be the result
of long, intense suffering apart.

"We should give them a minute," Rowan said huskily,
her eyes visibly wet as she dragged her gaze from the pair.
"Would you be an absolute hero and bring Evie into the
house for me?"

Gideon didn't like leaving Adara, but followed Rowan to
the kitchen where she began preparing a bottle. The baby
craned her neck and followed Rowan with her Oriental
eyes, beginning to strain against the confines of her seat,
whimpering with impatience.

"I know, you're completely out of sorts, aren't you?"
Rowan murmured as she released the baby while the bottle
warmed. Cuddling the infant, she nuzzled her cheek and
patted her back, soothing the fussing girl.

"We were supposed to be here all summer just enjoying
being a family," she said to Gideon. "Then it came up that I
could have a few pins taken out of my leg. I wanted to put
it off, but Nic said no, he could handle Evie for a couple
of nights while I was in hospital. But Evie decided to cut
a tooth and bellow nonstop. He didn't get a wink of sleep.
Then he found out Adara had come looking for him. He
didn't know which way to turn. Here, do you mind?" she
said as a *ping* sounded from the cylindrical bottle warmer.

She held out the infant and Gideon had no choice but to
take her so Rowan could retrieve the baby's bottle.

He held the sturdy little girl's rib cage between his
palms. Her dangling legs wriggled and her tiny hands

scratch-tickled his forearms while her doll's face craned to keep Rowan in view. She was the smallest, most fragile creature he'd ever held and fear that he'd break her made him want to hurriedly hand her back, but Rowan was occupied tipping the bottle to spray milk on her wrist then licking it off.

"I've used crutches so many times I can do a full tea service on them without spilling, but I haven't mastered juggling a baby. Yet." She smiled cheekily and hopped over to him. "Just rest her in the crook of your arm and—yes, I know you want that. You're hungry, aren't you? Uncle's going to feed you."

*No, I'm not,* Gideon thought, but found himself with a weight of soft warmth snuggled onto his forearm. As little Evie got the nipple in her mouth and relaxed, he did too. Her charcoal eyes gazed up at him trustingly and he felt a tug near his heart. Her foot tapped lightly onto his breastbone while she swallowed and breathed heavily with audible greediness. He felt like a superhero, making sure she wasn't going hungry.

"Shall we sit outside? I hope you've been comfortable here?" Rowan led him out of the kitchen to the patio.

"Very," he assured her, sincere. "You'll have to let us return the hospitality when our cruise ship launches next year. Now, how do we do this? Do you want to sit and take her—?"

A noise inside the house snapped Rowan's head around like a guard dog hearing a footstep. "That was Adara into the ladies' room. I'll just— Do you mind? I want to make sure Nic…" She *was* good on crutches, swooping away like a gull, a telling thread of concern in her tone as she disappeared into the house.

He snorted in bemusement, thinking that Nic Marcussen seemed the least likely man in the universe to require a mother hen for a wife, but apparently he had one.

While Gideon was literally left holding the baby.

He looked down at the girl, surprised to see how much of the bottle she'd drained. As her bright gaze caught his, Evie broke away from the teat to give him an ear-to-ear milky grin of joy and gratitude and trust.

A laugh curled upward from deep in his chest, surprising him with how instant and genuine his humor was. Little minx. They learned early how to disarm a man, didn't they? He was in very real danger of falling in love at first sight.

Adara wiped at her still-leaking eyes and tried to pull herself together so Gideon wouldn't worry. He had been right. It was okay. Nico was and always had been her big brother in every way that counted. Nevertheless, her heart was cracking open under the pressure of deep feeling. She desperately craved the arms of her husband to cushion her from the sensation of rawness.

As she went in search of him outside, she saw him settling into a chair at the patio table, his back to her. Biting her lips together, she tried not to burst into happy tears as she stepped through the door and moved to his side—

—where she found him holding a baby, smiling indulgently at the infant as if the tot was the most precious thing in the world.

The kick of pain blindsided her. For a second she was paralyzed by the crash back to the reality of their imperfect life, winded so much she wasn't able to move, let alone retreat, before Gideon glanced up and saw the devastated expression on her face.

If he'd been caught with Lexi in flagrante delicto, he couldn't have looked more culpable. *It wouldn't have hurt this badly.*

"She's on crutches. The baby was hungry. I couldn't say no," he defended quickly while his arm moved in the most subtly protective way to draw the baby closer to his chest. In the way of a natural father sheltering his young.

At the same time, his free hand shot out to take Adara's arm in an unbreakable grip.

"You look like you're going to fall down. Sit." He half rose, used one foot to angle a chair for her and maneuvered her into it.

Adara's legs gave out as she sank into the chair. She buried her face in her hands and frantically reminded herself that her emotions were pushed to the very edge of endurance right now. The bigger picture here wasn't that he was stealing an opportunity to cuddle a baby because she couldn't give him one. He was getting to know their niece.

Longing rose in her as she made that connection and a different, more tender kind of emotion filled her, sweet with the layers of reunion with family that had driven her here in the first place. She lifted her head and held out her hands.

"Can I hold her? Please?"

"Of course." He transferred the baby's weight into her arms and Adara nearly dissolved into a puddle of maternal love. "Her name's Evie. Adara, I wasn't—"

She shook her head.

His hand came up to the side of her neck, trapping her hair against her nape as he forced her to look at him and said in a fierce whisper. "I wasn't trying to hurt you."

"I know. It's okay," she assured him, rubbing her cheek on the hardness of his wrist. "I just wasn't expecting it, that's all. I'm not mad."

He cupped the side of her face and leaned across to kiss her once, hard. "You scared me. I thought I was going to lose you."

She had to consciously remember to hold on to the baby while her limbs softened and her heart shifted in her chest. Every time she thought they didn't have a hope in the world of making something of their marriage, he said something like that and completely enchanted her.

Voices made them break their intense stare into each other's eyes.

"I'm not being a grouch," her brother growled as he emerged from the house carrying his wife in the cradle of his arms. "But you were discharged early because you promised to keep it elevated, so I think you should do that, don't you?"

Gideon moved to pull out a chair so Rowan could slide down onto it, then he offered a hand to Nico. "Gideon."

"Nic," her brother said, completely pulled together after his tearful reassurances to her a few minutes ago. He'd never stopped caring or worrying about her all this time, just as she had for him. She was loved, was worth loving. It was a startling adjustment, like learning she wasn't an ugly duckling but a full-fledged swan.

Could Gideon see the change in her?

He wore a mask of subtle tension as he took his seat. No one else seemed to notice. Nic opened wine and Rowan stole the empty bottle of milk from her baby and handed Adara a burping towel.

When Nic set a glass of sparkling white before her, he smiled indulgently at Adara's attempt to pat a belch out of his daughter. "Looks like you know what you're doing. Do you have children?"

The canyon of inadequacy yawned before her, but Gideon squeezed her thigh and spoke with a neutrality she couldn't manage. "We've tried," he said simply. "It hasn't worked out."

"I'm sorry," Nic said with a grimace that spoke of a man wanting to kick himself for saying the wrong thing, but he couldn't have known.

"Not being able to get pregnant seemed like a horrible tragedy for me at first," Rowan said conversationally. "But we wouldn't have Evie otherwise and we can't imagine life without her. We're so smitten, we're like the only two people to ever have a baby, aren't we, Nic?"

"It's true," he admitted unabashedly while he settled into his own chair and absently eased Rowan's bandaged leg to balance across his thigh. His hand caressed her ankle, their body language speaking of utter relaxation and familiarity with each other. "I don't know what I did to deserve such good fortune."

The fierce look of deep love he gave his wife and the tender way she returned it was almost too intimate to witness, but Adara found herself holding her breath as yearning filled her. *I want that,* she thought, but even though she felt Gideon's fingers circle tenderly on the inside of her knee, she didn't imagine for a minute she'd get it.

The penthouse seemed cavernous and chilly when they returned from Greece. It was after midnight when they arrived after what had been a long, quiet flight.

They'd been through a lot since meeting up at the end of her brother's driveway, so she supposed it was natural they'd both withdraw a bit to digest it all, but the hint of tension and reserve Gideon was wearing bothered her.

They'd made love in the middle of the night and again first thing this morning. It had been wonderful as ever, but afterward, as they'd soaped each other in the shower, things had taken this turn into a brick wall.

Unable to get Gideon's look of paternal tenderness toward Evie out of her mind, she'd pointed out how her brother and his wife made adoption look like the most natural thing in the world.

"They do," he had agreed without inflection.

"It's something to think about," she had pressed ever so lightly. "Isn't it?"

"Perhaps."

So noncommittal.

Adara chewed her lip, completely open to the idea herself, but that meant staying married. Forever. To a man who didn't appear as enthused by the idea of children as she was.

He was such an enigma. Returning to New York was a cold plunge into her old marriage to a workaholic who liked his space and only communicated when he had to—if the scene she entered when she left the powder room was anything to go by.

Paul, their chauffeur, was exiting Adara's room where he would have left her luggage. Gideon was coming back to the living room from his own room, where he would have left his own. He swept his thumb across his smart phone as he gave Paul a rough schedule for the next few days, asking her absently, "Are you leaving early for the office with me tomorrow or do you want Paul to come back for you?"

Back to separate lives that revolved around their careers. She looked at her empty arms as she crossed them over her aching chest. "How early is early?"

He grimaced at the clock. "Six? The time change will have me up anyway."

Her too. "That's fine," she said, then thought, *Welcome back, Mrs. Complacent*. She'd obviously forgotten her spine back in Greece.

Paul wished them a good night and left. Gideon came across to set the security panel, then looked down at her as she stifled a yawn.

"Straight to bed?" he asked.

A bristling sensation lifted in the region between her shoulder blades and the back of her neck. His question was one of the shorthand signals they'd developed in this detached marriage of theirs. He was letting her off the hook for sex.

She was exhausted. It shouldn't bother her, but it left her

feeling abandoned and without hope for their marriage, a family, or a love like her brother had found.

"Yes," she said quietly, pulling on her cloak of polite endurance to hide how hurt she was. "It's been a long day and tomorrow will be longer." Smooth out all those rough edges, Adara. Make it seem as if you don't have a heart to break.

"Your place or mine?"

"I—what?" She blinked at him, trying to quell the flutter of sensual excitement that woke in her blood. A little embarrassed by how quickly she could bloom back to life, she murmured, "I'm genuinely tired."

Nevertheless, she seesawed with indecision, longing for the closeness she experienced in his arms, but fearful of how neglected she felt when he drew himself apart from her the way he had since meeting her brother.

"I'm freaking exhausted," he admitted with heartfelt weariness, "but we're not going back to separate bedrooms. Mine," he said decisively, catching her hand to lead her there. "Don't bother moving your clothes. The farther away the better."

"Gideon." She chuckled a little as she stumbled behind him, then was distracted by entering a room she'd rarely peeked into. It was scrupulously clean and not just from the housekeeper doing a thorough job in their absence. Gideon was a tidy man. Living on boats forged that habit, he'd told her once. He didn't like clutter. The decorator's palette for the walls was unmarred by paintings or photos. The night table held only a phone dock that doubled as a bedside light.

He stepped into his closet to set his shoes on a shelf.

"You need to find a few days in the next week to come to Valparaiso with me," he told her as he emerged, drawing his belt free as he spoke, then hanging it precisely alongside the rest.

"You've become very dictatorial in the last few days, do you realize that?" She wasn't sure where the cheeky comment came from, but it blurted out even as her voice tightened along with her blood vessels. He was undressing, shedding his shirt without reserve to expose tanned planes of muscle.

"You used to be a pushover. I didn't have to try very hard to get what I wanted. Now I do."

"Does that bother you?" A pang in her lip made her realize she was biting down as she awaited his answer, habitually fearful of masculine disapproval.

He moved toward her, pants open to expose the narrow line of hair descending from his navel, feet bare, predatory with his tight abs and naked chest and sober expression. His nipples were pulled into tight points by the air-conditioned room.

She tensed against a rush of uncertainty and sexual admiration.

"You were thinking of leaving me because you weren't getting what you wanted. That bothers me very much." He cupped the side of her neck and his thumb pressed under her chin, gently tilting her face up. "We can't meet each other's needs if we don't say what they are, so I'm pleased you're telling me what you want. I'm telling you what I want. I like feeling you next to me and waking up to make love to you in the middle of the night. I need to travel and when I do, I want you to know that no one is in my bed except you."

So he hadn't completely left her, this man who so easily found his way to the deepest recesses of her soul. She swept her lashes down to hide how moved she was.

"What do you want, Adara?"

She practically liquefied into one of those women she often saw following him with limpid eyes and undisguised yearning. Her heart was so scarred and scared she could barely acknowledge what she wanted, let alone articulate it, but she managed to say huskily, "You."

Instantly it felt like too huge an admission, like she was

confessing to a deeper need than the sexual ones he had. Unable to bear being so completely defenseless against him, she splayed her hands on his chest and tried to lessen the depth of the admission by saying in a stilted murmur, "I'm not a sexual person, but I want to be in bed with you *all the time*."

Something inscrutable flashed in his expression, quickly masked by excitement as his chest expanded under her touch with a big inhale.

Adara hid her sensitivity in a sexual advance she couldn't have made a week ago, but their constant lovemaking over the last few days had given her the confidence to lean forward and tease his nipple with her mouth.

He grasped a handful of her hair while his erection grew against her stomach, making her smile as she flicked with her tongue and made him groan with approval.

"I thought you wanted to sleep," he said through his teeth.

"We will," she said, scraping her teeth across to his other nipple. "In a bit."

Gideon checked inside the velvet clamshell box, giving the ring one more critical look. The cushion-cut pink diamond was framed on either side by half-carat white diamonds, two on each side. Like Adara, the arrangement had a quiet elegance that wasn't ostentatious or flashy. It was a rare find that held the eye a long time once you noticed it.

When he'd seen it, he'd thought, *Sunrise. A new beginning.* Then his sailor's superstition had kicked in. *Red sky in morning...*

No, there was no warning here. They were proceeding into the horizon on smooth waters, making this ring the perfect marker for their anniversary in a few weeks. He had considered waiting until the actual date to give this to her, but they had a gala tonight and it seemed the right time for Adara to show off a trinket from her husband.

A good time for him to show *her* off, he admitted to himself with a self-deprecating smirk. A funny pang hit him in the middle of his chest as he tucked the box into the pocket of his tuxedo jacket. Adara was the last person to walk around bragging, *Look what my husband gave me.* He was the one who'd coaxed her into accepting this invitation so he'd have an excuse to give her this ring and seal a deal they hadn't quite closed.

Moving into the empty living room to wait for her, he poured himself a drink and gazed at the lights bobbing across the harbor, disturbed by how insecure he still felt about their future.

If sex was an indicator, he had nothing to worry about. Horny as he may have been as a teenager, he hadn't had access to a female body often enough to be this sexually active. Since Greece, however, he and Adara had been living the sort of second honeymoon every man fantasized about. There shouldn't be an ounce of need left in him, but as he dwelled on waking this morning to Adara's curves melded into his side, and the welcoming moan she'd released when he'd slipped inside her, a flame of sexual hunger came alive in him again.

And it was so good. Not just the quantity, but the quality. Her old inhibitions were gone. She was outspoken enough that he could unleash himself with the knowledge that she'd slow him down if she didn't like it. The sex was a dream come true.

So he didn't understand this agitation in himself, especially when she'd become more open in other ways, making him feel even more special and privileged to wear the label "Adara's husband."

Like yesterday, when he'd swung by her office on impulse at lunch, catching her in a meeting. Through the glass wall he'd watched her hold court, standing at the head of a board table surrounded by men and women in suits, all glued to her words. He'd understood their fascination, hypnotized himself by the glow of—hell, it looked like happiness, damn it.

Adara had paused in sketching diagrams on a smart board to point the tip of her electronic pen at each person as she went round the table, soliciting comments, earning nods and building consensus.

Gideon had stood there transfixed, proud, awed, full of admiration while remaining male enough to enjoy the way her shirt buttons strained across her breasts, just a shade tighter than she used to wear them.

Maybe that wasn't entirely voluntary. She'd said something the other day about eating too much and being too sedentary while they were away. He'd dismissed the comment because who gained ten pounds in less than a week? And even if she had, he was quite happy with her curves, thanks. Studying that ready-to-pop button, he'd been torn between intense desire and the sheer pleasure of watching her work.

She'd turned her head and a flush of pleasure had lit up her expression. She'd bit back a smile, mouthing something about "my husband" to the crowd that turned their heads to the window.

He'd been busted and had to meet a pile of names he'd never remember. It had been worth it. Ten minutes later they had locked lips in the descending elevator and wound up doing a "snap inspection" on the family suite at one of her hotels, skipping lunch altogether.

It was all good. She'd even let him listen in to her calls to her younger brothers when she'd broken the news about looking up Nic. A few beseeching, helpless looks at Gideon while she walked through some difficult memories had kept him close, rubbing her back as she choked through the conversations, but afterward there'd been a level of peace in her that told him she was healing old wounds that had festered for years.

Tell her *your* secret, a voice whispered insidiously in his head.

He slipped his hand into his pocket to close his fist on the velvet box. *No.* It wasn't necessary. They were doing great. Her brother was on the other side of the world, not questioning where Adara's husband had come from. Gideon had dodged any curiosity from that quarter and there was no use rocking the boat.

Even though guilt ate him alive at the way Adara couldn't seem to get enough of watching her niece over the webcam. But what could he say? *Yes, let's allow strangers to dig into my past so we can adopt a baby*?

She hadn't brought it up again, but she didn't need to. It was obvious what she wanted and he couldn't do it.

Assaulted by a fresh bout of shame and remorse, he ducked it by glancing at his watch. It wasn't like Adara to keep him waiting.

Moving to her room where the bulk of her clothes and toiletries remained while their architect prepared renovation plans for a new master bedroom, Gideon was aware of a fleeting apprehension. He rarely checked in on her while she was getting ready. There was something about watching a woman put on makeup and dress to go out that triggered old feelings of being abandoned and helpless. He shook off the dark mood that seemed so determined to overtake him tonight, and knocked before letting himself into her room.

She was a vision of sexy dishevelment in a blue gown not yet zipped up her back. Her hair had ruffled from its valentine frame around her face, curling in soft scrolls around her bare shoulders while her flawless makeup gave her lips a sensual glow and added dramatic impact to the distempered expression in her eyes.

"Problem?" he asked, noting the splashes of color where gowns had been discarded over the chair, the bed, and even the floor. Perhaps they should rethink the room sharing. This kind of disorder could wear on him.

"I told you we were eating out too much. I look like a lumpy sausage in every one of these. This one won't even close and my makeup doesn't match..." She was whipping herself into quite a state.

He bit back a smile, aware that he'd be on the end of a swift set down if he revealed how cute and refreshing he thought this tantrum was.

"Maybe the zipper is just caught. Let me try."

"It's not caught. I'm getting fat." She stood still as he tried to draw the back panels of the silk together and work the zipper upward. *Oh, hell.* This wasn't just a snagged zip, and now he'd done it: put himself in the position of having to acknowledge to his wife that she had gained a pound or two. Might as well go up to the roof and jump right now.

"See?" she wailed when he kept trying to drag the zip upward.

"Honestly, I don't see any weight gain," he insisted while privately acknowledging that spending as much time as he did caressing this body, a small and gradual gain would go completely unnoticed. "You're probably just getting your period. Don't women feel puffy then? You must be due for one."

Even as he said it, he was caught by the realization that she hadn't had one since, well, it would have been before they'd become intimate in Greece. At least a month ago.

He bristled with an unwelcome thought that he dismissed before it fully formed.

While Adara stood very, very still, her color draining away in increments.

Instinctively, Gideon took hold of her arm, aware of the way she tensed under his touch, as if she wanted to reject it.

"I, um, never get back to normal right away after a mis-carriage," she summed up briskly, not looking at him while her brow furrowed. Her arm jerked to remove his touch as she shrugged into a self-hug. "You're probably right. It's just a particularly bad case of PMS bloating."

Except she'd also mentioned a few days ago that her breasts were sore because her bra was too tight.

Or tender because of something else?

He could see where her mind was going and it scared him because he really would lose her if she fell pregnant again.

"I use a condom every time, Adara. Every time." He'd been meaning to book a vasectomy, as permanent protec-tion, but hadn't been ready to take the necessary break from sex.

"I know," she said so quickly it was almost as though she was trying to shut down the conversation before the word could be said, but it was there, eating the color out of her so she was a bloodless ghost refusing to look at him.

"So I don't see how—"

"I'm sure it's impossible," she cut in crisply. "And I'd only be a couple of weeks, not starting to put on weight, but I won't be able to think straight until I'm sure." Peeling the delicate straps of her gown off her shoulders, she let it fall to the floor and stepped out of the circle of midnight blue. Her strapless green bra didn't match the yellow satin and lace across her buttocks, but it was a pretty sight anyway as she walked into the bathroom. "I think there's a leftover test in the cupboard…"

She closed him out, the quiet click of the door a punch in the heart. He rubbed his clammy hands on his thighs, insisting to himself it was impossible.

Even though Adara thought it *was* possible.

And she wasn't happy about it.

How could she be?

Bracing his hands on the edges of the bathroom door, he listened for the flush and heard the sink run. Then, silence.

He ground his teeth, waiting.

Oh, to hell with it. He pushed in.

She'd pulled on an ivory robe and stood at the sink, a plastic stick in her hand. It quivered in her shaking grip.

He moved to look over her shoulder and saw the blue plus sign as clearly as she did. *Positive.*

# CHAPTER EIGHT

THE VOLUME OF emotions that detonated in Adara was more than she could cope with. Dark and huge as a mushroom cloud, the feelings scared her into falling back on old habits of trying to compress them back into the shallow grave of her heart.

"The test is old, maybe. Faulty," Gideon said behind her.

"It was the second one in the box from when I tested myself a few months ago." She threw the stick away and washed her hands, scrubbing them hard, then drying them roughly before she escaped the bathroom that was luxuriously cavernous, but way too small when her husband was in it with her.

And she was pregnant.

Again.

Shock was giving way to those unidentified emotions putting pressure on her eyes and rib cage and heart. She didn't want him watching as they took her over and she had to face that *it was happening again.*

"You should go," she said briskly, keeping her back to him. "Make my apologies. Tell people I came down with the flu or something." She was distantly aware of the cold, slippery satin on her arms bunching under her fists, her whole being focused on listening for Gideon's footsteps to leave the room the way she was silently pleading for him to do.

"You're kidding, right?"

"I'm not in the mood to go out right now," she said sharply, grasping desperately for an even tone to hide how close she was to completely breaking down.

"Adara, I'm—"

"Don't you dare say you're sorry!" she whipped around to cry. Distantly she was aware of her control skidding out of reach, but the storm billowing to life inside her was beyond her ability to quell. "Maybe this is all the time we have with our children, but I won't be sorry they exist!"

Her closed fist came up against her trembling lips, trying to stem the flood that wanted to escape after her outburst.

"I'm not going anywhere," he said with quiet ferocity, moving toward her with what seemed like a wave of equally intense emotions swirling around him.

Their two force fields crackled with condensed energy as they met, heightening the strain between them. Adara looked into his face, really looked, and saw such a ravaged expression, such brutally contained anguish, her insides cracked and crumbled.

"Whatever happens, I'm staying right here." He pointed at the floor between their feet. "I won't leave you alone again. This is happening to *us*."

Emotion choked her then, overspilling the dam of denial to flood her with anguish and insecure hatred of this body that didn't know how to hang on to babies. Futile hope combined with learned despair to make her shake all over. She couldn't hold it back, had to say it.

"I'm scared, Gideon."

He closed his eyes in a flinch of excruciation. "I know," he choked out, and dragged her into his protective arms, locking her into the safety of a hard embrace. "I know, babe, I know."

It all came out in a swamping rush of jagged tears. She clung hard to him as the devastating sorrow she'd never shown him was finally allowed to pour out of her. Every hurt that had ever scarred her seemed to rise and open and bleed free, gushing until it ran out the toxins, gradually closing in a seal that might actually heal this time.

As her senses came back to her, she realized he'd carried her to the bed where he'd sat down on the edge to cradle her in his lap. He gently rocked her, making comforting noises, stroking her soothingly.

"Sorry," she sniffed, wiping her sleeve across her soaked cheeks. "I didn't mean to lose it like that."

"Shh." He eased the edges of his jacket around her, cuddling her into a pocket of warmth close to his chest. When she looked up at him, she saw his eyes were red and glassy, his mouth twisted in frustrated pain.

"I wish—"

"I know. Me too." He steadied his lips in a flat line, the impact of his one sharp glance telling her he knew deeply and perfectly and exactly what she wished for.

When his hand moved into the folds of her robe and settled low on her abdomen, she covered it with her own, willing their baby to know that Daddy was here too. Her heart stretched and ached.

Gideon swallowed loudly and drew in a heavy breath, things she felt viscerally with him as she rested her head against his heart. This is love, she thought. The knowing without words. The sharing of both joy and pain.

She sat in stillness a long time, wondering if it was true. Were they both here in this bubble of dawning heart-to-heart connection, or just her? Did he love her? A little?

Gideon swore softly and touched the pocket of his jacket. "Paul," he explained. "I should tell him we're not going. Is your phone in here?"

"On the dock in the living room."

"Here. You need to warm up." He dragged the covers back from the pillows before rising with her in his arms and neatly tucking her in.

Listless after her storm of weeping, Adara turned her back on his departure and let her eyes close and her mind go blank. She couldn't face that he'd walked out so dispassionately after holding her so tenderly.

She must have dozed because she woke still alone in the bed, but the bedside light was on and someone was rustling in her room. She opened her eyes to see Gideon fitting a hanger into one of her gowns and carrying it into the closet. A tiny smile dawned on her mouth as she surreptitiously watched him housekeep for her. He'd changed out of his tuxedo, which was always a pity because he made one look so good, but pajama pants were fine too. Even when they were obviously crisp and new from a package. Had he ever worn pajamas before tonight? she wondered.

His critical eye scanned the room for anything else out of place before he moved to the door.

Her heart fell. He wasn't going to join her. They were back to separate beds and separate lives.

But no. She heard the distant beep of him setting the alarm, then his footsteps padded back to her. He gently lifted the covers and eased into bed behind her.

She sighed and spooned herself into him.

"Did I wake you? I didn't mean to."

"It's okay. I won't be able to sleep anyway. I've already started thinking about doctor's appointments and taking vitamins and…" She sighed with heartfelt sadness. It seemed like such a futile effort to go through it all again. "…everything."

"I put in a call to Karen, letting her know we want an appointment tomorrow," he said, referring to her ob-gyn.

"Oh, um, thank you." His thoughtfulness startled her. She wouldn't have guessed that he even knew her doctor's name. Snugging herself a little more securely into him, she nuzzled the bent elbow beneath her cheek. "One less thing to worry about." Oddly, she found herself amused again.

"Especially because you might actually get me an appointment tomorrow. I'd take whatever they offered, something next week if that's all they had, but no one says no to you, do they?"

"Not unless it's the answer I want to hear."

She snickered and turned in his arms. "Why are you like that?" she asked with sudden curiosity. "What made you so bullish?"

"Having nothing and hating it. You should get some sleep." He rolled back to reach for the light switch.

"Honestly, if I try to sleep, I'll just lie here and worry. Tell me something to distract me. What were you like as a child? Before your mom died," she prompted.

"Scared," he admitted, letting her glimpse the flash of angry honesty in his expression before he doused the light and drew her body into alignment with his. Her robe was bunched, her bra restrictive and the fabric of his pajama pants annoying when she wanted to stroke her bare leg on his.

At the same time, she was caught by the single word that didn't seem to fit with a mother he'd described as "maternal."

"Why were you scared?" she asked gently.

Gideon sighed. "I really don't like talking about it, Adara."

"Mmm," she murmured in old acquiescence, then said into his chest, "But I told you about my childhood, unhappy as it was, and we're closer for it. Aren't we?"

He sighed and rolled onto his back, arms loosening from his hold on her. "My story's a hell of a lot uglier than yours. I don't know much about my mother except what I told you before. I give her credit for somehow getting us into a rented room by the time she died, but before that, I can remember her leaving me in, literally, holes in the wall. Telling me to stay there until she came back. Can you imagine a woman—a child—trying to keep a baby alive while living on the street? I never felt safe."

"Oh, Gideon," she whispered, reaching her hand onto his chest.

He clasped her hand in his, taking care not to crush her fine bones, but was torn between rejecting her caress of comfort and clinging to it. He was sorry he'd started this, but part of him wanted to lay the groundwork. If his past ever came out, he wanted Adara to understand why he'd become who he was.

"I hate remembering how powerless I felt. So when you ask me why I go after what I want however I have to, that's why."

"How did she die?"

The unforgettable image of his mother's weary eyes staring lifelessly from her battered face flashed behind his closed eyes. He opened them to the streaks of moon-light on the bedroom ceiling, trying to dispel the memory.

"She was beaten to death." By a john, if he'd pieced things together in his mind correctly.

"Oh, my God! What happened? Did the police find who did it? Where were you? Did you go into foster care after, or…?"

"I didn't stick around for police reports. I was so terri-fied, I just ran." All the way onto a ship bound for America, barely old enough to be in school.

"You *saw* her?"

"I told you it was ugly."

Her breath came in on a shaken sob. "I'm so sorry, Gideon. And you saw that other man, too. Your mentor."

"Kristor," he provided. Kristor Vozaras, but now wasn't the time to explain how they'd come to have the same name. "I knew I couldn't live like that, on the docks where crime is a career and a human life worth nothing. No matter what, I had to climb higher than carrying everything I owned in a bag on my shoulder. Whatever it took, I *had* to amass some wealth and take control of my destiny."

She moved her head on his chest, nodding in understanding perhaps. Her warm fingers stroked across his rib cage and she hugged herself tighter into him, the action warmly comforting despite his frozen core.

"I'm glad you didn't limit yourself," she said. "I've always admired you for being a risk-taker. I've never had the nerve to step beyond my comfort zone."

"Oh, Adara," he groaned, heart aching in his chest as he weaved his fingers into hers. "You're the most courageous woman I know." How else could she stare down the probability of another heartbreak with fierce love for their child brimming in her heart?

Maybe he couldn't control whether or not she kept this baby, but he was going to fight like hell to keep her. *No matter what.*

Adara woke in her old bed and thought for a second it was all a dream. She hadn't gone to Greece, hadn't found closeness with her husband...

Then he padded into her room, half-naked, hair rumpled, expression sober as he indicated the phone in his hand. "Karen wants to know if we can get to her office before the rest of her patients start arriving."

It all came rushing back. *Pregnant.* Fear clutched her heart, but she ignored the familiar angst and sat up, nodding. "Of course. I'll get dressed and we can leave right away."

"Um." Gideon's mouth twitched. "You might want to wash your face."

Adara went to the mirror and saw a goth nightmare staring back at her. "Right," she said with appalled understatement.

Gideon confirmed with Karen and left for his own room to dress.

Their lighthearted start became somber as Gideon drove them to the clinic, neither of them speaking while he concentrated on the thickening traffic and the reality of their history with pregnancy closed in on them.

Nevertheless, as urgently as Adara wanted to self-protect right now, she also really, really appreciated Gideon's solid presence beside her. He warmed her with a strong arm across her back as they walked up to Karen's office and kept a supportive hold on her as they stood numbly waiting for the receptionist, still in her street jacket, to escort them into an exam room.

Karen, efficient and caring as she was, was not pleased to learn Adara had miscarried two months ago without telling her.

Adara drew in a defensive breath, but Gideon spoke before she could.

"Let's not dwell on that. Obviously there was no lasting damage or Adara wouldn't be pregnant again. I'd like to focus on what we can do to help her with this pregnancy."

Karen was used to being the one in charge, but shook off her ruffled feathers as Gideon's obvious concern shone through.

"I'd like to say there was a magic formula for going to term. Mother Nature sometimes has other plans, but we hope for the best, right? Adara, you know the drill." She handed her a plastic cup.

A few minutes later, Adara was in a gown, sitting on the edge of the exam table while Karen confirmed her pregnancy. The frown puckering her brow brought a worried crinkle to Adara's and Gideon's foreheads as well.

"What's wrong?" Adara asked with dread.

"Nothing. Just our tests are more sensitive than the over-the-counter ones and…. Do you mind? I won't do an internal just yet, but can I palpate your abdomen?"

Adara settled onto her back and Karen's fingers pressed a few times before she set the cool flat of the stethoscope against her skin. "Tell me more about this miscarriage you had. When do you think you conceived that time?"

"Um, late April?" Adara guessed. "I can look it up on my phone."

"So fourteen, maybe fifteen weeks ago?" The cool end of the stethoscope was covering a lot of real estate.

"You're not thinking I'm still pregnant from then," Adara scoffed. "Karen, I know a miscarriage when I'm having one."

"I want you to have a scan. Let's go down the hall."

Gideon's face was as tight as Adara's felt. He held her elbow, but she barely felt his touch, limbs going numb with dread. Something was wrong. Really wrong. Karen's sobriety told her that.

Except that, five minutes later, they were looking at a screen that showed an unmistakable profile of a baby's head, its tiny body lounging in a hammock-like curve, one tiny hand lifting above its head to splay like a wishing star.

Gideon cussed out a very base Greek curse. Not exactly appropriate for such a reverent moment, but Adara had to agree. This was unbelievable.

"Is that a recording from someone else?" she asked, afraid to trust her eyes.

"This is why we put you through those procedures during a miscarriage, Adara," Karen said gently. "We look for things like a twin that might have survived. Given that this one has hung on past your first trimester, I'd guess he or she is exactly that. A survivor. This is a very good sign you'll go to term."

# CHAPTER NINE

IF THEY'D WALLOWED in disbelief and shock last night, and tension had been thick on their way to see Karen, it was nothing to the stunned silence that carried them back to the penthouse.

Adara sank onto the sofa without removing her jacket or shoes, totally awash in a sea of incredulity. She was afraid to believe it. They might actually have a baby this time. A family.

An expansion of incredible elation, supreme joy, as if she had the biggest, best secret in the world growing inside her, was tempered by cautious old Adara who never quite believed good things could happen to her. She might have a solicitous husband who felt every bit as protective and parental toward his offspring as she did, but he wasn't in love with her. Not the way she was tumbling into love with him.

Shaken, she glanced to where he stood with hands in his pockets, the back of his shirt flattened by his tense stance, the curve of his buttocks lovingly shaped by black jeans, his feet spaced apart for a sailor's habitual seeking of balance.

"What are you thinking?" she invited hesitantly.

"That I can't believe I let you climb down to that beach in Greece. I've been on you like a damn caveman…" He ran a hand over his hair and turned around. His face was lined with self-recrimination. "I wish to hell I'd known, Adara."

She set her chin, not liking the streak of accusation in his tone. Sitting straighter, she said, "I'm not going to apologize for refusing to see a doctor before today." Even though a lot of things would have been different if she had.

Would she and Gideon have come this far as a couple, though?

And was this far enough?

She clenched her hands and pressed her tightened mouth against her crossed thumbs, trying to process how this pregnancy changed everything. While Gideon had shown no desire to discuss adoption, she had kept divorce on the table. Now...

"It's done anyway," he said, pacing a few steps, then pivoting to confront her. "But moving forward, we're taking better care of you. Both of you. I'll start by informing your brothers you'll be delegating your responsibilities. I want you working four-hour days, not twelve. Travel is curtailed for both of us. Chile will have to wait and Tokyo will go on hold indefinitely. The architect needs to start over and you can't be here through renovations, so we'll have to hurry the Hampton place along."

"Karen said everything is normal, that this isn't a high-risk pregnancy," she reminded, tensing at all he'd said. "I can still work."

"Do you want to take chances?"

"Of course not. But I don't want to be railroaded either. You're acting like—"

Imperious brows went up. "Like?"

"Like it's actually going to happen," she said in a small voice. She watched the toes of her shoes point together. All of her shrank inward, curling protectively around the tiny flicker of life inside her.

"You just said yourself, it's not high risk." His voice was gruff, but she heard the tiny fracture in his tone. He wasn't as steady as he appeared.

"It's just…to make all these changes and tell people… What if something happens?"

The line of his shoulders slumped. He came to sit beside her, angled on the cushion to face her while he pinched her cold fingers in a tight grip. "I'm going to move whatever mountains need moving to ensure nothing does. We're going to have this baby, Adara."

She didn't look convinced. Her brow stayed pleated in worry, her mouth tremulous. A very tentative ray of hope in her eyes remained firmly couched, not allowed to grow.

Gideon clenched his teeth in frustration that sheer will wasn't enough. "I realize you're scared," he allowed.

"I may not be high risk, but there's still a risk," she insisted defensively.

She was breaking his heart. "I'm not disregarding that. But my coping strategy is to reduce the chances of any outcome but the one I want and go full steam ahead."

"And the outcome you want is…a baby?"

"Is there any doubt?" He sat back, unable to fathom that she'd imagine anything else.

"I asked you what you were thinking and you started talking about architects and Tokyo, like this was a massive inconvenience to your jam-packed schedule."

His breath escaped raggedly. "I'm a man. My first thoughts are practical—secure food and shelter. I'm not going to hang my heart out there and admit to massive insecurities at not knowing how to be a father, or reveal that I'm dying of pride."

Her mouth twitched into a pleased smile. "Or own up to whether you'd prefer a boy or a girl?" Underlying her teasing tone was genuine distress. Adara would have had more value in her father's eyes if she'd been a male, they both knew that.

That wasn't why he took her question like a lightning rod to the soul, though, flinching then forcing his expression smooth. "I've always wanted a girl," he admitted, feeling very much as if his vital organs were clawed from him and set out on display. "So we could name her Delphi, for my mother."

Adara paled a bit and he knew he'd made a mistake. He could practically see her taking on responsibility for never giving him that.

"Babe—"

"It's a lovely name," she said with a strained, sweet smile. "I'd like it very much if we could do that."

But she wasn't like him, willing to bet on long shots. Her cheekbones stood out prominently as she distressed over whether she could come through for him. He didn't know how to reassure her that this wasn't up to her. He had never blamed her, never would.

"Will you wait here a minute?" He kissed her forehead and stood, leaving to retrieve the ring he'd wanted to give her last night. When he returned, he sat on the edge of the sofa again, then thought better and dipped onto one knee. "I bought this to mark our fifth anniversary, but…"

Adara couldn't help covering a gasp as he revealed the soft pink diamond pulsing like a heart stone of warmth from the frozen arrangement of white diamonds and glinting platinum setting.

"No matter what happens, we have each other." He fit the ring on her right hand.

Her fingers spasmed a bit, not quite rejecting the gift, but this seemed like a reaffirmation of vows. She had been prepared to throw their marriage away a few weeks ago and didn't know if she was completely ready to recommit to it, but she couldn't bring herself to voice her hesitations when her ears were still ringing with his words about his mother. Every time she'd lost a baby, his mother had died for him again. Small wonder he didn't wear his heart on his sleeve.

Given time, would it become more accessible?

He kissed her knuckles and when he looked into her eyes, his gaze was full of his typical stamp of authority, already viewing this as a done deal. The impact was more than she could bear.

Shielding her own gaze, she looked at his mouth as she leaned forward to kiss him lingeringly. "Thank you. I'll try to be less of a scaredy-cat if you could, perhaps, let me tell my mother before calling the architect?"

She glanced up to catch a flare of something in the backs of his flecked eyes that might have been disappointment or hurt, but he adopted her light tone as he said, "I'm capable of compromise. Don't drag your feet."

For a woman battling through an aggressive cancer treatment, as Adara's mother, Ellice, was, the quiet of Chatham in upstate New York was probably perfect. For a man used to a nonstop pace through sixteen-hour days, the place was a padded cell.

It's only one afternoon, Gideon chided himself. Adara had tried to come alone, but he had insisted on driving her. Still reeling over yesterday's news, he already saw that the duration of her pregnancy would be a struggle not to smother his wife while his instinct to hover over her revved to maximum.

Letting her out of his sight when they'd arrived here had been genuinely difficult, but he respected her wish to speak to her mother alone. She had yet to bring up the topic of Nic. Ellice had been too sick for that conversation, but with doctor reports that weren't exactly encouraging, Adara was facing not having many more conversations with her mother at all.

Scowling with dismay at the rotten hands life dealt, Gideon walked the grounds of the property that Adara's father had bought as an "investment." The old man had really been tucking his wife away from the city, isolating her as a form of punishment because he'd been that sort of man. Gideon saw that now. Not that it had been a complete waste of money. The land itself was nice.

Gideon wondered if either of Adara's brothers wanted this place when their mother passed. With only a dried-up pond for a water view, it wasn't Gideon's style. He didn't need a rolling deck beneath his feet, but he did like a clear view to the horizon.

Maybe that was his old coping strategy rearing its head. Each time his world had fallen apart, he'd looked into the blue yonder and set a course for a fresh start. One thing he'd learned on the ocean: the world was big enough to run away from just about anything.

Not that he was willing to abandon the life he had here. Not now.

He stilled as he noticed a rabbit brazenly munching the lettuce in the garden. Bees were the only sound on the late-summer air, working the flowers that bordered the plot of tomatoes, beans and potatoes. The house stood above him on the hillock, white with fairy-tale gables and peaks. Below the wraparound veranda, the grounds rolled away in pastoral perfection.

It was a vision of the American dream and he was exactly like that invasive rabbit, feeding on what wasn't his.

His conscience had already been torturing him before Adara had turned up pregnant. Now all he could think was that he'd be lying about who he was to his son or daughter along with his wife.

But he couldn't go back and undo all the things he'd done to get here. He'd barely scratched the surface of his past when he'd told Adara he'd started working young. Child labor was what it had been, but as a stowaway discovered while the ship was out to sea, he could as easily have been thrown overboard.

Kristor had put him to work doing what a boy of six or

seven could manage. He'd swabbed decks and scrubbed out the head. He'd learned to gut a fish and peel potatoes. Burly men had shouted and kicked him around like a dog at times, but he'd survived it all and had grown into a young man very much out for his own gain.

By the time he was tall enough to make a proper deckhand, Kristor was taking jobs on dodgy ships, determined to build his retirement nest egg. Gideon went along with him, asking no questions and taking the generous pay the shady captains offered. He wished he could say he had been naive and only following Kristor's lead, but his soul had been black as obsidian. He'd seen dollar signs, not moral boundaries.

The ugly end to Kristor's life had been a vision into his own future if he continued as a smuggler, though. Gideon had had much higher ambitions than that. He'd been stowing his pay, same as Kristor, but it wasn't enough for a clean break.

Posing as Kristor's son, however, and claiming the man's modest savings as an "inheritance" had put him on the solid ground he'd needed. Kristor hadn't had any family entitled to it. Yes, Gideon had broken several laws in claiming that money, even going to the extent of paying a large chunk to a back-alley dealer in the Philippines for American identification. It had been necessary in order to leave that life and begin a legitimate one.

Or so he'd convinced himself at the time. His viewpoint had been skewed to basic survival, not unlike Adara's obdurate attitude when he'd first caught up to her in Greece. He'd been cutting himself off from the pain of losing Kristor in exactly the way he'd fled onto Kristor's ship in the first place, running from the grief and horror of losing his mother.

He couldn't say he completely regretted becoming Gideon Vozaras. At sixteen—nineteen according to the fresh ink on his ID—he'd sunk every penny he had into a rusting sieve of a tugboat. He repaired it, ran it, licensed it out to another boatman and bought another. Seven years later, he leveraged his fleet of thirty to buy an ailing shipyard. When that started to show a profit, he established his first shipping route. He barely slept or ate, but people started to call him, rather than the other way around.

Fully accepted as an established business by then, he'd still possessed some of his less than stellar morals. When he was ready to expand and needed an injection of capital, he started with a man known to let his ego rule his investment decisions. Gideon had walked into the Makricosta headquarters wearing his best suit and had his salesman's patter ready. He'd been willing to say whatever he needed to get to the next level.

He'd been pulled up by an hourglass figure in a sweater set and pencil skirt, her heels modest yet fashionable, her black hair gathered in a clasp so the straight dark tresses fell like a plumb line down her spine. She turned around as he announced himself to the receptionist.

He was used to prompting a bit of eye-widening and a flush of awareness in a woman. If the receptionist gave him the flirty head tilt and smooth of a tendril of hair, he missed it. His mouth had dried and his skin had felt too tight.

Adara's serene expression had given nothing away, but even though her demeanor had been cool, his internal temperature had climbed. She had escorted him down the hall to her father's office, her polish and grace utterly fascinating and so completely out of his league he might as well still have had dirt under his nails and the stink of diesel on his skin.

Three lengthy meetings later, he had been shut down. Her father had refused and Gideon had mentally said goodbye to any excuse to see her again. No use asking her to dinner. By then he had her full background. Adara didn't date and was reputed to be holding on to her virginity until she married.

When she had unexpectedly asked to see him a few weeks later, he'd been surprised, curious and unaccountably hopeful. She'd shown up in a jade dress with an ivory jacket that had been sleek and cool and infuriatingly modest, not the sort of thing a woman wore if she was encouraging an afternoon tryst.

"I didn't expect to see you again," he'd said with an edge of frustration.

"I…" She'd seemed very briefly discomfited, then said with grave sincerity, "I have a proposal for you, which may persuade my father to change his mind, if you're still interested in having him as a backer. May I have ten minutes of your time?"

Behind the closed doors of his office, she had laid out what was, indeed, a proposal. She had done her homework. She had information on his financials and future projects that weren't public knowledge.

"I apologize for that. I don't intend to make a habit of it."

"Of what?" he'd asked. "Snooping into my business or running background checks on prospective grooms?"

"Well, both," she'd said with a guileless look. "If you say yes."

He'd been self-serving enough to go along with the plan. The upside had been too good, offering access to her business and social circles along with a leap in his standing on the financial pages. And Adara had made it so easy. She had not only scripted their engagement and wedding, she'd known her lines. Their marriage had been perfect.

To the untrained eye.

He could look back now and see what a performance it had been on both their parts. From the reception to country clubs to rubbing shoulders with international bankers, they had set each other up like improv specialists, him feeding Adara lines and her staying on message.

And she'd conformed to brand like a pro, elevating her modest style to a timeless sophistication that had put both the hotels and his shipyard in a new class. She'd delivered exactly what she'd promised in terms of networking, opportunities and sheer hard work, putting in the late hours to attain the goals he'd laid out.

She had probably thought that's all he'd wanted from her, he realized, heart clenching. It had been, initially, but somewhere along the line he'd begun to care—about a lot of things. She was an excellent cook and she bought him shirts he liked. Whenever they were about to leave for work or an evening event, she invariably smoothed his hair or straightened his tie and said, "You look nice."

Part of him had stood back and called her actions patronizing, but a needier part had soaked up her approval. It was all the more powerful because he had admired her so much.

Adara set a very high standard for herself. Once he'd fully absorbed that, he'd begun taking it as a challenge to meet and exceed her expectations. Finally comfortable financially, he'd followed her lead and started helping others, selecting charities with thought for who he really wanted to help, creating foundations that benefited young mothers, street kids, and sailors unable to work due to disabilities.

Meanwhile, pride of possession had evolved into something so deep, Adara's seeming to cheat on him earlier this summer had shaken him to the bone.

It wasn't comfortable to be this invested. Sure he was a risk-taker, but not with his emotions. The way his heart had grown inordinately soft, especially in the last weeks, unnerved him, but he couldn't help the way his chest swelled with feeling and pride every time he so much as thought about his wife.

A screen door creaked, drawing his glance. Pressure

filled his chest as Adara appeared on the veranda and lifted a somber hand.

He didn't deserve her or any of this, but he'd do anything to keep it.

Adara's emotions were all over the place and that look of intense determination on Gideon's face as he looked up at her gave her a chill near her heart. He seemed so ruthless in that second, exactly as her mother had just accused him of being. She could clearly see the man who'd said, *Whatever it took, I had to amass some wealth and take control over my destiny.*

But maybe her vision was colored by everything she was dealing with. When she started down the stairs, he met her at the bottom, his scowl deepening as he took in her red, puffy eyes. His arm was tender as he crooked it around her and drew her into his solid presence.

"Pretty rough, huh?"

She began to shake. Until the last few weeks, she'd had to keep her sorrows or worries inside her where they ate like acid. Now she had Gideon. Her mother was so wrong about him. He wasn't cold and heartless like her father. Not at all.

"Can we stay out here a few minutes? I feel like I haven't had air in weeks." Not that the summer heat held much oxygen, but he obliged, ambling beside her as she took a turn around the pond. "This would have been a great place to grow up if my father had bought this earlier. And things had been different," she mused, imagining a swing set and a sandbox.

"If Nic had been your father's, you mean?"

Adara choked on a harsh laugh, voice breaking as she said, "Mom asked me if this baby was yours." Her hand moved to protectively cover their unborn child's ears. "What prospective grandmother has that as a first reaction?"

"*I* don't have any doubt he or she is mine," Gideon said with quiet resolution. "But even if you told me right now that it wasn't, I'd stay right here and work through it with you."

Adara checked her step, startled, thinking again, *whatever it took*… "You wouldn't be angry?"

"I'd be angry as hell, but I wouldn't take it out on you and the baby the way your father tortured you and your mother. I wouldn't push you out of my life to fend for yourself, either."

The way his mother had had to make her own way. Adara's surprise and apprehension softened to understanding. He might have a streak of single-mindedness, but there was a marshmallow center under his hard shell.

"You're a bigger person than me. Maybe it's the miscarriages and fear of infidelity talking, but I don't know if I could stay married if you had a baby with someone else."

"You're not sure you want to stay married, as it is, and the only woman having my baby is *you*."

Adara pivoted away from that and continued walking, startled by the shaft of fear his light challenge pierced into her. It would seem her ability to dissemble around him was completely gone. He knew every thought in her head, every hesitation in her heart.

"My mother said she'd understand if it wasn't yours," Adara said with a sheared edge on her tone, recalling how that conversation had spun into directions she hadn't anticipated any better than this one. Holding on to her composure had been nearly impossible as her mother had tried to find parallels in their two lives. "My parents had had a fight and the engagement was off. That's why she slept with Nic's dad. Olief was a journalist flying back to Europe. She had a layover. It was just a rebound thing. The sort of affair all her flight attendant friends were having. Then my father called and the wedding was back on."

"Even though she knew she was pregnant?"

"I guess paternity could have gone either way. She loved my father so she married him and deluded herself into believing Nic was his."

*At least you're not in love with your husband. I've always been proud of you for having that much sense, but children are a mistake, Adara. You have no idea how much power a man has over you once babies enter the picture.*

Adara had recoiled from her mother's words, finding it distasteful to be accused of having no feelings for Gideon even though that had been her goal for most of her marriage.

"I wanted her to be happy for us and she just took off on a bitter rant about my father." Hearing her mother refer to her grandchild as a "mistake" had been the greatest blow of all. Her entire childhood, void as it had been of parental pride and joy, had crawled out from under the bed, grim and dark and ready to swallow her.

"She's sick," Gideon reminded her.

"I know, but—" *But you lied to him*, she had wanted to say. Maybe her father wouldn't have twisted into such a cruel man if his wife had been honest from the start.

There was no use trying to change her mother at this point though. Challenging her, arguing and judging, were incredibly misplaced. Her mother wasn't just sick, she was dying.

"We'll do better by our child," Gideon vowed, pausing to turn her into him. He lifted her hand to graze his lips across the backs of her fingers. The ring he'd given her yesterday winked at her.

At the same time, his eyes held a somber rebuke. Gideon was a patient man, but this time he wasn't going to let her avoid his silent question. Even as she absorbed his earnest statement, her mother's voice whispered again, *You have no idea how much power a man has over you once babies enter the picture.*

But she wasn't her mother. There weren't any lies between her and Gideon. The secrets and recriminations that had surrounded her growing up, forcing her to close off her heart out of self-protection, were old news. Their child, unpolluted by any of that, gave her a chance to love cleanly and openly.

This fresh start with this man, who already stirred her so deeply, was a chance to build a truly happy life. If she dared believe she was entitled to it and opened herself to letting it happen. It was a huge leap of faith, but she'd taken one in marrying him at all. Maybe she was putting her heart at deep risk, but again and again he'd proven himself to be a man she could trust.

"We will, won't we?" she said in quiet promise.

Relief and a flicker of deeper emotion was quickly transformed into his predominant mask of arrogant confidence. For a second, he'd seemed moved, which made her heart trip, but now he was his typical conqueror self, nearly smug with triumph—which was familiar and oddly endearing, making her want to laugh and ignore her old self trying to warn her that she might be giving up too much too quickly.

But if she had a soupy, awed look on her face, he wore one of fierce tenderness.

"You're so beautiful." The kiss he bent to steal was as reverent and sweet as it was hard and possessive.

Her lips clung to his as he drew away.

"Don't get ideas," he chided, breaking contact from her look of invitation. "We're cut off until you deliver."

"That's you being overcautious. Karen didn't say we couldn't." She was still aggravated that they'd shared a bed last night but hadn't made love. She was nervous about doing anything to jeopardize her pregnancy, but they'd been making love without consequence until now.

"Karen doesn't know how insatiable we are once we get started. Just do me a favor and don't make this harder than it is."

"Pun intended?" She drifted her gaze down his front to the bulge behind his fly.

"This is going to be a very long pregnancy." He gritted his teeth, making her laugh as he guided her inside for an early dinner before driving home.

# CHAPTER TEN

AFTER YEARS OF being the one who micromanaged to ensure everything met her father's impossible standards, Adara was forced to let go and trust others to pull off top-notch work with minimal input. It wasn't easy, but she eased up and was pleasantly surprised by her very efficient teams. Despite her working from home for months, only checking in electronically, they were managing great things without her.

Staying away from the office had a drawback, however. Moving through the ballroom decorated in fall colors of gold, crimson and burnt umber, she couldn't help congratulating people on putting together a brilliant event to celebrate the Makricosta chain's thirty-fifth anniversary. They all reacted with great surprise and when Adara met up with Connie, a woman she'd worked closely with for years, she realized why.

Connie rocked back on her four-inch heels. "Wow, I've never seen a woman as pregnant as you act so happy and outgoing. When I got that big, I was a complete cow."

"Oh, I…" Adara didn't know what to say. Had her personality been frozen for so many years that a bit of friendly warmth was remarkable? Or was she really as big as she felt?

"That's meant as a compliment," Connie rushed to say, glancing with horror at Adara's guardian angel, Gideon.

They'd learned to give each other space in the confines of the penthouse as they worked from home, but tonight he was right beside her, his ripped masculinity nearly bursting out of his tuxedo. He didn't complain about their abstinence nearly as much as she did, but he spent a lot of time expending sexual energy in the weight room. It showed, making his presence all the more electric, while Adara's insecurity ballooned to match her figure.

"It's true," he said with a disturbing slide of his hand beneath the fall of her hair. His touch settled in a light, caressing clasp on the back of her neck, making her follicles tighten. "The pregnancy glow isn't a myth. You're gorgeous."

"I look like the *Queen Mary*," Adara sputtered. Her reports from Karen continued to be good, and weight gain was to be expected, but playing dress-up for this evening hadn't been as fun as it used to be. Her hair had developed kinks, she was too puffy for her rings and wearing heels was out of the question. Growing shorter and pudgier while her husband grew hotter and sleeker was demoralizing. All her excitement in having a date night deflated.

"I only meant that you seem very happy. When are you due?" Connie prompted.

Adara couldn't help brightening at the topic of delivering a healthy baby, her misgivings from early in the pregnancy dispelled by her baby's regular jabs and the closing in of her due date. Nowadays her fears were the natural ones of any mother, most specifically that her water would break while she was in public.

But a few minutes later, when Gideon interjected, "We should start the dancing," and guided her toward the floor, her self-consciousness returned. He must have felt her tension. As he took her in his arms, he chided, "Are you genuinely worried about how you look? Because I was being sincere. You're stunning."

Biting off another self-deprecating remark, she chose to be truthful. "We haven't been going out much, so I guess I wasn't expecting so many stunned expressions at how huge I am. And look around, Gideon. Wait, don't. There are far too many women with teensy waistlines and long legs and—"

"None with breasts like yours. Do you think I've looked anywhere but down your dress tonight? Unless it's at your lips. You're not wearing lipstick, are you? That's all you, ripe and pouty and pink. You're sexy as hell."

Said lips parted in surprise. Everything seemed to taste funny these days, lipstick included, so she'd opted for a flavorless lip balm and yes, had noted that even her lips looked fat. She might have bit them together in an attempt to hide them, but his wolfish fixation on her mouth sent tendrils of delight through her.

With a little moue she said, "Really? You're not just saying that?"

With a low growl, he stopped dancing and claimed her mouth with his own.

The kiss was devastating, making her knees want to fold so he had to tighten his hold on her, shifting her to an angle to accommodate her bump. That tilted her head just enough to seal their lips with erotic perfection.

He didn't keep it to a quick punctuation to prove a point, either. Adara put up a hand to the side of his head, thinking, *People are watching,* but he gave her tongue a wicked tag and she couldn't help letting the kiss deepen and continue.

Oh, this man could kiss.

A cleared throat brought her back to reality with a *thunk* that she felt all the way into the flats of her feet. A woman's amused Irish lilt said, "Don't interrupt them. They're adorable."

"Nic," Adara breathed in recognition of her older brother and his wife, growing hot with embarrassment as she realized what a show they'd been putting on. "Hi, Rowan. It didn't sound like you'd make it."

Her brother and his wife were beyond star power, Nic in a tuxedo and Rowan showing off her lithe dancer's body with an off-the-shoulder figure-hugging green gown.

"Evie got over her cold and we wanted to see you again," Rowan said.

Nic leaned in to kiss Adara's cheek before he shook hands with Gideon.

Something passed between the two men that she couldn't quite interpret and didn't get a chance to study. Having kept up via webcam, she and Rowan had become tight friends and that gave them plenty to talk about. The rest of the evening passed in a blur of catching up while also going through the routine of photo ops and speeches for the anniversary celebration, partaking of the buffet, and finally returning to the penthouse exhausted but still keyed up.

"That went well, don't you think?" she asked Gideon as she removed her earrings. They were enchanting cascades of diamonds commissioned to match her ring. She'd almost ruined her makeup when he'd presented them to her before they'd left earlier in the evening, she was so affected by his thoughtfulness.

Gideon made a noncommittal noise.

"No?" she prompted, alarmed that he might have noticed a flaw she'd missed.

"Hmm? No, it was fine. Perfect. Excellent. I'm a bit distracted. Look, you get ready for bed and I'll be in soon. I'd like a nightcap."

"Oh. Okay." Adara's startled confusion was evident, but Gideon didn't attempt to explain himself.

He breathed a small sigh of relief as she disappeared and didn't see the full measure of bracing whiskey he poured for himself or the rabid way he drained it. Despite the burn that promised forgetfulness, he wasn't able to stop replaying his conversation with her brother.

"I'd like a word," Nic had said when both their wives had been drawn across the room by some fashion marvel.

"Now is fine," Gideon had said, keeping one eye on Adara, premonition tightening his muscles.

"Understand first that I've always felt protective of Adara, even when the only thing she had to fear was a nightmare. Knowing what I abandoned her to, I'm sick with myself for not trying to contact her sooner. I'll be on guard for her the rest of my life."

"Reassuring," Gideon had muttered.

"The way you two were arguing at the end of my driveway wasn't," Nic retorted sharply. "When you first arrived in Greece. Not reassuring at all."

Gideon knew better than to show weakness, but he flinched involuntarily. "I thought she was meeting another man. Tell me how you would react if you thought your wife was stepping out on you."

"She wouldn't. But…" Nic shrugged, seeming to accept the explanation for Gideon's temper that day. "Regardless, I'm a man who collects the facts before he reacts."

Gideon had spilled a dry laugh at that point, enjoying the euphemistic phrase "collects the facts." "You mean you had me investigated."

"I don't have to hire people to do my legwork," Nic said disparagingly.

"No," Gideon snorted, wishing for a drink at that point. He'd known from the outset that Nic could be a threat, but he hadn't expected this. Not now when he and Adara had both found such happiness. "What did you learn?" He surreptitiously braced himself.

"What do you think I learned?" Nic asked, narrowing his eyes. "Nothing. Which doesn't surprise you, does it?"

"Of course it does," he'd lied. "I'm all over the internet."

"Gideon Vozaras is," Nic agreed. "He's never made a wrong move. Some of his early business dealings weren't as clean as they could have been, but that's every scrappy young man trying to make his mark. Those men don't usually appear out of thin air, though."

Gideon had calmly stropped his knuckles on his jaw, trying to disguise that he was clenching his teeth. "I'm fairly protective of Adara myself, you know." He flashed a glance from her laughing face to the vague resemblance of her features in her brother's rigid expression.

The other man wasn't intimidated, but there was a watchful respect. He didn't take the danger of Gideon's temper lightly.

"I can see that things between you are different from the way they first appeared," Nic said. "But secrets destroyed my life. I won't let that happen to Adara."

"It's not secrets that destroy. It's the exposing of them. You really want to do that to her when she's found the first bit of happiness she's known since you were children?" He jerked his chin toward the circle of women where Adara was holding court with a flush of pleasure on her face, allowing another woman to feel the baby kick. "Think about what you're doing, Nic."

"No, you think about it," Nic had retorted sharply. "Do you want to make it easy and give me a name? Tell her yourself before I get there? Because I will."

"You want a name? Start with Delphi Parnassus and happy reading." He'd bit out the words and smoothly extricated his wife from the party, claiming she needed her rest.

"Gideon? Are you all right?" Adara asked him, yanking him back to the apartment where she stood in the bedroom doorway, face clean of makeup. Her hair was brushed into sleek waves. She wore one of his silk shirts, the front crossed over her bulging tummy and pinned by her folded arms. Her bump shortened the shirt, offering such a tantalizing view to the tops of her thighs, he reacted like a drug had been injected into his loins.

"Why are you wearing that?" His voice barely made it up from the depths of his chest.

"I've grown out of all my nightgowns," she said with aggravation. "Do you mind?"

"It's criminal, Adara," he admitted with a scrape in his throat, polishing the last of his drink. "We promised not to tease each other. Let me get you my robe."

She tilted her head to a skeptical angle as he brushed past her. "I wasn't trying to tease. But, be honest, are my legs okay? Because they seem swollen. No wonder everyone was appalled."

*Be honest,* echoed in his head, but the whiskey was burning through blood that had abstained from alcohol the way the rest of him had been going without his wife. Fear, genuine fear of losing her—not this penthouse or their cruise ship or the other properties they owned—edged out conscience or logic. All he wanted was to hold on to her. Tightly.

"It's been a long night. You should be asleep," he told her when she followed him into the bedroom.

"I had a nap before we left," she reminded, scowling as he shook out his robe and held it for her. "Does it strike you that we act less like a married couple these days than a nanny and her charge? You don't need to dress me."

He patiently continued to keep the robe suspended by the shoulders, inviting her to shrug her arms into the sleeves. "If I treat you like a child, it's only to remind myself that's why I can't have you. You know I'm crazy about you."

"But how could you be? Look at me!" She flashed open the shirt she'd been hugging over her front.

He shut his eyes, but not before he took a mental photograph of creamy skin, nipples dark and distended, lush, plump curves and a ripe round belly with an alluring shadow beneath that was *not* concealed by any satin or lace. She was naked and gloriously fertile.

This was why ancient men worshipped the goddess who provided their young.

"You can't even look!"

"For God's sake, Adara." He hung the robe on its hook and moved into his closet to change, needing the distance or he'd bend her over the nearest piece of furniture and *show* her how badly he wanted her. "If I wanted to sleep with a stick, I would have married one. You've always had a nice round ass and I like it. Frankly, it's better than ever in my opinion. See how hot I am for you?"

He paused in hanging his tuxedo pants over a rod and moved into the doorway, showing her his straining erection barely contained by his boxers. Every cell in his body was primed for her and this fight was only shredding what little control he had left. It didn't help that he was also dealing with Nic's threats, feeling his grip on Adara and their life together slipping away. He wanted to cement their connection with a prolonged act of intimacy, but it wasn't possible.

Adara's gaze went liquid as she roamed it lovingly down his form, wetting her lips as she stared at the shape straining against the molding fabric of his shorts.

"I could—"

"I told you, we're in this together," he muttered, turning away from her offer even though it was like wrenching muscle tissue from his bones. But every time he thought of the way she'd gone down on him to protect this pregnancy in the first place, and that he'd resented not having all of her, he felt like the biggest heel alive.

He *was*.

He finished stowing his clothes and stepped into his pajama bottoms, returning to the bedroom to find her buttoning his shirt up her front, not looking at him.

He sighed, but what could he say?

A few seconds later, the lights were out and that delicious ass of hers was pressed firmly into his lap, driving him insane as she wiggled to get comfortable.

"Can I have your arm?" She lifted her head.

He obliged, sliding his arm under her neck the way she liked. As she settled and sighed, he smoothed her hair back from her ear and rested his lips against her nape. His other hand splayed on her belly and he let out a breath as well.

She was still tense though and it made it impossible for him to relax.

"Don't be angry," he cajoled. "This is only for a couple more months."

*"Months,"* Adara cried, nearly ready to burst into tears of frustration. Feeling his erection against her cheeks didn't help.

"Weeks," he hurried to say, even though they both knew it was eight.

"I'm dying." She covered his hand with hers and drew his fingers into contact with the wet valley between her thighs. "See?"

It was something she couldn't have even contemplated doing half a year ago, but they'd grown close and honest and sexual. Her body wasn't as visual as his when it came to showing how aroused she was, but she wanted him to know how badly she was suffering. She expected him to pull away and scold her, but he surprised her by burying a groan against her neck and stroking deeply and with more pressure. He explored her with the familiar expertise that always drove her directly to the edge.

Her hips rocked instinctively into his caress, then back into that teasing hardness behind the thin shield of fabric pressed against her bottom. His other arm shifted to clamp around her, clasping one full breast and caging her to the wall of his body while he bit her neck. His hips pushed against her and he pressed two fingertips where she felt it most, pinning her in a vise of sheer delight.

A quicksilver shiver was chased by a shudder and then the quaking poured through her, running like fire between her thighs and suffusing her whole body in sparkling waves of pleasure. The contractions were huge and stunning and incredible. She mindlessly prolonged them by grinding his hand between her legs and rocking her hips against his erection, loving everything about this wildly intimate act.

When the paroxysm receded, she gasped for a normal breath.

Gideon's caressing fingers left her. She protested with a little murmur. Her body wanted more and more and more, but a sweet lassitude filled her too. *Now* she felt sexy and adored.

She also realized her neck stung. Gideon had left a love bite there.

Dazed but determined to keep things equal between them, she tried to turn. He swore and rolled away.

"Don't be mad—" She realized there was also a wet patch on her back. Plucking at it, mind hardly able to comprehend how… "Did you—?"

"Yes," he said tightly. She sensed he was lifting his hips to remove his pajama pants. A second later the pants were dragged from beneath the covers and sent flying across the floor. "What the hell did you just do to me? I haven't done that since, hell, I don't think I've ever lost control like that. It's not funny."

Adara couldn't help the fit of giggles as she sat up to remove his shirt. "I was kinda caught up and didn't realize you were with me. That's nice. I'm glad."

"Yeah, I noticed you were enjoying it. That's why I was so turned on, but I didn't mean to lose it completely. Thank God it's dark. I'm so embarrassed—would you quit laughing?" He threw the stained shirt after the pants.

"I'm sorry," she said, unable to help convulsing with giggles as he spooned her into him again, skin to skin. It felt incredible and she snuggled deeper into the curve of his hot body. "Was it good for you?"

"What do you think? It was fantastic, you brat. How's baby? Did I hurt you? I was holding you pretty tight. Good thing you're not going anywhere tomorrow, with that giant hickey on your neck."

"We're fine. Both very happy." She smiled into the dark, melting as he caressed her belly and nuzzled her ear. "But you're not going to leave those clothes on the floor, are you?" she teased.

He stilled and let out a breath of exasperation. "They're fine till—oh, hell, it'll drive me crazy now you've said it and you know that, don't you?" He flung off the covers and gathered the shirt and pants to throw them in the hamper. "Enjoying yourself?" he asked as he returned to the bed that was shaking with her laughter.

Adara used the edge of the blanket to stifle her snickers. "I'm sorry. That was mean, wasn't it?"

"Yes, it was," he growled, cuddling her into him once more. They both relaxed. "But you must believe me now. About finding you irresistible?"

"I do," she agreed, sleepily caressing the back of his hand where it rested on the side of her belly. Tenderness filled her and she knew she'd never been this happy in her life. "And I can't help thinking... Gideon?"

"Mmm?" he responded sleepily.

"Are we falling in love?" Her heart stopped as she took that chance. It was such a walk straight off a cliff.

That didn't pay off.

Stillness transformed him into a rock behind her. Her postorgasmic relaxation dissipated, filling her with tension. His breath didn't even stir her hair.

Stupid, stupid, Adara. Hadn't she learned a millennium ago not to beg for affection?

"I'm not sure," he said in a gruff rasp.

"It was a silly question. Never mind. Let's just go to sleep. I'm tired." She resolutely shut her eyes and tried to force herself to go lax, to convince him she was sleeping, but she stayed awake a long time, a thick lump in her throat.

And when she woke in the night, he was no longer in the bed with her.

Gideon stood before the living room windows and saw nothing but his past. A dozen times or more over the years, he'd considered coming clean with Adara. Every time he'd talked himself out of telling her his real name, but this time he wasn't finding an easy way to rationalize keeping his secret.

At first it had been a no-brainer. She'd been all business with her proposal, selling him the upside of marriage in her sensible way. The hook had been deliciously baited with everything he'd ever wanted, including a sexy librarian-style wife. Telling her at that point that he was living under a false name would have deep-sixed their deal. Of course, he'd stayed silent.

His conscience had first pinched him the morning of their honeymoon though. She'd come to the breakfast table so fresh faced and shy, barely able to meet his gaze. He'd been incapable of forming thoughts or words, his entire being filled with excited pride as he recollected how trusting and sweetly responsive she'd been.

*"Any regrets?"* she'd asked into the silence, hands in her lap, breath subtly held.

*"None,"* he'd lied, because he'd had a small one. It had niggled that she was so obviously good and pristine and un-questioning. He'd soiled her in a way, marrying her under pretense.

He hadn't exactly been tortured by his lie, doing what he could to compensate, even forgetting for stretches at a time as they put on charity balls and cut ribbons on after-school clubs. He had let himself believe he really was Gideon Vozaras and Adara legally his wife. Life had been too easy for soul-searching and when the miscarriages had happened, well, things had grown too distant between them to even think of confessing.

Since Greece, however, the jabs to his conscience had grown more frequent and a lot sharper. Honesty had become a necessary pillar to their relationship, strengthening it as much as the physical intimacy. He respected her too much to be dishonest with her.

And he loved her too much to risk losing her.

*God, he loved her.* Last night when she'd asked him about his feelings, he'd been struck dumb by how inadequate the word was when describing such an expansive emotion. He'd handled it all wrong, immediately falling into a pit of remorse because he was misrepresenting himself. He *had* to tell her.

And he would lose her when he did.

He could stand losing everything else. The inevitable scandal in the papers, the legal ramifications, the hit to his social standing and being dropped from his numerous boards of directors... None of that would be easy to take, but he'd endure it easily if Adara stood by him.

She wouldn't. Maybe she would stick by a man who came from a decent background, but once he really opened his can of worms and she saw the extent of his filthy start, she'd be understandably appalled. It would take a miracle for her to overlook it.

Yet he had no choice, not with Nic breathing down his neck.

His heart pumped cold, sluggish blood through his

arteries as he waited like a man on death row, waited for the sound of footsteps and the call of his name.

Adara didn't bother trying to go back to bed when she woke at six. Swaddling herself in Gideon's robe, she went to find him, mind already churning with ways to gloss over her gaffe from last night. If she could have pretended it hadn't happened at all, she would have, but it was obvious she'd unsettled him. She'd have to say something.

She found him standing at the window in the living room, barefoot and shirtless, sweatpants slouched low on his hips. His hair was rumpled, his expression both ravaged and distracted when he turned at the sound of her footsteps.

He didn't say anything, just looked at her as if the greatest misery gripped him.

Her heart clutched. This was all her fault. She'd ruined everything.

"It was never part of our deal, I know that," she blurted, moving a few steps toward him only to be held off by his raised hand.

He might as well have planted that hand in the middle of her chest and shoved with all his considerable might, it was such a painfully final gesture of rejection.

"Our *deal*…" He ran his hand down his unshaven face. "You don't even know who you made that deal with, Adara. I shouldn't have taken it. It was wrong."

She gasped, cleaved in two by the implication he regretted their marriage and all that had come of it thus far. He couldn't mean it. No, this was about his childhood, she told herself, grasping for an explanation for this sudden rebuff. He'd confessed that before they married he'd had a low sense of self-worth. He blamed himself for his friend's death. He had probably convinced himself he wasn't worthy of being loved.

She knew how that felt, but he was so wrong.

"Gideon—" She moved toward him again.

He shook his head and walked away from her, standing at an angle so all she could see was his profile filled with self-loathing. A great weight slumped his bare shoulders.

She couldn't bear to see him hurting like this. "Gideon, please. I know I overstepped. We don't have to go into crisis."

"It's not *you* that's done anything. You're perfect. And I wouldn't do this if your brother hadn't threatened to do it for me," he said through gritted teeth, as if he was digging a bullet from his own flesh. "I would never hurt you if I had a choice. You know that, right?"

"Hurt me how? Which brother? What do you mean?"

"Nic. He's threatened to expose me to you, so I have no choice but to tell you myself."

His despair was so tangible, her hand unconsciously curled into the lapels of the robe, drawing it tightly over the place in her throat that suddenly felt sliced open and cold. She instinctively knew she didn't want to hear what he had to say, but forced herself to ask in a barely-there voice, "Tell me what?"

He solidified into a marble statue, inscrutable and still, his lips barely moving as he said, "That I'm not Gideon Vozaras."

After a long second, she reminded herself to blink, but she was still unable to comprehend. Her mind said, *Of course you are.* He wasn't making sense.

"I don't... What do you mean? Who is then?"

"No one. It's a made-up name."

"No, it's not." The refusal was automatic. How could his name be made up? He had a driver's license and a passport. Deeds to boats and properties. His name was on their marriage certificate. You couldn't falsify things like that. Could you?

She stared at him, ears ringing with the need to hear

something from those firmly clamped lips, something that would contradict what he'd already said.

He only held her gaze with a deeply regretful look. His brow was furrowed and anguished.

No. She shook her head. This was just something he was saying to get out of feeling pressured to love her because…

Her mind couldn't conjure any sensible reason to go to this length of a tale to escape an emotional obligation. Rather, her thoughts leaped more quickly to the opposite: that it would make more sense to pretend to love in order to perpetuate a ruse. The nightly news was full of fraudsters who pretended to love someone so they could marry a fortune.

Her throat closed up and she took a step backward, recoiling from the direction her thoughts were taking. It wasn't possible. She was being paranoid.

But she couldn't escape the way tiny actions—especially those taken since she'd asked for a divorce—began to glow with significance. They landed on her with a weightless burn, clinging like fly ash.

*I fired Lexi.*

*I had self-worth because you gave it to me. People respected me.*

His sudden turn toward physical attentiveness and nonstop seduction. No baby wasn't a deal breaker, he'd said.

But adoption wasn't worth talking about *because that would require a thorough background check.*

Her heart shriveled and began to hurt. She brought a protective hand to her belly. He must have thought he'd won the lottery when she had turned up pregnant and their marriage was seemingly cemented forever.

*I wouldn't do this if your brother hadn't threatened to do it for me.*

He would have let her just keep on believing he was Gideon Vozaras.

"Who are you?" she asked in a thin voice, thinking, *This is a dream. A bad one.* "Where did Gideon Vozaras come from?"

He scowled. "I took Kristor's surname so I could pose as his son and collect what savings he had. My first name came off the cover of a Bible in a hotel room." He jerked a shoulder, face twisting with dismay. "Sacrilegious, I know."

A fine tremor began to work through her and she realized she was cold. Too bad. There was no cuddling up to her husband for a warm hug. This man was a stranger.

The truth of that struck to her core.

"We're not married," she breathed. Somehow it was worse than all the rest. She was a good girl. Always had been. She'd saved herself for marriage. They'd had a wedding. Her father had finally approved of something she'd done. There were photos of them taking vows. All those witnesses had seen…a joke. A lie.

It was all a huge, huge lie.

Gideon—*the stranger*—flattened his mouth into a grim line. "In every way that matters, I am—"

"Oh my *God*," Adara cried, shaking now as her mind raced through all that this meant. He must have called his bookie and put everything he owned on a long shot when she turned up in his office asking to marry him. What a fantastic idiot she was! "You never loved me. You didn't even *want* me."

"Adara." His turn to take a step toward her and it was her turn to back away.

*Whatever it took, I had to amass some wealth…*

She remembered exactly how shocked he'd looked when she'd suggested marriage, how quick he'd been to seize the chance. How accommodating and willing to go with the flow of everything she asked, from waiting until the wedding night to keeping separate bedrooms.

She covered her mouth to hold back a scream. And last

night she'd had to *beg* him to touch her. She'd had to plead because he'd been avoiding lovemaking—

Humiliation stung all the way to her soul.

"You've been laughing at me all this time, haven't you?" she accused as emotion welled in her. Hot, fierce emotion that made her tremble uncontrollably. "No wonder you fought so hard to stay married. Where would all of this go if we divorced?" She flung out an arm to encompass the penthouse and work space and high living they enjoyed. "Who would half of it go to? Thank God I was pregnant, huh, Gid—" She choked, aware she didn't even know his real name. "Whoever the hell you are."

Gideon's world was dissolving around him, but it had nothing to do with penthouses in the top of a tower. "Calm down," he said, grasping desperately at control, when he wanted to crush her to him and show her how wrong she was. "You're going to put yourself into labor. We can get through this, Adara. Look how far we've come since Greece."

It was a weakly thrown life ring, one that failed to reach her.

"How *far?*" she cried, rising to a new level of hysteria. "I thought we were learning to be *honest*. You might have mentioned this little secret of yours."

"I'm telling you now," he insisted.

"Because my brother extorted it out of you! If he hadn't, I'd still be in the dark, wouldn't I?"

He grappled for a reasonable tone, worried about the way her face was reddening. Her blood pressure wasn't a huge issue, but they were monitoring it. She'd complained of breathlessness a few times and her chest was heaving with agitation.

"We were happy," he defended.

"The mark is always happy when she's well and truly duped," she cried. "How could you do that to me? To anyone? What kind of man *are* you?" She rushed him, looking as if she intended to pulverize him.

He caught her arms and held her off. He didn't care about his own safety. She could pummel him into the dirt if it made her feel better, but she and the baby were everything. If she didn't get hold of herself, she was going to hurt one or the other or both.

She struggled against his hold, but he easily used his superior strength to back her into the sofa, where he firmly plunked her into it, saying sternly, "Calm *down*."

"I have a criminal liar invading my home! I'm entitled to—oh, you bastard! I hate you." She tried to rise and strike at him. "How could you do this? How?"

He forced her back into the softness of the cushions. "You're giving me no choice but to walk out of here," he warned. "I'd rather stay and talk this out."

"And talk me round, you mean." She slapped at his touch. "Get out of here then, you scumbag."

The names didn't matter. The betrayal and loathing behind the words sliced him to the bone. He couldn't bear to leave her hating him like this, but even as he stood there hesitating, she was trying to rock herself out of the cushions and swipe at him at the same time, breasts heaving with exertion.

For her own safety, he couldn't stay. Every step to the door flayed a layer of skin from his body, but he moved away from her, waiting for a pause in her tirade of filthy names to say, "It was never my ability to love that was in question, Adara."

"You should have said it last night when I asked. I might have fallen for it then, but not now, you phony. Get out. And don't ever expect to see this child."

That was meant as a knife to the heart and it landed right on target, stealing his breath and almost taking him back into the fight, but as he glanced back, he could see how pale and fraught she was, obviously going into a kind of shock. He grabbed his cell phone on the way to the elevator and placed a call to Nic as the doors closed him out of his home.

"Get over here and make sure she doesn't lose our baby over this."

# CHAPTER ELEVEN

Adara had a very high tolerance for emotional pain, but this went beyond anything she'd ever imagined. Even the news that her mother unexpectedly succumbed to her cancer didn't touch it. Maybe because she'd prepared herself for that loss, she was able to get through it without falling apart, but in truth, she was pretty sure her heart was too broken to feel it.

At least dealing with the funeral and out-of-town family gave her something to concentrate on besides the betrayal she'd suffered. Moving like a robot, she went through the motions of making arrangements while all three of her brothers stood as an honor guard around her.

Nic hadn't been sure of his reception, but she didn't blame him for bringing Gideon's lies to her attention. Nic understood how unacceptable and wrong hiding the truth was. He'd been right to force it into the light.

As for the man she had thought of as her husband, she saw him once. He came to the service, not making any effort to approach her, but she felt his eyes on her the whole time.

After the first glimpse, she couldn't bear to look at him. All she could think about was how easy she'd been for him in every way, screwing up her courage to propose. Giving in to hormones and his deft proficiency with the female body. Feeling so proud to have a man at all, especially one who made women envy her. He'd played on all her biggest weaknesses, right up to his supposed shared pain over the miscarriages.

Here her heart stalled, torn apart by the idea he'd been faking his grief. It was too unfair, too cruel. Was even a shred of what he'd told her about his childhood true?

That thought weakened her, making her susceptible to excusing his behavior, so she cut herself off from considering it. She'd leaned on Theo's wide chest and focused on the inappropriate dress worn by Demitri's date. Leave it to her youngest brother to bring an escort to his mother's funeral.

Her brothers coped in very different ways, but they stayed close, protective in their way, getting her through those first few weeks of loss so she didn't have to dwell on the fact her marriage had been an unmitigated fraud.

But solitude arrived when they went back to work and Nic went home with his wife and baby.

Adara had to say one thing about her fake of a husband. He'd provoked a new sense of responsibility in both her younger brothers. Demitri was still a wild card, but he hadn't missed a single appointment in his calendar since he'd been informed of her pregnancy, and while she wasn't always comfortable with his newfangled marketing campaigns, they seemed to be working.

As for Theo, well, the middle child was always a dark horse, keeping things inside. Epitomizing the strong silent type, he didn't socialize or like people much at all. That's why she was so surprised when he dropped by the penthouse on his way home from the airport, took off his jacket and asked if he could make himself coffee.

"I can make it," she offered.

"Stay off your feet."

She made a face at his back, tired of a lifetime of being bossed by men, but also tired in general. Elevating her ankles again as she'd been instructed, she went back to studying a spreadsheet on her laptop.

"Why are you working?" he asked when he came back to pace her living room restlessly, steaming cup in his hand.

"I'm not checking up on you, if that's what you think."

"Go ahead. You won't find any mistakes. I don't make them."

She lifted her brows at his arrogance, but he only held her gaze while he sipped his coffee.

"We were never allowed to, were we?" he added with a lightness that had an inner band of steel belting.

Her first instinct was to duck. Were they really going there?

An unavoidable voicing of the truth had emerged in her dealings with her siblings once she'd pulled Nic back into their lives. With the absence of their mother's feelings to worry about, perhaps they were all examining the effects of silence, asking questions that might hurt but cleansed ancient wounds.

"No, only Demitri was allowed. And he made enough for all of us," she added caustically, stating another unspoken truth.

Theo agreed to that with a pull of one corner of his mouth before he paced another straight line across her wall of windows. "Which leaves me wondering if I should let you make this one."

Adara set aside her laptop and folded her hands over her belly. "Which one is that?"

"The same one our father made."

A *zing* of alarm went through her, more like a paralyzing shock from a cattle prod, actually, leaving her limbs feeling loose and not her own. She clumsily swung her feet to the floor but didn't have the strength to stand.

"If you're talking about Gid—that man who pretended to be my husband, he *lied*, Theo. That's why our father was the way he was. Because Mother betrayed him. Trust me when I tell you it leaves a bitterness you can't rinse out of your mouth." Her heart ached every day with loss and anger and hurt.

"Our father was a twisted, cruel bastard because he never forgave her. Is that what you're going to do? Punish Gideon and take it out on his baby?"

Adara set her hand protectively on her belly. "Of course not!" She wasn't being that cutting and heartless. Was she?

"Are you going to let him see his child, then?"

She swallowed, unable to say a clear yes or no. The thought of seeing Gideon made her go both hot and cold, burning with anticipation and freezing her with fear that he'd hurt her all over again. She couldn't bear the thought of facing him, knowing how he'd tricked her while part of her still loved the man she'd thought of as her husband. Deep down she knew she couldn't deny her child its father, but the reality of sharing custody with a charlatan was too much to contemplate.

Therefore, she was ignoring the need to make a decision, putting it off until she couldn't avoid it any longer.

"He'll always be in your life in one way or another. Are you going to twist the knife every chance you get? Or act like a civilized human being about it?"

"Stop it," she said, hating the way he was painting her as small and vindictive. He didn't understand how shattering it was to have your perceptions exploded like this. How much like grief it was to lose the man you loved not to an accident, but to duplicity. She rocked herself off the sofa and onto her feet. "Why are you defending him? What do you expect me to do? Lie down and let him wipe his feet on me the way our mother did? He abused my trust!"

"But he didn't abuse you. Did he?" It was a real question, one with a rare thread of uncertainty woven into his tone.

"Of course not," she muttered, instantly repelled by even

the suggestion. Why? What did she care what other people thought of Gid—that man?

"You make it sound like you wouldn't have stood for it, but we all hung around for it," Theo pointed out bluntly.

She didn't answer. There was nothing to say to that ugly truth. If she could see her toes, she knew they'd have been curled into the carpet.

"I was scared for you, you know," Theo said gruffly. "When you married him. We didn't know him, who he was, what he was capable of. I watched him like a hawk, and I would have stepped in if he'd made one wrong move, but he didn't. And you…" He narrowed his eyes. "You changed. It took me a while to figure out what was different, but you weren't scared anymore. Were you?"

Adara swallowed, thinking back to those first weeks and months of marriage, when she had been waiting for the other shoe to drop. Gradually she'd begun to trust that the even temper her husband showed her was real. If the ground was icy, he steadied her. If a cab was coming, he drew her back.

And she remembered very clearly the last time her father had touched her in anger, a few weeks after her wedding. She'd been trying to explain why the engineer needed to make changes to a drawing and he'd batted the pencil from her hand, clipping her wrist with his knuckles.

Mere seconds later, Gideon had walked into the room, arriving to take her home.

Her father had changed before her eyes, remaining as blustery as always, but becoming slightly subdued, eyeing her uneasily as she retrieved her pencil and subtly massaged her wrist.

She hadn't said a word, of course, merely confirmed with her father that they were finished for the day before she'd left with Gideon, but she'd realized she had a champion in her husband, passive and ignorant though he was to his role. As long as she had him, she had protection. Her father had never got physical with her again.

That sense of security had become precious to her. That's why she'd been so devastated when she had thought Lexi had snatched him from her, and now the hurt was even worse, when she knew his shielding tenderness had never existed at all.

"It was in his best interest to keep me happy," she said, voice husky and cold. "I was the facade that made him look real."

"Maybe," Theo agreed, twisting the knife that seemed lodged in her own heart. "In the beginning. But... Adara, I would have done everything I could to help you through this pregnancy regardless of any threats from Gideon. You're my sister. I know what this baby means to you. But the way he spoke to me when he called, that was not just a father speaking. He was worried about both of you. Protective. I've always had a healthy respect for him, but I was intimidated that day. There was no way I was going to be the weak link that caused anything to happen to you or this baby."

"Welcome to my world where you buy the snake oil and convince yourself it works," she scoffed.

He stopped his pacing to stare accusingly at her. "You fooled me, you know. Both of you. I looked at how happy you two were in the last few months and I was *hopeful*. I thought finally one of us was shaking off our childhood and making a proper life for herself. You made me start to believe it was possible, and now—"

"He *lied*, Theo."

"Maybe he had reason to," he challenged and moved to retrieve an envelope from the pocket of his raincoat. He dropped it on the coffee table in front of her. "That's from Nic. He asked me to come through on my way back from Tokyo and bring it to you. I didn't read it, but Nic pointed out that he changed his own name to escape his childhood so he shouldn't have judged Gideon for doing it. Maybe you shouldn't, either."

"He didn't convince Nic he'd married him, did he? He didn't sleep with Nic and make him believe in a fantasy!" He hadn't resuscitated Nic's heart back to life only to crush it under his boot heel. She could never, ever forget that.

"He didn't take over the hotels the way he could have," Theo challenged. "If anything, he kept us afloat until now, when we're finally undoing the damage our father did. He could have robbed us blind the minute the will was read. We all owe him for not doing that. I haven't slept," Theo added gruffly. "Call me later if you want any clarification on that balance sheet for Paris."

He left her staring at the envelope that seemed less snake oil and more snake, coiled in a basket and ready to strike the moment she disturbed the contents.

*Throw it in the incinerator,* she thought. Theo didn't know what he was talking about. The difference here was that their mother had loved and lied while Gideon had purely lied. He didn't love her. That final, odd comment he'd made about his ability to love not being in question had been a last-ditch effort to cling to the life he had built *no matter what he had to do.*

Thinking of their child growing up in the same hostile atmosphere she'd known made her stomach turn, though. She didn't want to wield her sense of betrayal like a weapon, damaging everyone close to her.

Maybe if she understood why he'd done it, she'd hate him less. Theo was right about Gideon always being connected to her, no matter how awkward that would be. She would have to rise above her bitterness and learn to be civil to him.

Lowering to the sofa, she opened the envelope and shook out the printed screen shots of clippings and police reports and email chains. Through the next hours she combed through the pieces Nic had gathered, fitting them into a cracked, bleak image of a baby born from a girl abused by her stepfather. The girl's mother had thrown her out when she became pregnant. A ragtag community of dockworkers, social services and street people had tried to help the adolescent keep herself and her beloved son clothed and fed.

It seemed Gideon had been truthful about one thing: his mother had possessed a strong maternal instinct. Delphi had been urged more than once to put him up for adoption, but was on record as stating no one could love him as much as she did. While not always successful at keeping a roof over their heads, she'd done all a girl of her age could, working every low-end, unsavory job possible without resorting to selling drugs or sex.

Sadly, a nasty element working the docks had decided she didn't have to accept money for her body. It could be taken anyway. Adara cried as she read how the young woman had met such a violent end. She cried even harder, thinking of a young boy seeing his mother like that, beaten and raped and left to die.

Blowing her nose, she moved on to the account of Delphi's friends from low places doing the improbable: going to the police and demanding a search for Delphi's son. Here Nic had done the legwork on a trail that the police had let go cold. Taking the thin thread of Delphi's last name, he had tied it to a crew list from a freighter ship dated years later. The name Vozaras was there too, but the first name was Kristor.

A side story took off on a tangent about smuggling, but nothing had been proven. The only charges considered had been for underage labor and somehow that had been dropped.

Adara wiped at a tickle on her cheek as she absorbed the Dickensian tale of a boy who should have been in school, learning and being loved by a family. He'd been aboard a freighter instead, doing the work of a man. No wonder he was such a whiz with all things sea related. He had literally grown up on a ship.

Considering the deprivation he'd known, the loss of his mother and lack of—as he'd told her himself once—anyone caring about him, it was a wonder he'd turned into a law-abiding citizen at all. When she thought of all the little ways he had looked out for her, even before Greece, when he'd do those small things like make sure she was under the umbrella or huge things like finagle her into running the hotel chain despite her father's interference from the grave, she was humbled.

Perhaps he had been self-serving when he'd agreed to marry her, but he'd treated her far better than the man who was supposed to love and care for her ever had.

She'd been avoiding thinking back to Greece and all that had happened since, but she couldn't ignore his solicitude and protectiveness any longer. He could have let her risk her neck climbing down that cliff alone; he could have sent her to her brother's alone. His actions had gone above and beyond those of a man only wanting to manipulate.

And when she recalled the warmth in his smile when he'd gazed at Evie, the pained longing in him when he'd talked about the loss of their own babies…

Even after that, when they'd been waiting out this pregnancy here, more than once she had glanced up unexpectedly and found a smile of pride softening his face. Half the time his eyes were on her bulging stomach, not even aware she was looking at him. Other times he was looking at her and always seemed to grin a bit ruefully after, as if he'd been caught in a besotted moment and felt sheepish for it.

He couldn't fake all of that. Could he? His shattered control, just from touching her that last night, hadn't been the response of a man who was unmoved and repulsed. He'd been as swept away as she had. Laughing, teasing, pulling her into him afterward as though she was his cherished stuffie.

She swallowed.

Theo was right about a few things. Despite the lack of a truly legal marriage, Gideon had been behaving like a husband and father so well, even she had believed they had a chance for a lifetime of true happiness.

Perhaps they had.

If she hadn't ruined it by throwing him out for daring to reveal the darkest secrets closest to his soul.

She bit her lip, distantly aware of the physical pain, but the emotional anguish was far sharper. It wasn't fair to imagine there had been another time in their lives when they'd been close enough to risk telling each other something so deeply personal. Look how long she'd masked that her father was a brute. If Gideon hadn't followed her to Greece, she might never have told him about that last miscarriage. He'd had as much right to know about their loss as she had to know his name.

Oh, God.

Scanning the scattered papers with burning eyes, she wondered if he even knew this much about himself. She hurt so badly for him, completely understanding why he'd wanted to escape being the boy who had gone through all this and become someone else.

She hadn't even given him a chance to tell his side of things. She *was* just like their father—a man she had never forgiven for the hurts he'd visited on all of them.

But after acting just like him, she couldn't ask Gideon for another chance. Not when he'd taken such a huge risk and she'd condemned him for it. How could she expect him to forgive her when she'd never forgive herself?

It killed Gideon to do it, but he put together the necessary declaration of his identity and the rest of what was needed to dissolve their fake marriage. Then he had the paperwork couriered to the penthouse.

Adara wasn't taking his calls. The least he could do was make things easier on her. Karen was reporting that everything was progressing fine, but all he could think was that Adara must be devastated by the loss of her mother on top of what he'd done to her. He was eating his heart out, aching every moment of every day, but he couldn't badger her for a chance to explain himself. What was there to explain? He'd lied.

He wasn't her husband.

So why was he personally reframing the apartment below their penthouse, executing the plans his architect had drawn up once they'd decided to stay in the city and expand their living space to two floors, creating a single master bedroom with a nursery off the side?

Because he was a fool. It was either this or climb on the next boat and never touch land again. The option kept tapping him on the shoulder, but for some reason he couldn't bring himself to take it.

He couldn't be that far away from the woman he regarded as his wife.

He stopped hammering, chest vibrating with the hollowness of loss.

Actually, that was his cell phone, buzzing in his pocket.

Setting aside the hammer, he saw the call was from Adara. His heart stopped as he hurried to remove his leather glove and accept the call.

"Babe?" The endearment left his lips as if he was sleeping beside her.

Nothing. Damn, he'd missed it. He started to lower the phone and reconnect, but heard a faint "You said you'd be here."

"What?" He brought the phone to his ear.

"You said I wouldn't have to go through this alone and

that you'd be with me every second and the pains have started but *you're not here*. You lied about that too."

Adrenaline singed a path through his arteries and exploded in his heart. "You're in labor?"

A sniff before she gritted out a resentful "Yes."

He threw off his hard hat and safety goggles. "Where are you?"

Silence.

"Adara!"

"In the apartment," she groused. "And you're not."

"Where in the apartment?" he demanded, running up the emergency stairs two at a time to the service entrance. "Don't scream if you hear someone in the kitchen. It's me. Did you change the code?"

"What? How are you in the kitchen? I'm in the bed—" She sucked in a breath.

He stabbed the keypad and the light went green.

He shot through the door, into the kitchen, and strode to her room, ears pounding at the silence. Her bedroom looked like a crime scene with clothes tossed everywhere, nylons bunched on the floor, slippers strewn into the corner, but no Adara. He checked the bathroom.

"Where are you?" he demanded.

"Here," she insisted in his ear. "By the bed."

He'd been on both sides of her bed and rounded it again, but she wasn't there. "Damn it, Adara." He lowered the phone and shouted, "Where *are* you?"

"Here!" she screamed.

Her voice came from the other side of the penthouse. He ran through the living room to his room. *Their* room. A faint part of him wanted to read something significant into that, but when he entered, he didn't see her there either.

Was she torturing him on purpose—?

*Oh, hell.* He spotted one white fist clinging to the rumpled blanket. Her dark head was bent against the far side of the mattress.

"Oh, babe," he said, and threw his phone aside to come around to where she knelt, bare shoulders rising and falling with her panting breaths. She had a towel around her, but nothing else. Her hair was dripping wet.

"Okay, I'm here. You're sure this is just labor?"

"I know what labor feels like, Gideon."

"Okay, okay," he soothed. "Can I get you onto the bed?" He was afraid to touch her. "Are you bleeding?"

"No, but my water broke. That's why I had a shower." She kept her forehead buried against the side of the mattress. "I'm not ready for this. It hurts. And I'm so scared the baby will die—"

"Shh, shh." He stroked her cold shoulder with a shaky hand. "Have you felt the baby move?"

She nodded. "But anything could happen."

"Nothing is going to happen. I'm right here." He prayed to God he wasn't lying to her about this. Shakily he picked up her phone and ended their call. "Have you called the ambulance? Karen?"

"No." She swiped her eyes on her bare arm, and peeked over her elbow at him, gaze full of dark vulnerability and a frightened longing that put pressure on his lungs. "I just thought of you, that you said you'd be here with me. Where were you? How did you get here so fast?"

"Downstairs," he answered, dialing Karen's personal line from memory. In seconds he had briefed her and ended the call. "She'll meet us at the hospital. An ambulance is on the way."

"Oh, leave it to you to get everything done in one call."

"Are you complaining?" He eased her to her feet and onto the bed, muscles twitching to draw her cold, damp skin against him to warm her up, but he drew the covers over her instead. Sitting beside her on the bed, he rested one hand on the side of her neck and stared into her eyes. "You know me. I won't settle for anything less than the best."

*Her,* he was not so subtly implying.

Her brow wrinkled and her mouth trembled. She looked away.

Now wasn't the time to break through the walls she'd put up between them though. He reluctantly drew away and stood.

"Where are you going?" she asked with alarm.

"Have you packed a bag?"

"No, but… You're coming with me, aren't you?" she asked as he moved to find an empty overnight case. "To the hospital?"

"You couldn't keep me away. Not even if you had me arrested." She must have wanted to. Why hadn't she? He glanced over and her hand was outstretched to him, urging him with convulsive clasps to return to her side. Her expression strained into silent agony.

He leaped toward her and grabbed her hand, letting her cling to him as he breathed with her through the contraction, keeping her from hyperventilating, staring into her eyes with as much confidence as he could possibly instill while hiding how much her pain distressed him. He hated seeing her suffer. This was going to kill him.

She released a huge breath and let go of his hand to throw her arm over her eyes. "I'm being a weakling about this. I'm sorry."

"Don't," he growled. Her apology made him want to drop to his knees and beg her for forgiveness. He packed instead, throwing in one of his shirts as a nightgown, a pair of her stretchy sweats, her toothbrush and the moisturizer she always used. "Slippers, hairbrush, lip balm. What else?"

Adara watched him move economically through the space they'd shared, demonstrating how well he knew her as he unhesitatingly gathered all the things she used every day: vitamins, hair clips, even the lozenges she kept by the bed for if she had a cough in the night.

"I—" *read about your mother,* she wanted to say, but another pain ground up from the middle of her spine to wrap around her bulging middle. She gritted her teeth and he took her hand, reassuring her with a steady stare of unwavering confidence and command of the moment, silently willing her to accept and ride and wait for it to release her from its grip.

His focus allowed her to endure the pain without panic. As the contraction subsided, she fell back on the pillow again, breathing normally.

"Those are close," he said, glancing at the clock.

"They started hours ago. I was in denial."

She got a severe look for that, but he was distracted from rebuking her by the arrival of the paramedics. Minutes later, she was strapped to a gurney, her hand well secured in Gideon's sure grasp as she was taken downstairs and loaded into the ambulance.

From there, nothing existed but the business of delivering a baby. As promised, Gideon stayed with her every second. And he was exactly the man she'd always known—the one who seemed to know what she wanted or needed the moment it occurred to her. When the lights began to irritate her, he had them lowered. When she was examined, he shooed extra people from the room, sensitive to her inherent modesty. He kept ice chips handy and gathered her sweaty hair off her neck and never flinched once, no matter how tightly she gripped his arm or how colorfully she swore and blamed him for the pain she was in.

"I can't do it," she sobbed at one point, so exhausted she wanted to die.

"Think of how much you hate me," he cajoled.

She didn't hate him. She wanted to, but she couldn't. She loved him too much.

But she was angry with him. He'd hurt her so badly. It went beyond anything she had imagined she could endure. And then she'd found out *why* he'd lied and it made her hate herself. She was angry most about his leaving her. Living without him was a wasteland of numbness punctuated with spikes of remembered joy that froze and faded as soon as they were recalled. He'd left her in that agonizing state for weeks and…

Another pain built and she gathered all her fury and betrayal, letting it knot her muscles and feed her strength and then she *pushed*…

Gideon stood with his feet braced on the solid floor, but swayed as though a deck rocked beneath him. His son, swaddled into a tight roll by an efficient nurse, wore a disgruntled red face. He wouldn't be satisfied with the soothing sway much longer, not when his tiny stomach was empty. He kept his eyes stubbornly shut, but let out an angry squawk and turned his head to root against the edge of the blanket.

Why that made Gideon want to laugh and cry at the same time, he didn't know. Maybe because he was overtired. He hadn't slept, his body felt as if he'd been thrown down a flight of stairs, his skin had the film of twenty-four hours without a shower and his own stomach was empty. This was like a hangover, but a crazy good one that left him unable to hold on to clear thoughts. And even though he had a sense he should be filled with regret, he was so elated it was criminal.

"I know, son," he whispered against the infant's unbelievably tender cheek. "But Mama is so tired. Can you hang on a little longer, till she wakes up?" He tried a different pattern of jiggling and offered a fingertip only to have it rejected with a thrust of the baby's tongue.

The boy whimpered a little more loudly.

"I'm awake," Adara said in the sweet, sleepy voice he'd been missing like a limb from his body.

Gideon turned from the rain beyond the window and found her lying on her side, her hand tucked under the side of her face as she watched him. The tender look in her eyes filled him with such unreasonable hope, he had to swallow back a choked sob. He consciously shook off the dream that tried to balloon in his head. *Get real,* he told himself, recalling why he was missing her so badly. His heart plummeted as though he'd taken a steel toe into it.

"He's hungry?" she asked.

"Like he's never been fed a day in his life."

Adara smirked and glanced at the clock, noting the boy was barely four hours into his life. With some wincing and a hand from Gideon, she pulled herself to sit up.

"Sore?" He glanced toward the door, thinking to call a nurse.

"It's okay. He's worth it." She got her arm out of the sleeve of her gown, exposing her swollen breast.

"Do you, um, want to cover up with something?" He looked around for a towel.

"Why?" She drew the edge of her gown across her chest again. "Is there someone else in here?"

"No, just me."

"Oh, well, that's okay then, isn't it?" She started to reveal herself again, but hesitated, her confused gaze striking his with shadows of such deep uncertainty, his heart hurt.

"Of course it's okay." He wanted to lean down and kiss her, he was so moved that she still felt so natural around him. It could only mean good things, couldn't it?

Adara could hardly look into Gideon's eyes, but she couldn't look away. He delved so searchingly into her gaze, as if looking for confirmation they stood a chance, but she'd treated him so badly, rejecting him for being as self-protective as she'd always been. She didn't know how to bridge this chasm between them.

Their son found his voice with an insistent yell and made them both start.

And then, even though she'd had a brief lesson before falling asleep, Adara had to learn to breast-feed, which wasn't as natural a process as some mothers made it look. She wasn't sure how to hold him. Her breast was too swollen for such a tiny mouth.

Their son surpassed his patience and grew too fussy to try. Gideon looked at her with urgency to get the job done as the baby began to wail in earnest.

"What am I doing wrong?" she cried.

"Don't look at me, I've never done it either. Here, I'll sit beside you and hold him so you can line him up— There, see? He's never done it, either, but he's getting it."

She didn't know what was more stingingly sweet: the first pull of her baby's mouth on her nipple or the stirring way Gideon cradled her against his chest so he could help her hold their baby. Adara blinked back tears, frantically wondering how she could be so close to Gideon and feel he was so far out of reach at the same time.

She tensed to hide that she was beginning to tremble, finding words impossible as emotion overwhelmed her. At least she had her back tucked to his chest and he couldn't see her face.

He seemed to react to her tension, pulling away with a grimace that he smoothed from his expression before she'd properly glimpsed it. Standing by the bed with his hands in the pockets of his rumpled work pants, he stared at the baby.

She did too, not knowing where else to look, then became fascinated by the miracle of a closed fist against her breast, tiny lashes, the peek of a miniature earlobe from beneath the edge of the blue cap.

A drop of pure emotion fell from her eye, landing on his cheek.

"Oh," she gasped, drying the betraying tear. "I'm just so overwhelmed," she said, trying to dismiss that she was crying over a lot more than the arrival of their son.

"I know." Gideon's blurred image took a step forward and he gestured helplessly. "I didn't expect it to be like this."

*Like this.* Those words seemed to encompass a lot more than a safe delivery after so many heartaches.

Adara blinked, trying to clear her vision to see what was in his face, eyes, heart, but all she could think was that she'd screwed up and thrown away something unbelievably precious. Her eyes flooded with despondent tears.

"Please come home," she choked out. "With us. We won't be a family without you and I miss you so much—" She couldn't continue.

"Oh, babe." He rushed forward, his warm hand cupping her face as he settled his hip beside her thigh and drew her into him, pressing hot lips against her temple, her wet cheek, her trembling lips. "I've been trying to think how I'd ever convince you to let me. I'm *sorry.*"

She shook her head, burying her face in the hollow of his shoulder as she tried to regain control. "It's okay." She sniffed. "It was never easy for me to tell you about my childhood horrors. I shouldn't have expected you to revisit yours without some serious prodding."

He massaged the back of her head, his chin rubbing her hair. "I didn't want to, but mostly because I knew it could be the breaking point of our marriage. I didn't want that. And not because it would expose me. I didn't want to lose *you*. Does it help at all to know that I've always felt married to you? Maybe it wasn't legal, but it was real to me. You're my wife, Adara."

She nodded. "I am."

He laughed a little, the sound one of husky joy. "You are." He drew back, cupping her face as he looked for confirmation in her eyes. "You are."

She bit her lips, holding back the longing as she nodded. "I am. It's enough."

The radiant pride in his expression dimmed. "Enough?"

"Knowing that our union matters to you. That you want me as your wife. That we can be a family."

He sat back, hands falling away from her. "What are you saying? What does all of that do for you?"

"What do you mean? It's good, Gideon. I want to carry on as we were, treating this like a real marriage. We don't have to change anything or bring up your past or involve any lawyers. My brothers know why we separated, but no one else does. You are Gideon Vozaras. I'm Mrs. Vozaras. It's all good."

He stood abruptly, his mood shifting to acute dismay. "And why are you staying married to that man? That name?"

"Because—" *I love him.* Her heart dipped. She wasn't ready to put herself out there again and get nothing in return. "There's no point in shaking things up. I read those papers you sent and they say that I have a case to take you to the cleaners, but I don't want that. I'm fine with us being married in a common-law sort of way. No use rocking the boat." There, she was using language he understood.

Or should, but his jaw was like iron as he moved to the window and showed her a scant angle of his profile and a tense line across his shoulders.

"You asked me if we were falling in love," he reminded.

"It was never part of our deal. I can live without it," she hurried to say.

"I can't."

His words plunged a knife into her. She gasped and looked wildly around as she absorbed what it could mean if he wanted a marriage based on love, but was stuck with her—

"For God's sake, Adara. Are you still not seeing what you mean to me?" He was looking over his shoulder at her, incredulous, but incredibly gentle too.

"What?" Her breast was cold and she realized the baby had fallen asleep and let her nipple slip from his mouth. She wished for extra hands as she tried to cradle the baby and cover herself at the same time.

Gideon walked over and grasped her chin, forcing her gaze up to his. A fire burned in the back of that intense gaze, one that sparked an answering burn in her.

She still wasn't sure, though...

"You're not bound to me legally, but that doesn't matter if I own your heart," he told her. "I want you, body and soul. If there's something standing in the way of your loving me, tell me what it is. Now. So I can fix it or remove it and have you once and for all."

"I—" She almost lost her nerve, but sensed it really was time to let go of the last of her insecurities and be open about what she wanted. Grasp it. Demand it. "I want you to love me back."

She wasn't just wearing her heart on her sleeve, she'd pinned it to the clothesline and wheeled it out into the yard.

A look of unbelievable tenderness softened his harsh expression. "How could I not?"

She slowly shook her head. "Don't make it sound like it's there just like that. I was awful to you. I know that you've lost people close to you and don't want to be hurt again. It's okay that you're not able to love me yet. I can wait." Maybe. She set her chin, determined it wouldn't tremble despite the fact her heart was in her throat.

If only he wasn't so confusing, smiling indulgently at her like that.

"You do love me." He cradled the side of her face in his

palm, scanning her face as if he was memorizing it, and she suddenly realized she must look like something the cat had coughed up. Her hair hadn't been washed, she'd barely rinsed her mouth with a sip of water.

Self-consciously she lifted the baby to her shoulder and rubbed his back, using him as a bit of a shield while she worked at maintaining hold of her emotions.

"I love you quite a bit, actually," she confessed toward her blanket-covered knees. "It's not anything like what I feel for the other men in my life. This one included." She hitched the baby a bit higher and couldn't resist kissing his little cheek, even as her soul reached out to his father. "I don't know how to handle what I feel for you. When my father was mean to me, it hurt even though I didn't care about him, but it's nothing compared to how much it hurts when you love someone and trust him and think they don't care about you at all."

"I know," he growled. "Losing someone to death is agony, but it's even worse knowing the person you love with all your heart is alive and doesn't want to see you."

Hearing how much he loved her was bittersweet. She stared at him in anguish, not wanting the power to hurt him that badly, but seeing from his tortured expression that she had. There were no words to heal, only an urge to draw him close so she could try to kiss away his pain.

"I'm sorry. I love you."

"I know, me, too. I love you so much."

Their mouths met in homecoming, both of them moaning as the ache ceased. He opened his lips over hers and she flowered like a plant tasting water. Heat flowed into her. Joy.

*Love.*

A door swished and a nurse said, "Bit soon for that, isn't it?"

They broke apart. Gideon shot a private smile at Adara as he reached to tie her gown behind her neck.

"And how is our young man? Does he have a name?" the nurse chattered.

Adara licked her lips, eyeing Gideon as she said, "Delphi's not exactly a boy's name, but I thought…Androu?" It was Gideon's real name.

His expression spasmed with emotion before he controlled it. "Are you sure?" he asked, voice strained, body braced for disappointment.

"He's someone I love and want in my life forever. I think, someday, he'd be really proud to know who he was named after."

"I don't deserve you," he said against her lips, kissing her resoundingly, right there in front of the nurse.

Adara flushed and smiled, bubbles of happiness filling her. "We do, you know," she contradicted him. "We both deserve this."

She didn't care that the nurse was smiling indulgently at them even as she took Androu and undressed him so she could weigh him.

"Well, you certainly deserve to be happy. Me, I just demand the best and get it." *You,* he mouthed. *Him.* He cocked his head toward the baby.

"A habit I'm adopting," she said with a cheeky wrinkle of her nose. "I know how possessive you are of the things you've built, too. I'm taking on that trait as well. *Us,*" she whispered, soft and heartfelt.

"Yeah, I'm going to hang on to us pretty tight too," he said in a way that made her heart leap. *"Agape mou."*

# EPILOGUE

GIDEON WALKED INTO his home office thinking he really needed to start spending more time in here. It wasn't that things were falling apart. He and Adara had put some great people in place when they'd first learned of the pregnancy. Her brothers were still running things like a well-oiled machine and he should have quit micromanaging years ago, so this was a timely lesson in letting go.

But there was a fine line between delegating and neglecting. Much more lolling about his home, playing airplane with his son and necking with his wife, and he'd be a full-fledged layabout.

Of course, he could blame finishing the renovations, putting in a staircase to the lower floor, painting and furnishing their new private space away from the main floor. That had taken time. There had also been his recovery from minor surgery, but that had really only been the one afternoon on headache pills and he'd been fine.

No, he might be getting up in the night to change diapers, but he wasn't breast-feeding or anemic from childbirth. He didn't have Adara's totally legitimate reasons for shirking work.

He certainly shouldn't be leaving confidential papers lying openly on his desk, whether the workmen were gone or not.

The block letters and signature tabs were a dead give-away that this was a contract, one he couldn't remember even pulling out to review, but— Ah. It was the separation agreement he'd sent to Adara. She must have left it here.

A pang hit him, but it was merely the remembered pain of thinking he'd lost everything and was quickly relieved by a rush of relief and happiness that they'd recovered. Her devotion was as steadfast as his, prompting a flood of deep love for her as he walked the papers toward the shredder. He didn't want this bad mojo in the house, but then he saw she'd signed it. His heart stopped.

Ha. That wasn't her name. Under the statement that began, *I, Adara Makricosta, hereby agree*...she'd scrawled with a deep impression, *Never,* and added a smiley face.

Quirking a grin at her sass, he decided this was a signed contract in its own right, definitely worth tucking in the safe. Suddenly, work didn't seem important after all. Was she finished feeding Androu? he wondered. They'd had co-inciding follow-ups at separate doctor clinics today. He'd returned to find her rocking a drifting Androu to sleep downstairs and decided to see what he could get done here, but…

He turned to find her in his office doorway, the baby monitor in her hand.

"He's asleep?" he asked.

She nodded and came to set the monitor on his desktop. "How did your appointment go?"

"Not swimmingly."

Her eyes widened in alarm.

"That's a joke," he hurried to assure her. "I'm saying there were no swimmers. I'm good. Shooting blanks."

She snorted, then sobered and cocked her head in con-cern. "You're sure it doesn't bother you? I really was fully prepared to have my tubes tied."

He tried to wave away the same worries he'd been trying to alleviate for weeks, but she kept her anxious expression.

He sighed. "I'd make ten more just like Androu if we could. We both would, right? He's perfect," he said, moving to take her arms in a warm but firm grasp of insistence. "But if we want more children, we can find another way. You can't risk another pregnancy."

"Exactly why I should have been the one having the permanent procedure. What if someday—"

"Are you going somewhere?" he challenged lightly. "I'm not. Therefore, my getting fixed is a solution for both of us. You've been through enough. And this was not a big moral struggle for me. I'm happy to take responsibility for protecting you."

She pouted a little. "Well, thank you then. I do appreciate it."

He caressed from the base of her throat to under her chin, coaxing her to tilt her head up so he could see those pillowy lips pursed so erotically.

"There was some self-serving to it, you know," he admitted, voice thickening with the many weeks of abstinence they'd observed. Now there'd never be any worries for either of them, no matter when or where they came together. And hell, if he hadn't inflicted pain down there to distract himself, he probably would have lost his mind waiting for this moment. "How did *your* appointment go?" he belatedly asked, reminding himself not to let the engine rev too high and fast.

"Oh." Her lashes swooped and her mouth widened into a sensual smile of invitation. "All clear to resume normal activities."

"If you can call how we make each other feel 'normal.'" He backed her toward the desk. "I was just thinking I haven't been spending enough quality time in here."

Her breath caught in the most delightful way, and even though she stiffened in surprise when her hips met the edge of his desk, she melted with reception just as quickly, hitching herself to sit on it. Her hand curled around to the back of his neck and she leaned her other hand onto the surface of his desk, watching without protest as he began unbuttoning her top.

"We do have a nice new bed downstairs that hasn't been used for one of its intended purposes, you know," she reminded in a sultry voice.

"I am quite aware," he countered dryly as he bared her chest and released her bra. Her breasts were bigger, pale and lightly veined, the nipples dark and stiff with excitement. "God, you're beautiful."

"They're kind of majestic, aren't they?" She arched a little.

"They kind of are," he agreed with awe, tracing lightly before he bent to touch careful kisses around her nipples.

"Gideon?"

Her tone made him raise his head. "What's wrong?"

"I know we should savor this because it's been a really long time and we kind of started over with our marriage so this is a bit of a honeymoon moment, but I've really missed making love with you. I thought about walking in here naked. I don't want to wait."

Ever willing to accommodate, he stripped her pants off without another word, taking her ice-blue undies with them. Spreading her knees, he only bothered to open his jeans and shove them down as far as necessary, before he carefully pushed inside her.

Adara gasped at the pinch and friction of not being quite ready, but his hot, firm thickness was the connection she'd been longing for. With a moan, she twined her legs around him and forced his entry, drawing a deep hiss from him.

They fought a light battle, him trying to slow her down, her urging him as deep into her as she could take before she sprawled back on his desk and let him have his way with her.

It was raw and quick and powerful, over in minutes, but they were shaking in each other's arms as they caught their breath. Her vision sparkled and she felt as if she radiated ecstasy.

"You okay?" he murmured as he kissed her neck. "That was pretty primal."

"That was an appetizer," she said, languidly kissing him and using her tongue. Her fingertips traced the damp line through his shirt down his spine. "*Now* you can take me downstairs and show me your best moves."

"You're sounding pretty bossy there, Mrs. Vozaras." He straightened and gently disengaged so he could hitch up his jeans and scoop her off the desk into a cradle against his chest.

"Only a problem if we want different things, and I don't think that's true."

He cocked his head in agreement. "You're so right. Monitor," he prompted, dipping his still-weak knees so she could grab it off the corner of the desk.

She craned her neck over his shoulder as he carried her through the door. "You gonna leave my clothes on the floor like that?"

"Do I look stupid? We're on the clock. He could wake up any second."

She traced his lips with her fingertip. "But if the boat rocks, they'll be thrown all over the place," she teased.

He paused on the stairs. "I am dry-docked and landlocked, sticking right here with you, my siren of a wife. We're on solid ground. Nothing is going anywhere."

"Aw." Touched, she kissed him. It grew deeply passionate. He let her legs drift to find the step above him so he could roam his hands over her naked curves, lighting delicious fires in her nerve endings.

She worked on divesting him, caressing heated skin, leaving a few more articles of clothing on the stairs before she led him below to christen their new bed.

* * * * *

# A DEBT PAID
# IN PASSION

Generous readers, you're my valentines. Thank you for making all those hours in my stuffy attic writing room worth it.

# CHAPTER ONE

*LOOK AT ME,* Raoul Zesiger willed Sirena Abbott.

He had to lean back in his chair to see her past the three men between them. He should have been looking at the judge, but he couldn't take his eyes off Sirena.

She sat very still, face forward, her profile somber. Her absurdly long gypsy lashes had stayed downswept as his lawyer had risen to speak. She didn't even flick a glance in his direction when her own lawyer stood to plead that jail time was counterproductive, since she needed to work to pay back the stolen funds.

Raoul's lawyers had warned him this wouldn't result in incarceration, but Raoul had pressed hard for it. He would see this treacherously innocent-looking woman, with her mouth pouted in grave tension and her thick brunette locks pulled into a deceptively respectful knot, go to jail for betraying him. For stealing.

His stepfather had been a thief. He had never expected to be taken advantage of again, especially by his reliable PA, a woman he'd come to trust to be there, always. But she had dipped her fingers into his personal account.

Then she had tried to manipulate him into going easy by *being* easy.

He didn't want the flash of memory to strike. His ears were waiting for the judge to state that this would progress to a sentence, but his body prickled with heat as he recalled the feel of those plump lips softening under his. Her breasts, a lush handful, had smelled of summer. Her nipples were sun-warmed berries against his tongue, succulent and sweet. The heart-shaped backside he'd watched too often as it retreated from his office had been both taut and smooth as he had lifted her skirt and peeled lace down. Thighs like powdered sugar, an enticing musky perfume between that pulled him to hard attention as he remembered how tight—almost virginal—she'd been. But so hot and welcoming.

Because she'd known her criminal act was about to come to light.

His gut clenched in a mixture of fury and unparalleled carnal hunger. For two years he'd managed to keep his desire contained, but now that he'd had her, all he could think about was having her again. He hated her for having such power over him. He could swear under oath that he'd never hurt a woman, but he wanted to crush Sirena Abbott. Eradicate her. Destroy her.

The clap of a gavel snapped him back to the courtroom. It was empty save for the five of them behind two tables, both facing the judge. His lawyer gave Raoul a resigned tilt of his head and Raoul realized with sick disgust that the decision had gone in Sirena's favor.

At the other table, partly obscured by her lawyer, Sirena's spine softened in relief. Her wide eyes lifted to the heavens, shining with gratitude. Her lawyer thanked the judge and set a hand under Sirena's elbow to help her rise, leaning in to say something to her.

Raoul felt a clench of possessiveness as he watched the solicitous middle-aged lawyer hover over her. He told himself it was anger, nothing else. He loathed being a victim again. She shouldn't get away with a repayment plan of six hundred pounds a month. That wasn't reparation. That was a joke.

Why wouldn't she look at him? It was the least she could do: look him in the eye and acknowledge they both knew she was getting away with a crime. But she murmured something to her lawyer and left the man packing his briefcase as she circled to the aisle. Her sexy curves were downplayed by her sleek jacket and pencil skirt, but she was still alluring as hell. Her step slowed as she came to the gate into the gallery.

*Look at me,* Raoul silently commanded again, holding his breath as she hesitated, sensing she was about to swing her gaze to his.

Her lips drained of color and her hand trembled as she reached out, trying to find the gate. She stared straight ahead, eyes blinking and blinking—

"She's fainting!" He shoved past his two lawyers and toppled chairs to reach her even as her own lawyer turned and reacted. They caught her together.

Raoul hated the man anew for touching her as they both eased her to the floor. She was dead weight. He had to catch her head as it lolled. She hadn't been this insubstantial the last time he'd held her. She hadn't been *fragile.*

Raoul barked for first aid.

Someone appeared with oxygen in blessedly short time. He let himself be pushed back a half step, but he couldn't take his eyes off the way Sirena's cheeks had gone hollow, her skin gray. Everything in him, breath, blood, thought, ground to a halt as he waited for a new verdict: that she would be okay.

It was his father all over again. The lack of response, the wild panic rising in him as he fought against helplessness and brutal reality. Was she breathing? She couldn't be dead. *Open your eyes, Sirena.*

Distantly he heard the attendant asking after preexisting conditions and Raoul racked his brain. She wasn't diabetic, had never taken medication that he'd seen. He reached for the phone he'd turned off while court was in session, intent on accessing her personnel file, when he heard her lawyer answer in a low murmur.

"She's pregnant."

The words burst like shattered glass in his ears.

Sirena became aware of something pressed to her face. Clammy sweat coated her skin and a swirl of her ever-present nausea turned mercilessly inside her.

She lifted a heavy hand to dislodge whatever was smothering her and a voice said, "You fainted, Sirena. Take it easy for a minute."

Opening her eyes, she saw John, the highly recommended lawyer who'd been perfunctory until she'd almost vomited in his wastebasket. She'd told him the father's identity was irrelevant, but Raoul was glaring from beyond John's shoulder with all the relevance of an unforgiving sun on a lost soul in the desert—and he appeared about as sympathetic.

She had tried hard not to look at Raoul, former boss, brief lover, unsuspecting father. He was too…everything. Tall, dark, unabashedly urbane and sophisticated. Severe. Judgmental.

But of their own accord, her hungry eyes took in his appearance—her first opportunity to do so in weeks. She cataloged his razor-sharp charcoal suit, the solid black tie. His jaw was freshly shaved for his morning appointment, his dark hair recently cut into the sternly simple style of a successful businessman.

And there were his eyes, the gray irises stormy and full of condemnation as they snared hers in an unbreakable stare.

John asked, "Is there any pain? We've called an ambulance."

Sirena flashed a terrified glance back at Raoul. It was

a mistake. She realized immediately that he'd read it for what it was: an admission of guilt. A betrayal of truth.

Clenching her perfidious eyes closed, she willed him not to pick up on what had been revealed, but he was the most acutely intelligent person she'd ever met. He missed nothing.

If he knew she was carrying his baby, there'd be another fight. Considering what this current contest had taken out of her, she wasn't ready for another. She wouldn't, *couldn't*, let him think he had a right to custody of her child.

"Sirena," Raoul said in that dark chocolate voice of his.

Her skin rippled in a pleasurable shiver of recognition. Two years of hearing every intonation in that voice left her with the knowledge that her name on his lips right now was an implacable warning.

"Look at me," he commanded.

Sirena reached blindly for John's hand, clenching her icy fingers on his warm, dry ones. Beneath the oxygen mask, her voice was hollow and whisper thin.

"Tell him to leave me alone or I'll take out a restraining order."

# CHAPTER TWO

THE FIRST VOLLEY of the second war was waiting when she got home from the hospital. More tests had been scheduled, but for the moment her doctor was putting her faint down to stress and low blood sugar resulting from her unrelenting nausea.

Sirena thought nothing could be more stressful than facing prison while dealing with an unplanned pregnancy, but Raoul knew no bounds when it came to psychological torture. She read the email John had forwarded:

My client has every reason to believe your client carries his baby. He insists on full involvement in the care through pregnancy and will take sole custody at birth.

Her blood congealed, even though this was no surprise. Raoul was possessive. She'd learned *that*. This reaction was fully expected, but having anyone try to take this baby from her was unthinkable.

Blinking the sting of desperation from her eyes, she typed, It's not his, saying aloud, "And tell him to go to hell."

She didn't let herself dwell on the fact that Raoul wanted his baby. It would make her weaken toward a man she needed to believe was a monster—even though she'd spent two years falling into deep infatuation with not just a dynamic tycoon, but a man who was a caring son and protective older stepbrother. In some ways he was her mirror image, she'd often thought fancifully. They'd both lost a parent and both wanted the best for their younger siblings. She had come to believe him to be an admirable person with a dry wit and standards that put her learned habits of perfectionism to shame.

*No,* she reminded herself as she prepared a slice of toast she would force herself to eat. He was a cruel, angry, small person who felt nothing. For her, at least. He'd proven it when he'd made passionate love to her one day, then had her arrested the next.

A black hole of despair threatened to open beneath her feet, but she was safe now. That part was over. She'd made a horrible mistake and the judge had accepted her remorse, even if Raoul hadn't. She had no idea how she would come up with six hundred pounds a month, but that was a minor worry against convincing Raoul the baby wasn't his.

There was no way she could live with having another loved one wrenched from her life. The fear of her baby growing up without its mother, the way she had, had given her the strength to fight tooth and nail against Raoul's determination to put her in jail. Somehow she would rally the strength to oust him from her life for good.

Which left her feeling incredibly bereft, but she ignored it.

Taking tea, toast and a tablet for nausea to the sofa, she scanned her laptop to see if any transcription jobs had come in. The legal bills were appalling and being fired three months ago had decimated her very modest savings.

If only she could take back that one awful moment when she had thought, *Raoul will understand.* She rubbed her brow where it crinkled in lament. Borrowing from him had seemed the most simple and obvious thing to do when her sister had been in tears, saying, *I guess I'm not meant to be a teacher.* Their father was expecting payment from a big customer any day. Ali had struggled so hard to get her marks up and be accepted into the specialized program. The tuition was due, but the cash was not in hand.

*I can cover it,* Sirena had assured her, confident the balance would move out and come back into Raoul's account on the same statement. He probably wouldn't even notice, let alone care. He paid *her* to worry about little details like that.

Then her father's customer had gone insolvent.

Not overnight, of course. It started with a delay of a few more days. A week. Sirena had begun chasing it herself, right up to the monthly cutoff date, not wanting to mention her self-approved loan to her boss until she had the funds to repay it.

The money hadn't appeared and the opportunity to explain hadn't arisen, not before other events.

And since she didn't want to involve her father when his livelihood was nose-diving, she had shouldered the fallout herself, keeping her motives from Raoul and not revealing to her family what she'd done or that she was facing jail time for it.

This had been the most crushingly lonely and frightening time of her life.

A muted beep announced an incoming email. From Raoul. Her heart leaped in misplaced anticipation. It was one word.

Liar.

He wasn't buying that the baby wasn't his.

Gritting her teeth against an ache that crushed her chest, she added Raoul to her email block list and sent a missive to John.

Tell him that contacting me directly is out of line. If the baby was his, I would sue for support. I would have asked for leniency when he was trying to put me in jail. This baby is not his and he must LEAVE ME ALONE.

Hitting send was like poking herself in the throat. She drew a pained breath, fighting the sense of loss. But life hit you with sudden changes and you had to roll with them. She had learned that when her mother had died, and again when her stepmother had whisked her father and half sister to Australia with brutal speed as soon as Sirena graduated and enrolled in business school.

People *left,* was what she'd learned. They disappeared from your life whether you wanted them to or not. Sometimes they even fired you and tried to lock you away in prison so they'd never have to see you again.

Making a disgusted noise at herself for indulging in what amounted to emotional self-harm, she turned her thoughts to the little being who wouldn't leave her. With a gentle hand on her unsettled abdomen, she focused on the one person she'd do everything in her power to keep in her life forever. She didn't intend to smother the poor thing, just be his or her mother. She couldn't countenance anyone taking that role from her. And Raoul would try. He was that angry and ruthless.

She shivered as she recalled seeing that side of him for the first time, after making bail. The only thing that had gotten her through the humiliating process of being arrested, fingerprinted and charged was the certainty that Raoul didn't know what was happening to her. Some accountant had done this. A bank official. They didn't understand that Raoul might be gruff on the outside, but she was his best PA ever. His right hand. They'd become intimate. He would be furious that she was being treated this way.

She had believed with all her heart that as soon as she told him what had happened, he'd make it right.

He hadn't. He'd made her wait in the rain at the gate of his mansion outside London, eventually striding out with hard-hearted purpose, his severe expression chilly with distaste as he surveyed her.

"I've been trying to reach you," Sirena had said through the rungs of the security gate, frightened by how unreachable he seemed. "I was arrested today."

"I know," Raoul replied without a shred of concern. "I filed the complaint."

Her shock and stunned anguish must have been obvious, but his mouth had barely twitched in reaction. Cruel dislike had been the only emotion in his scathing expression. Sirena's stepmother had been small and critical, but she hadn't outright hated Sirena. In that second, she realized Raoul reviled her, and that was more painful than anything.

Guilt and remorse had made her want to shrivel up and die, but she couldn't—wouldn't—believe she'd ruined her career and her budding relationship with the man of her dreams over one tiny misstep.

"But…" Everything she wanted to say backed up in her throat. They'd developed friendship, reliance and respect over two years of working together and just yesterday they'd taken that relationship to a new level. He'd been tender and teasing and…

God, she had believed he'd been *loving*.

"But what?" he challenged. "You thought sleeping with me would make a difference to how I'd react when I found out you had stolen from me? I was bored. You were there. That's all yesterday was. You ought to know better than to think it would make me go easy on someone who was cheating me. Get a lawyer. You need one."

Swallowing the rock that her crust of toast had become,

Sirena pushed the betrayal firmly away. Raoul was in her past and somehow she had to make a future for herself and her baby. She turned her attention to putting out more feelers for work.

But over the next several weeks, the attacks from Raoul kept coming. Settlement offers that increased in size. Demands for paternity tests. Time limits.

Pacing John's office, she bit back a rebuke at him for revealing her pregnancy that day in the courtroom. She hadn't admitted to anyone that Raoul was the father and she was determined she never would.

"Here's what I would like to know, John. How am I supposed to pay more legal bills I can't afford when it's not even my wish to be talking to you about this?"

"Your wish may be coming true, Sirena. He's stated clearly that this is his final offer and you're to accept it by Monday or forever go empty-handed."

She stopped and stilled. Loss again. Like watching the final sands drifting through the neck of an hourglass, unable to stop them. Pain in her lip made her aware she was biting it to keep from crying out in protest. Rubbing her brow with a shaking hand, Sirena told herself it was what she wanted: Raoul gone from her life.

"Look, Sirena, I've told you several times this isn't my area of expertise. So far that hasn't mattered because you've refused to admit the baby is his—"

"It's not," she interjected, keeping her back to him. She wasn't a great liar and didn't like doing it, but she justified it because this baby was *hers.* Full stop.

"He obviously thinks it's possible. You and he must have been involved."

"Involvement comes in different levels, doesn't it?" she snapped, then closed her mouth, fearful she was saying too much.

"So you're punishing him for bringing less to the relationship than you did?"

"His mistresses spend more on an evening gown and he tried to send me to prison for it!" she swung around to blurt. "What kind of relationship is that?"

"You're punishing him for his legal action, then? Or not buying you a dress?"

"I'm not punishing him," Sirena muttered, turning back to the window overlooking a wet day in Hyde Park.

"No, you're punishing your child by keeping its father out of the picture—whether that father is Raoul Zesiger or some other nameless man you've failed to bring forward. I'm a father, so even though I don't practice family law, I know the best interests of the child are not served by denying a parent access just because you're angry with him. Do you have reason to believe he'd be an unfit parent?"

*Completely the opposite,* she silently admitted as a tendril of longing curled around her heart. She had seen how Raoul's stepsister adored him and how he indulged the young woman with doting affection while setting firm boundaries. Raoul would be a supportive, protective, exceptional father.

Her brows flinched and her throat tightened. She *was* angry with him. And secretly terrified that her child would ultimately pick its father over its mother, but that didn't justify keeping the baby from knowing both its parents.

"Have you thought about your child's future?" John prodded. "There are certain entitlements, like a good education, inheritances…"

She had to get this baby delivered first. That's where her focus had really been these last several weeks.

Sirena's fists tightened under her elbows as she hunched herself into a comfortless hug. Her mother had died trying to give birth to the baby who would have been Sirena's little brother. Sirena's blood pressure was under constant monitoring. Between that and the lawyer meetings, she was barely working, barely making the bills. The stress was making the test results all the more concerning.

She tried not to think of all the bad things that could happen, but for the first time she let herself consider what her child would need if she couldn't provide it. Her father and sister were all the way in Australia. It would be days before they could get here—if her stepmother let either of them come at all. Right now Faye was taking the high ground, sniffing with disapproval over Sirena's unplanned, unwed pregnancy. No one would be as emotionally invested as the baby's father...

"Sirena, I'm not trying to—"

"Be my conscience?" she interjected. He was still acting as one. "I have a specialist appointment on Monday. I don't know how long it will take. Tell him I will give his offer my full attention after that and will be in touch by the end of next week."

John's demeanor shifted. "So he is the father."

"That will be determined by the paternity test once the baby is born, won't it?" Sirena retorted, scrambling to hold onto as many cards as she could because she was running out of them, fast.

Raoul's mind had been going around in circles for weeks, driving him mad. If Sirena was pregnant with his child, she would have used that to keep him from trying to incarcerate her. Since she hadn't, it must not be his. But she could have used her condition for leniency during the proceedings and hadn't. Which meant she wanted to keep the pregnancy from him. Which led him to believe the baby was his.

Most troubling, if he wasn't the father, who was?

Raoul sent baleful glances around his various offices as he traveled his circuit of major cities, aware there were a plethora of men in his numerous office towers with whom Sirena, with her voluptuous body and warm smile, could easily have hooked up.

The thought grated with deep repugnance. He'd never heard the merest whisper of promiscuity about his PA, but she'd obviously led a secretive life. It wasn't as if she'd been a virgin when he'd made love to her.

She'd been the next thing to it, though, with her shy hesitancy that had turned to startled pleasure.

Biting back a groan, he tried not to think of that afternoon in a house he'd toured as a potential real estate investment. Every day he fought the recollection of their passionate encounter and every night she revisited him, her silky hair whispering against his skin, her soft giggle of self-consciousness turning to a gasp of awe as she stroked him. The hum of surrender in her throat as he found the center of her pleasure nearly had him losing it in his sleep.

Every morning he reminded himself he'd used a condom.

One that had been in his wallet so long he couldn't remember when or for whom he'd placed it there. He'd only been grateful to find it when a downpour had turned Sirena from the open front door into his arms. A stumbling bump of her pivoting into him, a gentlemanly attempt to keep her on her feet, a collision of soft curves against a body already charged with sexual hunger.

When she'd looked up at him with wonder as her abdomen took the impression of his erection, when she'd parted her lips and looked at his mouth as though she'd been waiting her whole life to feel it cover her own…

Swearing, Raoul rose to pace his Paris office. It was as far as he was willing to get from London after trying to settle with Sirena once and for all. The remembered vision of her passion-glazed eyes became overlaid with a more recent one: when her lawyer had mentioned her pregnancy and she had shot that petrified look at Raoul.

*The baby was his.* He knew it in his gut and if he'd been ruthless with her for stealing money, she had no idea the lengths he'd go for his child.

Doubt niggled, though. If the baby was his, and she was the type to embezzle, then try to sleep her way out of it, why wasn't she trying to squeeze a settlement out of him?

None of it added up and he was losing his mind trying to make sense of it. If she'd only *talk* to him. They used to communicate with incredible fluidity, finishing each other's sentences, filling in gaps with a look…

Lies, he reminded himself. All an act to trick him into trusting her, and it had worked. That's what grated so badly. He'd failed to see that she was unreliable, despite his history with shameless charlatans.

And how the hell had he turned into his father? Was it genetic that he should wind up sexually infatuated with his secretary? He'd successfully ignored such attractions for years. His father had killed himself over an interoffice affair, so he'd made it a personal rule to avoid such things at all costs. It was a matter of basic survival.

His surge of interest in Sirena had been intense right from the beginning, though. He'd hired her in spite of it, partly because he'd been sure he was a stronger man than his father. Maybe he'd even been trying to prove it.

It galled him that he'd fallen into a tryst despite his better intentions. But he might have come to terms with that failing if she hadn't betrayed him. Suddenly he'd been not just his father, but his mother, naively watching the bank account drain while being fed sweet, reassuring words to excuse it.

*I was going to pay it back before you found out.*

He tried to close out the echo of Sirena's clear voice, claiming exactly what any dupe would expect to hear once she realized her caught hands were covered in red. That he'd seen her as steadfast until that moment left him questioning his own judgment, which was a huge kick to his confidence. People relied on him all over the world. His weakness for her made him feel as though he was misrepresenting himself, and more than anything he hated being let down. It galled him. Mere repayment wasn't good enough to compensate for that. People like her needed to be taught a lesson.

Staring at his desktop full of work, he cursed the concentration he'd lost because of all this, the time wasted on legal meetings that could have been spent on work.

And the worst loss of production was because he was trying to replace the best PA he'd ever had!

Seemingly the best. His only comfort was that he hadn't given her the executive title he'd been considering. The damage she could have done in a position like that was beyond thinking. She was doing enough harm to his bottom line no longer employed by him at all.

It couldn't go on. He'd finally, reluctantly, sent her a strongly worded ultimatum and his palms were sweating that she would reject this one, too. She knew him well enough to believe that when he said final, he meant final, but he'd never had anything so valuable as his flesh and blood on the table. If she refused again…

She wouldn't. Sirena Abbott was more avaricious than he'd given her credit for, but she was innately practical. She would recognize he'd hit his limit and would cash in.

As if to prove it, his email blipped with a message from his lawyer.

Sirena Abbott had an appointment on Monday and wanted the rest of the week to think things through.

Raoul leaned on hands that curled into tight fists. His inner being swelled with triumph. Silly woman. When he said Monday, he meant *Monday.*

\* \* \*

As Sirena entered the alcove that housed the front of her building, she was still preoccupied by the lecture from the obstetrician about taking time to relax. She needed to read up on side effects of the medication he'd prescribed, too.

Distracted, she didn't notice anyone until a lean, masculine body stepped out of the shadows. Her pulse leaped in excited recognition even as she jerked in alarm.

Her keys dropped with a clatter. Pressing herself into the glass door, she pulled her collar tighter to her throat. His familiar scent overwhelmed her, spicy and masculine beneath a layer of rain. The late-afternoon gloom threw forbidding shadows into the angles of his features and turned his short, spiky lashes into sharp blades above turbulent eyes. He was compelling as ever and she was as susceptible as always.

"Hello, Sirena."

*That voice.*

"What are you doing here?" Her knuckles dug into her neck where her pulse raced with dangerous speed. She was supposed to be avoiding this sort of elevation of her heart rate, but Raoul had always done this to her. Thank God she'd spent two years perfecting how to hide her girlish flushes of awareness and awestruck admiration. With a tilt of her chin she conveyed that he didn't intimidate her— even though she was in danger of cracking the glass at her back, she was pressed so hard against it.

"You didn't really think I'd wait until Friday," he said, uncompromising and flinty.

"I didn't think you'd be waiting at my door," she protested, adding with admirable civility, "I'll review the documents tomorrow, I promise."

Raoul shook his head in condescension. "Today, Sirena."

"It's been a long day, Raoul. Don't make it longer." Her

voice was weighted with more tiredness than she meant
to reveal.

His eyes narrowed. "What sort of appointment did you
have? Doctor?"

A little shiver of premonition went through her. Something told her not to let him see how unsettling the news
had been, but the reality of all those tests and personal history forms had taken a toll. If she had thought she could
avoid signing a shared custody agreement with Raoul,
today she'd learned it was imperative she do so.

"Is the baby all right?" Raoul demanded gruffly. The
edgy concern in his tone affected her, making her soften
and stiffen at the same time.

"The baby is fine," she said firmly. If the mother could
keep herself healthy enough to deliver—and ensure there
was at least one parent left to rear it—the baby was in a
great position for a long and happy life.

"You?" he questioned with sharp acuity. Damned man
never missed a thing.

"I'm tired," she prevaricated. "And I have to use the loo.
It's only five o'clock. That gives me seven hours. Come
back at eleven fifty-nine."

Raoul's jaw hardened. "No." Leaning down, brushing
entirely too close to her legs, he picked up her keys and
straightened. "No more games, no more lawyers. You and
I are hammering this out. Now."

Sirena tried to take her keys, but Raoul only closed his
hand over them, leaving her fingers brushing the hard
strength of his knuckles.

The contact sent an electric zing through her nervous
system, leaving her entire body quivering over what was
a ridiculously innocuous touch.

She'd been too stressed and nauseous to have sexual
feelings these last months, but suddenly every vessel in
her body came alive to the presence of *this* man, the aveng-

ing god who had never had any genuine respect for her in the first place.

Tamping down on the rush of hurt and disappointment that welled in her chest, Sirena found her spine, standing up to him as well as a woman in flats could to a man who was head and shoulders taller than she was.

"Let's get something clear," she said, voice trembling a bit. She hoped he put it down to anger, not weak, stupid longing for something that had never existed. "Whatever agreement we come to is contingent on paternity tests proving you're the father."

Raoul rocked back on his heels. His negotiation face slid into place over his shock. In the shadowed alcove, Sirena wasn't sure if his pupils really contracted to pinpoints, but she felt his gaze like a lance that held her in place. It made her nervous, but she was proud of herself for taking him aback. She couldn't afford to be a pushover.

"Who else is in the running?" he gritted out.

"I have a life beyond your exalted presence." The lies went up like umbrellas, but she had so few advantages.

He stood unflinching and austere, but there was something in his bearing that made her heart pang. She knew he was the father, but by keeping him guessing she was performing a type of torture on him, keeping him in a state of anxious inability to act. It was cruel and made her feel ashamed.

*Don't be a wimp, Sirena.* He could take care of himself. The only thing she needed to worry about was her baby.

"Let's get this done," she said.

# CHAPTER THREE

RAOUL HAD NEVER been in Sirena's flat. When he entered he was surprised to immediately feel as though he was returning to a place both familiar and comfortable. It was so *her*.

She was a tidy person with simple taste, but her innate sensuality came through in textures and easy blends of color. The open-plan lounge-kitchen was tiny, but everything had a place, houseplants were lush and well tended. Family snapshots smiled from walls and shelves. He had time while she was in the powder room to take in the miniscule bedroom kept as scrupulously neat as the rest, the bed notably a single.

Sirena cast him a harried glance as she emerged and shrugged from her coat, draping it over the back of a dining chair.

Her figure, voluptuous as ever, had a new curve that made him draw in a searing breath. Until this moment, *pregnant* had been a word bandied through hostile emails and legal paperwork. As he cataloged the snug fit of leggings and a stretchy top over a body that hadn't filled out much except in the one place, he felt his scalp tighten.

*Sirena was carrying a baby.*

Her pale, slender hand opened over the small bump. Too small? He had no idea about these things.

Yanking his gaze to her face, he saw defensive wariness

and something else, something incredibly vulnerable that triggered his deepest protective instincts.

Thankfully she glanced away, thick hair falling across her cheek to hide her expression. Raoul regrouped, reminding himself not to let her get to him, but he couldn't take his eyes off that firm swelling. He'd spent two years fighting the urge to touch this woman, had given in to a moment of weakness once, and it took all his self-discipline not to reach for her now. His hands itched to start at that mysterious bump then explore the rest of her luscious shape. He shoved his fists into his overcoat pockets and glared with resentment.

"I'm having ice water and an orange. Do you want coffee?" she asked.

"Nothing," he bit out. No more foot dragging. He was still reeling from her coy remark about paternity, played out so well he was entertaining a shred of uncertainty. He couldn't begin to consider what he'd do if he wasn't the father.

The not knowing made him restless, especially because he couldn't understand why she was tormenting him. Yes, his position would be strengthened if she admitted he was the father, but so would hers. He would do anything for his child. One glimpse of a pregnant belly shouldn't affect him this deeply, but all he could think was that his entire life had changed. Every decision from now on would be weighed against its effect on that tiny being in Sirena's center.

She took her frosted glass and plate of sectioned orange to the table, opening a file as she sat down. One glance invited him to take the chair across from her. They didn't stand on ceremony. He didn't hold her chair; this wasn't a date. It was reminiscent of the times they'd planted themselves on either side of a boardroom table and worked through projects and tasks until he'd cleared his plate and loaded hers full, confident it would all be completed to his exacting specifications.

He tightened his mouth against a blurted demand for answers. *Why?* If she had needed money, why hadn't she asked him for a loan? A raise? The salary he'd been paying her was generous, but he'd seen she was ready for more responsibility and the compensation that went with it. Had *this* been her plan all along? Pregnancy and a custody settlement?

The thought occurred as she opened the file and he glimpsed a copy of a contract filled with notations and scribbles.

"You *have* read it," he said with tight disgust.

"I do my homework, same as you," she retorted, ice clinking as she sipped. Her skin, fine grained as a baby's, was pale. Weren't pregnant women supposed to glow? Sirena didn't look unhealthy, but there were shadows under her eyes and in them. She touched her brow where she used to complain of tension headaches. He could see the pulse in her throat pounding as if her heart would explode.

The precariousness of his position struck him. He wanted to be ruthless, but not only was he facing a woman in a weakened condition, her condition affected a baby. As he absorbed the raised stakes, his tension increased. The scent of the fresh orange seemed overly strong and pungent.

"I want medical reports," he said with more harsh demand than he would typically use at the opening of a negotiation.

Sirena flinched and laced her fingers together. Without looking at him, she said, "I don't have a problem sharing the baby's health checkups. So far it's been textbook. I have a scan on my laptop I can email you once we've signed off." Now her eyes came up, but her gaze was veiled. She was hiding something.

"Who are you?" he muttered. "You're not the Sirena I knew." His PA had been approachable and cheerful, quick to smile, quick to see the humor in things. This woman was locked down, serious and more secretive than he'd ever imagined.

Like him, which was a disturbing thought.

"What makes you think you ever knew me, Raoul?" The elegant arches of her dark brows lifted while bitter amusement twisted her doll-perfect lips. "Did you ever ask about my life? My plans? My likes or dislikes? All I remember is demands that revolved around your needs. Your intention to work late. Your bad mood because you hadn't eaten. You once snapped your fingers at me because you wanted the name of the woman you'd taken to dinner, maybe even bed, the night before. She needed flowers as a kiss-off. On that note, as your former PA I'm compelled to point out that your new one dropped the ball. I didn't get my lilies."

Her audacity tested Raoul's already dicey mood. His inner compass swung from contempt to self-disgust that he'd slept with her at all to a guilty acknowledgment that no, he hadn't spent much time getting to know her on a personal level. He'd wanted too badly to take things to an intimate level, so he'd kept her at a distance.

Not that he had any intention of explaining when she was coming out swinging with two full buckets of scathing judgment and brutal sarcasm.

"That ice water seems to have gone directly into your veins," he remarked with the smoothness of a panther batting a bird from the air.

"Yes, I'm a kettle and so much blacker than you." She pivoted the file and pushed it toward him. "You might as well read my notes and we'll go from there."

Cold. Distant. Unreachable. She wasn't saying those words, but he'd heard them from enough women to know that's what she was implying.

Oddly, he hadn't thought Sirena saw him that way, and it bothered him that she did. Which made no sense, because he hadn't cared much when those other women said it and he hadn't once put Sirena in the same category as his former lovers. She was never intended to be his lover at all. When he took women to his bed, it was without any sort of expectation beyond an affair that would allow him to release sexual tension. Sirena had already been too integral a part of his working life to blur those lines.

Yet he had. And she seemed to be holding him to account for his callous treatment of her—when she had only slept with him for her own gain! Possibly for the very baby they were fighting over.

Drawing the papers closer, he began taking in her notations. The first was a refusal to submit to paternity tests until after the birth, at which point this contract would come into effect if he was proven to be the father.

He didn't like it, but in the interest of moving forward he initialed it.

Things quickly became more confusing and audacious. Distantly he noted that she'd circled a formatting error—one more eagle-eyed skill he regretted losing from his business life.

"Why the hell is everything to be held in trust for the baby?"

"I don't want your money," she said with such flatness he almost believed her.

*Don't get sidetracked,* he warned himself. Obviously she had wanted his money or she wouldn't have stolen from him, but arguing that point was moot. Right now all that mattered was getting paternity resolved and his right to involvement irrevocable.

He lowered his gaze to the pages in front of him, trying to make sense of her changes when they all favored the baby's financial future and left her taking nothing from him. Raoul cut her a suspicious glance. No one gave up this much…

"Ah," he snorted with understanding as he came to the codicil. *"No."*

"Think about it. You can't breast-feed. It makes sense that I have full custody."

"For *five* years? Nice try. Five days, maybe."

"Five days," she repeated through her teeth, flashing an angry emotion he'd never seen in her. Her eyes glazed with a level of hatred that pierced through his shell with unexpected toxicity, leaving a fiery sting.

And was that fear? Her generous mouth trembled before she pressed it into a firm line. "If you're not going to be reasonable, leave now. You're not the father anyway."

She rose and so did he, catching her by the arms as she tried to skirt past him. The little swell at her belly nudged into him, foreign and disconcerting, making his hands tighten with a possessive desire to keep her close. Keep *it* close, he corrected silently.

"Don't touch me." Fine trembles cascaded through her so he felt it as if he grasped an electric wire that pulsed in warning.

"Sure you don't want to try persuading me into clemency again?" he prodded, recognizing that deep down he was still weakly enthralled by her. If she offered herself right now, he would be receptive. It would change things.

"I didn't sue you for sexual harassment before, but I had every right to."

Her words slapped him. Hard.

Dropping his hold, he reared back, offended to his core. "You wanted me every bit as much as I wanted you," he seethed. His memories exploded daily with the way her expression had shone with excitement. The way she'd molded herself into him and arched for more contact and cried out with joy as the shudders of culmination racked them both.

"No, you were *bored*," she shot back with vicious fury that carried a ring of hurt.

It shouldn't singe him with guilt, but it did. He'd been saving face when he'd said that, full of whiskey and brimming with betrayal. The news that she had been released had been roiling in him like poison. Having her show up at the end of his drive had nearly undone him.

Now he teetered between a dangerous admission of attraction and delivering his brutal set-down for a second time.

"Get out, Raoul," Sirena said with a pained lack of heat. She sounded defeated. Heartbroken. "I'm sorry I ever met you."

The retort that the feeling was mutual hovered on his tongue, but stayed locked behind teeth clenched against a surprising lash of...hell, why would he suffer regret?

Pinching the bridge of his nose, he reminded himself the woman he'd thought he'd known had never existed. He threw himself back into his chair. "We'll hire a panel of experts to work out the schedule of the baby's first five years based on his or her personal needs. At four years we'll begin negotiating the school years."

"A panel of experts," she repeated on a choking laugh. "Yes, I've got your deep pockets. Let's do that."

"If you're worried about money, why are you refusing a settlement?"

Her response was quiet and somber, disturbingly sincere. "Because I don't want money. I want my baby." She moved to the window. It was covered in drizzle that the wind had tossed against the glass. Her hand rested on her belly. Her profile was grave.

Raoul dragged his eyes off her, disturbed by how much her earnest simplicity wrenched his gut. It made him twitch with the impulse to reassure her, and not just verbally. For some reason, he wanted to hold her so badly his whole body ached.

That wasn't like him. He had his moments of being a softy when it came to his mother or stepsister. They were beloved and very much his responsibility even though they weren't as helpless these days as they'd once been. He still flinched with guilt when he remembered how he'd been living it up his first year of college, drinking and chasing girls, completely oblivious to what was happening at home. Then, despite how brutal and thoughtless his stepfather's gambling had been, the man's death had shattered the hearts of two people he cared for deeply. Faced with abject poverty, it had been easy for Raoul to feel nothing but animosity toward the dead man, but the unmitigated grief his mother and Miranda had suffered had been very real. He'd hated seeing them in pain. It had been sharply reminiscent of his agony after his father's suicide.

But as supportive as he'd tried to be while he took control and recovered their finances, he'd never been the touchy-feely sort who hugged and cuddled away their pain.

Why he craved to offer Sirena that sort of comfort boggled him.

Forcing himself to ignore the desire, he scanned the changes she'd made to the agreement, thinking that perhaps he was more self-involved than he'd realized since he had been focused this entire time on what the child meant to him, how his life would change, how he'd make room for it and provide for *his* progeny. What *he* wanted.

Suddenly he was seeing and hearing what Sirena wanted and it wasn't to hurt him. She had ample ways to do that, but her changes to this document were more about keeping the baby with her than keeping it from him.

"Did you think about termination at all?" he asked with sudden curiosity.

"Yes."

The word struck him like a bullet, utterly unexpected and so lethal it stopped his heart. Until his mind caught up. Obviously she'd decided to have the baby or they wouldn't be here.

He rubbed feeling back into his face, but his ears felt filled with water. He had to strain to hear her as she quietly continued.

"I was only a few weeks along when I found out. There's a pill you can take that early. You don't have to go into hospital, there are fewer complications… There seemed to be a lot of good reasons not to go through with the pregnancy." Her profile grew distressed and her fingertips grazed the pulse in her throat.

Reasons like the threat of prison and having a man she didn't want in her life demanding access to her baby. Raoul's sharp mind pinned up the drawbacks as quickly as her own must have. His blood ran cold at how close he'd come to not knowing about this baby at all.

"I couldn't bring myself to…expel it from my life like that. I want this baby, Raoul." She turned with her hand protectively on her middle again, her eyes glittering with quiet ferocity. "I know it's foolish to let you see how badly I want it. You'll find a way to use it against me. But I need you to believe me. I will *never* let anyone take my baby from me."

His scalp tightened with preternatural wariness and pride and awe. Sirena was revealing the sort of primal mother instinct their caveman ancestors would have prized in a mate. The alpha male in him exalted in seeing that quality emanating from the mother of his child.

While the cutthroat negotiator in him recognized a tough adversary.

"You're trying to convince me I can't buy you off," he summed up, trying not to let himself become too entranced by her seeming to possess redeeming qualities. She had fooled him once already.

"You can't. The only reason I'm speaking to you at all is to give my baby the same advantages its father might provide its future siblings, whether that's monetary or social standing or emotional support. Consider what those things might be as you work through the rest of that." She nodded at the contract and slipped into the powder room again.

*Future siblings?* Raoul's mind became an empty whiteboard as he bit back a remark that he hadn't expected *this* child; he certainly wasn't ready to contemplate more.

Three months later, Raoul was taking steps to ensure he was prepared for the birth, looking ahead to clear his calendar in six weeks. He rarely took time off and found even Christmas with his mother an endurance test of agitation to get back to work. Anticipation energized him for this vacation, though.

Because it was a new challenge? Or because he would see Sirena?

He shut down the thought. The baby was his sole interest. He was eager to find out the sex, know it was healthy and have final confirmation it was *his*.

Not that he had many doubts on any of that. True to their agreement, Sirena had sent him updates on the baby's progress. Nothing concerning her own, he had noted with vague dissatisfaction, but he expected he would be informed if there were problems. The second scan later in the pregnancy had not revealed an obvious male, so he'd assumed the baby was female and found himself taken with the vision of a daughter possessing dark curls and beguiling green eyes.

As for paternity, to his mind, the fact Sirena had signed made the baby his. The final test after the birth was a formality that would activate the arrangements, that was all.

But that was a month and a half from now and he had people to organize. People who were abuzz with the news that the driven head of their multinational software corporation was taking an extended absence.

Only a handful of his closest and most trusted subordinates knew the reason, and even they didn't know the mother's identity. The scandalous circumstances of his father's infidelity and suicide had made Raoul a circumspect man. Nothing about his involvement with Sirena, their affair, her being fired for embezzlement or her pregnancy was public knowledge. When people asked—and she'd made enough of an impression on associates and colleagues that many did—he only said she was no longer with the company.

Part of him continued to resent that loss, especially when the assistants he kept trying out turned out to be so *trying.* The highly recommended Ms. Poole entered the meeting with a worried pucker in her magic-marker brows.

"I said life or death, Ms. Poole," he reminded, clinging to patience.

"She's very insistent," the spindly woman said, bringing a mobile phone to him.

"Who?" He tamped down on asking, *Sirena?* Her tenacity was something he'd come to respect, if not always appreciate.

"Molly. About your agreement with Ms. Abbott."

He didn't know any Molly, but something preternatural set an unexpected boot heel on his chest, sharp and compressing, causing pressure to balloon out in radiant waves. Odd. There was no reason to believe this was bad news. Sirena hadn't contacted him directly since he'd left her looking wrung out and cross at her flat that day, neither of them particularly satisfied with the outcome of their negotiations, but possessing a binding document between them.

"Yes?" He took the phone in a hand that became nerveless and clumsy. As he stood and moved from the table, he was aware of the ripple of curiosity behind him. At the same time, despite everything that had passed between them, he experienced a flick of excitement. His mind conjured an image of Sirena in one of those knitted skirt-and-sweater sets she used to wear.

"Mr. Zesiger? I'm Sirena Abbott's midwife. She asked me to inform you that the baby is on its way."

"It's early," he protested.

"Yes, they had to induce—" She cut herself off.

He heard muffled words and held his breath as he strained to hear what was said.

She came back. "I've just been informed it will be an emergency cesarean."

"Where is she?" he demanded while apprehension wrapped around him like sandpaper, leaving him abraded and raw.

"I understood you were only to be informed and that a paternity test be ordered, not that you would attend—"

"Save me the phone calls to find her so I can come directly," he bit out.

A brief pause before she told him. "But the results won't be known for days."

"Tell her I'm on my way," he said, but she was already gone.

# CHAPTER FOUR

A WOMAN MET him in the hospital reception area. She wore red glasses and a homespun pullover. Her ditch-water hair was in one thick plait, her expression grave.

"Raoul? Molly." She held out a hand and offered a tight smile. "Sirena told me I'd know you when I saw you. The baby is a girl. They've taken the samples and should have the results in a few days." Her manner was disconcertingly strained.

Because she didn't want to get his hopes up? The baby was here, the moment of truth at hand. He shouldn't be so stunned given the nature of the call or the time it had taken to fight traffic to get here, but the swiftness of the procedure surprised him. At the same time, he was aware of a gripping need to see the infant and *know* she was his.

A girl. He hadn't realized how much he wanted one. And safely delivered. The abruptness of the call and lack of details had unsettled him, but they were fine. Everything was fine.

"Good," he heard himself say, finally able to breathe. "I'm pleased to hear they came through all right." He gestured for her to lead the way, assuming she'd show him to their room.

Molly didn't move. "Premature babies always have certain hurdles, but the pediatrician is confident she'll progress as well as the best of them." She seemed to ponder whether to say more.

"And Sirena?" he prompted. Some unknown source of telepathy made him brace even as the question left him. A kind of dread that was distant but gut-churningly familiar seeped into his bloodstream like poison, unwanted and tensing him with refusal and denial before he even knew what she would say.

Molly's eyes became liquid. "They're doing all they can."

For a long moment nothing happened. No movement, no sound, nothing. Then, from far off, he heard a torn inhale, like a last gasp of life.

*No.* Her words didn't even make sense. He suddenly found himself bumping into a wall and put out a hand to steady himself. "What *happened?*"

"I wondered if she had told you about her condition." Molly moved closer. Her touch was a biting grasp on his upper arm, surprisingly strong and necessary as he wondered if he'd stay on his feet. "It's been a risky pregnancy from the start. High blood pressure, then early-onset pre-eclampsia. She's been managing that condition these last few weeks, trying to buy the baby more time. Today they couldn't wait any longer without risking both their lives, so the doctors induced. After she had a seizure, they stopped the labor and took her for surgery. Now she's lost a lot of blood. I'm sorry. I can see this is hard for you to hear."

Hard? All his strength was draining away, leaving him cold and empty. Clammy with fear. Her life was about to snap free of his and she *hadn't even told him.* She might as well have swallowed a bottle of pills and left herself for him to find when he got home from school. Suddenly he was nine again, barely comprehending what he was seeing, unable to get a response out of the heavy body he was shaking with all his might. Not there soon enough. Helpless to make this right.

"Why the hell didn't she *say something?*" he burst out, furious that she'd given him no indication, no warning, just left him tied to the tracks to be hit with a train.

Molly shook her head in bafflement. "Sirena didn't talk about the custody agreement, but it's been my impression things have been hostile."

So hostile she kept from him that her life was on the line?

"I don't want her to *die!*" The word was foul and jagged in his throat. He spoke from the very center of himself, flashing a look at Molly that made her flinch. He couldn't imagine what he looked like, but his world was screeching to a halt and everything in it was whirling past him.

"No one does," she assured him in the guarded tone developed by people who dealt with victims. It was the same prudent nonengagement with explosive emotions that the social worker had used as she had steered his young self from his father's body.

"Take me to her," he gritted out. A horrible avalanche of fear like he'd never known crushed him. He wanted to run shouting for her until he found her. This wasn't real. It couldn't be.

"I can't. But—" She seemed to think twice, then gave him a poignant smile. "Maybe they'll let us into the nursery."

He forced one foot in front of the other, walking as if through a wall of thick, suffocating gelatin as he followed Molly to the preemie clinic, ambivalence writhing like a two-headed snake inside him. Was it his fault Sirena hovered on the brink? Or another man's? He adamantly wanted his child, but the idea that one life could cost another appalled him.

He came up to the tiny, nearly naked being in the incubator, her bottom covered in an oversized nappy, her hair hidden by a cap. Wires extended from her bare fragile body and her miniature Sirena mouth briefly pursed in a kiss.

He couldn't see anything of himself in her, but a startlingly deep need to gather and guard the infant welled in him. Pressing his icy hands to the warm glass, he silently begged the little girl to *hang on*. If this was all that would be left of Sirena…

He brutally refused to entertain such a thought, turning his mind to sending a deep imperative through the walls of the hospital to the unknown location of this baby's mother. *Hang on, Sirena. Hang on.*

Sirena had the worst hangover of her life. Her whole body hurt, her mouth was dry and nausea roiled in her stomach. In her daze, she moved her hand to her middle, where the solid shape of her baby was gone, replaced with bandages and a soft waistline.

A whimper of distress escaped her.

"Lucy is fine, Sirena." His voice was unsweetened cocoa, warm and comforting despite the bitter taint.

"Lucy?" she managed, blinking gritty eyes. The stark ceiling above her was white, the day painfully bright. Slowly the steel-gray of Raoul's gaze came into focus.

"Isn't that what you told Molly? That you wanted your daughter named for your mother, Lucille?"

*You don't mind?* she almost said, but wasn't sure where the paternity test was. When she had signed the consent forms, they'd told her the kind of proof he'd requested, the kind admissible in court, was a more complex test that would take several days. She wondered if waiting on that had been the only thing keeping him from whisking Lucy from this hospital before she woke.

She didn't ask. She could barely form words with what felt like a cotton-filled mouth. It took all her concentration to remain impassive. Seeing him gave her such a bizarre sense of relief she wanted to burst into tears. She reminded herself not to read anything into the shadow of stubble on his jaw or the bruises of tiredness under his eyes. The man was a machine when it came to work; he could have been at the office late and dropped by on his way to his penthouse.

Still, that scruff of light beard gave her a thrill. She'd seen him like this many times and always experienced this same ripple of attraction. The same desire to smooth a hand over his rough cheek. He would be overworked yet energized by whatever had piqued his ambition, his shirt collar open, his sleeves rolled back and soon, a smile of weary satisfaction.

But not today. Today he was sexily rumpled, but his demeanor was antagonistic, making a shiver of apprehension sidle through her as he spoke in a rough growl. "You should have told me you weren't well."

The harsh accusation in his tone was so sharp she flinched. All she could think about were those harrowing moments when they'd told her the baby had to come out. Not for Lucy's sake, but her own. The fear in her had been so great, she'd been on the verge of begging Raoul to come to her. The Raoul she had once imagined him to be anyway. He was so strong and capable and she'd instinctively known she'd feel safe if he was near.

He hated her, though. He wouldn't care. Like always, she'd been on her own.

She'd gone through the induction and the beginning of pains without anyone at her side, only calling Molly when the nurse confirmed that yes, labor was properly started. That was when she'd been required to notify Raoul. She had been explaining that to Molly when something went wrong.

She didn't even know what had happened. Having a

huge blank like that was frightening. His blaming her for not advising him it was a possibility added insult to injury, putting her on the defensive.

"Why would I tell you anything?" she challenged from her disadvantaged position, flat on the bed, tied down with wires, voice like a flake of yellowed onionskin. "You can't be happy I pulled through."

"You haven't yet," he said, snapping forward in a way that made her heart jump. He set his big hands on either side of her and leaned over her, promising reprisal despite her pathetic condition. "And don't ever accuse me of anything so ugly again."

Sirena tried to swallow and couldn't even feel her dry tongue against her arid lips. "Can I have some water?" she begged in a whispered plea. "Please? I'm so thirsty."

"I don't know if you're allowed to have anything," he said with a scowl, something avid and desperate flickering through his eyes before he bent with the sudden swoop of a hawk going for a kill.

His mouth covered hers for the briefest second. His damp tongue licked into the parched cavern of her mouth to moisten the dry membranes. The relief was incredible, the act surprising and intimate beyond measure.

"I'll tell the nurse you're awake." He walked out, leaving her speechless and tingling with the return of life to her entire body, mind dazed and wondering if she was still unconscious and hallucinating.

Sirena had thought nothing could make her melt so thoroughly as the vulnerable sight of her premature daughter. Then she began hearing the stories of Raoul learning to diaper and feed her. Raoul, who didn't even know for sure he was the father, had paced a path between Lucy and Sirena, talking unceasingly to Sirena when they had feared she would slip into a coma. He'd only gone home for a shower and sleep now that Sirena had woken, nearly seventy-two hours after the birth.

She told herself not to read it as a sign of caring. If Raoul was tending to Lucy, he was only stamping a claim while trying to prove Sirena was dispensable. To some extent she was. She quickly learned she could hold her baby, but she was too sick and weak for anything else. She was pumping her breasts, but only to keep her thin milk supply going while she waited for the cocktail of medications to leave her system. She couldn't feed Lucy or do anything else a mother ought to do.

Dejected, she was fretting over how useless she was as she headed back to bed the next morning, wiped out by the tiny act of brushing her teeth.

Raoul walked in on her attempt to scale the bed, finding her with one hip hitched on the edge, bare legs akimbo as she quickly tried to stay decent under her hospital gown.

Aside from faint shadows under his heavy eyes, he looked fantastic in casual pants and a striped shirt. He brought a wonderfully familiar scent with him, too. For a second she was back in the office welcoming her freshly shaved boss, sharing coffee with him as they discussed how they'd tackle the day.

He eyed her balefully, but that might have been a reaction to the ferocious scowl she threw at him. She hadn't been allowed coffee since early in the pregnancy and he was sipping from a travel mug tagged with a ProZess Software logo. He was a picture of everything she couldn't have.

"Why are you here?" she asked, struggling to use her severed stomach muscles to heft herself onto the bed.

He smoothly moved to her side, set down his coffee and helped her.

"I don't—" She stiffened in rejection, but he bundled her into his crisp shirt anyway. The press of his body heat through the fabric burned into her as he used a gentle embrace to lift her. His free hand caressed her bare, dangling leg, sliding it neatly under the sheet as he slid her into bed as if she weighed no more than a kitten.

Shaken, she drew the sheet up to her neck and glared at him.

He picked up his coffee and sipped, staring back with his poker face. "Your doctor said he'd have the paternity results when he did his rounds this morning."

Her heart left her body and ran down the hall to bar the door of the nursery.

She wasn't ready to face this. Last night had been full of sudden jerks to wakefulness that had left her panting and unable to calm herself from the nightmare that Raoul would disappear with their daughter.

That *he* would disappear from her life again.

Why did it matter whether he was in her life? She felt nothing but hatred and mistrust toward him, she reminded herself. But the weeks of not seeing him while she waited out her pregnancy had been the bleakest of her life, worse even than when her family had left for Australia.

Logic told her he wasn't worth these yearning feelings she still had, but she felt a rush of delight that he kept showing up. When he was in the room, the longing that gripped her during his absences eased and the dark shadows inside her receded.

She couldn't forget he was the enemy, though. And she was running out of defenses.

He must have seen her apprehension, because he drawled, "Scared? Why?" The question was like a throwing star, pointed on all sides and sticking deep. "Because I might be the father? Or because you know I am?"

The stealthy challenge circled her heart like a Spanish inquisitor, the knife blade out and audibly scraping the strop.

She noticed her hands were pleating the edge of the sheet into an accordion. What was the use in prevaricating? She licked her numb lips.

"Are you going to try to take her from me if you are?" she asked in a thin voice.

*If? You bitch,* he thought as the tension of not knowing stayed dialed high inside him. The last three days had been hellish as he'd grown more and more attached to that tiny tree frog of a girl while cautioning himself that she might belong to another man.

Just like her mother.

"I could have taken her a dozen times by now," he bit out. "I should have."

It wasn't completely true. The hospital had accommodated his visiting the baby, but only because he was the kind of man who didn't let up until he got what he wanted. They wouldn't have let him leave with her, though.

If Sirena believed he could have, however, great. He wanted to punish her for the limbo she'd kept him in.

Her hands went still and pale. All of her seemed to drain of color until she was practically translucent, her already wan face ashen. Fainting again? He shot out a hand to press her into the pillows against the raised head of the bed.

She tried to bat away his touch, but in slow motion, her tortured expression lifting long enough to let him glimpse the storm of emotions behind her tangled lashes and white lips: frustration at her weakness, a flinch of physical pain in her brow, defensiveness that he had the audacity to touch her and terror. Raw terror in the glimmering green of her eyes.

Rolling her head away, she swallowed, her fear so palpable the hair rose on the back of his neck.

*Advantage to me,* he thought, trying to shrug off the prickling feeling, but guilty self-disgust weighed in the pit of his stomach. All he could think about was the hours he'd spent right here, telling her how unfair it was for a child to grow up missing a parent. The questions Lucy would have, the empty wedge in the wholeness of her life, would affect the child forever.

Blood ties hadn't mattered at that point. He and Lucy had been linked by the prospect that she would suffer his pain—an unthinkable cruelty for an infant just starting her life. The whole time he'd been urging Sirena to pull through, he'd been mentally cataloging everything he knew about her, wanting to be Lucy's depository of information on her mother.

While all he'd heard in the back of his mind had been Sirena's scathing, *What makes you think you ever knew me, Raoul?*

His heart dipped. She wanted her baby. He knew that much. As he'd gleaned all the details of this pregnancy that had nearly killed her, he'd wondered about her feelings for the father. Did the lucky man even know how stalwartly determined she'd been to have his child?

If that man was him… His abdomen tensed around a ripple of something deep and moving, something he didn't want to acknowledge because it put him in her debt.

The specialist swept in, taking in the charged tension with a somber look. "Good morning. I know you've been waiting, Raoul. Let me put you at ease. You are Lucy's biological father."

Relief poured into him like blood returning after a constriction, filling him with confidence and pride in his daughter, the little scrap with such a determined life force.

No reaction from Sirena. She kept her face averted as though he and the doctor weren't even in the room.

"I don't have plans to take her from you," Raoul blurted. The impatient words left him before he realized they were on his tongue, leaving him irritated by how she weakened him with nothing but terrified silence.

She gave him a teary, disbelieving look that got his back up.

The physician distracted her, asking after her incision and leaving Raoul to face a cold, stony truth: he couldn't separate mother from daughter.

Her accusation when she'd woken yesterday that he would have wished her dead had made him so sick he hadn't had words. His own father's absence had been self-inflicted—he'd *left* Raoul and his mother—but it didn't make the idea of Sirena's baby accidentally being motherless any less horrific. Raoul wouldn't be able to live with himself if he was the instrument that divided a parent from a child.

"When can I take her home?" he heard Sirena ask the doctor.

An image flashed into Raoul's mind of her collapsing the way she had at the courthouse, but without anyone to catch her or the baby in her arms.

"You're not taking her to your flat," he stated bluntly, speaking on instinct from the appalled place that was very much aware of how ill and weak she was.

Sirena's gaze swung to his, persecuted and wild. "You just said—"

"I said I wasn't so low I'd steal your baby from you. But you're more than prepared to keep Lucy from me, aren't you?" That reality was very raw. "You're the one who steals, Sirena, not me."

A humiliated blush rolled into her aghast face.

The physician broke in with, "Let's get you and Lucy well first, then we'll talk about where she's going." It was a blatant effort to defuse their belligerent standoff.

The doctor departed a few minutes later, leaving Sirena trying to decide which was worse: having Raoul in the room, where his presence ratcheted her tension beyond bearing, or out of the room, where she didn't know what he was up to.

"The contract is in effect now," she reminded him in a mutter. "I'll adhere to it."

"Will you? Because you've done everything possible to keep me from even knowing she's mine." His temper snapped. "How could you do that? I lost my father, Sirena. I know how it feels to grow up without one."

"And I lost my mother," she cried, then cringed as the force of such harsh speech sliced pain across her abdomen. "Why do you think I stood up to the most pitiless man in the world?" she asked in a thick voice, clenching her eyes shut as she fought for control, so emotional from everything that she verged on breaking down. "You really know how to put a woman through hell, Raoul. I can't even get myself down the hall to her and you're playing stupid mind games. *I won't take her, but you can't have her.* Maybe you would deserve a place in her life if you just once showed an ounce of compassion."

Silence.

She threw her heavy arm over her closed eyes, pressing back weak tears, concentrating on her breathing to pull herself together. The worst part was, she felt horrible about trying to keep him from Lucy. He had a right to be angry about that—along with the stealing—but she couldn't undo any of it. Her life was a giant mess and she had no idea how she was going to fix it and carry on.

"Let's go," Raoul said in a gruff tone that was too close to the bed.

Sirena lowered her arm to eye him, startled to see he'd brought the wheelchair to her side.

"I'll take you to see Lucy. We'll both calm down and maybe start communicating like adults."

"Don't be nice," she groaned. "It makes me feel awful."

"You should feel awful." He braced her as she slid off the bed and into the chair.

She slumped into it and dropped her face into her hands. "I love her more than you can know, Raoul. And you've been horrid, trying to take her from me the instant you heard I was pregnant. What else could I do except lie about paternity?"

The chair moved and she lifted her head, glad she didn't have to face him, especially when he said with quiet sincerity, "You're wrong. I do know how much you love her. I feel the same way. That's why I've been so tough about it. I didn't know about your mother. I thought this was all payback for the court case."

"No," she breathed, shoulders slumping. "I'm angry about that, but—" her voice hitched with yearning "—I just want to be her mum."

"What happened to yours?" His voice sounded deeper and quieter than she'd ever heard it, making her feel small for trying to cut him from his daughter's life. She didn't know how he'd lost his father, but that nascent connection she'd always felt toward him over their shared grief extended from within herself, like a strand of spiderweb drifting behind her, searching to anchor itself to him.

"This." She waved a trembling hand at her pathetic physical state. "Her complications were different so this wasn't hereditary, but it was always in my mind that having a baby isn't as simple for some as it is for others. I was only six when she died, so I don't have a lot of memories, but that's why losing her hurt so much. I can't bear the idea of Lucy going through all her life markers of puberty and boyfriends and childbirth without her mother there for her."

He stayed silent behind her, giving no indication whether her words had any impact. She wasn't able to twist around and look and didn't want to anyway. He might be interpreting her confession as a plea for sympathy when it was the kind of opening of her heart that left her feeling so raw and exposed she could hardly bear it.

She was grateful they entered the quiet warmth of the nursery at that point. Seconds later, as she cuddled Lucy into her chest, her world righted, becoming achingly perfect, even with Raoul's commanding presence hovering over them. Maybe because he was here. Much as she resented him, she wanted Lucy to have her father.

After feeding and changing and getting an update on Lucy's progress, Raoul returned Sirena to her room. She was quiet, visibly exhausted, their silence no longer hostile. When he helped her into bed, she only murmured, "Thank you," before plummeting into sleep.

Such a ferocious scrapper and now he understood why. The way she'd talked about missing her mother had made something lurch in his chest. It was a renewed snag of guilt at not really knowing her. His resentful *I never dreamed she was capable of stealing* was shifting into *still waters run deep.*

The way his father had quit on him made him highly susceptible to exalting a woman who had fought so hard to give her child life and to be in it.

He didn't like this shift in him. It made him wonder about her motives for stealing, and he didn't want to develop compassion and forgiveness for that. Opportunists took advantage of weak emotions like affection and trust. Next thing you knew, you were on the streets with two dependents—a social pariah—and your path forward was a broken cliff into an abyss.

He couldn't doubt Sirena's love for their daughter, though. While in the nursery, the old Sirena had returned, all warm smiles and soft laughter, her expression open and her wit quick, making the nurses laugh. He'd had to bite back his own chuckle more than once, fighting a desire to let go of his defenses and fall under her spell again.

Scowling, he tried to imagine how this impossible situation would play out. A foolish idea was taking hold in the back of his mind, one that looked ridiculous as a thought bubble. It would be outrageous in real life. He needed distance, not more exposure to her, but they were both coming from the same place with regard to Lucy. He couldn't ignore that. In fact, as the days passed, it was *all* he could think about.

Their truce lasted through the week as Raoul spent most of the day with them. Sirena stopped using the chair and started breast-feeding, even brought Lucy into her room with her overnight, which was a struggle she tried not to reveal, fearful of winding up in a fight with Raoul that she didn't have the energy to win. The rapport between them might be guarded and impersonal, but it was safe. As long as she didn't give him anything to criticize, they got along fine.

Meanwhile, the reality of taking a baby back to her flat when she couldn't even properly care for herself ate at her. When her doctor cleared her for discharge, she should have been elated, but she was so overwhelmed she hardly contained her tears.

Of course Raoul arrived at that exact moment. He was wearing a suit and tie, the shoulders of his jacket speckled with damp spots of late-spring rain. No time to worry how she'd cope when she had bigger concerns confronting her from the foot of her hospital bed. Dark, handsome, vengeful concerns.

"I told you a week ago you I won't let you take her to your flat," he said unemotionally.

It was the fight she'd been dreading, but she still wasn't prepared for it.

"And I'm pretty sure we signed an agreement that said I could," she replied, trying not to let him stir her temper. "I have nights with Lucy. You can visit during the day, exactly as we're doing here. Are we ignoring the panel of experts you hired?" Her quick sarcasm was a show of strength she didn't have. She had just gotten back from walking down the hall and that snappy reply was the extent of the spunk in her.

"You have the stamina of a trampled daisy. What if something happened? No. You're coming home with me," Raoul pronounced.

For a few seconds, she couldn't even blink. A tiny voice deep in her soul asked, *Me? Not just Lucy?* Her pulse tripped into a gallop and tingling excitement raced all the way to her nerve endings.

*Get a grip, Sirena!*

"I have staples, Raoul. It's not nice to make me laugh," she retorted, trying to gather thoughts that had scattered like shards of glass from a broken window. Stay in his house? With him? She already felt too vulnerable seeing him during the day. Living off him would decimate her pride and put her in his debt.

"You do," Raoul agreed with edgy derision. "Staples and tubes and a unit of someone else's blood. You're on medications that make you light-headed and have appointments for follow-up and a baby to care for. You can't do it alone."

In her heart of hearts she'd been counting on a miracle with her sister, but of course that hadn't panned out. Her father wasn't working, so he couldn't foot the bill for plane fare and God knew she couldn't afford it. Besides, Ali was in her first semester at uni—that had been the whole point of Sirena sending the money so many months ago.

Sirena had friends she could call for the odd thing, but

not the sort of steady help she needed these first weeks at home. Frustration made her voice strident.

"Why would you even suggest it? You don't want anything to do with me," she accused, voicing the fear that was a dark plague inside her.

He tilted his arrogant head to a condescending angle. "You may not be my ideal choice as the mother of my child, but I can't overlook the fact that you are, or that you love her as much as I do. We both want to be with her and you need looking after. Bringing you into my home is clearly the most practical solution."

That uncouthed *not be my ideal* stung like mad. She knew she looked awful, hair flat and dull, no makeup. Her figure would remain a disaster until she could start on the treadmill again.

Was he seeing anyone, she wondered suddenly? It was the sort of thing she hadn't been able to avoid knowing when she'd been working for him—and bizarrely, after being fired she'd found the not knowing even worse. How would she feel to learn he was with another woman while she was sleeping under his roof?

She broke their locked gazes, deeply repelled by the idea of him in bed with other women. "We don't even like each other. It would be a disaster."

"We're going to have to get past that for Lucy's sake, aren't we?" he countered.

"And my being dependent on you will foster goodwill? I doubt it," she argued, even as she mentally leaped to the pro of still being able to do her transcription jobs if he was on hand to care for Lucy for an hour here and there. That would mean she could keep her flat. The prospect of losing her home had become a genuine concern.

Raoul folded his arms as he put his sharp mind to work finding the argument that would clinch what he wanted.

Not that he *wanted* her in his home, he reminded himself. It was his daughter he was after.

"If I were to have another child, I would look after the health of that child's mother. Didn't you tell me you expect me to offer Lucy the same considerations I would offer all my children?"

He was pleased to recall the demand she'd thrown at him weeks ago. It justified taking her into his home. He didn't need a volatile mix of leftover attraction and betrayal confronting him with his eggs every morning, but Lucy's needs trumped his.

Sirena heard the logic, but couldn't bring herself to acknowledge it. His dispassionate reasoning was exactly that: lacking in feeling, practical. Cold.

It was also a perfect out, allowing her to accept a crazy arrangement for sensible reasons, but she feared she was only giving in to temptation. She knew why, too. Deep down, a grossly foolish part of herself believed that if she could just have his attention long enough, she could explain and earn his forgiveness.

The loss of his good opinion crushed her, not abating despite the months that had passed since the lawsuit. Experience with her stepmother told her that imagining she could earn Raoul's admiration was pure self-delusion, but that didn't alter the fact that she desperately wanted him to stop hating her.

While he wanted unfettered access to his daughter. That's all that motivated him and he was trying to make it happen with his typical brook-no-arguments leadership and infinite resources, standing there casually impeccable and vaguely bored, certain he had the entire thing sewn up.

"Did I ever tell you how annoyingly bigheaded you can be when you think you've had the last word?" she muttered while casting for a suitable reason to refuse.

"I don't *think* I've had it, I know it. The doctor won't release you unless you have a care plan in place. I'm it."

"You're my get-out-of-jail card? When you put it like that…"

Every muscle in his body seemed to harden. "Be careful, Sirena. I'm taking into account you're still only half-alive. Once you're back to full strength, I won't be nearly so charitable. I've forgotten nothing."

A futile yearning swelled in her chest and burned in the back of her throat. He had every right to be angry, but to have her arrested when she'd been like an appendage for him for two years, then had given herself to him without hesitation…?

"You know I can't have sex for another five weeks, right?" she threw at him. "If you're thinking to have a convenient outlet on hand, it won't happen."

He swept her with one pithy glance that reminded her she was far beneath her best. She hated both of them in that second. Why did she care whether he was attracted to her or ever had been? He hadn't. He'd been horny and she'd been handy. He'd told her so. Apparently having her underfoot wouldn't be handy enough to tempt him again. That should be a comfort, not a knife in the heart.

"Just until the doctor clears me to live alone," she muttered, bolstering her humiliated blush with a level glance into his implacable face. "I'm only staying until I'm back to full strength. Then Lucy comes to my flat with me."

"We'll burn that bridge when we get to it."

Despite the welcome of blooming gardens at the house in Ascot, Sirena was icy cold as they drove past the gates where she'd stood waiting for Raoul in the rain, begging him over the intercom to speak to her.

Finding him here that day had been a matter of calling in a favor with an out-of-the-know workmate. After that she'd been shut out completely, her personal items from her desk returned and her keys, company ID, equipment and expense cards taken back.

Unable to look at him, she set a light hand on the warm shape of the baby between them and rocked numbly with the car when the chauffeur halted under the portico. As she reached to unclip the child seat, Raoul's adept fingers brushed hers away.

"I'll bring her." He relayed the diaper bag to his chauffeur and lifted Lucy out the opposite door, coming around to meet Sirena where the chauffeur had opened her door.

She tried to climb from the low-slung car and was more resentful than grateful when Raoul reached to help, offering his arm so she could cling to it with a shaky grip. Her muscles burned at the strain of pulling up and steadying herself on her weak legs. Pain sliced across her middle where her incision was healing.

As they went up the steps, he slipped his arm around her and half carried her.

She made a noise of protest, but couldn't help leaning into his support, both bolstered and weakened by his lean hardness. She finally gave in to the pull of attraction and let her head loll into his shoulder for just a second before he spoke, his tone flatly shoving her back to reality.

"You shouldn't have been discharged."

"I don't want to be this feeble," she grumbled, pulling away as they crossed the threshold. The loss of his touch made her feel weak and sorry for herself. "Even that time in Peru I managed to keep going. I'll get better. I have to." She sank down on the velvet-upholstered bench in the foyer and cupped her swimming head in her hands.

"When were you sick in Peru? That time half the conference came down with food poisoning? You didn't get it."

"I did! But someone had to take charge, extend the arrangements with the hotel and rebook the flights. I didn't hear you volunteering."

He grew an inch in height and his mouth opened, but she waved a hand against whatever scathing response he was on the verge of making.

"It was my job. I'm not complaining, just saying that's the most wretched and useless I've ever felt, but this is worse. I hate being like this."

"You should have told me. This time *and* then."

"It was my job," she repeated, ignoring his admonition in favor of reminding him her work ethic had been rock solid. She looked up at him and he met her gaze with an inscrutable frown and a tic in his cheek.

"I expect you to tell me what your needs are, Sirena. I'm not a mind reader. We'll go to your room now so you can rest. Can you manage these stairs with me or shall I have a room prepared down here?"

"Upstairs is fine, but Lucy will need a feed before I lie down." She deliberately kept her gaze on the baby and not on these beloved surroundings. Silly, naive fool that she was, she used to host fantasies about one day being mistress here. She loved everything about its eclectic style.

The lounge where she moved to nurse was one of her favorite rooms, with its Mediterranean colors, contemporary furniture and view to the English garden. Raoul had a lot of worldly influences in his life, from his Spanish mother's ancestry of warmth and sensuality to his father's Swiss precision. He had been educated in America, so he brought those modern, pop-culture elements into his world with contemporary art and futuristic electronics. All of his homes were classy, comfortable and convenient.

And all contained the one ingredient to which she was drawn inexorably: him.

He stood in profile to her, lean and pantherish, thumb sweeping across the screen of his mobile as he dealt with all the things she used to do for him. Her heart panged. She had loved working for him, loved the job that challenged her. Transcribing had put her through business school and kept her fed these last months, so she couldn't knock it, but it didn't take her off her steno chair, let alone around the world.

"Are you going in to the office this afternoon?" she asked, of two minds whether she wanted him to leave. Being on guard against him drained her, but another secret part of her drank up his nearness like a cactus in a rare rain.

"They're asking the same. Things are in disarray. When you delivered, I had only starting to put things in place for an absence I thought would happen next month."

"I'm sorry," she said, feeling the habitual words leave her lips and thinking, *Why are you apologizing? It's not your fault!*

"A warning that premature delivery was a possibility would have been helpful."

The supercilious remark got her back up. "I didn't need the extra stress of you hanging over me telling me what to do," she said with acerbity. "I followed doctor's orders and tried to go to term, which is all I *could* do. If you're inconvenienced by the early birth, well, welcome to parenthood. I believe we're both in for adjustments."

"A little communication goes a long way, is what I'm saying. Keeping things to yourself is a theme that keeps getting you into trouble." His deceptively silky tone rang with danger.

"Oh, and you gave me ample opportunity to communicate after informing me *through the arrest charges* that you knew money had gone missing?"

"Before that," he snapped. His jaw was like iron, his gray eyes metallic and locked down, but he did darken a shade with something that might have been culpability.

"You could have told me you were having financial troubles and we could have worked something out. Stealing from me was unacceptable."

"I agree. That's why I only borrowed."

"So you've said," he ground through his teeth. "But if you—"

Lucy made a little sputter. Sirena quickly sat her up, glancing at Raoul to finish his sentence, but he had stopped speaking to stare openly at her nude breast. She'd come to the demoralizing realization that there was no dignity in childbirth and there wasn't much more afterward. You needed two hands on a newborn, leaving none for tucking yourself back into a bra that had more jibs and sails than a yacht.

"You burp her," she ordered out of self-conscious embarrassment, screening herself with an elbow and quickly covering up once he'd taken the baby. It was an awkward moment on the heels of a deeper fight that promised her stay here would be a dark corner of hell.

When he helped her up the stairs a few minutes later, draped a coverlet over her and set a baby monitor on the nightstand, tears nearly overwhelmed her. A confusion of gratitude and relief with a hefty dose of frustration and fear of the unknown filled her. This wasn't the way she'd expected her life would turn out and she didn't know which way it would bend next. She couldn't trust Raoul, but she had to, at least for an hour while her body recovered enough to take him on next round.

Struggling to keep her heavy eyelids open, she said, "I didn't look to see which room you're putting her in. I won't know where to go if I hear her."

With a sardonic quirk of his mouth, he said, "The monitor is so I can hear you. I have a cot in my office for Lucy."

She really did want to cry then. He was the capable one and she would never measure up. She closed her eyes against the sting and clamped her trembling lips together, praying he couldn't tell how vulnerable she was.

Sirena fell asleep like a blanket had been dropped over her.

Raoul frowned, wanting to set a hand alongside her face to check for temperature, but he didn't want to disturb her. She needed the rest too badly.

Yet she insisted on wearing herself out by fighting him at every turn. What would she be like full strength? He kept seeing glimpses of the old Sirena in her sharp wit, but the hostility and challenges were new and disconcerting. How much of her real personality had she repressed while she had worked for him because he was the boss and she the employee?

And because she had wanted to lull him into not missing stolen money?

He scowled. That act didn't fit with the woman who had pushed herself to work when she was sick. Or pushed herself through a difficult pregnancy to give the best start in life to a baby whose birth could have killed her.

The sight of Sirena unconscious and white, tubes and wires keeping her alive, would never leave him. For that act alone, he owed her consideration. A chance to recover, at least.

Her obvious love for their daughter played on him too. Her worry after each medical checkup. The way she looked to him for his interpretation and reassurance. A cynical part of him warned against being taken in again, but her connection to their baby was too real to be manufactured.

Then there was the sexual attraction that was as bad as ever, despite how pale and weak she was. He hadn't been able to stop himself ogling her naked breast. Her ass was gorgeously round and begging to be fondled. Every time he got near enough to catch her scent, he wanted to pull her close and kiss the hell out of her plump, smart mouth.

He rubbed his face, more preoccupied than ever by a woman he never should have touched. Work was what he needed. Studying had been his escape from the struggle to understand his father's suicide. From age twenty, once his stepfather's perfidy came to light, he'd been immersed in recovering their finances. The urgency of that task had been a type of salvation from emotional angst as well.

Thankfully, despite having to drop out of university, he'd had a basic version of a software program more than halfway through development. Taking it to completion and selling it had staved off his sense of failure over not realizing what his stepfather had been doing. Piling up dollars and assets like points on a screen ever since had become enormously satisfying. It always reassured him to know he was creating not just a financial umbrella, but a giant, inflated mattress of protection for his family.

A family that now included a helpless infant. That gave him more motivation than ever.

And that baby's mother?

He took his seat at his desk and angled the baby monitor, staring hard at it until he heard her whispery breath, wondering where Sirena would fit into his life long-term.

# CHAPTER FIVE

IN SOME WAYS, living with Raoul was too easy. The sub-liminal communication they had developed working to-gether laid the groundwork. She knew his moods, picked up the small cues that meant his call would be a long one and already knew his boundaries when it came to making a space for her within his. Plus, he was such a work hound she was able to sneak away to quiet corners until he took a breather and came looking for his daughter.

But being out of his sight didn't mean he was out of her mind. Why, oh, why did she have to track him with in-ternal radar, her entire being called by his dynamic pres-ence? No matter how many times she told herself to get over him, knowing how close he was made her mind trail back to a rainy afternoon's passionate coming together. So stupid! Daydreams like that made her a pushover for what had been an impersonal coupling on his part. It's what had gotten her into this mess.

She should move back to her flat, but that circumstance was being influenced by other ones, putting a pleat in her brow.

"Was that the doctor?" he asked, startling her with a jolt of unexpected excitement because she had been cer-tain he was in his office down the hall.

Trying to downplay the way she exploded with joyful awareness, she walked the cordless phone across the lounge to return it to its cradle.

"Indra. My neighbor." Her skin tingled despite her internal willing of the heat to leave her cheeks. These encounters in lounges and dining rooms were unbearable.

"Did something happen? You're frowning."

*Don't study me,* she wanted to cry. Never had she imagined she would long to go back to when she'd been one more piece of equipment in his high-tech office, but his aloof attitude had been a lot easier to deal with. Nowadays he watched her every move as though trying to read between her lines and catch her in a lie.

"Everything is fine," she said with false nonchalance. "She was asking how long I'd be out of my flat. We always had an arrangement when I was traveling that if she had family staying, they could use my place. Her niece is arriving with her new husband and, not surprisingly, they would love the privacy."

Awkward sexual awareness poured through her in an infuriating blush. She hadn't been cleared for sex and Raoul had made it plain he wasn't interested. Talking about intimacy shouldn't cause her to simmer with responsiveness, but she became enormously conscious of his masculine silhouette—so wide across the shoulders and narrowing down to those powerful thighs. She desperately wished she could swallow back her reference to the intimate things that happened between a man and a woman.

While Raoul flicked a glance down the T-shirt and yoga pants that were snug on her still-plump body. "What did you tell her?" he asked, his voice so devoid of any hint as to his thoughts she only felt more ill at ease and anxious to disappear.

"That I wished I could help her, but I'll need it sooner rather than later." There. She'd drawn the line.

He met her stare with one equally as steady. "What has the doctor said?"

"Stay out of the pool for another week but short walks are fine. Sleep." She gave him a dry look. "Apparently he's unaware that babies are night creatures."

He frowned. "Why didn't you say? I can get up with Lucy."

"What's the point? You don't have functioning breasts." Again with the dirty talk. Now all she could think of was his naked, very masculine chest, layered with muscle and sprinkled with fine, springy hairs. *Stop!* She turned to hide her flaming face.

"I can change her and settle her back to sleep as well as you can," he pointed out.

She tensed. He was proving himself to be the generous, involved parent she had known he would be, but after so many years without any sort of support, it was ingrained in her to do things by herself.

"I need to manage on my own," she dismissed. "Soon I'll have no choice. And you're working. You need your sleep."

"What do you call transcribing?" he asked with the irritated tone he'd taken the first time he'd found her at it. "You're courting a setback, pushing yourself like that." He spoke in the lofty way that made him a confident company president and a completely annoying adversary.

"I'm not overdoing it. My recovery is my priority. I know my freedom with Lucy hinges on it." She flashed a meaningless smile. "Don't worry. I won't be underfoot any longer than necessary."

That didn't seem to reassure him. His frown deepened. Fortunately Lucy woke and Sirena had a reason to escape the intensity of his inscrutable presence.

Raoul's perfectly functioning libido watched Sirena's curvy behind zip from the room. He was highly attuned to the meaning behind sudden blushes and flustered disappearing acts. They were the kind of signals that provoked any man's interest and he was already interested. Way too interested.

Back when he'd first hired Sirena, he'd seen the same little betrayals of attraction. It hadn't meant anything to him, since women always reacted to him. He had money, worked out, dressed well and groomed daily. Sirena's suppressed awareness had been routine.

He'd ignored it and his own sexual curiosity right up until That Day. Since then, she'd been spitting and hissing and so washed-out he'd felt like a lecher for any less than pure thoughts. Today, however, her nervously smoothing her hair and standing straighter while seeming ultraperturbed by her aroused senses was insanely seductive.

Emphasis on *insane*. So what if her body was recovered enough to feel a flash of chemistry? He couldn't act on it. They were barely capable of civility. Sex would make an already complicated relationship completely unworkable.

It would be easier on his libido if she left, he acknowledged grudgingly. Her involuntary reaction had pulsed male arousal through him so strongly he was drawn taut, his erection thrusting against the confines of his pants, throbbing with imperative to hunt down the woman who had incited him and find relief in the wet depths that had welcomed him deliciously almost a year ago.

There was the problem. It had been a year, he dismissed, trying to forget the whole thing.

He remained edgy into the late hours, though, even after he had accounted for his long spell of abstinence with time spent at work and with lawyers. He'd been too busy to date. It wasn't that he was so bewitched by one particular woman that only she would do.

Hell. He should visit the city and exercise his urges.

Yes, that was the solution. He loathed the idea of Lucy moving out, so—

He paused in dousing his bedroom light, hearing Lucy start crying again. Sirena kept telling him the nights were hers, but this was silly. They shared parenting well enough through the daylight hours. She was being stubborn to prove a point that was totally lost on him.

By the time he moved down the darkened hall, Lucy was quiet again and Sirena was gently closing the nursery door. She jumped as his shadow joined hers on the wall, gasping as she swung around to confront him.

Clutching her heart, she scolded in a whisper, "You scared me to death!"

"I live here," he drawled, not the least bit scared even though his heart began to pound. She stood eye level to his naked chest, her bewildered expression burnished gold by the night-light. She was braless under a sleeveless tank and a pair of loose shorts that looked like men's boxers, her nipples sharply peaked against light cotton.

Damn. This was the wrong kind of night sharing, but he couldn't stop the bombardment of erotic signals that plowed into his sexual receptors. Her hair was loose and wavy. She was lightly scented from the bubble bath she'd taken earlier. Her breath hitched behind invitingly parted lips while her hungry gaze swept across his pecs, stinging him like licks from a velvet whip.

He wore loose pajama pants that drew a relaxed line across his flat abdomen, but they began to tent—

She yanked her gaze to his, embarrassed and deeply apprehensive.

And, if he wasn't mistaken, as dazed with repressed sexual need as he was.

"It didn't sound like she was settling," he managed gruffly, recalling why he was here. "I was coming to take over so you could go back to bed." *Bed.* It was all he could think about. They'd used a sofa that other time and for less than an hour. He wanted more. Hours. Days.

Raoul's voice made the hairs stand up all over her body. His scent was charged and aggressive, as though he hadn't quite made it to bed yet, while she was sleepy and befuddled. She became screamingly aware that her hair was everywhere and her thin tank and loose shorts weren't exactly sexy lingerie. That was probably a good thing, but she secretly wished she looked attractive.

*Idiot.*

"She's sleeping now," she mumbled and sidestepped at the same time he did, almost coming up against him as he loomed before her.

It was the foyer in Oxshott again. Her startled gaze came up in time to see his focus drop to her mouth. Her heart soared and her mind blanked, just like last time.

*Not again,* she thought, but couldn't move, paralyzed by attraction and wonder.

His hand came up and hesitated. The bare skin of her shoulder waited, nerve endings reaching out in anticipation. Raoul started to bend his head.

*Don't let it happen,* she warned herself with anxious intensity, but her self-preservation instincts were flashfiring so rapidly she couldn't figure out if she should retreat the wrong way down the hall, barrel through him or exit into Lucy's room.

His big hand cradled the side of her face, tilting her mouth up to his as his mouth crashed down on hers on an aggrieved groan.

*Don't— Oh, do...*

Everything about him was strong and the way his mouth covered hers, so confident and hungry, overcame her willpower. The shape of his lips fit hers perfectly. When the tip of his tongue parted her lips, she shuddered in renewal. *Oh, please.* She melted into him. She couldn't help it. She knew how good it could be between them. Her body remembered the virile feel of his muscles gathering, the fullness of him inside her...

His forearm angled across her back with proprietary strength, tugging her into a soft collision that made her release a throaty cry that he swallowed. Their nightclothes were no shield. She felt *everything.* The hot roughness of his chest, the flat muscles of his waist under confused hands that didn't know where to land and the fierce shape of his supremely eager erection.

Her hands splayed on his smooth waist while her thoughts receded behind a kiss that began to consume her. Sweet, deep arousal, a sensation she hadn't felt in months, twined through her, coiling deliciously. It felt so good to be held. The way his breath hissed and he plundered her mouth as though he was slaking a lifetime of need caught her as nothing else could, making her strain to match his voracious desire.

As his hands slid over her shape, she wriggled and pressed into his touch, reveling in the way he shifted her into the hard plane of the door so he could sandwich her with his weight. When his hot hand rode up her bare thigh under the leg of her shorts and found no underpants, he groaned and nipped a line down her neck while his flat hand shaped the globe of her bottom, squeezed gently, massaged and claimed.

She arched her breasts into his chest and her hands went to where his rampant stiffness was nearly piercing a hole through the light silk of his pants.

"Yes, touch me," he said raggedly and bared himself, wrapping his hand over hers with a crushing grip. His mouth came back to catch her cry of surprise while his own hand went up the front of her thigh, fingertips unerringly finding her plump, aching center and drawing a line into the wet slickness. The circling touch of his fingertip against the tight knot of nerves struck bolts of need into her core, driving her to push against his touch, squeeze him tight, kiss him with complete abandon.

He bared her breast and bent his head. She thought, *I'm nursing.*

The reality of what they were doing crashed into her. She shoved him back a step, dislodging his touch, making him stagger and lift his head.

There were so many reasons to be aghast. Her appalled fear must have shown on her face. His glazed eyes met hers and he drew in a breath of shock.

Maybe he was equally horrified to see whom he'd accidentally fallen into kissing.

Just the nearest woman. The one who was *handy.*

Hurt knifed into her abdomen, twisting painfully. Freshly humiliated, Sirena elbowed past him and fled to her room.

She slept late. That beastly man had sneaked into her room after she fell asleep and stolen the baby monitor. He was at the breakfast table when he should have been in his office. Why he wasn't going into the city to work escaped her. It had been nearly a month since he'd had a full day there.

"Lucy?" she prompted, looking past him.

"I gave her a bottle, but she didn't take much. She's down, but probably not for long."

At least that gave her an excuse to avoid him while she disappeared to pump the ache out of her swollen breasts. He was still at the table when she returned. He wore his I've-got-all-day-so-don't-bother-stalling face.

"I don't want to talk about it," she said flatly, veering her gaze from the way his muscled shoulders filled his ice-blue shirt. If only she wasn't so hungry. She folded a leg under her as she took a seat and reached for a piece of cold, buttered toast, biting into it mutinously.

He set aside his tablet and leaned his forearms where his place setting had been cleared.

"I know you can't make love yet. I wouldn't have taken it that far. I didn't have protection either and I sure as hell don't want to get you pregnant again."

The bite of toast in her mouth turned coarse and bitter. All the hurt she'd been bottling and ignoring rose in the back of her throat to make swallowing difficult. She rose up from her chair with what she hoped was enough indignation to cover her wounded core.

"Do you think I don't wish every day that Lucy's father was anyone but you?" She heard the cut of his breath and knew she'd scored a direct hit, but there was no satisfaction in it. She had zero desire to stick around and gloat.

She was almost to the door when he said with sharp force, "Because I don't want to risk your life again. Given how dangerous I've learned childbirth can be, I don't intend to put any woman through that ever again."

The statement was shocking enough to make her hesitate. She glanced back, certain he couldn't be as serious as he sounded. His still posture and set jaw told her he was incontrovertibly sincere.

"Millions of women sail through pregnancy and deliver without any trouble," she pointed out. "You don't know how you'll feel in future, with a different woman."

He only gave her that shuttered look that told her any sort of discussion on the matter was firmly closed. She was wasting her breath if she thought she could reason with him. His rigid expression was so familiar, his certainty that he was right so ingrained and obvious, she felt her lips twitch in amusement.

It was the last reaction she expected. Her body was still humming with unsatisfied arousal, which only increased her aggravation and trampled self-worth. Her heart had shriveled overnight into a self-protective ball, but for some reason his misplaced, oddly gallant statement uncurled it a bit. He was showing the protectiveness she so admired in him, and it was directed at her. Well, all women, maybe, but it still felt kind and yes, there was even a weak part of her that took comfort in knowing he wasn't likely to fill his life with children by other women. The thought of him making babies with someone he actually loved had been quietly torturing her.

"What's funny?" he demanded.

"Nothing," she assured him, pressing a hand to her hollow stomach as it growled.

He rose with impatience to hold her chair. "Sit. Eat. You need the calories."

She returned to slide into her chair as his housekeeper brought a plate of eggs and tomato.

To her consternation, Raoul sat down again.

The memory of last night blistered her as the housekeeper left them alone. She had tossed and turned after their rendezvous, trying to figure out how it had happened. For her it was simple: she still reacted to him. For him… convenience? It had to be. He wasn't going into the city to work *or* to work out his kinks.

Blushing with anger and remembered excitement, she stared at her plate, picking at her food with the tines of her fork. That wild moment was going to sit between them like the wall of resentment over the missing money, filling all of their interactions with undercurrents. She needed her own space.

"I should be able to move into my flat after my next appointment," she said.

He made a noise of negation.

She set her chin to disguise the leap in her heart. She was still processing that he hadn't actually insulted the hell out of her a few minutes ago. Was he resisting her leaving because he wanted her here?

Pressing her knotted fists into her lap, she asked, "Sooner, then?"

"Never. I want Lucy full-time. That means you have to stay, too."

The words went through her like a bomb blast, practically lifting the hair off her head and leaving her ears ringing. Unexpected yearning clenched in her and last night's excitement flared like stirred coals reaching toward a conflagration. Warning bells in her head clanged *danger, danger*.

"There you go testing my incision again," she said, and scooped eggs into her mouth as though the matter was closed. It was. "No," she added in case he needed further clarification.

"Why not?" His challenge was almost like idle curiosity. Pithy and confident he'd eventually get his way.

She goggled at him. "That train wreck last night for starters," she blurted, face seared with a mask of humiliated embarrassment. If he'd made a pass and she'd rejected him, that would be one thing, but the way she'd responded had been horribly revealing. She dropped her gaze, wishing she could take back her reaction, especially when it occurred to her he might use it to get what he wanted.

"So the chemistry between us is alive and well. We've successfully ignored it in the past. Maybe we'll even look at resuming that side of our relationship once you're fully recovered. It's got nothing to do with my desire to raise my daughter."

Sirena choked. "What relationship? What chemistry?" Incredulous, she leaped to her feet without being aware of it. Her entire being rejected everything he was saying. It was so cruel she couldn't bear it. "I'm moving back to my flat as soon as the doctor clears me." She threw her napkin on the table and started to walk out again.

"You're going alone," he said in an implacable tone that chilled her to her marrow. "Lucy is staying here."

*Slam.* Here it was. The brick wall she had always known he would push between her and her child. Had she actually felt herself softening toward him? He was a bastard, through and through. And it hurt! He was hurting her by treating her this way and he was hurting her by not being the man she wanted him to be.

"That is not what our *legally binding* agreement says," she whirled to state.

"Keep your lawyer on retainer, sweetheart. We're going to rewrite it."

He wasn't bluffing. Her heart twisted while the rest of her, the part that had lost to a bully once before, put up her dukes. She had never wanted to physically harm anyone in her life, but at this moment a swelling wave of injustice pushed her toward him in aggressive confrontation, muscles twitching with the desire to claw him apart because he was striking at her very foundation.

He rose swiftly as she approached, surprised and instantly guarded, taking on a ready stance, his size the only thing that stopped her from lashing out with everything in her.

"Well, isn't that like you," she said with the only weapon available: a tongue coated with enough resentful hatred it wielded itself. *"I want you, Sirena,"* she mocked. *"Touch me, Sirena.* And the next morning it's, take everything that matters to her and kick her to the curb. Go ahead. Send me into John's office for another pile of legal bills I can't afford. I'll raise the stakes and take this to the court of public opinion. I'll hurt you in every way I can find. I'll take your daughter, because I will *not* let her be raised by someone who treats people the way you do."

She wiped the back of her wrist across her lips, her incensed emotions deflating to despair as she heard her own words and knew that she was bravado against his arsenal of money, position and power. What did she have? Charges against her for theft.

She couldn't continue to face him without breaking down.

"Where do you get the nerve to judge *me?*" she managed as a parting shot before she decamped to higher ground.

Raoul stood in astonished silence as he listened to Sirena's retreat. He felt as though he'd just surprised a wounded lioness and barely escaped still clutching his vital organs. Adrenaline stung his arteries and he had to consciously tell his muscles to relax.

None of that closed what felt like a giant chasm in his chest. *Touch me, Sirena. Kick her to the curb.* Shame snaked through him, keeping his jaw clenched even though he wanted to shout back at her in defense. *He* was the one with the right to trust issues. Where did she get off accusing *him* of manipulation?

His housekeeper came through, startling him. "More coffee?" she asked, obviously surprised to see the table deserted.

"No," he barked, then pulled himself together. "No, thank you," he said with more control, rubbing his face then disheveling his hair. "Please make up some sandwiches for Sirena, since she didn't finish her breakfast. I'll be in my office."

He went there for privacy, to work through their confrontation, not to make a dent in the work that piled up every minute he was distracted by this new family of his.

Just a daughter, he reminded himself. Not a partner.

*Touch me.* His gut tightened in remembered ecstasy as he felt again her light fingers encircling him. Desire had exploded in him last night. For her. Despite all his attempts to make excuses, the sad truth was no other woman tempted him. Even before conceiving Lucy, he'd been taking women to dinner without taking anything else.

He didn't want Sirena to be the only one he wanted. He ought to have more control over himself. As he'd eschewed sleep this morning in favor of forming arguments to keep Sirena and Lucy living with him, he'd convinced himself it was a convenient solution to their custody battle, nothing to do with sexual attraction.

While he'd relived her soft mewling noises and passionate response to his kiss in the hallway, her body incapable of lying.

Sirena didn't want anything to do with him, though. Maybe she was physically attracted, but her ferocity this morning warned him that she would rather smother him in his sleep than share his bed for lovemaking.

He stared blindly at the colorful gardens beyond his office window, his mind's eye seeing her savaged expression the day at the gate, then again this morning. A hard hand closed around his heart, squeezing uncomfortably. A million times he'd told himself she was as jaded and detached as all the rest of his lovers, but today something admonished him. He feared he'd hurt her in a way he hadn't realized he could. But how was his treatment of her any different than hers of him? She had gotten him depending on her, then backhanded him with theft. She'd ruined him for other women and was completely wrong for him at the same time.

Movement caught his eye. Sirena had brought Lucy into the garden. She wore a summer dress and bare feet. Her hair hung in a damp curtain down her back, its curls weighted into subtle waves that would spring up as the sun dried it. Folding one leg under herself the way she often did, she sat on the covered swing and kicked it into a gentle rock, head tilting back as she inhaled deeply.

She was pure woman in that moment, sensual yet maternal. Beautiful.

The want in him took on a new, disconcerting depth. It wasn't just sexual. He remembered her efficiency, her smooth handling of difficult people, her quick smiles.

He wanted the Sirena he'd believed her to be before his dented bank balance had proved she wasn't.

Damn it, he didn't *do* complex relationships. Motherson. Simple. Protective big brother. Easy. Boss and employee. Black-and-white.

With one noted exception.

His father's suicide over what had seemed to be a sordid yet standard affair was earning some of his empathy. If his father had struggled with things like overstepping boundaries in the workplace and a lust that battled strength with his love for his child, Raoul could see where he'd felt torn in too many directions. Raoul wasn't anywhere near killing himself over it, but he wasn't getting much sleep.

But if he was about to be exposed for his perfidy, he might start thinking drastic thoughts. Sirena had threatened a publicity backlash and he believed her. He was learning there was a no-holds-barred quality when her basic rights were threatened and part of him respected her for it.

And if there was one thing he prided himself on, it was upholding his end of a bargain.

Cursing, he opened the French doors onto the patio and strolled across to Sirena, footsteps whispering across the grass. Her eyes opened, but only to slits.

"I'm floating down the river of denial. Don't kill the mood," she warned with a chilly edge to her soft tone.

The corner of his mouth quirked. She had always caught him off guard with her colorful expressions. There was a hidden poet in her, he suspected. A romantic.

He frowned, unable to fit that with the calculating vamp he knew her to be.

"Look," he said, sweeping her multiple facets aside to work at keeping things simple. He'd been angry when he'd thrown his ultimatum at her, grumpily aware that he wanted her rather desperately while she thought he was trying to manipulate her. The manipulating factor was this infernal chemistry!

"I was wrong to say I'd go back on our agreement. You're right. You negotiated in good faith and things between us will only get ugly if we don't talk these things through without using Lucy as leverage."

"Are you on drugs? I thought you said I was right." Her eyes stayed shut, not revealing any of the willingness to compromise he was looking for.

"Where is all this sass coming from?" he demanded. "You never used to say things like that to me."

"Sure I did. In my head. Now that you've fired me, I can use my outside voice."

He accepted that with a disgruntled press of his lips, pushing his hands into his pockets as he rocked on his heels. The sun on his back was so hot he could feel the burn through his shirt. Sirena and the baby were in the shade, though, so he didn't insist they go back into the house yet.

"Will you stay? You know what my workload is like. I have to travel and I don't want to be half a globe from Lucy, not for weeks at a time."

"So when you say stay, you mean follow you around like nomads?" Her eyes opened, lashes screening her thoughts, but the indignant lift of her brows said plenty.

"Why not? You liked the travel when you worked for me, didn't you?"

Sirena pursed her lips. "When I got out of the hotels to see the sights."

He frowned, sensing criticism when he was well aware

she'd enjoyed visiting foreign cultures, welcoming new people and perspectives with excited curiosity, always ready with small talk full of well-researched questions about museums or local wonders, always craning her head at markets when they passed. She made good use of all she learned too, providing tidbits that informed his negotiations through foreign bureaucracy, but he wondered suddenly if he'd kept her too busy to actually experience all she'd wanted to.

They'd been there to work, though. That's what he did and who he was.

He scowled as he contemplated how little of those countries *he'd* seen.

"It doesn't matter what I want," she sighed. "Lucy will have school—"

"Years down the road," he argued, not letting her finish. "I'll make allowances for that, but you know as well as I do it will take time to put things in place. For the next few years, as long as she has us, she'll be happy anywhere. I'm not talking about leaving tomorrow. I realize you have medical checkups. We'll stay here as long as you need, but later in the year I don't see why we can't take a few weeks in Milan. My mother is already asking when I'll bring her to New York."

"I can't live with you permanently. How would we explain it to people? Your future bedmates sure wouldn't like it, and what if one of us wants to get married?"

Irritated by the mention of bedmates and life mates, he dismissed both. "I've never been interested in marriage and see even less point now. As for bedmates, for Lucy's sake, we should keep that in-house."

Sirena suddenly stopped the swing. Raoul sensed refusal so tangibly he bristled.

"Wow. For Lucy's sake I ought to have sex with you?

That's the kind of reasoning even someone with my damaged morals has trouble following."

"If we sleep together, it'll be because we both want to," he snapped, aware he was handling this badly, but she was frustrating the hell out of him. "That train wreck last night was a head-on crash from both sides. You want me and when you get cleared by the doctor, you'll be cleared for sex. Think about *that*."

# CHAPTER SIX

SIRENA DIDN'T HAVE much choice about whether to think on it. Her body was enamored with the idea of falling into bed with her old boss. Her mind drifted in that direction at the least bit of encouragement. Asleep, awake... He was always nearby, smelling like manly aftershave or endearingly like baby powder, telling family secrets to Lucy or speaking in some sexy foreign language on the phone, the syllables drifting teasingly into her ears...

She got so she conjured reasons not to trust him in order to counter the attraction, which wasn't healthy. *I've never been interested in marriage and see even less point now.* That certainly told her where his interest in her as a *bed-mate* started and stopped.

They wound up having abbreviated conversations punctuated by glances of awareness and stubborn avoidances. She *had* to move back into her own flat.

The trouble was, her neighbor's niece was still begging to take it over. Sirena began thinking that if she could find a decent job in a less-expensive part of London, she might be able to keep renting out her existing flat and take something smaller for herself. Her flat was an asset she didn't want to lose and without a better income soon, she would. Even at that, she wasn't sure how she'd pay for day care so she could work.

Which was the sort of worn path of worry that made her

circle back to what Raoul was offering. But it would be so *wrong*. He had wronged her and continued to feel wronged *by* her. She might have drunk herself into oblivion out of frustration if she didn't have a baby to think of. At least she could meet a friend for a small one.

Raoul didn't know what to make of her announcement that she was going out for the evening. His brows almost went through his hairline, but she didn't let that deter her.

"Amber is a friend who moved to Canada years ago. She's coming into London tonight. It's her only free time, so I'd like to join her for tapas and a drink and leave Lucy with you."

"Are you sure you're up for it?" he asked with one of those sweeping glances that lit fires all over her.

"Of course," she said more stridently than she intended, but the way she tingled every time he so much as turned his head in her direction was driving her crazy. She couldn't wait to get Amber's objective view of this situation.

With a shrug, Raoul said, "Pack a bag and we'll stay at the penthouse. That way you won't be so late getting in and I can go into the office in the morning. We'll test-drive one aspect of this arrangement I've suggested."

One aspect. Part of her wanted to refuse on principle, but she liked the idea of a shorter trip home. Her doctor was pleased with her progress, but between Lucy's needs and her body's wants, she wasn't sleeping enough.

And by the time she'd packed, driven in, unpacked and settled the baby, she was ready for bed, not a night on the town. She put on a black skirt and ruffled green top anyway. Both were a bit tight. At least her hair was an asset. She'd been clipping it up for months and hadn't realized how much it had grown. She rather liked it clouding around her shoulders, drawing attention from her still-thick waist. Wearing heels and makeup for the first time in ages, she looked pretty good.

Echoes of her stepmother's critical voice swept through her, cataloging her flaws and bringing Sirena down a smidge, but she had been practicing how to block that painful denigration for years. She stood straight and ignored the whispers of insecurity, jumping when Raoul appeared in her bedroom doorway.

"*Who* is this Amber?" he asked in a dark growl.

"A friend from school." Sirena turned from the mirror, a wicked slide of excitement careening through her as she took him in.

He wore jeans and a button-down shirt open at his throat, cuffs rolled up to his forearms. He was the man who always made butterflies invade her middle.

"You dress like this for a woman?" His gaze made a slow, thorough study of her from collarbone to ankles.

"This is all that fits. I can't show up in my sweats and trainers. Or do you mean I look like a pile of socks pushed into a leg of tights? Should I change?" Her hand went to the zip of her skirt.

His expression was dumbfounded. "Yes. *No,*" he insisted. "You look fine. Excellent. Beautiful. You're not meeting a man?"

"Because my dating profile of 'unemployed new mum with custody issues' is so irresistible? No. I'm meeting a *girl*friend. I wish you would quit calling me a liar."

"I called you beautiful," he said with a raking glance of masculine hunger, his frown both askance and…not critical, but not pleased.

She curled her toes in her shoes, disconcerted by how admiring and possessive he seemed. "I wasn't fishing for flattery."

He barred the door with his arm.

An uncomfortable silence stretched as her stepmother's voice did a number on her again, cataloging the extra pounds and shadows under her eyes and lack of a manicure, but as Raoul skimmed his gaze down her figure once more, and his expression reflected nothing but male approval, she felt quite beautiful.

The swirling sensation in her abdomen redoubled and little sensors in her body began reaching out toward him, tugging her with magnetic power toward him.

She forced herself to stand still, but he dropped his arm and stepped forward until he was standing right in front of her, towering despite her heels. His gray eyes shone with a startlingly warm regard as he scanned her face and hair. Strong hands came up to frame her face with disconcerting tenderness.

Her breath stalled in her lungs as he started to bend his head, his gaze on her mouth.

"What are you doing?" she managed, pressing against his chest.

He paused, gaze smoky with intent. "Reminding you that if a man comes on to you tonight, you have one right here willing to satisfy your needs."

He began to lower his head again but she leaned away.

"Don't smudge my lipstick," she argued shakily, the best protest she could rouse when her whole body wanted to let his take over. Her breasts ached for contact with the hardness of his chest and heat pooled between her thighs. A fine trembling invaded her limbs, making her weak. Her arms longed to reach out and cling to him.

At the last second, he veered to bury his lips against her neck. His light stubble abraded her skin while his open mouth found a sensitive spot on her nape that took out her knees.

"What are you doing?" she cried, melting into the arms that caught her. Her nipples sharpened into hard points as he applied delicate suction, marking her.

She should have stopped him, but she was held not just by his strength, but by a paralysis of physical joy. Her mouth ached for the press of his while her mind became a turmoil of unconscious thoughts, processing only the sensations of knowing hands skimming her curves as he laid claim to her hips and bottom. He was hard, ready, so tempting—

"You make me lose my mind," he growled, steadying her before he released her. "Do not start anything with anyone tonight. The car is waiting. That's what I came to tell you." He walked out.

Raoul didn't resent Sirena taking a night out, but he didn't like having no right to question her comings and goings and suspected the reason was old-fashioned jealousy. *Not* an emotion he'd ever experienced, and definitely unwelcome, but she was so hot. As sexy as a year ago, but less buttoned-down and professional. With her hair loose and her full breasts brimming her top, he'd seen what every man in London would see: a beautiful woman.

And he wouldn't be there to warn them off with a don't-even-try-it stare.

He shouldn't have kissed her, but he hadn't been able to resist imprinting her with the knowledge he wanted her. She'd been skittishly avoiding him since their kiss outside Lucy's bedroom and he'd been trying to ignore how badly he craved her, but his hunger grew exponentially every day.

It was frustrating as hell, but no matter how uncomfortable they both were with each other, they were equally devoted to Lucy. He couldn't countenance anything more than a few hours of separation from his child, so he kept coming back to sharing his house with her mother.

Disgruntled, still smelling of her perfume, he waited in the foyer to watch her leave, arms folded.

Sirena appeared, checked her step and flushed. Ducking her head, she opened her pocketbook. "I have my phone if Lucy needs me."

"We'll be fine. Do you have David's number?" he asked, mentioning his London driver.

"Yes, it's programmed—" She swept her thumb across the screen and frowned. "Oh, I missed this from Amber. She's sick. That's disappointing."

More like devastating, if her body language was anything to go by. Raoul was disgustingly relieved, but as he watched her shoulders fall and the pretty glow of excitement extinguish from her expression, he couldn't help feeling sorry for her.

She tempered her sad pout into a resigned quirk. "All dressed up and no place to go," she said wryly. "Sorry to drag you all the way to London for nothing. I guess it'll be sweats and trainers after all. I'll just let her know I got the message…" She ducked her head to text a reply.

"You were really looking forward to this," he commented as she finished.

She shrugged. "We chat online, but it's like with my sister. Sometimes I want to see her and it's frustrating when I can't." She blinked and he thought he glimpsed tears, but she started back to her room.

"Sirena."

She stiffened, not turning. "Yes?"

He'd surely regret this, but there was something about the brave face she was putting on and hell, she looked amazing. He couldn't let this butterfly crawl back into her shapeless cocoon.

"Come have a drink with me." He jerked his head toward the unlit lounge.

"What? No. Why? I'll be feeding Lucy later. I can't."

How many shades of refusal was that, he wondered with a twinge between amusement and exasperation.

"We'll stick to the plan," he countered. "Have the glass of wine you were planning to have with your friend and

I'll feed Lucy a bottle when she needs it. Going out was obviously something you were anticipating."

"It wasn't the wine." She rolled her eyes. "I wanted to see my friend."

"So come tell me why she's so special to you." He herded her toward the lounge and suspected she only let him because she was trying to pull away from contact with his palm against the small of her back.

"I don't understand why you'd want me to." She scuffed her spiky heels as he crowded her into the room with the sunken conversation area and the wet bar in the corner. He gave up trying to steer her and walked ahead of her, turning on a lamp on the end table before he brought the track lighting over the bar up to half power, keeping the mood soothing and intimate.

"You keep accusing me of not taking time to ask about your life. And…" He gestured at where her leg peeked from the slit in her skirt to the ruffles that framed her cleavage. "I can't stand the idea of this going to waste. I'd take you out, but unlike you I haven't arranged a sitter. Here. Have a seat and tell the bartender about your day."

He held one of the high stools and she hesitated before warily scooting her hip onto it. He let his gaze linger on the curve of her pert backside as it flowed into the slope of her lower back. Damn, but he wanted to stroke and claim.

*Thief,* he reminded himself, but it didn't do much to quell his hunger. Rounding the bar, he looked for a suitably light white wine in the small cooler.

"I should tell David he's off for the night," she said in a tone that put him back a year. Efficient, forward with responsibility and attention to detail, lilting just enough to invite a correction if she was off course. She rarely ever had been, except—

As she placed the call, he gestured for the phone.

She handed it across, brows lifted with inquiry.

He enlightened her as he made his request of David. "We've had a change of plans. Can you run to Angelo's and ask them to make us a couple of plates? Whatever they have on special, but no mushrooms for Sirena. You can go home after that."

"Are we working late?" she mused facetiously.

"I don't feel like cooking. Do you?"

"*Can* you cook? I've never seen you try."

"I can grill a steak." He was currently polishing glasses like a pro, having picked up both skills working in restaurants for much-needed cash a long time ago.

"But a man in your position never *has* to do anything, does he?" Her lips curved in a deprecating smile, niggling him into a serious response.

"I'm always irritated by the suggestion I haven't worked for what I have. I might have been born into a life of privilege, but that bottomed out thanks to my stepfather. Everything I have I built myself, and it comes with obligations and responsibilities that take up time. If I can delegate the small things, like cooking a steak, so I can negotiate a union contract to keep myself and a few hundred people working and fed, I will." He poured two glasses and pushed one toward her.

She looked at her wine, then gave him a glance of reassessment. Lifting her glass, she awaited the soft clink of his.

"To pleasant conversations between old friends," she said with gentle mockery.

He leaned back on the far side of the space behind the bar, eyeing her through slitted lids. "I can't get used to this."

"Used to what?" She set down her glass and rotated her knees forward so she faced him, elbows braced on the bar's marble top.

"This woman full of backchat and sarcasm. The one with secrets and a double life. The real you."

She might have flinched, but her chin quickly came forward to a defiant angle. Her gaze stayed low, showing him a rainbow of subtle shadows on her eyelids. "You're attributing me with more mystery than I possess. Yes, I'm being more frank with you than I was, but you can't tell your boss he's being an arrogant jerk, can you?" She lifted her lashes to level a hard stare at him. "Not if you want to pay the bills."

He thought about letting this devolve into something serious, but opted to keep things friendly. "I wouldn't have fired you for saying that," he assured her, waiting a beat before adding, "I would have said you were wrong."

Her mouth twitched, then she let the laugh happen and he experienced a sensation like settling into your own sofa or bed. *Definitely a bed,* he thought as a tingle of pure, masculine craving rose inside him. He let himself admire her painted lips and graceful throat and the exposed alabaster skin on her chest to the swells of her breasts. Why had he never taken her to dinner before?

Oh, right. She had been working for him.

It was freeing not to have that obstacle between them anymore.

*Slow down,* he reminded himself as she sobered and flicked a glance in his direction. The sexual undercurrents might be acknowledged, finally, but just because he wanted to bed her didn't mean he should.

Sirena couldn't take the intense way Raoul was staring at her. Every single day of working for him, she'd longed for him to show some sign of interest in her. Now that he had, it scared the hell out of her. But then, she knew better than to trust he was genuinely interested.

Accosted by harsh memories, she slid off the bar stool and took her wine to the expansive glass windows where the London Eye and the rest of the waterfront stained the river with neon rainbows.

"So is this how you start all your flashy dates? Or do they end here?"

"Flashy?" His image, only partially visible in the dim reflection on the glass, came around the bar to stand like a specter behind her.

"Women line up for the privilege, so I assume a date with you is pretty fantastic. Are they impressed when you bring them back here for a nightcap?" And a thorough seeing to? *Don't think about it.*

"I don't go out of my way to impress, if that's what you're implying. Dinner. A show. Does that differ hugely from one of your dates?"

She cut him a pithy look over her shoulder. "Since when do I have time to date?"

He absorbed that with a swallow of wine. "You've suggested a few times that I overworked you, but you also want me to believe your private life included a man who could have fathered Lucy. Which is the truth?"

"I was saving face when I said that," she admitted to the window.

"So I was an ogre who demanded too much? You could have said something."

Sirena hitched a shoulder, bothered that she felt guilty for not standing up for herself. "I didn't want to let you down or make you think I couldn't handle it." There was her stepmother walking into the room again, tsking with dissatisfaction, setting the bar another notch higher so Sirena would never, ever reach it, no matter how hard she tried. But oh, how she tried, hating to fail and draw criticism. "Some of that's my own baggage. I'm a workaholic. You can relate, I'm sure."

He moved to stand beside her. "I thought you were

happy with the workload. It didn't occur to me I was kill-ing your social life. You must have felt a lot of resentment."

He was jumping to the conclusion that that's why she'd stolen from him.

"No." Annoyed, she walked to the far end of the win-dows. "I never had a social life, so there was nothing to kill."

"You weren't a virgin. There was at least one man in your life," he shot back.

"One," she agreed, staring into the stemmed glass. "His name was Stephan. We lived together for almost two years, but we were both starving students, so date night was mi-crowave popcorn and whatever movie was on the telly." Stephan had had about a thousand allergies, including al-cohol, so even a cheap wine or beer had been out of the question. "Sometimes we went crazy and rented a new release, but my hand-me-down player said 'bad disc' half the time, so it wasn't worth the hassle."

"You *lived* with him?" Raoul's brows went up in askance reaction.

"It's not the same as dating," she hurried to argue. "It was—" Convenient. A desperate act in a lonely time. A mistake.

*"Serious?"* he supplied in a honed voice. He moved a few steps closer, seeming confrontational, which discon-certed her.

"Why are you judging me?" She rounded the conver-sation area, circling back to the bar, where she took a big gulp of wine before she set down her glass. "All I'm say-ing is that I never dated. This is turning into a long con-versation about nothing."

"You lived with a man for two years. That's not noth-ing, Sirena. Did you talk about marriage?"

"I—" She didn't want to go there, still feeling awful about it. Crossing her arms, she admitted, "He proposed.

It didn't work out." There, that was vague enough to keep her from looking as bad as she felt.

"You were *engaged*—"

"Shh! You're going to wake Lucy," she hissed. "Why are you yelling? I'm sorry I said anything." She looked for her watch, but she'd removed it because it didn't go with this outfit. "David should be here with the meals soon, shouldn't he?"

Raoul could barely compute what he was hearing. Another man had been that close to locking Sirena into marriage forever. How could he not have known?

"Did working for me cause the breakup?" he asked with a swift need to know.

"No." She sounded annoyed.

"What then?" For some reason this was important. He needed to know she'd severed all ties with this other man, irrevocably. "Do you still have feelings for him?"

"I'll always love him," she said with a self-conscious shrug.

The words rocked him onto his heels, like the back draft from a semitruck that nearly flattened him.

"In a friend way. That's all it ever was. A friend thing. Do you really need all the gory details?"

"I do, yes," he said through lips that felt stiff and cold. He wondered how he'd kept his wine from spilling, because he'd forgotten he held the glass. He moved to set it on an end table before giving Sirena his full attention, still reeling with shock when really, it wasn't as if people living together was a scandal. He just hadn't realized she had been so deeply involved with anyone. Ever.

When he lifted his gaze to prompt her into continuing, a shadow of persecution clouded her expression.

"It was a lonely time in my life. Amber was in Canada, my family had left for Australia. Stephan was the first boy who'd ever noticed me—"

"I find that hard to believe," Raoul interjected.

"The first boy I'd ever noticed had noticed me, then. Maybe there were crushes before that, but I wasn't allowed to go out when I was living at home—not even to spend the night at Amber's, in case we snuck out to a party. My stepmother wasn't having a pregnant teenager on her watch, so there were chores and a curfew and a little sister to babysit. When I enrolled at college, Stephan was the first boy I had the opportunity to spend time with. He was nice and I was romantic enough to spin it into more than it was." She shrugged again, looking as though she wanted to end there.

"It was obviously more if he proposed."

"That was impulse on his part. I decided to quit my degree and go with the business certificate so I could start earning proper money, rather than temping and doing transcription around my courses. He was afraid I'd meet someone else and I realized I wanted to, so we broke up."

Raoul felt a shred of pity for the man's desperate measure that hadn't paid off. At the same time, he was relieved, which unsettled him. He saw nothing but misery and remorse in her, though. "A puppy love relationship isn't anything to be ashamed of. Why do you feel guilty?" he asked.

"Because I hurt him. Part of me wonders if I wasn't using him because I was broke and didn't have anywhere else to turn. I didn't mean to lead him on, but I did."

The buzzer announced David with their meals.

Raoul turned to let him up, but all he could think was, *You used me. Do you feel bad about that?*

# CHAPTER SEVEN

TYPICAL OF ANGELO'S welcoming charm as a restaurateur, he had sent along a single white rose with a silk ribbon tied to the stem. *We've missed you,* the tag read.

Sirena stifled a pang of wistfulness as she picked up the budding flower from where it sat next to her plate and searched for a hint of scent in the tightly closed petals.

David had brought the basket of chinaware and scrumptious smells to the table beside the pool, setting it out in a way she imagined he'd done for countless of Raoul's paramours. Everything glittered, from the silver to the candles flames to the stars and city lights winking in the warm night air. Raoul set relaxing acoustic guitar music to come through the outdoor speakers and arrived with their glasses.

His brows went up with silent inquiry.

"Fast asleep," Sirena answered. She had known Lucy would be, but checking on her had been a timely excuse to leave Raoul's intense presence. She wasn't sure she was ready to face him again.

A distant beep sounded, signaling that David had left the apartment. They were alone again. *Round two,* she thought and reached for the wine Raoul set above her knife tip. He had topped up her glass, bringing the temperature of the pinot grigio down a degree so it soothed her throat as she drank.

She hesitated to start eating, even though the food was Angelo's typical appetizing fare of creamy pasta, bright peppers and fragrant basil. This wasn't like all those other times when she and Raoul had a tablet or laptop between them and she had chewed between typing and answering calls. They'd never stood on ceremony while working, but this was anything but casual. More than ever, she was aware of Raoul's potent masculinity, his quiet habits of sharp observation, his undeniable air of command.

And she was hyperaware of her dolled-up attire, the way even Angelo seemed to know this was different and had added the extra touch of silver and china.

This felt like a date.

"Problem?" Raoul asked.

She shook her head, chastising herself for falling into old fantasies of romance. "Just thinking I should put this in water," she said, gesturing to the rose.

"It can wait until we've eaten," he said.

He seemed to be waiting for her to start and that made her nervous. She searched for a neutral topic to break what felt like a tense silence. He spoke first.

"Why didn't you go to Australia with your family?"

Oh, hell, they were going there, were they? It wasn't enough to pry open the oyster, making her feel as though her protective shell was snapped in half and left with jagged edges. No, he wanted to poke a finger into her vulnerable center and see if there was a pearl in there, one glossed over for years, but gritty as obsidian at its heart.

She licked sauce from the corner of her mouth, stating plainly, "I wasn't invited."

He lowered his fork as his brilliant mind absorbed what was a logical and sensible answer, yet didn't make sense at all. He frowned. "Why weren't you invited?"

She held back a rude snort at a question she'd never been able to answer. Picking up the napkin off her lap, she dried her lips, wondering if she'd be able to get through this plate of food when her appetite was fading so quickly.

"I had just started school," she said, offering the excuse Faye, her stepmother, had used. "My father had given me some money toward tuition, about the same amount as air-fare. It didn't make sense to throw it away."

"So you were given a choice between school and going with them?"

"No." She couldn't help the bluster of resentment that hardened the word. Old, angry tension started clenching up her insides and she had to make a conscious effort not to let it take her over. Picking up her fork, she deflected the subject a little.

"This is why I was looking forward to dinner with Amber. She knows my history with my stepmother and lets me vent about whatever is bothering me, without my having to lay the groundwork and examine how much is my fault and whether I'm being paranoid. Amber takes my side, which is refreshing, whereas if I try to explain it all to you—" she waved a hand toward him, feeling herself getting worked up, but unable to stop it "—you'll be like Stephan and say maybe Faye didn't mean it that way, that I'm being oversensitive and her reasons make sense and I'm misinterpreting. Her reasons *always* make sense, Raoul. That's the beauty of her dictatorship."

*Oh, God, shut up, Sirena.*

She clenched her teeth, intending to drop the subject, but she couldn't hide the way her hand trembled as she tried to twirl noodles onto the tines of her fork.

"Why don't you give me an example," he suggested in a tone that echoed with reasonability, as though he were trying to talk a crazy person off a window ledge.

Sirena crammed too big a bite into her mouth, but he waited her out, saying nothing as she chewed and swallowed. The pasta went down like a lump of coal, acrid and coarse.

"For instance," she said tightly, "when I was so pregnant and swollen I could hardly get myself out of bed, worried I would *die,* I asked if my sister could come and was told that my father's plumbing business had fallen off and Ali had exams and the doctors were keeping an eye on Faye's thyroid so the timing really didn't work."

She glanced up to see a frozen expression on his face. "You should have called *me.*"

A pang of anguish struck. She'd been tempted a million times, but replied, "The people who were supposed to love and care about me wouldn't come. What was the point in asking you?"

He jerked back as if she'd thrown her pasta in his face.

She looked away, trying to hide the fact she was growing teary over old conflicts that would never be resolved. Her stepmother cared nothing for her while she, Sirena, loved her father and sister. There was nothing that could be done except manage the situation.

After a few seconds, he inquired in a stiff tone, "What about Amber? Why didn't you call her, if you're such good friends?"

"She's in a wheelchair." She cleared the huskiness from her throat. "Which isn't to say she wouldn't have been a help, but my flat is a walk-up and she has other health problems. That's what brought her to London. She's seeing a specialist then heading straight home."

His silence rang with pointed surprise. "I really don't know anything about you."

She wasn't touching that with a ten-foot pole.

They ate in silence for a few minutes until he asked, "Your father wasn't worried about you?"

"Of course, but he remarried because he didn't know

what to do with a little girl. He wasn't about to play mid-wife to a grown woman."

"And your sister? She can't make her own decisions?"

Sirena let out a poignant sigh, bristling at his judgment because if he didn't understand Ali's vulnerability and how much she needed support, he'd never understand why she'd taken his money for the young woman.

"Ali's young for her age. She struggles in school, so exams are a real issue for her. Pitting her against her mother has never seemed right, no matter how much I've wanted to. I adore her like I can't even tell you and I miss her terribly. I practically raised her. Faye wouldn't change a nappy if I was around to do it. Homework was me, running flash cards and spelling lists. The questions about puberty and sex and buying her first bra all came to me. But they left nearly eight years ago and I haven't seen her since. Faye had been cooking up the move the whole time I was applying to school, never mentioning it until my plans were sealed. Tell me that's not small-minded and hurtful."

"You could have gone to see them."

"Oh, with all my spare time working two jobs while studying? Or do you mean after you hired me? Go all the way to Australia for one of those generous single weeks you'd allow me? Every time I asked for more than five days you'd get an expression on your face like you were passing a kidney stone. I tried taking a stretch after that trade fair in Tokyo, but the database melted down in Brussels, remember? I had to cancel."

A muscle ticked in his cheek. "You might have explained the circumstances."

"To what end, Raoul? You never once showed the least bit of interest in my private life. You wanted an extension of your laptop, not a living, breathing woman."

"Because you were my employee," he bit out, pushing away from the table in a minor explosion.

She'd seen him reach the limit of his patience, but usually within the context of a business deal going south. To have that aggressive male energy aimed at her made her sit very still, but he wasn't throwing his anger at her. He paced to the edge of the pool, where he shoved his hands into his pockets and scowled into the eerie glow of the blue-green depths.

"You have no idea what it's like to lust after your co-worker, knowing that's the one person off-limits."

*I beg to differ,* she thought, but swallowed it back because… She shook her head. "How can you say something like that when you made it quite clear—"

"I know what I said that day. Stop throwing it in my face," he growled. "Why do you think I let it go so far so fast in Oxshott? I'd been thinking about it for two solid years. And the next day—" he gestured in frustration "—the very next day, I found you'd been stealing. You betrayed my trust and you used me. What the hell was I supposed to say? Admit you'd hurt me? It was too humiliating."

She'd *hurt* him?

No. She didn't let herself believe it, not after all these months of scouring the joy and tenderness from her memories, reframing it as a meaningless one-afternoon stand. Maybe in her mind their day in Oxshott had been special, but all he was saying was that he'd had sexual feelings for her while she'd been employed by him. That was only a fraction more personal than being *handy.* His ego had been damaged, not his heart.

"I was trying to behave like a professional as well," she said thinly. "Not dragging my personal life into the office. I don't see the point in sharing it now." She plucked her napkin from her lap and dropped it beside her plate. "You still don't care and I still can't see my family."

"What makes you think I don't care?" he swung around to challenge.

His naked look of strong emotion was a spear straight into her heart. She averted her gaze, tempted to dissect what sort of feelings underpinned his intense question, but refusing to. That way lay madness.

"Don't," she said through a tight throat. "You hate me and I'm fine with that because I hate you, too." *Liar,* a voice whispered in her head, but she ignored it along with the hiss of his sharp inhale. "Let's just keep things as honest as possible. For Lucy's sake."

It was hard to look at him, but she made herself do it. Made herself look him in the eye and face his hatred with stillness and calm while she wrapped tight inner arms around her writhing soul.

"I wish it was that simple." He surged forward to grip the back of his chair. "I want to hate you, but now I understand why you felt you couldn't come to me. You didn't know I was acting uninterested to curb my attraction, but it was there all along."

She recoiled, swinging from disbelief to heart-pounding excitement to intense hurt that he had treated her the way he had regardless of having feelings for her. They weren't very strong if he could behave like that, were they?

Speaking very carefully, crushing her icy fingers together in her lap, she stated the obvious. "Lust is not caring, Raoul."

He straightened to an arrogant height.

"No, listen," she rushed on, fearing he thought she was begging for affection. "I didn't think one hookup meant we were getting married and living happily ever after. I'm just saying I thought you had some respect and regard for me. But even a dismissal slip would have been better than having me arrested without speaking to me. That was…"

She faltered. He was staring at her with an expression

that had gone stony. Steeling herself, she forced herself to continue, even though her voice thinned.

"Discovering I was pregnant, knowing they'd take the baby from me in prison—" She stood in a shaken need to retreat, very afraid she was going to start to cry as the memories closed in. "Even my stepmother didn't go that far to hurt me."

"I didn't know you were pregnant," he reminded her ferociously.

"Exactly! And if you did, you would have gone easy for the baby's sake, not mine. You didn't care about *me*. Not one bit."

# CHAPTER EIGHT

Raoul felt as though he was pacing in London's infamous fog. The walls of his penthouse were clear enough, the sky beyond the windows dull with a high ceiling, but his mind wouldn't grasp a lucid concept. He kept replaying everything Sirena had said last night, which had him writhing in a miasma of regret and agitation.

Lucy squirmed in his hold.

He paused to look at her, certain she must be picking up his tension. That's why she was so unsettled. He was pacing one end of his home to the other trying to soothe her, but neither of them was finding any peace.

*How peaceful would Sirena have felt pacing a twelve-by-twelve cell?*

His stomach churned.

He hadn't let himself dwell on that picture when he'd been trying to put her away, but now he couldn't get it out of his head. Vibrant Sirena who craned her neck with excited curiosity from the airport to the business center in every city they visited, locked in a cage of gray brick and cold bars.

*You hate me and I'm fine with that because I hate you, too.*

"What are you doing in here?"

Her voice startled him, causing a ripple of pleasure-pain down his spine. He blinked, becoming aware he'd wandered into the small flat off the main one. It was meant for a housekeeper or nanny, but stood empty because his maid service came daily to his city residence.

"Just something different for her to look at." He stopped rubbing Lucy's back and changed her position so she could see her mother. "She's fussy."

Sirena's brow crinkled as she took in the rumpled clothes he'd been wearing since their unfinished dinner by the pool.

His neutral expression felt too heavy on his cheekbones, but he balked at letting her see the more complex emotions writhing in him—uncertainty and yearning that went beyond the simply sexual. Pain. There was a searing throb inside him he couldn't seem to identify or ease.

"Have you been up all night? You should have brought her to me." She came forward to take the baby and was greeted with rooting kisses all over her face. She laughed with tender surprise, a sound that his angry attempt to jail her would have silenced forever. His heart shriveled in his chest.

"Did Daddy forget to feed you?" she murmured as she moved to the sofa.

"I tried a few minutes ago. She wasn't interested." His voice rasped.

She flinched at his rough tone, and flicked him an uncertain glance. "Giving him a hard time, are you?" She shrugged out of one side of her robe and dropped the strap of her tank top down her arm to expose her breast.

He had walked in on her feeding so many times she was no longer self-conscious about it. He didn't think of it as sexual, but seeing her feed their daughter affected him. It was the softness that overcame Sirena. Her fingers gently swirled Lucy's dark hair into whorls as the baby relaxed and made greedy noises. Her expression brimmed with such maternal love his breastbone ached.

He hadn't known she was pregnant when he'd pushed for jail time, but she had. She must have been terrified. While he, the first person she should have been able to rely on, had been the last person she would ever consider calling.

She glanced up. Her smile faded. Last night's enmity crept back like cold smoke, suffocating and dark. "I've got her," she said, dropping her lashes to hide her eyes. "You can get some sleep or go in to the office like you planned."

"No. I can't."

He ran a hand through his hair, becoming aware of a persistent headache and a general bruised feeling all over his body. His breath felt thick and insufficient. He spoke in a voice that very reluctantly delivered what he had to say.

"Sirena, you know I lost my father. What I never tell people…I found him. I came home from school and there he was, overdosed. Deliberately. He'd been having an affair with his secretary." He paused. "I called an ambulance, tried to revive him, but I was only nine years old. And it was too late."

Sirena's eyes fixated on him, the green orbs wide with shock. "I had no idea."

"I hate talking about it. My mother doesn't speak of it either."

"No, the few times she mentioned your father she sounded as if…"

"She loved him? She did. I only know about the affair because I found the note in the safe when we moved. It was full of assurances that he loved us both, but he still chose death because he couldn't live without this woman. I can't help blaming her." He knew it wasn't logical, but nothing about his father's death made sense to him.

"The note was the only thing left in the safe," he continued. "My stepfather had emptied it of everything else. My mother loved him, too, and he appeared to love her back.

I thought she'd found some comfort with him after our loss, but my stepfather was using her. He gambled away every cent we had. I came home from university because he'd had a heart attack and that's when I found the phones were about to be cut off and the electricity was overdue. We lost him and the house in the same month. My mother was a mess, grief stricken, but also feeling guilty for having trusted him and giving me no indication things were sliding downhill so fast."

He pushed his hands into his pockets, seeing again his mother's remorseful weeping and hearing her broken litany of, *He said he would turn it around.*

"You mentioned last night he was the reason you started over. I didn't realize it was that grim. What did you do?" Her voice was all softness and compassion, her bared shoulder enhancing the picture of her as vulnerable and incapable of causing harm.

"I developed a deep animosity toward anyone who tries to rob me," he admitted with quiet brutality.

She paled. Her gaze fell and her expression grew bleak.

"Maybe it doesn't excuse my having you arrested without speaking to you first, but I felt justified when it happened. I was… Damn it, Sirena, it was a perfect storm of my worst nightmares, falling for my secretary the way my father had, then being betrayed by someone I had come to rely on. I lashed out hard and fast."

She gave a little nod as she drew the sleepy infant off her breast and shrugged her robe into place. "I understand."

How many times had he seen that look on her face, he wondered, taking in the lowered lashes and stoic expression. He was tough to work for, he knew that. He pushed himself hard and was so overcommitted he didn't have time for mistakes. She'd always been the first to hear about any he found.

The phrase *long-suffering* came to mind as he saw past

her impassive expression to the self-protective tension in
her body language. For the first time he heard the stark
despondency in her voice. It had the same underlying incomprehension he felt when he talked about his father's
suicide. She didn't understand. She was merely accepting
what she couldn't change.

His heart lurched. He prided himself on supporting his
family and living up to his responsibilities, but he had
leaned heavily on Sirena when she worked for him. Where
was her pillar of support, though? Her talk last night of
being scared and ill and forsaken by her family had terrified and angered him anew. He wondered why she had
needed the money. She had never said, but he was damned
sure it wasn't for gambling debts or high fashion or drugs.

"Why did you steal from me, Sirena?"

She flinched at the word *steal,* then a kind of defeat
washed over her, shutting her eyes and making her shoulders slump. "My sister needed money to pay her tuition
fees."

The words left a bang of silence like a balloon popping
into jagged pieces. He hadn't expected it, but it seemed
oddly predictable after the fact.

She rushed on. "She was so upset after working so hard
to get accepted to her degree program. They have a huge
waiting list. She couldn't just wait a semester and apply
again. And she'll make an amazing teacher, because she
understands what it's like to struggle. I honestly thought
it would only be for a few days until Dad got payment
from his customer— Please don't go after him for repayment," she said with sudden stark alarm. "Things happened with his business. He doesn't have it and he's really
struggling. It would kill him to know how much trouble
I got myself into."

Her misery was real, her regret so palpable he could
taste it. There was no struggle over whether to believe her.

The explanation fit perfectly with her revelations last night about her love for her sister. He'd always seen her as loyal. It was why he'd been so blindsided by and furious about her dishonesty. It was exactly like the woman he knew to step up and fix things as expediently as possible.

None of that excused her behavior, but at least he understood it.

"I think she'll go down for a while now." She rose, pale and not meeting his eyes.

He should have let her leave him to his thoughts, but put out his hand to stop her.

She halted, eyes downcast. Subtle waves of tension rolled off her. He could tell she wanted to be away from him, but she wasn't willing to allow contact with his outstretched arm even to brush it aside so she could leave the room.

Her refusal to touch him spread an ache of dismay through him. They'd torn the curtains back and exposed their motives for treating each other the way they had, but it didn't change the fact that she'd stolen and he'd wanted her jailed her for it. Those sorts of injuries took a long time to heal.

But they had to ignore the pain and make this work in spite of it.

"The simplest, most advantageous solution for Lucy would be for us to live together permanently," he began.

Her shoulders sagged. "I know, Raoul. But it wouldn't work. We don't trust each other."

She seemed genuinely distressed. He felt the same, but he couldn't give up. It wasn't in his nature.

"We can start over. We've cleared the air. Damn it, Sirena," he rushed on when she shook her head. "I want to be with my daughter and you feel the same. You can't tell me you'd rather put her in day care for most of the time you'd have her. And when she's with me, I'm hiring a nanny to watch her so I can work? It makes no sense."

"But—"

"We put this behind us," he insisted, overriding her. "You just have to be honest from now on. Swear to me you'll never steal from me again. I want that promise," he stated firmly. More of an ultimatum, really.

Her eyes welled. He was coming at her from so many angles and she was still muddled from a rough sleep. She'd been deeply hurt last night. She'd tossed and turned, convinced that telling him anything about how badly he'd wounded her had been a mistake. What would he care? He would find a way to use it against her.

When she'd risen, she'd been determined to start the move back to her flat.

Then she'd found him looking like a pile of forgotten laundry, hair rumpled, sexy stubble on his cheeks and tortured shadows under his eyes. Her heart had been knocked out of place and was still sitting crooked in her chest. Everything he'd said had put her determination to leave him into disarray.

*Falling for my secretary...*

That barely there hint of regard shouldn't make her blood race, but it did.

"We've managed until now and we were furious with each other," he cajoled.

"I'm still furious," she interjected with more exasperation than heat. A lot of her bitter loathing was dissolving. She couldn't help it. Getting that peek into his past explained so much, not least his single-minded determination to succeed.

And it did nothing to dissipate the attraction she felt toward him. If anything, it was worse now. The thick walls she'd built against him were thinning and little fantasies of somehow finding a future with him, earning his trust and maybe his love, sparkled like fairy dust in the edges of her vision.

*So* dumb.

Given what he'd just told her, it was time to accept that he would never, ever love her. The best she could hope for was this, a truce and a fresh start.

Injustice sawed behind her breastbone like an abrasive file.

Lucy grew heavy in her arms. She started to change her position, then let Raoul take her, watching as the limp infant was tucked lovingly into her father's chest.

Folding her empty arms, she tried telling herself she could manage alone, but she couldn't ignore his point about day care.

"My mother wants to see her," Raoul added in quiet insistence. "You know how hard travel is on her. Lucy obviously hates the bottle. We could force the issue—"

"No!" she blurted, hating thinking of Lucy being distressed about anything. If she preferred to breast-feed, well, this was a finite time in both their lives.

"You'll come to New York with us, then."

"Don't start with your pushy tactics! I know how you work, getting a small concession and turning it into a major one," she said with mild disgust. "I'll *think* about New York. And if I go, it won't be as your—"

Lover? Mistress? Girlfriend? The words all sounded so superficial and temporary, paring her self-worth down to nothing.

"Nanny?" he prompted, mouth quirking briefly, then he sobered. "I'd have to hire one if you don't go. I'd prefer to pay you. You could quit the transcription."

"Don't make it sound easy. It's not."

One long masculine finger touched her jaw, turning her face to his. "What's hard? Making the promise about not stealing? Or keeping it?"

His challenge pinned her so she felt like an insect squirming in place, unable to escape even though she wanted to scamper away. Dying by increments, she felt the spasm of hurt reflect in her face before she was able to mask it, but a pierce of pain stayed lodged in her heart like an iron spike.

Looking him straight in the eye, she defiantly said, "I will never take anything from you. Ever."

He held her gaze for so long she almost couldn't stand it. Tightness gripped her chest and her skin felt too small for her body.

He nodded once.

As he walked away, she hung back, trembling. Had she lost or won?

Raoul's mother cried when she held Lucy for the first time.

"I never imagined he'd give me a grandchild. He's such a workaholic." Beatrisa was a tall, slender woman who dressed well and bound her silver hair into a figure eight behind her head. Her subtle makeup enhanced her aristocratic features and she wore elegant jewelry that Sirena suspected were gifts from her son.

Beatrisa had always seemed to lack a real spark of life and now Sirena understood why. She felt a tremendous need to be kind to the older woman, and was glad she'd conceded to the trip, even though everything about staying in this house was awkward.

"She thinks we're a couple," she hissed when they were given a room to share.

"What a crazy assumption, with the baby and all," he drawled.

"You should explain to her."

"How?" he countered with exasperation.

Oh, that attitude of his grated. Especially since she could see how it would go. Beatrisa was being incredibly polite, plainly trying not to pry as she accepted their "modern" relationship with a murmur about admiring independent women. Any attempt to clarify would crack open the marriage question and Raoul *didn't see any point in that.*

Not that she wanted to marry him. No, they might have found a truce and a crooked understanding with their revelations about their past, but it wasn't as though he'd magically fallen in love with her. For her part, she was too aware of how easily she could tip back into crazy infatuation with him, making her vulnerable to his dominant personality. He'd broken her heart once already. She couldn't let him do it again.

"I'll use the bed in Lucy's room," she said.

His sigh rang with male frustration. "The doctor cleared you for more than travel, didn't he?"

"So I'm supposed to fall into bed with you?" She swung around to glare at him across the foot of the enormous, inviting bed with its plump pillows and slippery satin cover. "I realize you think I slept with you to hide my crime, but sex isn't that mindless for me. I need feelings on both sides."

A chill washed over her as her words rang in her ears. Nausea threatened, the kind that came from deep mortification. She was an independent woman, all right, one whose only solace against her obsession with her boss was that he'd never known how deep it went, but she'd just snapped her way into humiliation. Her clothes might as well be on the floor around her ankles, she felt so naked and exposed.

He stood arrested, but the wheels were spinning fast behind his inscrutable stare.

Trying to stay ahead of any conclusions he might draw, she gathered her toothbrush and pajamas from her bag, aware she was shaking but unable to control it.

"Of course, I'm given to self-deception," she stammered. "And thank God, or we wouldn't have Lucy, would we? But we both know how we feel about each other now and I make enough fresh mistakes without having to repeat old ones, so…"

She practically ran from the room before locking herself into Lucy's, where she threw herself facedown on the bed and quietly screamed into a pillow.

# CHAPTER NINE

RAOUL HAD GROWN up in New York, but he didn't care for it. Too many dark memories. The climate didn't help, always socked in with rain or buried in snow or suffocatingly humid with summer heat. The place forced on him a heavy feeling of a weight inside him that he couldn't shift.

He was already struggling with that when he paused on his way into a meeting and instructed the receptionist to interrupt him if Sirena called.

"Ms. Abbott? I thought she'd left the company! How is she?" The woman's warmth and interest were sincere.

His blunt "Fine" was rude. And a lie. He'd left the house before he'd seen her this morning, but he knew from the way Sirena had blanched last night that she was not fine. He almost suspected she was injured in a way he hadn't considered.

Brooding while he half listened to his engineers develop a workback schedule, he did some math. He hadn't added everything together since their talk over drinks that night by the pool because he'd been distracted by other revelations, but if it was true she hadn't dated after that boy in college, she'd had exactly one lover since her first, ill-fated relationship.

Him.

*...sex isn't that mindless for me. I need feelings on both sides.*

The way she'd practically grabbed the voice bubble from the air and gobbled it back indicated pretty clearly that she'd never meant to admit that to him. Which made it disturbingly sincere.

*Of course, I'm given to self-deception,* she'd added to cover up, but that only made him grind his teeth, wondering if he was as well. Despite her motives for stealing unfolding into a picture of a woman who hadn't believed he'd help if she asked, he'd never wavered from believing she'd slept with him to cover up what she'd done.

He needed to believe it. Anything else was too uncomfortable. He wasn't a womanizer. He didn't take advantage of the vulnerable. He didn't lead women on.

She hadn't expected one hookup to be a marriage proposal, she'd said, but had expected to be treated with respect.

At the time of their affair, he'd been way past respect into genuine liking. Affection. Something deeper he'd never contemplated letting himself feel.

God, when he thought back to how those twenty-four hours had gone, it was like another lifetime. The sweetness of her, the relief of finally giving in to touching her, the powerful release that had shaken him to the core…

The doors opening inside him, a sensation like footsteps invading the well-guarded depths of his soul. Even as their damp, half-clothed bodies had been trembling in ecstasy, he'd crashed back to the reality of what they'd just done. Whom he'd done it with. How vulnerable he felt.

His inner panels had lit up with alarm signals. While Sirena's plump lips had grazed his throat, he'd been withdrawing, deeply aware of a sense of jeopardy. His father hadn't killed himself because he'd fallen for his secretary. He'd killed himself because he'd *fallen.* In love. Deep emotions drove men to desperate acts.

What he'd felt for Sirena in those loaded minutes of sensual closeness had scared the hell out of him.

He'd pulled away, said something about the rain having stopped. By the time he'd dropped her at her building and returned to his own, he'd been primed for a reason, any reason, to knock her so far away from him she'd never reach him again.

And he had.

*...Even my stepmother didn't go that far to hurt me.*

Rather than killing himself, he'd destroyed what had been growing between them.

It was a sickening, horrid vision of himself. He lurched to his feet, needing to escape his own pathetic weakness, but only drew the attention of the room.

"Problem, sir?" The group stood back to look between him and the Smart Board where the schedule could have been written in Sanskrit for all the sense it made.

"I have to make a call," he lied, and strode through the maze of cubicles clattering with keyboard strikes into his office. It contained two desks, one that was a bold, masculine statement and the other a stylish work space that, for a time, had been the first place he glanced. Now it stood as a monument to his colossal overreaction.

He rubbed his face, hating to feel this tortured, this *guilty.* The fact remained, she had stolen from him, he reminded himself.

But he hadn't lashed out at her for that. She'd angered him, yes, but her real crime had been moving him in the first place. Sirena had dared to penetrate walls nobody else had dared breach.

*Lust isn't caring.*

No, it wasn't, but what he felt wasn't mere lust.

Sirena was grateful that Raoul had left for the office before she rose. Of course, she was also hypocrite enough to miss him despite her chagrin over her revelation last night. There was also envy and disgruntlement that he still worked in one of the many dynamic, ever-changing offices she had loved so much. Who had taken her place? She hated her usurper on principle.

Chatting with Beatrisa, hearing stories of Raoul's childhood became a nice distraction from her muddled emotions.

When he returned unexpectedly at lunch, it was with a surprise: tickets to a matinee. "Musicals aren't my speed. I'll stay with Lucy. You ladies have fun."

It was an incredible treat, the sort of thing Sirena used to wish for every time they visited New York, but had never found time or funds for. Afterward they had tea and scones in a glitzy café until Raoul texted that his daughter had inherited his stubborn streak.

Giggling over his self-deprecating assessment, they rushed back so Sirena could feed their starving baby. Full of excitement about their afternoon, she was disappointed when Raoul said, "I'm glad you enjoyed it. Start dinner without me. I have a call to make."

When he found his way to the table, he was wearing his cloak of remoteness. His mother didn't pick up the signals of his distraction, but Sirena did. While Beatrisa talked about their day, the feeling of being left out of his world struck Sirena afresh, but she supposed his turning aloof was better than another clash like last night's.

As Beatrisa wound down over coffee, Raoul finally said, "I'm afraid we've had a change of plans, Mother. We won't be able to stay the week. The company has been nominated for an award in L.A. I have to fly out to pick it up."

"You hate those things!" Sirena blurted. It had always been her job to figure out who could show up in his place, make the arrangements and prepare a speech.

"Surely you could do that without dragging Sirena and the baby across the country? They can stay here with me," his mother said.

Sirena shrugged. Lucy was out of sorts enough with the time change from London. She didn't need another one.

Raoul only gave his coffee cup a quarter turn and said, "They've specifically asked if Sirena would attend. It's that bunch we worked with for the special-effects software," he told her. "You always made an impression with my associates. You've been sorely missed by a lot of them."

Sirena flushed hot and cold, not sure how to respond. She missed everything about her job, but she couldn't go back to it, so she tried not to think of it.

As she considered all those beautiful women he'd taken to galas and cocktail parties, she also felt too inadequate to be his date. "I never attended that sort of thing with you before—" she started to dismiss.

"Things are different now, aren't they?"

*How?* She lifted a swift glance and collided with his unrelenting stare, like he was pushing his will upon her. She instinctively bristled while the fault line in her chest gaped and widened. "There's no one to watch Lucy."

"Miranda's agreed to fly in and sit with her."

"You want to fly your stepsister to L.A. to babysit?" It was ludicrous—and the way he briefly glanced away, as though he wasn't being honest with her, put her on guard.

"She flies all the time doing those trade shows. We'll need to leave early, but we'll come back here for a day or two on our way back to London." He rose, putting an end to the discussion in a completely familiar way.

Old habits of accommodating his needs collided with the newer ones of taking care of her baby's needs and her own. "Raoul."

"This is important to me, Sirena. Please don't argue."

Wow. Had he just said *please?* Shock struck her dumb long enough he was able to escape without her raising another argument.

By morning, it was too late. When he said early, he meant early, coming into her room to begin packing Lucy's things while shooing Sirena's sleepy head into the shower. Being naked and knowing he was just beyond the door made her senses flare, but he was completely indifferent. They were on the plane within the hour.

Lucy didn't enjoy the altitude climb, so they were well in the air before Sirena caught her breath. She gratefully embraced a cup of coffee while Raoul swept and tapped his way across a tablet screen.

"I liked that crew from the film, too, but I can't believe you shook us out of bed for them. What's really going on?" she asked.

"Use the stateroom if you want more sleep." He didn't even look up.

"No, I've had coffee now. You'll have to entertain me," she volleyed back.

His gaze came up with pupils so big his eyes were almost black. After a checking glance to their sleeping infant, he swung a loaded *"Okay"* to her.

In a blink, he'd transformed from the distracted man intent on his work that she'd seen a million times to a predatory male thinking of nothing but sex.

Her skin tightened and a flush of excitement flooded her with heat. Most betraying of all, tingles pooled in a swirl of sharp desire deep between her thighs.

His tense mouth eased into a smile of approval while he took a slow visual tour to her breasts, where her nipples stung with need. He didn't move, but suddenly he felt very close. He knew exactly what was happening to her.

She yanked her gaze away, but the picture of his masculine beauty stayed with her. The man had a chest to absolutely die for and she ached to see it again, run her hands over his smooth shoulders and taut abs.

Embarrassed by her shortened breath and prickling arousal, she swallowed and said a strangled, "I think we've covered that. It's not on."

Silence. And when she risked a glance at him, his jaw was clenched.

"Because you think I don't have feelings for you," he growled.

"I don't expect you to," she stated stiffly, then had to dip her face to stare into her empty mug, hiding that she was going red with indignity. "Obviously you've been very decent, taking me in when I was sick, but that was more to do with Lucy, wasn't it? And yesterday was nice, but it was a treat for your mother. Shows like that aren't your thing, you said. So you sent me, which isn't to say I didn't enjoy it, just that I realize it wasn't about me."

"You have a stellar opinion of me and my motives, don't you?"

"I'm not trying to insult you."

"You're doing a helluva job of it anyway. Let's hope this trip redeems me in your eyes." He went back to his tablet, shutting her out, which was probably a good thing.

He'd disconcerted her, sounding almost injured. A tiny worm of ambiguity niggled in her. Was she working so hard to protect herself she was failing to see the softer feelings she'd once been convinced were there? Or was that delusion a short trip to another painful tumble?

Despite the caffeine in her system, she wound up dozing and before she knew it, they were in California. They didn't stay in the suite they'd used two years ago, when he'd been working with the special-effects company. This was a new, ultrachic building designed on a curve, like a giant glass-and-bronze half cylinder with its back to the ocean.

Inside the penthouse, the floor-to-ceiling windows were framed in gray-and-white geometric squares. The tiles and carpet marked severe paths through the open plan of lounge, kitchen and dining area. All of the furniture was angular and modern, but luxury softened the hard edges. Jewel-colored pillows and billowy curtains gave it a sexy, romantic feel and the stunning three-sixty views to mountains and ocean and cityscape were breathtaking. Sirena's first thought was of the bath she'd take after dark, surrounded by the twinkling lights of the city.

As was her habit, she ran a brisk inventory as she explored, ensuring all the standard arrangements for Raoul were made.

"No Chivas and no cord for the secure internet connection." She adjusted the drapes in the main room to let in more of the brilliant sunshine and view of the ocean. "I'll call down. Did you want extra of that rain forest coffee you like to take home?"

He didn't answer, so she turned to see him watching her with a bemused expression. "I would love that, thank you."

His appreciation poured sunlight directly into her soul. A huge smile tried to take over her face and she had to turn away to hide how easily he flipped her inside out. What the hell was she doing? No way was she begging for a shred of affection. She needed to nip this craziness in the bud.

Fortunately their daughter woke and demanded attention, then a stylist showed up with a measuring tape and color swatches.

"What? Why?" Sirena argued as Raoul took the baby so she could lift her arms.

"We have that red carpet thing in a few nights," he reminded.

"You didn't say red carpet! I thought it was a cocktail party." She hadn't gained a ton of baby weight, she'd been too sick, but even though she'd started back on the treadmill, she was soft and had bags under her eyes. She'd never clean up like the stunners who usually hung off his arm.

Muddled and anxious, she got through the rest of the day and took some air on the balcony after her bath. A clean breeze off the water had swept away the pollution and the air smelled sultry, helping ease her unsettled mind.

Raoul joined her, making her stomach quiver in awareness. She ignored it.

"What do you think? Should I buy this unit?" he asked her.

"They're treating you to entice you?" she guessed, then rejected the luxurious surroundings with a haughty shake of her head. "I came out here to see the fireworks over the happiest place on earth and I don't, so it's no good. A major disappointment."

"I'll make the purchase contingent on their moving the building to the next county," he drawled.

"Ha!" She laughed at herself. "I guess I should look at a map. It's just always been on my bucket list to come to L.A., visit the theme parks, wear the ears…I thought I'd at least see the castle and fireworks while I'm here."

"You can. We'll be here a week. Take—" He cut himself off.

"Lucy isn't old enough to appreciate it," she scoffed, predicting what he had almost said. "No, I can wait for another time." To avoid his casually rumpled masculine appearance, she looked to the glowing blue of the pool jutting off to the right on their patio, a few steps down. It was surrounded by orange trees in oversized planter pots and twined with pinpoints of white lights. "If we come here again."

She pursed her lips, wondering if this would become her life. She suspected so and took a second to self-examine.

"Honestly, Raoul? I don't know if I would have enjoyed the travel half so much if we'd been staying at cheap motels and taking shuttle buses through dodgy back alleys. You live very well. It makes me very tempted to stay with you indefinitely."

"That's the only thing that tempts you?" he asked with mild disgust.

"Oh, please! You're not that insecure." She was glad it was dark and he couldn't see how she took in his physique with a swift glance and a hard blush. "You could drive shuttle buses for back-alley hotels and still be appealing. But I've been in a relationship for practical reasons. They aren't as great as they look. I knew from the outset I wouldn't be with Stephan forever and it made me feel trapped. I don't want to start something unless I know we can both live with it for a very long time."

"I hate hearing you talk about him." He gave her a pointed look that landed like a spear in her heart, sticking and vibrating. "This is the least practical or convenient relationship I've ever been in, but I still want it. I want *you*."

"You mean you—"

"Don't," he interrupted, stepping so close she pressed back into the rail.

She gripped it, heart zooming into flight as his potent masculinity clouded around her like a spell. "Don't what?"

"Don't say I only want my daughter. I do, but that's not why I'm out here. I saw you walk by with this robe clinging to your damp skin…" His nostrils flared as he seared his glance down her front. One hand came out to hook into her belt, tugging lightly.

She should have let him draw her forward, but she resisted and the belt gave way.

Something flared in his silver eyes.

"Raoul." She meant it as a protest, but it was more an enticing whisper.

"Let me," he growled, and with slow deliberation parted

the edges of her robe. She was naked beneath and he swore softly before murmuring, "You're so beautiful."

She desperately needed to hear that. No one ever complimented her and seeing the way he ate up her figure was intensely gratifying, filling up a hollow part of her soul.

The cool night air made her skin pimple, knotting her nipples into tight buds and swirling to the warm places on her abdomen and thighs. A suffusion of heat followed, one incited by the hunger and admiration in his long study of her nude body.

"Raoul," she moaned again, this time on a helpless whimper.

He groaned and stepped closer, shod feet bracketing her bare ones. His hot hands sought her waist and circled to her back, pulling her into contact with his clothed body.

She let her head fall back and met his open mouth with her own, moaning at how wrong this was, but she wanted it so badly. Her hands eased their death grip on the rail and rose to stroke over his shoulders, following the rippling flex of his shoulder blades as he swooped his hands over the small of her back, cupped her naked bottom and pressed her aching pelvis into firm contact with the ridge of his erection.

There was no buildup, no mental debate as she wondered if her desire would catch. Everything about this man turned her switches on. All he had to do was touch her. Her hips tilted, seeking more intimate contact with his hardness.

He thrust his tongue into her mouth in a bold claim, cupping the side of her face to hold her for his devastating kiss. She pulled him into her, wanting more, loving the stroke of his restless hands, the way he clasped her breast and gently crushed and massaged and softly bit her lips before he lifted his head.

"Bedroom," he said, starting to pull her with him.

She came to her senses and pressed a hand to his chest. "We can't."

"Why not?"

For the life of her, she couldn't think of anything but feeling him inside her, but that's all it would be. Physical feelings. For him. As much as she wanted the release, she knew she'd never be able to keep it that dispassionate.

As he read her rejection, his expression shuttered. With a feral noise, he lurched away and grasped the rail to the lower balcony and vaulted to the pool deck below.

"What—?"

He landed between a pair of loungers, took three long strides and dove straight into the pool.

Sirena slapped a hand over her mouth, astonished as she watched his blurred image move with surprising speed down the length of the pool, all underwater. He was halfway back before he rose to gasp for air.

"What on earth are you doing?" she cried.

"What the hell are you doing?" he shot back, kicking himself to the far edge and hefting himself onto the ledge. Yanking at his wet shirt, he struggled out of it and dropped it beside his hip with a splat. "Get inside or I'm coming after you and this time I'm not stopping."

She spun and ran to her room, where she hugged a pillow and told herself she'd made the right decision.

Even though it felt like the stupidest choice in the world.

"Sirena!"

*It was about time.* Odious man. First he made her so crazy she spent the night hating herself for not sleeping with him when she would have hated herself more if she *had.* Then he left without writing a note, giving no indication of where he was going or when to expect him back—although he had prepared the coffee machine so all she had to do was push the button. But that didn't excuse barging in here, yelling her name when she was trying to settle their daughter.

"Sirena, where—? Oh, here you are."

She glared at him. "She was almost asleep." She lightly bounced the baby to ease her drowsy eyes closed again.

"I'll take her," he said, moving forward in that battle-ship way of his.

"Fine, take her. Maybe she'll sleep for you," she muttered, grouchy because she needed a nap as badly as the baby. Maybe going to bed with him *now....*

*Shut up, Sirena.*

"I don't want you to drop her," he said, "when you see who I brought with me."

She sidestepped to see a young woman in the doorway. She was blonde, slender, achingly sweet-looking in her innocent way, yet tall and curvy without a hint of the preadolescent she'd been the last time Sirena had seen her.

Allison's soft brown eyes pooled with giant tears while a great, mischievous grin widened her mouth. She thrust out her arms. "Me," she burst out. "Surprise!"

A scream built in Sirena's throat and locked it, making pressure expand so hard her eyes filled. She choked, try-ing to gasp a breath, and began to shake. She wanted to move forward, but her knees started to sag.

Raoul caught her, swearing under his breath. "I should have warned you, but I didn't want to build expectations if anything went wrong—"

"It's okay, it's okay," she babbled, wanting to lean into him, but forcing her legs to take her weight. She passed through a thick mist that was pure sparkle and magic. As she reached the familiar yet very grown-up sister she hadn't seen in the flesh for so long, she realized her cheeks hurt because she was smiling bigger than she ever had in her life.

"You don't look this tall when we talk on my tablet,"

she managed to joke even as a sobbing laugh rattled her voice. Her arms wrapped around her baby sister.

Ali's wiry embrace crushed her. The physical contact was so deeply moving, Sirena thought she'd break into pieces.

The women held on to each other a long time, making Raoul's throat close. Ali, as she had said she liked to be called, had chattered excitedly in the limo, her gestures and tone oddly Sirena-like despite the faint accent and fair coloring. She had a measure of Sirena's steely core, too. When he'd asked why her parents hadn't come, she'd only said, "Mum can be funny sometimes," and lifted her chin. He had the impression this trip was a bit of rebellion and wondered if it would have repercussions for Sirena.

He'd found Faye oddly obstructive, considering he was offering an all-expenses-paid trip to America. It had been hard to sidestep her demand to speak to Sirena, which he suspected might have called off Ali's visit.

Navigating future altercations with Sirena's family was a concern for another time, he decided. This moment, seeing how happy he'd made Sirena, was worth any trouble down the road.

The women pulled back to stare at one another, glowing in an aura of happiness.

Ali's gaze dragged toward him. "Can I meet Lucy? I've been dying to hold her." She took her niece and sighed with adoration. "Oh, Sin, she's beautiful."

*Sin,* he silently repeated, liking the nickname immediately.

"Isn't she?" she agreed shamelessly. Eyes damp and lips trembling, she cupped her flushed cheeks in her hands.

She looked so taken aback and overwhelmed Raoul couldn't help moving toward her, but he was almost afraid to touch her. She seemed to be struggling to contain her emotions. Gently he smoothed her hair back from the side of her face. "I didn't realize this would be such a shock. Are you all right?"

She flashed him one glimpse of the naked emotions brimming in her, then threw herself at him.

He took the hit of her soft weight with a surprised "Oof," then closed his arms around her.

She buried her face in the middle of his chest, clinging tightly, barely audible as she said, "You have no idea what this means to me. I can't ever thank you enough."

All the sexual heat of last night's embrace came back as he felt the press of her breasts and was surrounded in her feminine scent of green tea and pineapple. An incredible wash of tenderness accompanied it. He had wanted to do something nice, but had never suspected such a small thing would have such magnificent impact.

Governed by instinct, he enfolded her and stroked her hair. His chin caressed her silky locks and he had to swallow the emotion from his throat. He'd forgotten this perk in letting yourself feel for another person. When they were happy, you were happy. He should have done this sooner. He'd healed a crack in her heart, filled it with joy, and it had taken nothing. A couple of phone calls and a plane ticket. What did that say about how lonely she'd been?

"You two," Ali trilled. "You're so cute."

Sirena realized she was all over Raoul like a coat of paint. After last night she didn't know where they stood. She always felt this pull around him and at this moment felt positively anchored to him, heart to heart. Misreading their connection had gotten her where she was today, though.

Pulling away, she swiped her fingertips under her eyes, trying to get a grip. Her overwhelmed emotions weren't just shock and joy over seeing her sister. There was a huge part shaken to the core that Raoul had done this for her. She tried to remind herself that the cost was nothing to him, but to think of it and make it happen...

Did he feel something for her after all?

She was afraid to look at him, fearful of seeing nothing and being disappointed. She was also terrified that her shields were so far gone he'd see right into her soul and the special place she reserved for him beside it.

"This is like Christmas," she said, clearing her throat and searching for a stronger voice. "It really puts to shame that tie I haven't even bought Raoul."

They all laughed and the day became a celebration, California-style. Raoul ordered brunch and mimosas and joined them on and off as they sat by the pool, taking turns holding Lucy and catching up.

By evening, the excitement and time change had caught up to all of them and they had an early night. The next morning, she met Raoul in the kitchen.

"Can't sleep?" she said with an attack of nerves, feeling defenseless without Lucy or Ali to still the sexual vibrations that immediately flared between them. "Me, either."

"I have a heavy morning before everyone in Europe goes home, but I wanted to give you these." He showed her some tickets. "I almost spilled the beans about Ali when you were talking about this the other night. I came this close to suggesting you take her."

Sirena gasped as she caught sight of the iconic fairy circling the castle with dust. "Raoul!"

"For the record, these are not for her, although I hope she enjoys the day as much as you do. These aren't for Lucy either." The bright tickets came alongside her jaw as he crooked his finger under her chin, making her lift her eyes to his. "These are for you, because it's something you've always wanted."

He kissed her. The gesture was so sweet she couldn't help clinging to his lips with her own. His taste made goose bumps lift all over her body.

She swallowed and tried to hide how touched she was

by joking, "I really don't know what to think of all this." Her heart rate picked up, daring to conjecture there might be a hint of tenderness or affection driving him after all. "You're going to a lot of trouble just to keep things *in-house*."

"Sirena—" His quick, defensive blurt of her name made her wave a quick hand.

"I'm sorry. I'm being cheeky because I don't know what else to say, not because I think you have ulterior motives," she hurried to excuse.

He sighed. "I realize I'm not demonstrative." Leaning near the sink, he studied her, his body language heavy. A range of emotions ran across his usually stoic face. They were intimate and, she suspected, indicative of deep scarring.

She instantly wanted to reach out with reassurance, but felt too shy and uncertain so she wound up standing there with her hands wringing, the silence thick and awkward. What could she say anyway? That a couple of kisses and nice gestures had won her over? They hadn't. She had tons of misgivings.

He ran a hand over his face. "After my father, I pushed everyone to a safe distance. What he'd done was too cruel. He was a good man, a good father. We played catch, went fishing. It was a perfect childhood. I'll never understand why he killed himself or how anyone could say they love someone and hurt them that badly. Letting down my guard with anyone since then…it's not something that's comfortable for me."

Outwardly she handled what he was saying, taking it on the chin without flinching, even though she was screaming inside. Even though she was pretty sure she paled and her bones turned to powder. Somehow she stayed there, nodding circumspectly, saying, "I understand."

Her words seemed to hurt him. He winced.

"No, I do," she assured, being as honest as he was. "I have my own baggage that makes me worry you'll pull up stakes without a moment's notice. It makes me scared to let things move to…" She swallowed, trying to find a description that wouldn't reveal too much. "To a level of deeper dependence."

"I'm not going anywhere. This is everything I want, right here." He pointed to the floor between them, suggesting the domesticity of waking every morning with her and their little family, which was nice, but it wasn't the fairy tale on the tickets.

She had to let go of that. Better to keep her expectations realistic even if it hurt. And it hurt so much to know he would never love her. Not the way she loved him.

*Oh.* The knowledge of how deep her feelings had become went through her like a sweet, potent potion. This wasn't infatuation with the boss. It wasn't hormones raging for the wrong man. It was the evolution of feelings and attraction she'd always felt toward him. They had tumbled into deep devotion and longing to make a life with him.

Swallowing the lump that came into her throat, she hid her angst with a smile. "Even though you seem to do everything and I haven't done one thing for you? How about breakfast, at least?" She turned her back on him as she peered into the refrigerator, defusing the charged moment.

The spoiling didn't stop, however. After their day at the park, he appalled the upscale clientele of a rooftop restaurant by daring to bring a baby, of all things, into their exclusive establishment. They saw the fireworks from their table, of course. A trip to the beach was arranged the next day and a drive along the coastline the following. They lunched on fresh seafood and local wines and scouted art studios for bargains.

Then the preparations for the technology awards started.

Raoul escorted them into a design house on Rodeo Drive and handed over his credit card to a stylist.

"Ali, find some things for yourself and if you see something your mother would like, put that on there too. I'm having a prototype of my new gadget flown in for your father. You can take that back for him, but if you see something for him…" He leaned to kiss Sirena's cheek, trailing off as he prepared to take his leave.

"Dad's tastes are pretty simple," she said blankly, startled by his casual affection. He'd been so solicitous these last few days, a hand often finding its way to the middle of her back or resting at her waist, but she still wasn't used to it.

"Whatever you think is best. I'll be at Armani, having my tux fitted. Because I need another one." He rolled his eyes. "I'll come back for Lucy when I'm done."

They seated Ali in an overstuffed armchair and offered her champagne. Sirena leaned down to give her Lucy so she could have her fitting and Ali whispered, "It's like we're living *Pretty Woman.* You're going to marry him, right?"

"Sweetie, I keep telling you, it's not like that. We just had a moment that got us into a situation and we're trying to make the best of it." She didn't know how else to explain her circumstances without revealing details that were far from romantic.

Back when she'd been pregnant and under suspicion, she'd kept the arrest from her family. It hadn't been her father's fault, but he would have felt responsible. She certainly didn't want her sister feeling guilty about pursuing her teaching dream.

Now, well, she didn't want to tell Ali everything for fear she'd think badly of Raoul. The things Raoul had shared with her were deeply personal and without being able to balance his actions against his motives, he would look like a cold, unforgiving monster. Which was miles from the truth.

Sighing a little, she had to admit he was actually what she'd always admired him for being: a strong, ambitious man with a deep streak of responsibility and loyalty to his family. He was gallant after growing up around women, innately desiring to protect and provide for his own. Even if he had been toothless, dirt-poor and overweight, he'd still open doors and show incredible patience for women who couldn't decide which shoes or lipstick to wear. He'd still walk a baby all night and start the coffee for her mother.

And she'd still love him.

"Oh, Sin, you're gorgeous," Ali murmured as Sirena walked back to her.

With a pinch in her heart, she studied the emerald gown and thought about how she was the complete opposite of Raoul. She could dress up in world-class finery, have her teeth whitened, love their baby and he'd still only see her as a thief.

# CHAPTER TEN

RAOUL WENT IN search of Sirena, hearing Ali saying with exasperation, "She'll be fine. We both will. I swear."

"But call if you need to. Or text. You have Raoul's number if I don't hear mine?"

Suppressing a grin, he stepped into the doorway of the room operating as their nursery. Vaguely aware of Ali efficiently changing his daughter's nappy, he caught an eyeful of Sin and felt as though his breath had been punched out of him.

She had her back to him, but he was transfixed. He took in the curls pulled away from one ear to cascade like a waterfall over her opposite shoulder. Her off-the-shoulder gown in gypsy-green dipped to reveal one shoulder blade. A cutout on the other side offered a peek of her waist and spine. The skirt draped gracefully over her rounded hips to puddle sumptuously behind her. Distantly, he realized he wasn't getting any air, and that she hadn't even turned around, but she'd stolen his breath.

"Your date is here. Quite a dish, too," Ali said, cocking her chin in his direction.

He barely noticed the girl as the woman turned. Her plump bottom lip was caught in her teeth while her mossy eyes were pools of uncertainty. Always beautiful, Sirena didn't need makeup and the stylist had known it, only enhancing her stunning bone structure and opulent lashes with a streak of frosted jade and shimmering gold.

A wink of emeralds dangled from her ears and encircled her wrist. They were loaners, but he decided to buy them. They matched her eyes too perfectly to allow them to go to any other woman.

"I'm sorry," she said faintly. "Have you, um, been waiting for me?"

*All my life.*

"Get her out of here," Ali said with a nudge into Sirena's back. "She's being a nervous Nellie even though I keep telling her I babysat all of Sydney until I finally got a proper job at the real estate office."

Raoul held out his arm, not trusting his voice to tell her how beautiful she looked, then winced as she got there first, saying, "You look nice."

Her light touch curled into the curve of his elbow and a subtle mix of aromas filled his senses with floral and berry notes underscored with tangy citrus and a mysterious anise.

He waited until they were in the elevator, where he let the doors close without choosing a floor, before he gave in to temptation and reached to adjust the drape of her gown, revealing her leg and a shoe with a dominatrix heel.

"What are you doing?" She started to step her foot back inside the skirt, but he set a hand on the bared skin of her waist.

"Don't move, *Sin.*"

She gasped, cocking her hip to escape his touch as though it burned, but the flush of color that flooded under her skin and the spark that invaded her glistening eyes told him it was a more erotic reaction.

"You look amazing," he murmured as he removed his phone from his breast pocket.

Her eyes widened in surprise and her wicked mouth

twitched before she screened her thoughts behind a tangled line of mink. "Really?" She settled into a pose with the confidence of a woman who knew she looked her best and was having fun with it. Her shoulders went back, her breasts came up, her hips slanted and her feet parted just far enough to be provocative. "Men are so predictable."

She tossed her hair and offered a screen-legend smile.

"It's true," he agreed, snapping the photo. "We're simple creatures. Now take it off."

She laughed and hit the button for the lobby. "I'm keeping it on at least as long as it took me to get into it. Let me see." Her cool fingers grazed his in a soft caress as she urged him to slant the screen of his phone.

As he studied the photo with her, he saw what he hadn't meant to reveal. He'd liked the way the mirror showed the back of the gown and had angled the frame to catch it, but he hadn't noticed his own expression was caught in the reflection. Lust tightened his face. He wasn't ashamed of it, but his expression held something else.

He tucked the phone away, not wanting to examine the naked emotion on his face.

Discomfited, Sirena told herself she ought to be used to Raoul's mercurial moods, switching from warm familiarity to all business in the space of a heartbeat. With a pang near her heart, she tried to calm her racing pulse and quit building this into something it wasn't. But Ali's romantic nature was contagious. *He's going to propose. Why else does a man go to all this trouble?*

Ali didn't realize this level of luxury wasn't trouble for Raoul. It was completely normal and he probably took photos of all his dates, inserting them into his iLittleBlackBook so he could keep track of who was who.

The biting thought was wiped clear by another and she cringed inwardly. She really was the most misguidedly devoted ex-PA if she had to bite back remarking to him, *You know what might be a cool idea for an app?*

She was trying so hard to ground out her electric excitement she didn't realize the elevator doors had opened onto the opulent lobby.

"What's wrong?" he prompted.

*Idiot.* Trying to make light of her distraction, she quoted Julia Roberts under her breath. "If I forget to tell you later, I had a nice time tonight."

He didn't get it. In his typically classy fashion, he said very sincerely, "So did I."

*Oh.*

Her bones went soft as she took the hand he offered and let him lead her to the limo. It was like sitting down to an IMAX film where scenery rushing by became more intense and colorful, pulling her into a surreal world she had seen from a distance before, but that now drew her in three dimensionally.

Bulbs went off as they walked the red carpet. Action stars were everywhere and this wasn't even a big awards show. *Just Hollywood indulging itself,* Raoul had said. Still she could hardly keep her jaw from dropping.

The show was a pageantry of talent, one woman's singing almost bringing Sirena to tears. During a break, Raoul said, "You're really enjoying this."

"How could I not? I don't have any natural talents of my own, so I'm in complete awe of those that do."

"You're an excellent mother, Sirena."

"Oh, please," she deflected, uncomfortable with flattery. "Having a baby nearly killed me and I'm bumbling my way through colic and feeding. I'm hardly gifted."

"Don't joke about that," he said with gravity. "Ever."

Like all criticisms, deserved or not, she took his remark to heart and hid her abraded soul by sitting straight, chin level. His category was called next anyway, putting an end to the short conversation.

He won, of course, which was well deserved. As he rose, he clasped her hand and tried to bring her up with him.

"No!" she said, horrified. Her emotions were right there under the surface, barely contained. She wasn't standing under massive lights when she was this close to tears.

Setting his mouth into a displeased line, he went to the podium and waited for the applause to die down.

"This innovative software came out of a need for a specific effect. It wouldn't have been developed if not for the people who demanded it. But I think the entire team will agree that we wouldn't have delivered on time, on budget without the support of my exceptional assistant at the time, Sirena Abbott. She refused to come on stage with me because she's more comfortable in a supporting role than in the spotlight. I've come to realize that about you, Sin."

The nickname was a tiny endearment, but the intensity of his gaze picking her out across the crowded auditorium was monumental. Later she would realize heads and cameras had turned her way, but in this moment, all she saw and felt was Raoul's undivided attention.

"You recently did the hard work on a very special project in which I played a very small role. I won't take credit for the beautiful baby girl you made us. If we were giving golden statues for that tonight, this would be yours."

Now her makeup was going to run, vexing man! She blinked, trying to hold back the tears.

He was escorted offstage by handlers for photos. He'd warned her that would happen and she gratefully grasped the chance to slip into the ladies' room to collect herself. No one had ever made such a production of appreciating her. She didn't know how to cope with it. Criticism was hurtful, but she was comfortable with it. She knew what to do after receiving it. The path to Better was right there and she always took it.

Arriving at Well Done made her look around in confusion. Part of her wanted to dismiss what Raoul had said as empty flattery, but she knew that wasn't healthy and she loved their daughter too much to reduce the sweet things he'd just said about her, even if that meant accepting praise for her own contribution.

She *did* try to be a good mother and a good person. Was it so far-fetched that he might have noticed and come to value those things about her?

With her breath still hitching, she left the ladies' room and ran straight into Raoul. He was clutching his award in one fist as he paced. He stopped when he saw her.

"I was about to come in there looking for you."

"Shoes and a dress like this are challenging," she joked to hide her discomfiture.

Someone else came into the short hallway and he nudged her farther into the moderate privacy of an area where a bank of outdated pay telephones still hung. That was the millionth time he'd stroked his fingers over the bare skin at her waist and it was totally short-circuiting her brain.

"Are you upset with me?" he asked.

"For what?" She ducked her head to the snap on her pocketbook, not wanting him to see how gauche she felt, unable to take one little compliment.

"For telling the world we have a baby together."

"Oh. That." She pressed her freshly painted lips together, mouth quirking wryly. "It's not the way I would have done it, but I'm not going to pretend she doesn't exist."

"It's not the way I meant to reveal her either. I was fielding some awkward questions backstage about whether we're getting married. It made me realize we should. Then you wouldn't worry about whether you could depend on me."

Stunned, Sirena could only stare at his bow tie, eyes burning as she reflected that it was even less sentimental than Stephan's awkward "Maybe we should get married."

"And before you accuse me of saying it purely for practicality's sake—" He clunked his heavy award onto a shelf and crowded her into a corner. "Let me remind you there's a reason we wound up with an unplanned pregnancy."

There went that hand again, possessively sliding to the small of her back, fingers dipping behind silk as he curved her into him, bumping her thighs into his.

She automatically caught at his sleeve for balance, but her other hand braced her pocketbook into his shoulder. Her head fell back a little, lips parting on a shocked gasp as her entire front lit up with seeking tingles, wanting contact with his.

"Fresh lipstick," she managed as his mouth neared hers.

"I don't care." He pressed hard lips over her trembling ones, both soothing and inciting the ache spreading through her body. Heat rose like a circle of flames around them, burning her alive as they pressed together, spinning and hurtling directly into the sun.

She groaned and met his tongue with hers, lifting on tiptoes to increase the pressure and even diving her fingers into his short hair to pull him down, urging him to kiss her harder. He did, rocking his mouth on hers with feral hunger. Hard fingers dug into her buttock and spine as he crushed her to him.

His erection imprinted her through the fabric of his pants, making the ethereal layer of silk gown seem nonexistent. She didn't want it between them. She wanted to feel nothing but satin skin over hard flesh, flexing muscle and the slam of his heartbeat against hers. She whimpered, almost sobbing in her need for him.

Drawing back a fraction, he muttered, "This is crazy." He had a hand tangled in her hair, clenching a handful in a way that kept her immobile. It would have been too cave-man and primitive if he wasn't also holding her as if he was saving her from a shipwreck and dropping hot kisses down the side of her face to her nape.

She trembled, mortified by how close she was to losing it in public. It was no consolation that he had her buried in a corner. People were coming and going behind him. They had to be glancing this way. Her hands had burrowed beneath his jacket, but they were flexing on his shirt, try-ing to pull it from his waistband so she could stroke the indent of his spine.

"Raoul, we have to stop."

"I know. I'm about to drag you into a janitor's closet." He straightened and pulled his snowy handkerchief from his pocket. He swiped it across his mouth, then asked her with a look if he'd gotten all the color off.

She thumbed a tiny smudge from the corner of his mouth and stole the cloth for herself, thinking to take it into the ladies' room, but he caught her hand and his award and started for the exit.

"What—?"

"Don't make me pick you up, Sin."

"I have a feeling you just did," she mumbled and heard him chuckle as he snapped for a limo.

"That one's not ours," she said.

"Ours will find us when we're ready," he assured her and had them driven about four blocks to the palatial entrance of a hotel. Throwing his platinum card on the counter, he got them a key in record time and seconds later they were walking into the decadence of the honeymoon suite.

Sirena stopped a few steps in, wondering what she was doing. It was one thing to be swept away, quite another to book a room and take off her clothes with deliberation.

Raoul unbuttoned his tuxedo jacket, shrugging out of it and throwing it across the arm of a wingback chair. "Second thoughts? I've had a vasectomy, if that's what you're worried about."

"What?" Her pocketbook hit the floor before she realized her fingers had released it. She quickly crouched to retrieve it, but couldn't take her eyes off the man with his hands pushed into tight fists in his trouser pockets. "When?"

"About a week after we fought about it. You asked if I'd pulled a hamstring on the treadmill and I said, 'something like that.'"

"You should have said—" She was floored, unable to process it. "Why would you do that? I'm a fluke. Other women—"

"I don't think about having sex with other women. Only you."

Her heart stumbled and she had a hard time rising to stand on her weak knees.

"I have condoms, too." He extracted a length of conjoined foil squares from his pocket. "In case you're worried about anything else. I've been tested and have never, ever not used one of these. Which frankly makes me nervous of my performance without one, given it's been so long since we were together."

Her mouth opened. Her lips and tongue wanted to form words, but no air moved from her throat. Her voice had left the building. He hadn't been with anyone else?

"We're good together, Sin." He crossed to her with a laconic scuff of his shoes on the tiles. "Even without taking this to the bedroom. We always were."

"Because I did as I was told," she managed to counter.

He took her chin, forcing her to look into his eyes. Her hair practically lifted off her scalp at his touch. His nearness and the way he studied her mouth caused her breath to stutter.

"I can't stand being around idiots or sycophants or

women who act helpless. You're bright and funny and incredibly competent. I've always been as attracted to that as the knockout body and gypsy looks."

Her lips began to quiver. "I still feel like anything could happen and it would all fall apart and you'd hate me again."

A sharp spasm seemed to take him. "You know what I hate? Not having you in my life at all. Oh, hell, don't cry. There's a lot to build on here, Sin."

"I know," she murmured, fingering the tail of his bow tie, wishing she had the courage to boldly yank it free. "Not to mention how much it would mean to me that Lucy would never wind up with a stepmother like my own."

His bearing hardened before her eyes, taking umbrage.

"Oh, please, you don't really need to hear that's not my only motive. I've been insanely attracted to you for years."

"I do need to hear that," he said with a tight white line around his mouth. "I need to hear it, see it, *feel* it…"

When he covered her mouth with his, the passion behind his kiss was cataclysmic. If she had wanted to be swept away, the tsunami of desire was here, lifting her so she found herself clutched to his chest and carried to the bed. But there an odd, intent stillness took him over. Everything slowed.

He sat beside her to run light fingers from her bare shoulder to her wrist, lifting her hand to his mouth. Hot, damp lips pressed into the thin skin of her inner arm, following the faint blue line to the crease of her elbow.

She compulsively wove her fingers into his silky hair, enjoying the play of the short strands on the sensitive spaces between her fingers. He smelled faintly of aftershave and firmly of himself. The compelling scent overwhelmed her as he nuzzled the hollow of her shoulder, then grazed his lips over the upper swell of her breast.

His shirt was a crisp annoyance as she sought the heat

beneath his collar, restricted by the tight buttons and bow tie and his refusal to crush her under his weight.

"I want to feel you," she complained, restively scraping her fingers up from his waistband to free his shirt, crumpling the fine silk.

He sat up. His narrow eyes glittered with something smug and arrogant, but his movements were urgent as he pulled at his clothing.

*He does need to hear it,* she thought, even as she rose on an elbow and picked at his buttons, trying to hurry him. As he threw off the shirt, she stroked across the twitching muscles of his chest, lightly scratching with her nails as she stroked from his collarbone to his abs.

"You're so hot," she breathed, thinking, *figuratively and literally.* He epitomized an underwear model's fine physique, but radiated heat from his swarthy, flush-darkened torso. His pure male sexuality weakened her. She was glad she was lying down, but a distant part of her was flinching in alarm. She'd done this once, stroked and satisfied her curiosity and his libido, and the next day her world had been devastated.

"Every time you clip up your hair, I want to let it down," he said in a sensuous rumble, gently seeking pins to release the hair pulled back from her temple. As he finger-combed, he bent to let his hot breath tease the delicate whorls of her ear. "I think of you doing very erotic things to me with this hair," he said, words and lips sensitizing her to screaming pitch before he took her to a new level of shivering excitement, dabbing his tongue and lightly biting and sucking her lobe. By the time he moved to the flesh at her nape, she was head-to-toe goose bumps, forehead pleated in an agony of delicious excitement. He further paralyzed her with soft bites into the incredibly responsive tendons of her neck, making her moan and arch to offer herself.

"What are you doing to me?" she gasped, making no

protest as he slid her wrists upward and clasped them in one of his hands.

"I haven't even got your dress off," he husked, seeking and finding the zip at her side. Slowly he released it, watching her pant as she waited, completely absorbed, wanting nothing except to belong to this man.

"You're like a goddess. A fantasy coming true, making me insane. I can't think of anything but having you." He released his grip on her to peel the one shoulder down her arm, exposing her breasts and avidly looking at them.

"Raoul." She brought her elbows down and forward, forearms wanting to shield herself, but his undisguised desire was a type of seduction. A deep part of her wanted to please him and if the thrust of her breasts excited him, she wanted to give him that.

He clasped the full globes in splayed hands and anointed them with reverent kisses. "So beautiful. So perfect." His hands slid to push the fabric down further and she lifted her hips, letting him take the gown off her legs, leaving her naked but for her slutty shoes and a nude thong that wasn't any kind of cover.

She'd been waxed, plucked, exfoliated and moisturized today, but she still held her breath, fearful he'd make note of her imperfections.

He chuckled with gruff pleasure and drew a wickedly teasing fingertip over the silk covering her hot and pulsing mound. His sure hands skimmed away that defense and suddenly she was painfully aware of wearing only shoes on a broad bed while she writhed in arousal before a half-dressed man.

"Raoul."

She didn't know what she wanted to say, but he said, "Shh," with quiet command.

His brows lowered in concentration as he cupped her hip in one hand, stilling her. His other hand moved to smooth a testing fingertip over her C-section scar. It was the starkest mark left by childbearing, even more pronounced than the faint stretch marks and the fading brown line descending from her belly button.

"Don't," she said, wriggling self-consciously and trying to brush his hand away.

"Tender?"

The scar was oddly both oversensitive and numb, but mostly his touch felt too personal. He bent to touch a kiss there and she gasped, shocked and moved and flooded with embarrassed excitement.

Then he shifted to blow softly over her mound. He'd been seducing her so gently, she'd overlooked how powerful and forceful he really was. Her contracting thighs smoothly parted for his superior strength as he made room for his wide shoulders, settling low to press licking kisses high on the insides of her legs.

"You don't have to…"

"Oh, sweet, hot Sin, I do. I really, really do."

She clenched her eyes shut as knowing fingers caressed. This was the sort of intimacy she'd never been able to relax for, knowing he was looking at her— *Oh, God.* Her muscles clenched on the finger that slid in to test her slippery depths.

"Tell me when I get it right," he said, taking a soft bite of her flesh. At the same time he withdrew his touch, then filled her with the span of two thick fingers. His tongue flicked and she couldn't bite back her keening moan. Everything in her gathered to this one bundle of pure sensation, paradise beckoning with each languid caress that he lazily bestowed on her, as if they had all the time in the world.

It was pure torture and so good she was dying, losing herself, growing wanton, inviting more with a tilt of her hips, encouraging him in gasps of sobbing murmurs.

"I can't take it," she cried, pulling mercilessly at his hair.

He reared back onto his knees with a near-primal growl, making her wail with loss even though she'd forced the issue.

Jerking at his trousers, he freed himself, shoving them off and away before he crawled over her. Her legs instinctively twined up to hitch her ankles behind his waist, trying to draw him down as he clasped the sides of her face and kissed her, hard.

His weight settled, crushing her pelvis before he lifted to allow her seeking hand to clasp his sleek shaft and guide him into her.

He slid home with a delicious plunge that turned his whole body to granite. For a few seconds he was a blistering, immovable cage around her, mouth locked to her lips, his heart the only movement as it pounded the wall of his chest, trying to reach hers.

A sigh of pure bliss left her. It felt so good to have him in her, filling the hollow ache she'd thought would be with her the rest of her life.

Then he eased back, pulling at her nerve endings as though they were harp strings, drawing her taut with ecstatic tension before he thrust again. Joy expanded within her.

The crescendo built, both of them clasping to be closer even as they fought to make the strokes harder, deeper, more irrevocable. This wasn't just her, she knew distantly. He was as lost to need as she was, clawing for satisfaction as if their lives depended on it. It did. She needed this, him, the raw hunger and the sweet struggle and the fight to hold on, hold back, to never let this end, to give and take…

The pinnacle arrived, holding them balanced on its tip, breath caught as they swayed between anguish and joy.

Elation won, tumbling them into the maw. He crushed

her as he throbbed with his final thrusts making deep contractions pulse rapture from her center to the tips of her fingers. Deaf, dumb, blind, she could only feel. She was in heaven.

# CHAPTER ELEVEN

RAOUL HAD NEVER feared for his life during sex, but tonight came pretty close. His heart still felt as though it was under enormous pressure. Taxed. Too full.

Sitting on the foot of the bed, he wanted to believe a trip to the cardiologist would fix him, but it wasn't the answer. The woman avoiding his gaze as she pulled the green gown over her head and let it fall into place was the shard of glass piercing his chest.

"Are you all right?" he asked, voice burning like whiskey in his throat.

"Of course." She flipped her hair free of the gown and bent her attention to the narrow zipper along her side.

She'd been the one to hear the chime announcing a text from her sister while he'd been brain-dead from the most powerful orgasm in history. His legs wouldn't hold him, his skin wanted nothing but the silken brush of Sirena's smooth nudity and all his libido could think was *more*.

This sort of dependence scared the hell out of him, making him want to retreat, maybe do some work for a few hours. Definitely remove himself from her presence until he'd recovered his equilibrium.

At the same time, he was disturbed by Sirena's emotional withdrawal. She'd been as caught up as he, it had been incredible, but now she was subtly tense, offering to text the limo driver to pick them up.

He did it, then said what was top of mind before he thought better of it. "I'm not ready to share you. Maybe if we stayed in here a week—"

Like magic, her force field of aloofness fell away and a sweet smile appeared. "If these breasts were detachable, I'd send them ahead and have the driver collect the rest of me tomorrow."

The medieval clamp on his heart eased. Her humor made it easy to amble across to smooth her hair off her shoulder and admit, "That was incredible. Thank you."

"I thought so, too." Her tiny voice tightened the follicles all over his body.

But the way she shyly ducked her head made this all feel too fleeting. He wanted this new circumstance locked into place. Couldn't she see how simply right this was?

"We're getting married," he said with quiet assertion.

Sirena felt something in her ease. She'd been quietly fighting terror that paradise would swing one-eighty into hell again, but his arrogant order let her know he wasn't planning to dump her as quickly as he'd seduced her. Still, she didn't hear anything about love and that tightened her heartstrings to a point near breaking.

Reminding herself they'd come a long way and she shouldn't expect too much, she said lightly, "Let me guess. I have two choices? Say yes now or say yes later?"

He blinked, not revealing what was going on in his quicksilver brain.

"Do you want to say no?" His instant air of detachment pushed her heart to the edge of a plank, but she supposed he could be having as much difficulty dropping his defense mechanisms as she was.

"No." The word came out a bit forlorn. Never had she imagined marrying a man who didn't love her, but if he couldn't see himself having sex with anyone else, she couldn't see herself marrying anyone else. There were enough bonuses to balance the limitations, she promised herself.

"Then it's settled," he said.

She bit lips that wouldn't stop trembling.

They reached the penthouse and Ali eagerly perched across from her in the lounge, practically bouncing with excitement as Sirena sat down to feed Lucy.

"Well?" Ali demanded.

"Well, what?" Sirena asked, inwardly tracking Raoul to the bar.

"Oh, you're hopeless. Raoul, did you propose or didn't you?"

He paused with his glass half raised to his lips, gaze flicking to Sirena's.

"We decided to marry, yes," Sirena said with as little inflection as she could manage.

"I *told* you a man doesn't go all out like this without a ring in his pocket. Let's see it." Ali clapped her hands then held them out, wiggling her fingers to coax Sirena to show her own.

"I—"

To her right, she heard the bottom of a glass hit the bar top with a firm *clunk,* but she refused to look in his direction.

"Sweetie, we have a baby," she said to Ali. "Getting married is a formality. I don't need an engagement ring for the few days it will take to get a license and sign some papers."

"You're not having a real wedding? But you always planned the full dress and fancy cake and Dad walking you down the aisle—"

"I was a kid when I talked like that! No, listen." She hurried to forestall her sister beating this particular dead horse. "Dad and Faye have made it plain they're not up to traveling and Raoul has lost a lot of time with Lucy coming early. It was very sweet of him to arrange for us to have this visit—" she made a point to let him see she was utterly sincere in her appreciation of that, but his inscrutable expression and unmoving stature cowed her "—but we don't need any more disruptions," she finished.

Ali didn't want to let it go, that was her nature. She might be nineteen, but she was still a little girl in some respects. Sirena had grown up enough to realize you had to move past childish dreams and be realistic. She got Ali to drop it and Raoul left the room.

It was Ali's last night, so Sirena wasn't entirely sorry they'd been called back early. She settled Lucy, took off her makeup, then she and Ali had tea and talked about the stars Sirena had rubbed elbows with. Deep inside, she hugged close the secret of all that had happened with Raoul. Ali would never understand if she told her how far they'd come, but the closeness they'd achieved was huge. No brilliantly cut chunk of stone or fancy frock would ever mean as much to her as the way he'd held her as if he didn't want to let her go.

It was late when they finally said good-night and sought their beds.

Sirena came up short as she found hers occupied.

Raoul set aside his tablet as she stopped inside her door. The lamps slanted golden light across his bare chest, making a relief map of his muscled shoulders and abdomen. She couldn't decipher everything in his austere expression, but there was no mistaking the possessiveness of his quick glance from her lapels to her naked legs.

Tremendous self-consciousness struck. Playing with the tie of her kimono, she tried for nonchalance as she said, "I didn't know you were waiting for me."

"I was trying to fix that situation in Milan." His scowl

told her he was still trying. "I'll give my schedule a hard look and figure out when we can get to Australia. Do you want to put off the wedding until then?"

"No," she said firmly, hurrying to the bathroom to brush her teeth, hoping he'd take it as a signal to end the subject, but he didn't. When she returned to the bedroom, he continued as if she hadn't left.

"I've booked a jeweler to bring some engagement rings before we have to drop Ali at the airport."

"I won't wear one." The words came out with more vehemence than she meant, but the sort of wedding she'd always dreamed of had been a celebration of love and this relationship wasn't that soul mate connection. Yes, she loved him and he'd come a long way toward showing more than lust for her, but going through all the hoops and barrels of a big wedding would feel fake. It was vitally important they keep things as honest as possible considering their rough start.

He had one knee crooked beneath the sheet and one strong wrist braced on its point. "Do you intend to wear a wedding band?" His tone held a stealthy note of danger that made her tummy flutter.

She was shocked by how defenseless yet wonderful the idea of wearing his wedding band made her feel. An engagement ring was a romantic gesture; a wedding band was a lifetime commitment. Her throat thickened and she grew warm all over as she murmured, "Of course."

Trying to cloak how disturbed she was, she clicked off the lamp and gestured toward the one on his side.

He didn't move. "Why won't you wear an engagement ring, then?"

"Jewelry with stones isn't practical around babies. And—" She hugged herself. A tiny part of her still hated for him to think she was avaricious, but it was more than that. "I'm not interested in being a bride. I just want us to be a family."

His unapproachable vibes dissipated. He reached to flick the sheet back, motioning her into the bed beside him. She hesitated, unable to be casual despite how intimate they'd been a few hours ago. He was naked and despite her exhaustion, she was dying to feel him against her, but shedding her robe as if they'd always been sleeping like this was impossible.

Amusement curled his masculine lips into a sardonic smile. "Really?" He turned away to click off the light.

"Don't laugh," she grumbled as the darkness made it safe to drop her robe and slide into bed.

Warm hands pulled her into contact with his hot, ready body. "I have better things to do than laugh, Sin."

They married in Las Vegas on the way back to New York. Sirena made all the arrangements over the internet and this time, when they were given a shared room at his mother's, she didn't hesitate. Despite the perfunctory ceremony, the state of being married felt surprisingly natural.

They fell easily into old patterns. Within days of returning to London, Raoul had talked her into giving up her transcription customers and taking charge of his personal calendar instead. It came with an allowance similar to her old salary, which was rather generous considering her flat was paying for itself in rent and she didn't have any other living expenses. Still, taking his money needled her. It would probably be healthier for them if she remained financially independent, but she accepted because she loved being part of his day-to-day life.

"And hire me a decent PA, would you?" he added as they finished up breakfast one of their first mornings back.

"Perhaps they have a two-for-one special at the nanny agency," she mused, flicking the screen on her tablet, not looking up even though she was aware of him pausing after rising from the table.

"Do you think you're funny?" he asked above her in the ominous tone that used to make her quake, but now made her grin.

"You just handed me a list that includes booking you a play date—" for squash, but she overlooked that "—and buying your mother a birthday gift. Throw in a nappy change and I'm spot-on."

He was silent, then said, "This is the sort of thing you used to say in your head when you were afraid I would fire you if you said it aloud?"

She kept her chin tucked and lifted only her lashes. "I'm just having fun, Raoul."

"Are you?" She knew him well enough to recognize when he was completely serious, but she was distracted by the way his stern natural handsomeness gave him an air of commanding masculine authority. Her nerve endings came alive in tingling pulses and the rest of her wanted to melt into a puddle of undying adoration.

"Yes," she croaked, and tried to clear the huskiness from her throat, not quite remembering what they were talking about.

"Because there was a time when I planned to offer you a position on my executive. If you'd rather pursue your career, you can have a job with me and it won't be nepotism. You're qualified. Or look for something else that appeals. I would hate trying to navigate the two schedules," he said with a significant pause to let the downside sink in, "but we could make it work if this isn't challenging enough for you."

She warmed, wistful about the reasons her promotion had never come about, but she wasn't sure she would have taken it even if he had offered it. With her nose wrinkled in self-deprecation, she admitted, "I like working directly with you, being part of the action without having to take the lead. It makes me feel needed. Is that bad?"

"You are needed." He nodded at their daughter in her bouncy chair. "By both of us. If I took you for granted before she came along, well, rest assured I came to realize what I'd lost and very much appreciate all you do for me now."

She softened all over. Her smile wouldn't stay pinned. "Thank you for that."

He bent to steal a swift kiss that turned into a lingering one, sweet as molasses. As he straightened and gathered his things, he added, "And you should know by now that my fantasies run to sexy secretaries over naughty nannies."

She was so in love it was hard to remember he didn't feel the same.

Working for him, she had been one of many distant moons in his dynamic orbit. Now she was a part of his world in a way she hadn't expected could happen. Raoul didn't try to cram her into a corner of his busy life. He made a space for her and Lucy that gave them priority over everything else. When work demanded his time outside the office, he made every effort to include her, keeping her firmly at his side, not the least awkward about the fact she used to be his PA.

Tonight's cocktail party was different from an award ceremony or the meet and greet he'd had with his new clients last week, though. No one there had known she used to be his employee. Here, the hosts would likely remember her as the girl with the quick-draw tablet and Bluetooth earplug who had brought them coffee and arranged their lunch.

Sirena braced herself when Paolo Donatelli, an international banker, and his wife, Lauren, welcomed them into the luxurious foyer of their Milan penthouse. They were a stunning couple, Paolo casually elegant in a gorgeously Italian way, his wife tall and warmly glowing in the family way.

"Congratulations on your happy news! You took everyone by surprise. Even Paolo," Lauren said, kissing both Sirena's cheeks.

"You're misquoting me, *bella*," Paolo said, copying his wife's affectionate gesture toward Sirena. "I said if you two were involved, no one would know unless Raoul wanted it known. He's the most discreet man I've ever met."

Sirena blushed, throat going dry as she felt their curiosity for more details on how their marriage and baby had slid under the radar the way they had.

"We surprised ourselves," Raoul said, drawing her closer as he looked into her eyes. The reassurance in his gaze warmed her, easing her past the discomfiting moment. "And discretion is what you pay for, Paolo," he added, neatly halting further prying.

"This is true," the Italian said wryly. "On that note…"

The men disappeared into Paolo's study. Before Lauren drew Sirena into the gaggle of guests, she clasped her arm. "Did we put you on the spot? I'm sorry. The truth is, I'm thrilled. I don't always feel a connection to the spouses of Paolo's associates, but you've always been so nice. I'm glad I'll be seeing more of you."

"Don't think I won't cash in on that," Sirena said, relaxing as she sensed a genuine offer of friendship. "I'm dying to shop with you. You always look amazing and here I am in Milan, but I don't speak Italian."

Lauren's eyes widened in excitement. "I would love that!"

It was the boost of acceptance she needed. Lauren also helped her find her own style, so Sirena's confidence grew as she spent more time on Raoul's arm. Their days were busy and their nights incredible, building tiny bridges of connection she began to trust were sturdy and reliable.

That developing sense of closeness and familiarity brought her into his London office tower one afternoon simply because she was missing him.

"Hello," she said, using her weight to press the door shut behind her while she took in the familiar sight of him at his massive desk against the wall of windows, London's skyline behind him.

"This is an unexpected pleasure." He leaned back.

"Lucy had her photo shoot this morning. I wanted to show you the proofs. It could have waited, but since I was only a few blocks away…" She dug the flash drive from her coat pocket as she came around to the side of the desk where the outlets were mounted. "And I wanted to see your face when you see them rather than—oh!"

Tumbled into his lap, she took a breathless second to figure out how she'd wound up here. As if there was any mystery, when her husband was looking at her as though he wanted to eat her alive. An appreciative smirk twitched his mouth while an intriguing tension made his cheekbones taut.

"Where's Lucy?" He drew the chopsticks from her hair so her waves tumbled free.

Grinning, she toyed with the knot of his tie. "Watching her new nanny try to flirt with your new PA, completely oblivious to the fact she's barking up the wrongly oriented tree."

"Lucy or the nanny?" He released the zip on her calf-length boot and slipped his hand inside. His warm touch cupped her calf then circled to fondle her knee.

She purred, losing track of the conversation. Settling into him a little more, she felt the press of his growing arousal. His light caress climbed to the side of her thigh beneath her suede skirt. When she pressed her lips into his throat, she felt him swallow.

"Did you lock the door?" His hand was well under her skirt now, moving insistently beneath the tight, unforgiving cut, delving to the top of her leg.

"A detail-oriented girl like me? What do you think?"

"I think I'm about to lose all ambition for the rest of the day." He bent his head to kiss her and the phone rang. The heat flaring in his eyes sparked to frustration. "Only you and my mother have that line."

"I might be pocket-dialing you, if that's my phone digging into my hip."

He chuckled, "Smart-ass," and leaned to tap the button for speakerphone. "Mother?" he prompted.

"Yes, it's me."

"Good timing. Sirena is here." The ironic face he made had her catching back laughter with a hand against her mouth.

They exchanged pleasantries before his mother got to the reason for her call: a misplaced bracelet.

"I know it's silly to ask if you remember seeing where I left it, but I've been up and down through the house and it hasn't turned up."

Raoul flashed a glance to Sirena. It was a quick, unexpected slide of a knife between her ribs, barbed with *Again?*

He recovered quickly, even showed a hint of culpability in the way his gaze wavered and flicked away. "I remember you wearing it to dinner," he said to his mother.

"Sirena?" she prompted.

Her ears rang with all that had just gone unsaid. Her skin chilled and the heart that had been flowering open shriveled to a poisoned husk. The bleak world she had inhabited for so many months crept toward her like dark clouds closing in from the horizon.

"Same," she said through a tight throat, all too aware she'd admired the tennis bracelet openly, listening intently to Beatrisa's story of how touched she'd been to receive it from her son for her sixtieth birthday.

It was all going to start happening again and this time it would hurt even more.

Raoul was aware of his wife turning to marble as he finished with his mother—which he hurried because Sirena's growing tension needed to be addressed. She tried several times to climb off his lap, but he held her in place until he'd ended the call.

"Let me up," she said icily.

"I don't suspect you of taking that bracelet," he growled. Doubt might have flickered through his mind, but he was entitled, wasn't he?

She dug her elbow into the middle of his chest. Her legs determinedly tried to find the floor. "Get your hands off me," she snarled.

He lifted his grip, angry that she was angry. He didn't help her rise, just protected his genitals as she scrambled to her feet and zipped her boot. Flushed, with her hair loose and disheveled, she located her purse and would have walked out without another word.

Leaping up, he met her at the door. "You're not walking out like this."

"Oh, you expect me to stay here and put out so you can accuse me of using my body for leniency again?"

The muscles in his abdomen were so tight there shouldn't have been room for his stomach to compress under a blow, but his gut knotted as though she'd kicked him.

He clenched his fist where he'd braced his arm across the closed door, aware that his wife was incredibly passionate, but the lack of inhibition she showed him was the result of weeks of building on their connection out of bed as much as in it. She still had morning-after blushes and charming as they were, they reminded him that physical intimacy was still new to her. She wasn't capable of using sex for any kind of manipulation. It was purely joy and pleasure for both of them.

"No," he bit out, shamed anew that he'd ever reduced her generous giving of herself to such a low transaction. He knew how much damage his accusation had done to her acceptance of his desire and need for her. Bringing it up again only pushed them farther apart than they already were and he felt a cold, anxious sweat break over him, not wanting to be here in this uncertain place. "I do expect you to talk this out like an adult, though. Not storm off in a fit," he insisted.

"I'm the one reacting badly? Your first thought was that I'd stolen again! I knew you didn't trust me when you set up my account without giving me access to any of yours, but to look at me like that, so blatantly accusing me—"

"You did it once before, damn it. Is it so surprising—"

"Once," she cried, holding up a single finger. "One time I thought I'd lean on someone else's resources instead of trying to do everything myself. It was wrong, I know that, but it was *one time*. Have I taken anything from you before or since? Not even a few bob for nappies from the change on your night table. But you can't wait to find fault! Does it feel good? Does it justify the way you hold back your heart and don't trust me? God, I knew it would be a mistake to get this involved with you!"

She turned away, so she didn't see the way he was knocked back, as if her outburst had been a spray of bullets. He couldn't even defend himself, aware that subconsciously he *was* waiting for a sign that his growing feelings for her were misplaced. She was coming to mean far too much to him. Every time he thought the level of emotion between them was as much as he could handle, his attachment grew. The more you cared, the more you risked and he was getting in so deep there was no self-protection left. He didn't like it, he couldn't deny that.

But to hear her call their relationship a mistake was a brutal blow. He hated seeing her shoulders buckle, hated knowing that she was only standing here in this room with him because he was barring the door.

"Look, the thing with the account I set up for you—"

"I don't want to hear it, I really don't. Would you let me take Lucy home? She needs her nap."

"I'll come home with you." He moved to fetch his laptop. As he did, she walked out. Beyond the door, Lucy let out a sudden cry.

"I'm sorry," the nanny said anxiously as he emerged to find Sirena trying to comfort the baby. "She scratched herself."

An urgent call came in at that second and Sirena wound up leaving without him. When he managed to fight traffic and get home, he was relieved to find them there, even though Sirena was pale and frazzled. Mother and baby were both out of sorts. He was beginning to think Lucy had Sirena's sensitive nature for undercurrents, because she was obviously unsettled by her mother's tension.

He took over soothing the fussy infant and, despite his urgent need to sort things out between them, suggested Sirena take a bath. It was late when they sat down to a quiet dinner, just the two of them. Sirena picked at her food.

The silence built.

"Sin—"

"I don't want to talk about it."

"I called her back," he said, overriding her hostility. "Her housekeeper is sure she saw it on her dresser top after we left. It's fallen behind some furniture or something."

"So it's not that you believe me. You believe the house-keeper."

He drew patience into his lungs with a long inhale. "You barely wear the jewelry I give you and don't spend half the money in the account I opened for you. I have no reason to believe you'd want or need that bracelet."

Her mouth stayed pinched while she rearranged her food.

"I've put what happened behind us. Today was a slipup on my part, that's all."

"Fine," she said in the way women did when they meant, *Like hell,* but he took her at her word, determined to get them back on the comfortable footing they'd been enjoying. When they went to bed, he reached for her as he did every night.

She didn't melt her body into his the way he'd come to expect.

He wanted her. Badly. This break in their connection needed to be reestablished with the physical joining that brought him a kind of pleasure and sense of accord he couldn't even articulate. But while she didn't outright push him away, she didn't open to his kiss and heat to his touch the way she usually did.

With urgency riding him, he slowed his touch, trying to reassure her and himself that nothing had changed. He knew all her trigger points and lightly stimulated them: the dimples at the small of her back that made her shiver, the tendon in her neck that turned her to pudding when he scraped his teeth against it, the underside of her arm that was ticklish, but also made her turn into him and twine her leg around his waist.

When she moaned softly and combed her fingers into his hair, he shuddered with relief, but kept the pace gradual and thorough, wanting her to know how much he revered this bond between them. He didn't know how else to express his feelings for her. They were too deep and disturbing to even try to voice. Surely when they were like this, she felt it and understood?

Her hand moved restlessly on his shoulder and he kissed his way down the inside of her arm. Her wrist was sweetly feminine, the fine pulse beating frantically against his tongue, her fingers trembling against his mouth. He lightly sucked one, then another, anointing all her sensitive places, biting into the mound below her thumb until he'd imprinted himself on her lifeline.

She arched, the seeking signal enough to blast through his control, but he was determined to have every inch of her before she had one inch of him. He rolled her onto her stomach and used his leg to pin hers, then stroked her body with his. Her skin was soft and smooth, her form lovely with its curves and nectarine-scented skin. He kissed his way down her spine as he stroked her legs and buttocks, intensely turned on as she gasped and lifted into his touch and moaned his name.

Pushing the mane of her hair away from her neck, he settled on her, letting her feel how aroused he was. The slam of his heartbeat was like a piston trying to stamp into her. He slid a hand beneath her, cupping her breast then moving lower to the wet heat that was all his.

"I can't get enough of you," he admitted in a hot whisper against her bared ear. "I think about this all the time, giving you pleasure, feeling you melt for me." She was close to shattering, straining beneath him, making gorgeous noises that had the hairs all over his body standing up as he fought losing it without even entering her.

Easing away, he rolled her to face him.

She was trembling, her arms shaking as she tried to draw him over her. Her thighs fell open, but he only kissed down her breastbone to her navel.

"Raoul, I'm dying," she moaned, trying to draw him back up to her.

He was hanging by a thread, but took his time settling on her. Easing into her was like immersing himself in heaven. He went slowly, savoring every heartbeat while fighting the threatening eruption. Catching her inciting hands in his own, he held them still and let her feel him in complete possession of her.

"I will never be careless with you," he told her, deeply aware of the effect he was having on her, the twitch of her thighs scissoring his waist, the clasp of her sheath, the shaken breaths sawing between her lips. "This is too important to me."

He swallowed her gasp as he covered her trembling lips with his, wanting to crush her with all the passionate hunger in him, but venerating her instead, doing everything in his power to transmit that she was pure sweetness, utter joy to him. Perfect.

But he wasn't superhuman. The connection so vital to him was also his lifeblood and he needed to stoke it. The withdrawal and thrust sent a wave of intense pleasure down his back, pulling him tighter and harder, making the need to drive himself into her unbearable. He basked in the sheer magnificence of her, moving with gentle deliberation as he savored the effect she had on him, the way she responded to his strokes.

Their struggle was long and slow and deep. Impossible to give up and impossible to prolong. When the high keening noise came into her throat and her teeth closed on his earlobe, when her climax was only a breath away, he let himself fall, his wife clutched firmly in his arms.

# CHAPTER TWELVE

As Raoul knotted his tie, he wasn't sure if he should feel smug or sorry. Over his reflected shoulder, Sirena was motionless on their ravaged bed, deeply asleep.

Last night had been intense. Even after he'd fetched Lucy for a feed a couple of hours ago and come back fully expecting they'd both finally catch a few winks, Sirena had reached for him as though they hadn't been colliding all night. They'd nearly killed each other with the force of their most recent release.

Then they had finally passed out. When his body had woken him out of habit at six, he'd considered canceling today's meetings, but two very in-demand people had flown in on his request. He had to make time for them.

He didn't like leaving Sirena without saying goodbye, but he was loath to wake her when he was the reason she needed her rest. Shrugging on his suit jacket, he moved closer to gauge how deep into REM she was.

Her face was contorted with agony and her limbs gave a twitch of sleep-paralyzed struggle. Alarmed, he sat to grasp her shoulder, sharply saying, "Sin!" to snap her awake.

"Nooo!" she cried and her hand came up so fast it caught him in the mouth before he knew it.

"What the hell?" He dabbed a finger against his lip, expecting she'd split it.

Her wild eyes came to rest on him, terror slowly receding as she curled her offending hand into her chest. "Did I hit you? Oh, my God, I'm so sorry." Her horror was as real as the remnants of panic still whitening her lips.

"You were having a nightmare. What was it?"

Shadows of memory crept into her eyes before she shielded them with her lashes. Without enlightening him, she drew the blankets up to her neck, shivering and looking to the clock. "What time is it? I didn't realize it was so late. Did your alarm go off?"

"Sin?" He smoothed her hair away from her sweaty temple. "Tell me."

"I don't want to think of it. Will you check Lucy while I have a quick shower?"

"You should sleep in."

"I don't want to try in case it comes back." She slid from the far side of the bed, leaving him uneasy.

Despite the passion that remained acute as ever between them, Sirena couldn't shake the sense of an ax about to fall. She brushed aside her worries by day, telling herself to trust that Raoul really had put his suspicions away, but her subconscious tortured her at night. He woke her from horrible nightmares at least once a night, bleak, frightening dreams where he wrenched Lucy from her arms and condemned Sirena to utter abandonment. Sometimes she was in prison, sometimes she was outside his gates, rain soaking her to the skin, cold metal numbing her fingers, his feelings for her completely beyond her reach.

He'd reassure her and be considerate and affectionate and would make love to her so sweetly she thought she would die, but she still wound up alone and rejected when she closed her eyes.

"I don't know what else I can say," he bit out over a

week later after a sullen dinner when he had remarked on the dark circles under her eyes.

They were in Paris, the city of lovers, sharing after-dinner coffee in the lounge. The nanny had taken an evening off with friends. The housekeeper had tidied up the dishes before leaving for the night. Outside the rain-specked window, the ink-black path of the Seine wound in gilded streaks past the purple and red and yellow lights of the buildings on the far shore.

"Tell me the bracelet has turned up," she said with a melancholy shrug, trying to be dismissive but actually feeling quite desperate.

Thick silence. He'd made her tell him what the dreams were about, but it hadn't helped either of them cope. His lack of response almost sounded accusatory to her.

"It's not like I want to be like this," she pointed out defensively.

Her phone rang in the depths of her purse. She stood to find it, hoping to avoid another dead-end conversation about something she couldn't control.

"You could try trusting me. That's what this comes down to."

She caught back a snort and insisted, "I do," but her heart twisted as though it knew she was lying. What could she do about that? If he loved her, she might be able to believe that he wasn't on the verge of rejecting her. But what he felt for her was passion—and that wasn't a forever type of feeling, was it?

"You don't even trust me enough to talk about this without seizing any excuse to walk away," he said pointedly.

"What is there to say?" She dropped her purse onto the sofa and folded her arms. "I'm supposed to ignore the fact there's no one else it could be? Is your mother losing her memory? Not a bit that I've noticed. Could it be the housekeeper? The one who's been with her for ten years?

Oh, I know, it's Miranda, who gets paid a fortune on top of that trust you set up for her."

A flash of something moved in his eyes. She didn't try to interpret it, too busy rushing on with the facts piled up against her.

"Did a thief break in and steal one bracelet in a house-ful of electronics and art? No! Unless *you* took it, the only other person it could be is *me*." She pointed to her chest. "I'm ready to confess just to get the breakup and court proceedings over with."

A cloak of such tangible chill fell over him, he virtu-ally turned gray and breathed fog. "A divorce? Is that the kind of court proceedings you're referring to?"

Her fingernails clawed into her upper arms. It wasn't, but if he reached for the D-word that quickly, it must be something he was considering. The pain that crept into her then didn't even have a name, it was too all encom-passing and deadly.

Into their staring contest, his phone rang. He didn't move, but it broke the spell. She looked away, body puls-ing with anguish.

"Is it?" he demanded through his teeth, ignoring his phone.

"How else will you react when it never turns up?" she said in a strained voice.

When she dared to look at him, he was so far inside himself there was no reaching him. It was as if the man who had been her protector and sounding board and part-ner had checked out and left the brute from the end of his driveway.

Her heart retracted into a core of ice, cracking from its own cold density.

His phone went silent and her tablet burbled.

"Oh, for God's sake!" she cried, rounding to the coffee table and glancing at the screen to see it was her sister. A different chill moved into her chest. The timing was wrong for a friendly visit—

She swiped at the screen. "Ali?" she asked before the vision of her sister came into focus, crying.

"It's Dad. He's had a heart attack. Mum's in the ambulance. I'm going to meet them at the hospital."

Sirena wasn't aware of swaying, only felt herself steady as firm hands grasped her and eased her onto the sofa. Raoul caught the tablet as it tumbled from her numb fingers.

"She'll be there as soon as I can make arrangements," he said in a rasping voice, ending the call. He tried to take her hands, but Sirena jerked from his touch, practically leaping to her feet.

"I have to pack."

"You're in shock."

"I need to do something."

"Fine. I'll order the flight." He ran a hand over his face, looking surprisingly awful. Maybe it was memories of losing his own father.

That thought made her stomach bottom out. Not dwelling on it, she went through the motions of packing, counting nappies for Lucy, fretting about the time it would take to circle half the globe. Would she reach her father in time?

Calling back the nanny didn't make sense. As nice as she was, she wasn't family. Sirena just wanted Raoul. For all their horrid conflict, he was a pillar. She couldn't dismiss how supportive he was as he booked a private jet, bundled them into a limo and buckled Lucy securely beside her in the plane's cabin.

"Text when you land so I know you arrived safely," he said.

"You're not coming?" Her barely there control shredded to near nothing.

"There's something I have to do."

*Divorce.* The ugly word came back, more noxious than ever. This was it, the expulsion from his life she had feared. Or rather, expected. Bile rose to the back of her throat, sitting in a hot burn despite her convulsive swallow. At least she had Lucy.

Without saying a word, she set her hand on their daughter and looked straight ahead. Funny how after all this time of aching for forgiveness, she didn't care what he believed. She only wanted him to be with her, but he walked away.

As she watched him depart, everything in her was mute and bereft. Minutes later the plane was climbing and the delicate silken ropes binding her to him stretched, thinned and finally snapped.

Forty-eight hours later, the only good news in her life was that her father's surgery had gone well and he would recover in time.

On the other hand, she had a baby who cried if she so much as thought about putting her down. As if the awkwardness of reacquainting with Faye wasn't hard enough without the buffer of her father to smooth the way, her sister insisted on returning to school on the other side of Sydney to be with—*don't tell Mum*—her boyfriend.

"This way you can use my bed," Ali insisted in front of her mother, putting Sirena on the spot. It was Ali's way of being helpful. She was oblivious to the undercurrents.

A cot for Lucy had already been borrowed from the neighbor and Sirena didn't want to appear churlish, but it only took one remark from her stepmother to put Sirena squarely back into her broadly criticized childhood.

"I imagine she'd be sitting up if she wasn't so fat."

Lucy was going to have a figure like her mother's. Not everyone thought that was a problem, Sirena bit back retorting. *Ask my husband.*

Her chest burned as she wondered how long she'd be able to refer to him that way.

He stunned her by contacting her at that moment, through her smartphone.

Highly conscious of her stepmother listening in, she bounced the baby on her hip and tried not to reveal how put out she was that the Wi-Fi she'd scrimped to pay for all those unemployed months, so she could contact her father and sister as often as she liked, had been canceled. *Ali's gone to school. What do we need it for?*

The phone screen was a poor substitute for her tablet and this conversation would cost her a fortune. She felt her scowl and Raoul gave her a forbidding look right back, killing any remote hopes she entertained that they weren't on the skids.

He was in his New York office, the dull sky behind him. His queries about her father and hope for his quick recovery were delivered in a strained rumble that was barely audible over her stepmother bashing dishes.

Sirena could only swallow, such deep emotions were accosting her, and she didn't know what to say with prying, critical ears a few steps away.

"You'll be there until he's released?" Raoul presumed.

"Yes, I—" She was aware of the temperature dropping to arctic levels as Faye absorbed the notion of unwanted houseguests for the indefinite future. "I have a lot to figure out. I'll call you once I know what I'm doing."

"Very well." He sounded about as friendly as Faye.

Ending the call, she endured an oppressive evening where it took everything in her not to reveal her misery and sense of failure to a woman who would dance a jig over her suffering. She barely slept, but when she woke, it was with a fresh sense of purpose.

She was not the unwanted stepchild any longer. Maybe her marriage was a disaster, but she was still a woman with resources and skills. After popping by the hospital to photograph her weak but proud father holding his grand-daughter, she called a real estate agent.

It would be a fresh start in a place that wouldn't remind her of Raoul. An hour later, she was shown into a building under redevelopment.

"This is available immediately?" she asked, thinking that trading on her husband's name had its perks.

"As soon as your credit is approved, hopefully later today," the agent told her.

Money would be tight. She doubted Raoul would con-tinue her allowance if they separated, but she hadn't let on to the agent that a breakup was in the cards. She was using her London flat, which was solely in her name, as leverage. She'd have to rely on transcription to make her payments until she found a decent job, but Raoul had said she had executive potential. She wouldn't sell herself short. None of this would be easy, but living with Faye and her father was not an option and neither was returning to her husband.

She needed her own space. Her heart was breaking into little pieces to match her marriage. She'd always known it wouldn't last, but she still needed solitude to come to terms with it.

After her and Lucy's first night in the quiet of their new flat, they woke early for their morning visit to the hospi-tal. They picked up groceries on the way back and, as a distraction from her misery, invited Faye to see the place. Sirena had concocted a story about Raoul wanting them to have a condo for their visits here, unwilling to confess to her imminent divorce. Unfortunately, that gave Faye carte blanche to show up with paint chips and a pile of unsolicited decorating advice.

"It's just been painted," Sirena argued.

"This oxblood is far too loud for a baby. Look at this eggshell. It will keep her calm. Book the painters to come in after you go back to London. It'll be finished and the fumes gone before your next visit."

She wasn't going back to London.

A knock at the door relieved Sirena from having to explain. She expected the building manager. He had promised to take care of some finishing items today.

As she reached the door, she hoped she could use this excuse to encourage Faye on her way—

"Oh!" Her heart leaped into her throat as she found Raoul outside her door.

He narrowed bleary eyes on her. Bleak lines were carved into his face, barely disguised by a cantankerous expression. When he raked his avaricious gaze down her simple blue capris and collared top, her pulse reacted with a dancing skip, but he looked so forbidding she could only stare dumbly at him.

"I didn't expect you," she said stiltedly.

"No?" He shouldered his way into the tiny flat, taking in the bare walls, the clean but dated furniture and the woman trying to tease a pacifier into his daughter's jabbering mouth.

Faye left off as Raoul approached, coming to attention in the instinctual way most did when confronted with his authoritative presence.

He nodded at her before he set a wide hand on his daughter's tummy. "How are you, kitten?"

Lucy kicked in excitement, grinning toothlessly with recognition and joy, arms flailing.

"I missed you, too," he said, hand staying on her while he took a better look around the flat. Disapproval blazed off him, like sharp, aggressive, glinting knives. No tender welcome or affectionate nickname for her, Sirena noted with a hollow ache.

"You must be the father?" Faye said haughtily when his gaze came back to her.

"My husband, yes," Sirena hurried to interject, pulling herself out of her shock. "Raoul, my stepmother, Faye."

"Nice to meet you," he said without inflection. "Would you be kind enough to watch Lucy while Sirena and I have a private conversation?"

Sirena's stomach hardened into a knot. She could practically hear Faye's, *I told you men expect to make these decisions themselves,* but Faye's opinion was the least of her problems. She hadn't really thought Raoul would give her Lucy, had she?

No, she might have hoped in her heart of hearts that their daughter would be a connection that brought him to her, but this didn't feel as though they were bridging differences. A huge chasm separated them, full of mist and frost.

"I can't walk her in this heat," Faye began, but Raoul negated the suggestion with a flick of his hand.

"We'll be upstairs, viewing the penthouse." His tone was so much that of a confident tycoon, even Faye didn't argue.

Sirena took a moment to set her phone to dial his so Faye could reach them, then accompanied him into the elevator, watching nervously as he punched the P.

"I don't understand—"

"Your agent called to clear your finances and within five minutes was trying to sell me the top floor. It seemed the most expedient way to get into this building if you refused to let me up, so I took the codes and said I'd look at it."

The elevator stopped and her knees weakened. She steeled her spine, but her voice was wobbly. "Of course I'd let you up. We're on perfectly friendly terms."

"Are we?" he rasped, holding the door while she exited, then moving to tap a code into the penthouse's security panel. The half-renovated space was empty of workmen, the concrete floor bare but for a few paint spatters, the walls down to timber frame and the plumbing extracted.

"I can't live with Faye," she blurted, arms flailing defensively. "I've tried to explain how she and I—"

"I understand that," he said with an inscrutable stare. "But you could have gone to a hotel."

She looked away. "That would have been expensive."

"And you weren't about to ask me to cover it, were you?"

Her throat tightened as she tried to swallow, unable to look at him because that topic was just too raw.

"And it would be too temporary," he said in a tone that made her feel wobbly inside. "Because you're staying here. Not coming back to me." It wasn't a question and the graveled way he said it made her flinch.

"There's no point, is there? I realize this seems like I've chosen the farthest place I could get from London, but my family is here, Raoul. Surely you understand why I'd prefer it?" She needed something, someone. They'd never take his place in her heart. The hole was too big, but she couldn't live with this ashen emptiness.

"Oh, I understand." His harsh laugh cut through the tense air. "Run as far from London as you want. I'll follow. If you're adamant about living in that flat you just bought, I'll be in this one."

The words struck like a burst of hot, dusty wind, choking and dry, making her eyes blink. *I'll follow,* but he was following Lucy.

She resisted the desire to rub where her breastbone rang in disappointment. It should be an enormous comfort to her that he hadn't arrived with threats to rend their child from her arms, but all she could think was how jealous she was of her daughter's ability to draw this man's eternal, all-encompassing love.

*She* might be selfish enough to take their daughter from her father, but he wouldn't separate mother and child.

She touched her brow where it was crinkled, aware of him pacing to the space under the floating staircase near the balcony doors. His footsteps were hollow, everything about this place echoing with the same emptiness she felt. His intention to live here was both pleasure and pain, but she'd had a baby with this man. Their lives would be linked forever. She'd never be given a chance for distance and space and getting over him. They would circle each other for eternity, two planets in the same solar system that never touched.

"Every working cell in my brain is telling me I have no right to keep you from leaving me, but the thought of letting you go makes me sick."

Her heart took a stumbling leap in her chest. She caught back any jumps of joy. It was Lucy he was worrying about losing. Lucy, and maybe a passionate bedmate and a scrupulously organized life.

"I…" She trailed off, realizing she'd been so focused on how anguished she felt, she hadn't noticed how broken he looked. If he'd slept since they'd been in Paris, it hadn't been much. He looked as if he'd aged and his shadow of stubble gave her that same old desire to smooth her hand on his rough cheek.

"Miranda had the bracelet," he spit out, as though the words were so bitter he could hardly keep them in his mouth. "I went to New York to confront her. When you threw her name at me in Paris, I realized immediately it was something she would do. She borrowed it for a night out and forgot to return it." He added in a mutter that his stepsister was a "bloody scatterbrain."

Sirena winced, glad to have the question answered, but in the big scheme of things, what did it matter? He had said he didn't think she'd taken it, but he'd had to go all the way to New York to have it confirmed. That hurt. Blinking, she fought back the burn of head-to-toe agony, willing her mouth to stay steady and the constriction in her chest to ease, but she didn't know what to say.

"No more nightmares, all right?" he said gruffly. "It's resolved. You're not in danger of going to prison. I'm never going to try putting you there and I won't let anyone else do it. Do you understand that, Sirena? That threat is gone. Forever."

His implacable tone and the way he tried to impose his will on her was so endearingly familiar she wanted to cry. She shrugged a fake acceptance, because what did he know about it? She woke up crying because the bed was empty beside her. He wanted to live apart. Her life was missing a giant, ornery, wonderful piece and she could barely stand here absorbing his closeness, knowing they'd never again be *close*.

"I've caused you so much pain, haven't I? And why? Because I was afraid to feel any!" He knocked his fist into his chest with self-disgusted violence, making her start. His ragged voice held her very still, frightened, but not of him. Of how angry he was with himself. He was deeply agonized and it both startled and shook her.

"You were right when you said I was looking for every reason to keep you from affecting me. Your nightmares are my punishment. Tell me they're over now, Sin, because they're beyond anything I can stand. Every night I'm confronted by what a thoughtless, cruel bastard I was to you. How I let you down so grossly. When I think of what I tried to do when you were so fragile, killing yourself to keep our child—"

"Don't," she urged, rushing forward a few steps, anguished by how tormented he was. His remorse was too intense to witness.

"It was worse being away from you, not there to wake

you," he said with a dazed affliction. His voice was like someone whose spirit was dead. "I only left because I wanted the mystery solved once and for all, so you'd finally sleep peacefully again. I was arranging the flight, anxious to get here and ease your mind, when your damned agent called and I learned you never intended to let me share your bed again."

"The dreams weren't that bad—"

"Don't downplay what I did to you!" His near shout made her jump again and he ran a hand over his face, visibly trying to bring himself back under control. "Damn it, do you ever think of yourself? That generosity of yours is exactly what gets to me and makes you necessary in my life every second of every day." His hand came out in a plea. "I've always been aware of it, but I never valued it the way I should have. It's why you risked your job to help your sister. I should have seen you'd never do something like that for personal gain. I didn't need protecting from you. It was the other way around." His face twisted with agony. "Don't let your soft heart forgive me. I don't deserve it. Make me live six floors apart from you and suffer like a soul in hell."

For all the jagged pain in his voice, there was a shred of hope in his eyes. He was looking at her as though she were a lifeline just beyond his reach.

She began to tremble, so confused and shaken she could only blurt, "I *can't*. I want to live with you. You're the one who brought up divorce. You're the one who put me on a plane and sent me away! The nightmares are about you not loving me and I love you so much I can't bear it!" She had to bury her face in her hands then because she was revealing too much. This swell of emotions was too much to hold inside.

Hard hands bit into her arms and she was crushed into his chest. His ragged groan vibrated through her as he held her so hard she thought he'd splice them into hybrid branches on a single trunk. A moan of relief from pain escaped her and she let her hands close on his back in pinching handfuls that had to hurt, but she was ravaged by such deep emotions she needed this embrace to keep from splintering into pieces.

"I love you, Sin. I've been sick without you and all I could think about was my father feeling this way and how deep his pain must have been at not having the woman he loved. It's even worse when I had her and ruined everything…"

"No, you didn't," she moaned and cradled his stubbled face to bring his mouth to hers, cutting off his self-recrimination with a tender kiss, wanting to taste that glorious word he'd used.

He opened his mouth on hers with a groan of greed. Their chemistry flared, but it was so much more. They kissed with aching hunger, shuffling to press tighter, thighs weaving, hips rubbing with shiver-inducing friction.

Cupping her head, he drew his own back, hissing a breath at the ceiling. "I'm not taking you on a damned concrete floor where anyone could walk in."

The landing at the top of the stairs caught his gaze and for a second he considered… When he glanced at his wife, she was bringing her sultry gaze back from the same direction. Her body leaned with heart-swelling pliancy against his.

Tempted nearly to breaking point, he hugged her close and reminded himself how incredibly lucky he was to have this second chance. No way was he screwing it up.

Pressing a kiss to her temple, he said, "I don't deserve you. Let me try to do something right, rather than repeat Oxshott."

Her gaze fell and he feared she took it as rejection, even

though he wasn't able to quit stroking her, filling his hands with the reality of her when he'd been sure they were over.

"I liked Oxshott," she murmured, pouted lips nearly touching his breastbone.

"I loved Oxshott," he said softly, stroking her hair back from her face and looking into her eyes, so moved, so bewildered she could love him, he could barely find words.

"I love you," he repeated, even though it was an inadequate description of the depth of regard and adoration he felt toward her.

A misty look came over her face, but a specter moved behind the gaze she lowered. "You don't have to say it if it's not true. I still want to live with you."

"It's not a conscious choice, Sin," he snorted softly. Looking back on how hard he'd fought against feeling this way put a chill in his blood.

"But you're not happy." Her bottom lip moved unsteadily until she caught it in her teeth.

"It hasn't been a comfortable journey, but right now I couldn't be happier."

Her mouth twitched and she nudged against the erection imprinting her abdomen. Her brow cocked as though to ask, *are you sure about that?*

On the verge of becoming distracted, he cupped her jaw, urging her with a caress of her peach-flushed cheek to look into his eyes. This was too important. He saw the hesitancy and vulnerability she was trying to hide behind her flirty smile. His heart lurched.

"I want to make love to you so much I can hardly breathe." A pleasant shiver chased over him at the mere thought of burying himself in her. "Holding you and touching you is the most incredible experience of my life." He caressed her almost convulsively, reassuring himself that he was touching this beautiful woman who meant so much to him. "I was really scared, Sin. I didn't know how I was going to convince you to give me another shot."

Something stark flashed in her eyes before she ducked her head. "I've loved you from practically the minute we met. You're the only man I'll ever want to be with."

Loyal to a fault and so emotionally brave. He would be a lonely coward if he didn't emulate her.

"And you're the only woman I can imagine spending my life with. You believe that, don't you?" he prompted, rather desperate to know her subconscious wouldn't put her through the wringer ever again.

"Of course," she said, adding cheekily, "I have Lucy."

"Don't joke." He leaned back a fraction, waiting for her chastised gaze to come up to his. "I mean it. I want to spend my life with you. I want to marry you. A proper wedding this time. Your dad can give you away…"

She shook her head, trying to forestall him.

"Why not?" he demanded. "You don't want to be the center of attention?" It was the only excuse he could accept. He wouldn't force her into something that made her uncomfortable.

"Those romantic dreams were a young girl's rescue fantasy." She waved them away as she disentangled herself from his embrace. "I've grown up, got my head on straight. I don't need some empty gesture because you feel guilty. I'm fine. We're fine." Her smile was soft and lovely and tried hard to disguise a deep insecurity.

He stared at her, aware he only had himself to blame. "You still don't trust me," he accused gently.

"Of course I do."

"You don't believe my feelings for you are as strong as yours are for me." He was insulted to the core by that, but this wasn't about him. It was about the fragile self-worth he'd damaged too many times.

"I—" What could she say? It was true. "I'm not trying

to start a fight. I know things will only get better from now on."

He allowed the conversation to end there and they returned to Lucy, then went to the hospital for an introduction to her father. By the time they crawled into bed, she truly felt they were on their way to a stronger relationship than ever. He made love to her with the same sweet power as always and held her all night long.

And then he took over in that mildly annoying way of his, throwing Faye for a loop, checking to see if their house needed modifications for when her father came home. He had a man-to-man chat with her father about his finances, too.

*"Don't hurt his pride,"* she urged before he left for the hospital, and got a pithy look.

*"I want him to know he has a fallback if he doesn't get on his feet right away. I take care of my family,"* Raoul said.

For the first time in a very long time, she began to feel she had a cohesive family. With her confidence renewed in her position as a mother and his wife, she tried to let go of her baggage and enjoy her time with her father and sister. Faye became someone she shook her head over, rather than taking her words to heart, especially after her father remarked on their relationship.

"After your mother died, I saw you growing up so fast, trying to take on all her responsibilities. I married the first woman who looked like she'd have me, hoping to give you back your childhood, but it didn't work. You two never connected. You were so independent. Faye didn't know what to make of you. Moving here, I honestly didn't think you'd miss us or that it would be so long until I saw you again. You sounded happy with your job and traveling…"

Startled by this view of herself, she asked Raoul later, "Do I take charge of everything?"